Praise f ... ...**Kenna**

"McKenna provides heartbreakingly tender romantic development that will move readers to tears. Her military background lends authenticity to this outstanding tale, and readers will fall in love with the upstanding hero and his fierce determination to save the woman he loves."
—*Publishers Weekly* on *Never Surrender*

"Talented Lindsay McKenna delivers excitement and romance in equal measure."
—*RT Book Reviews* on *Protecting His Own*

"Lindsay McKenna will have you flying with the daring and deadly women pilots who risk their lives... Buckle in for the ride of your life."
—*Writers Unlimited* on *Heart of Stone*

Praise for *New York Times* bestselling author Joan Johnston

"A guaranteed good read."
—*New York Times* bestselling author Heather Graham

"Joan Johnston does short contemporary Westerns to perfection."
—*Publishers Weekly*

"Joan Johnston continually gives us everything we want... fabulous details and atmosphere, memorable characters, a story that you wish would never end, and lots of tension and sensuality."
—*RT Book Reviews*

NEW YORK TIMES BESTSELLING AUTHORS

LINDSAY McKENNA

& JOAN JOHNSTON

THE LAST COWBOY
&
HAWK'S WAY: GARTH

HARLEQUIN®

ISBN-13: 978-1-335-58012-2

The Last Cowboy & Hawk's Way: Garth

Copyright © 2020 by Harlequin Books S.A.

The Last Cowboy
First published in 2011. This edition published in 2020.
Copyright © 2011 by Lindsay McKenna

Hawk's Way: Garth
First published as The Wrangler and the Rich Girl in 1993.
This edition published in 2020.
Copyright © 1993 by Joan Mertens Johnston

Recycling programs for this product may not exist in your area.

For questions and comments about the quality of this book, please contact us at CustomerService@Harlequin.com.

Harlequin Enterprises ULC
22 Adelaide St. West, 40th Floor
Toronto, Ontario M5H 4E3, Canada
www.Harlequin.com

Printed in U.S.A.

CONTENTS

Lindsay McKenna is proud to have served her country in the US Navy as an aerographer's mate third class—also known as a weather forecaster. She was a pioneer in the military romance subgenre and loves to combine heart-pounding action with soulful and poignant romance. True to her military roots, she is the originator of the long-running and reader-favorite Morgan's Mercenaries series. She does extensive hands-on research, including flying in aircraft such as a P3-B Orion sub-hunter and a B-52 bomber. She was the first romance writer to sign her books in the Pentagon bookstore. Visit her online at lindsaymckenna.com.

Books by Lindsay McKenna

Shadow Warriors

Running Fire
Taking Fire
Never Surrender
Breaking Point
Degree of Risk

Jackson Hole, Wyoming

Out Rider
Night Hawk
Wolf Haven
High Country Rebel
The Loner

Visit the Author Profile page
at Harlequin.com for more titles.

THE LAST COWBOY

Lindsay McKenna

To Susan Hamilton of High Country Raptors, Flagstaff, Arizona, as well as Marchiene Reinstra, Tricia Speed, Patricia Comfort, Monica Amarillis (Milan, Italy), Sunday Larson, Naomi C. Rose and Maureen Wolverton. All strong, intelligent and compassionate women. Our world needs positive, healthy role models for women. It takes a state of mind, a confidence in yourself, to be treated as an equal in today's society. I'm privileged to be a part of your lives as you are a part of mine. My wish is that someday soon there will be equality for all women in our world.

CHAPTER ONE

"BOSS! LOOK OUT!"

Slade McPherson was in a rectangular corral at his Jackson Hole, Wyoming, ranch with the meanest Hereford bull he'd ever dealt with. He heard Shorty, his wrangler, give a cry of warning. There was sudden movement behind him. Diablo, the bull, had been walking toward the chute to receive his yearly set of shots. Slade never allowed any horses in such a confined area with the bull. Diablo hated men. Slade wasn't about to allow one of his prized horses to be butted and injured by Diablo.

Whirling around, he saw Diablo toss his massive white-and-rust head, drool flinging in all directions out of his mouth. The bull had decided not to go into the chute and, instead, wheeled his one ton body around and charged Slade who was ten feet away. The bull bellowed, lowered his head and attacked.

Slade was five feet away from the steel-pipe fence. There was no way he could stop such a charge. All he could do was run like hell. And that's exactly what he did. Because he was six-foot-two inches in height and he had a long stride. Adrenaline shot through him as he dug the heels of his cowboy boots into the dusty floor of the corral. In two strides, Slade hit the fence, made a huge leap and landed on the third rung of the five-rung corral. The ground shook from Diablo's charge. As he jerked his leg up, still climbing to get away from the angry bull, Slade felt the brush of the bull's head against the heel of his boot.

It took a matter of two seconds before it was all over. Diablo roared and galloped around the small enclosure, tossing his head in frustration. Slade balanced himself on the fifth rung of the fence, watching his prized breeding bull bawl and race around the enclosure. *That was close!* Slade had lost count of the times Diablo had planned and waited until he'd get near enough to trample him to death. The bull had great genes for putting good meat on his offspring, but his personality sucked.

"Boss," Shorty panted, running over and looking up at Slade, "you okay? He grazed you."

Taking off his tan Stetson hat, the crown damp with sweat from the July day, Slade grinned and lifted his forearm. He wiped his brow with the back of his arm. "I'm fine," he drawled. "Close but no cigar." The sun was bright as it climbed higher in a deep blue sky. He glanced down at Shorty. The man was only five-foot-six inches tall, lean as a whippet and didn't look as if he could even make it as a wrangler, but he was one of the best. He came from good Irish stock with sandy-colored short hair and dancing green, elfish eyes.

"Good thing," Shorty muttered, worry in his tone. He stepped aside as Slade clambered off the pipe fence and landed on the dusty earth. "I'll tell ya, that bull seems to hate us humans more and more every year." Shorty's small face grew pinched as he watched the bull continuing to trot in circles, the drool from the corners of his opened mouth flying out like thin, glittering spider webs around his head and massive shoulders.

"Bad personality genes for sure," Slade agreed, set-

tling the dusty, sweat-stained Stetson back on his head.
He watched Diablo. Once the bull seemed cooled down,
the animal walked quietly into the chute. For the Hereford, it was a game, Slade realized as he walked around
the outside of the corral. At the chute, he dropped the
rear slat that would keep the bull confined. Going to his
green Chevy truck, Slade picked up the syringe lying
on the seat. Once a year, Diablo got his necessary vac-
cinations. Shorty followed him to the stout pipe chute
that now enclosed the twenty-five-hundred-pound bull.

"Boss, remember you got a new client comin' out
here this afternoon," Shorty reminded him. The wrangler had been with Slade since he'd taken over the ranch.

Slade grunted. He really didn't want to hear that.
Going to the chute, he said, "Stand by Diablo's head and
distract him for a moment."

Grinning, Shorty moved to within a foot of the metal
chute where the bull stood. "I'll be the decoy," he chortled.

Slade nodded and positioned himself at the rear of
the bull. Diablo lived to find a human to trample. In
the bull's mind, humans were a threat to his territory.
And Diablo would never allow another male on two legs
within the pastures he roamed with his herd of cows.
If they came near, all bets were off, and he became enraged and would charge them. Good thing he thought
four-legged horses were not threatening. Diablo snorted,
his ears moving forward and back as Shorty slowly approached.

"Perfect," Slade murmured as he sank the needle into
the thick, muscled area of the bull's well-padded hip.
Diablo's entire attention was on Shorty's approach. As
Slade withdrew the needle, he glanced forward to get the

bull's reaction. There was none. His angry brown eyes were fixed on Shorty. "We're done," he called. Placing the emptied syringe back in the box on his truck seat, Slade said, "Release him back out into the pasture."

"Right, Boss," Shorty said with a quick nod. "He ain't gonna be happy, though. All his ladies are in the pasture across the road from him."

Pulling his leather gloves back on, Slade nodded. "Too bad. He can look, but not touch." Slade had a small herd of Herefords, fifty in all, that Diablo bred in early fall. It took nine months for gestation. In the early summer months, the calves were born. At that time, Diablo was separated from his band, a dirt road plus a stout metal-pipe rail fence between them. One never kept a bull with newly born calves. The chances of them being injured or killed by the bull was very real.

And Slade needed every calf that was birthed because after they reached a certain age, they would be sold to the meat market. And that meant money to pay a mortgage that was always a monthly nightmare to him. Above all, Slade never wanted to lose this ranch. He lived on the razor's edge of doing just that. Being a small-time rancher meant a constant balancing act with the bank mortgage on a monthly basis. Miss one payment and he'd be foreclosed upon. *It can't happen!*

Slade watched Shorty open the chute. Instantly, Diablo bellowed and shot out of it at a full gallop. The Tetons Ranch that Slade had inherited from his parents after his uncle died was only fifty acres in size. A very small ranch, all things considered. Diablo thundered out of the opened gate. Ahead of him was lush green pasture. And farther to his left was the stout pipe fence and a dirt road. All his ladies and their babies grazed peacefully on the other side. Diablo would pace for a while, walking up and down the fence line, tossing his head and reestablishing he was boss of his herd. Slade knew that the territorial bull would eventually settle down. Diablo would do his best to follow his herd, but the pipe fence and road always stood between them. Once the bull quieted, he would graze and watch his band from afar.

Shorty came back. He took off his dusty black Stetson and brushed it against his thigh. Dust poofed away from it. "Boss," he said as he pulled a crinkled piece of notebook paper from his back pocket, "here's whose comin' at 1:00 p.m."

Slade didn't like new clients, but they were his bread and butter, necessary to meet his financial obligations for the Tetons Ranch. "Okay, thanks," he grunted, taking the paper. Shorty managed Slade's endurance-training appointments. Carefully unwrapping the note, he saw Shorty had scribbled a name and phone number. Frowning, he tried to read it. Shorty was thirty-five years old, single and had never been married. He'd worked for Slade's Uncle Paul shortly before he'd died, and the ranch had been willed to Slade and his fraternal twin brother, Griff. Slade was now thirty-two, and he was grateful for Shorty's loyalty to the ranch and his family. He glanced up—Shorty's thin, narrow face was set in a grin.

"I 'spose you can't read my writin', Boss?"

"Got that right," Slade growled. He handed the note back to his wrangler. "Want to translate it for me?"

Chortling, Shorty read it and said, "Dr. Jordana Lawton is bringing her mustang mare named Stormy here this afternoon at 1:00 p.m." Shorty handed him back the note.

"A doctor?"

"Yes, Boss. She's an emergency-room physician, and Gwen Garner told me that Dr. Lawton is also a func-tional-medicine specialist and has her clinic near the hospital."

Mouth quirking, Slade asked, "What'd you do? Have a cozy chat with Gwen?" Her son, Cade Garner, was a deputy sheriff. She was the town gossip, but she was careful on what she said and made sure her informa-tion was correct before she passed it on to anyone else.

Turning red, Shorty shrugged. "Hey, Gwen said Dr. Lawton was a nice lady, Boss. I guess because Dr. Law-ton is used to chattin' with her patients, she's real easy to talk to."

"You weren't her patient."

"No, but when we talked on the phone, she made me feel special," Shorty said, challenging him.

Shrugging, Slade muttered, "I don't care who she is so long as she can pay for the training. What's this about a mustang mare? Is she wanting endurance training?"

"For both of 'em, Boss. The doctor wants to know if her mare is capable of being an endurance-horse pros-pect from a conformation standpoint. So, I told her to trailer the mare out here and you'd take a look at her."

In Slade's business of endurance riding, of which he was many times a champion, people often brought their horses out for him to check out. "Okay. Anything else she wants?"

Shrugging, Shorty said, "The doc said if her mare's conformation was okay, she wanted to hire you to train both of them for level one riding."

Nodding, Slade interpreted this as money coming into his coffers to keep the bank at bay. He had weekly training sessions with nine male students. He knew how to get a horse ready for an endurance ride, whether it was a twenty, fifty or a hundred-mile challenge. And he also knew how to get the rider in shape, as well. "Okay, that sounds good. She got a background in endurance racing?"

"A little," Shorty hedged. "I really didn't get into much of a discussion with her on that, Boss. I figure you'll sort it out with her when she arrives here this afternoon."

"Okay," Slade said. Tucking the paper with the doctor's name and phone number into his dark red cotton cowboy shirt pocket, he said, "Let's get back to work. We need to start separating the calves from their mothers, branding and vaccinating them." That would be a weeklong activity. And Slade only had one wrangler. He worked from four in the morning to midnight every day. And every hour of daylight was precious.

"Right," Shorty murmured, following him to where their horses were tied to the corral fence.

As Slade mounted his buckskin quarter horse, Dude, his mind wandered back to Dr. Jordana Lawton for just a second. Slightly curious if she was a good endurance prospect, Slade hoped that it would work out so he had more money flowing in. He'd find out soon enough.

JORDANA LAWTON CAREFULLY negotiated the rutted dirt road. She drove her dark blue Ford three-quarter-ton pickup truck as if she was driving over hens' eggs. Behind her in a dark blue two-horse trailer was her gray mustang mare, Stormy. One never took a deeply rutted road with a horse trailer at a high speed. It would bounce the horse around so much that it could either cause an injury or send the animal into a frantic emotional state akin to trauma.

And trauma was something Jordana knew inside and out as an emergency-room physician. Glancing at the clock on the dash, she knew she was going to be late. She hadn't anticipated the dirt road being in such bad shape, but thunderstorms coming over the Tetons last week had made a gooey mire of every ranch road in the valley. And she wasn't going to hurry in order to get there on time. Slade McPherson, the national-champion endurance rider and trainer, would just have to wait.

The windows were down in the cab, and her shoulder-length black hair flew in wisps across her face. Jordana pulled the errant strands away and then placed both hands back on the steering wheel. In the two years that she had lived in Jackson Hole, Wyoming, she had come to find that the majority of ranch roads in the valley were not paved. Most of the owners had a tractor, and they would drive out with a blade attached and smooth out the ruts.

Frowning, her focus on her driving, she worried that Stormy might lose her footing on the thick rubber mats. Jordana wanted this experience for the mare to be a good one. It only took one bad ride in a trailer to spook some horses. After that, the horse would refuse to ever enter the trailer again. That couldn't happen because Jordana had high hopes that this mustang mare would be good enough to start competing at the top endurance level in the United States. And she wanted Stormy always to look forward to entering the trailer, instead of dreading it. *Slow but sure...*

SLADE GRITTED HIS teeth as he looked down at the watch on his thick wrist. He'd just rode in from the pastures where he and Shorty had been separating cows from calves. It was hard, sweaty work. And he didn't want to waste time. Dr. Lawton was already ten minutes late. Slade didn't like people who weren't punctual. He had gone in and checked his answering machine to see if she'd called and canceled the appointment. There were no calls. Wasn't that just like a woman? Isabel, his ex-wife, had always been late.

He hated dealing with women in general. He much preferred working with men who wanted to train for endurance riding. Ever since his divorce from city slicker Isabel Stephens four years ago, Slade had taken on a distinct dislike of the opposite sex. Isabel hailed from New York City, had rich parents and possessed the emotional maturity of a sixteen-year-old girl. She had never been on time for anything except their impromptu wedding. Slade had developed an intense dislike of city dwellers, New York City types, in particular. Isabel had left a bad taste in his mouth. She'd hired a rich New York City attorney and had taken him to the cleaners during their divorce proceedings.

Grimacing, Slade kicked the red dirt with the toe of his scarred cowboy boot. Isabel was the reason his beloved ranch was teetering on the edge of foreclosure. She'd taken him for every penny he'd ever earned. All his savings that had kept the ranch on sound financial footing had gone to her. Now, four years later, Slade continued to wrestle with every penny that came in on a monthly basis. He had nightmares about losing his parents' ranch. It had been in the family for over a hundred years. There was no way he could lose it. Being a rancher was all he knew. Anger stirred in him as he relived the divorce from petulant, spoiled Isabel.

Pulling in a deep, ragged breath, Slade recalled how

he'd fallen in love with the sleek, beautiful Isabel. A dressage rider from the East Coast, she'd come out to Jackson Hole for a two-week vacation with her rich corporate friend who owned a ten-million-dollar home here in the valley. Isabel had met Slade at the Tetons fifty-mile ride, her first endurance contest. Isabel knew her horses. And when Slade had seen her in the crowd as each rider rode up and waited to be released by the judge every five minutes, his heart had pounded. Slade could never remember a woman who had affected him so profoundly as Isabel had.

And it hadn't hurt that he'd won that race on his flashy medicine-hat mustang stallion, Thor, either. Isabel had had stars in her eyes for him as he'd rode in first among a hundred other contestants. They'd had dinner and gone to bed that night. And Slade, stupid idiot that he was, impulsively married her a week later.

"What a loco decision," he groused, looking at his watch again. The dirt road to Tetons Ranch curved, so he wouldn't see a truck and horse trailer until the last moment. He saw no one driving around that corner. "Damn," he added, now walking angrily back to his ranch house. Where the hell was this woman? If she couldn't even be on time for this first meeting, what would it be like if he accepted her as a student later? If her horse had the potential? *Not good. Not good at all. Damn her. Why couldn't she call and let him know where she was at?*

JORDANA GAVE A gasp of surprise. As she slowly pulled around the last curve, she saw the iconic Marlboro Man cowboy from the cigarette ads. Oh, she'd seen photos of Slade McPherson, but in real life… *My God…*

Most things didn't unsettle Jordana one way or another. But the fierce-looking, rugged cowboy did. As she drove her horse trailer between the barn and the ranch house where he stood, Jordana felt her heart unexpectedly begin to pound. This wasn't adrenaline. She was a physician, and she knew the difference. No, this was her womanly side wildly responding to the man she saw standing there, his hands tense on his narrow hips, watching her approach.

Jordana knew Slade McPherson was a loner. Everyone in Jackson Hole had told her that. A strong, gruff, even antisocial rancher who knew more about breeding endurance horses than anyone else in the nation. She'd done her research. And in her eyes, after learning all she could about this hardened, rugged cowboy, he was the best at what he did: a champion endurance rider and breeder.

Not expecting to have such a powerful physical reaction to seeing him in person made Jordana feel giddy like a teenager. As she put on the brake, she saw his large gray eyes narrowing speculatively upon her. Suddenly vulnerable beneath that incisive, probing gaze, Jordana felt like Jell-O melting out in hot sunlight. Even her lower body was reacting to him! *Good grief!* What was this all about? Unhinged, Jordana suddenly felt unsure in this man's towering presence. He wore a set of dusty Levis that perfectly outlined his long, powerful legs and thick thighs. His hands were long and large, draped over his narrow hips. The dark red cotton cowboy shirt did nothing but emphasize his square face that was burned dark by the sun. The slashes at the sides of his full mouth and the crow's feet at the corners of his eyes told her this man regularly challenged the weather in any condition—and won.

Her intuitive sense told Jordana he was armored up. The realization hit her in the solar plexus. Unexpectedly, her hands shook as she gathered up items from the seat in preparation to leave the truck. Jordana suddenly was taken back to when she was fifteen years old. It was at that age she had been struck by love for the first time. And how she felt then was how she felt now. Compressing her full lips, she tried to gather her strewn emotions. As hard and implacable as Slade McPherson appeared to be in person, Jordana knew she had to put on her physician's face: strong, confident and detached. It would hide her present emotions that were a mix of excitement, desire and curiosity.

Climbing out of the truck, Jordana hastily walked around the front of it. As she faced the stony-looking Slade McPherson, she heard him snarl, "You're late…"

CHAPTER TWO

JORDANA FELT AS if she'd just been physically slapped by the rugged-looking cowboy who towered over her. She was only five foot six inches tall. He was like a Sequoia compared to her pine-tree height. Compressing her full lips, Jordana weathered his icily spoken words. As a trauma physician, she'd encountered people in all states of anger and irritability. Knowing that a soft, steady voice and appearing unflappable calmed emotional storms, she smiled and said, "I'm sorry. I'm Jordana Lawton. The road to your ranch was a little more rutted than I'd anticipated, and I slowed down so my mare wouldn't get thrown around in the trailer." She put her hand forward.

Slade absorbed the apology in her husky voice. The sound flowed over him like melting honey. Jordana's hand was extended, and he stared down at it. She had long fingers, her hand as delicate-looking as her face. Obliquely he wondered if she had the stamina it took to gut out a fifty- or hundred-mile endurance ride. In appearance, she didn't look like much more than a pretty black-haired, blue-eyed woman with a curvy body in all the right places. The sunlight danced across her shoulder-length hair, highlighting some of the reddish strands.

"Slade McPherson, Dr. Lawton." He monitored the amount of strength as his hand engulfed hers. To his surprise, he found her hand strong and firm, just like his. Swallowing that discovery, he instantly released her fingers because red-hot tingles were soaring from his hand up into his lower arm. What the hell was happening? Slade had no idea.

"Call me Jordana," she insisted. Giving him a bit of a wry smile, she added, "I am a trauma doc, but that's my job. Out here, I'm just like anyone else. Please call me Jordana?"

Slade felt as if he was being pulled into her dancing, sky-blue eyes. There was warmth and understanding glinting in them like dapples of sunlight across the lakes found in the Tetons range. Her pupils were large and black, eyelashes forming a dark frame around them. Again, he swallowed hard. There was nothing to dislike about Jordana. She appeared to be around his age, although her face appeared to be that of a young twenty-something. Slade knew that doctors didn't really get out of training until they were twenty-eight to thirty years old.

"I haven't got much time," he said abruptly, and he waved his hand toward the horse trailer. "Shorty said you have an endurance prospect you wanted me to evaluate?"

Wincing internally, Jordana had to stop the comparison between her former boss, Dr. Paul Edwin, who'd had the exact same acid, remote and cold personality as McPherson. That made her cringe inside. After a two-year sexual harassment lawsuit, Jordana had won the court case but she'd lost her position at a prestigious New York City hospital. That was why she'd decided to start all over and moved from there to Jackson Hole, Wyoming. Now, she was being tested by a man who looked as harsh as the mighty Tetons range itself.

"Yes, I have a mustang mare named Stormy. I'd like you to evaluate her conformation. See if she has what it takes."

"At what level?" he demanded, stalking around the back of the trailer and opening the latches.

Jordana quickly followed him. He flowed like water over rock. There was a fluidity to Slade that mesmerized her. She realized he was in top athletic shape to be able to move with that kind of boneless grace. "Level one, the Nationals," she said. Jordana moved forward as the doors swung out and pulled out the ramp. Stormy whinnied.

Reaching up, Jordana patted the sleek gray rump of her mare. "It's okay, Stormy. I'm going to get you out of there." She walked to the side of the trailer and opened a smaller door. This allowed her to go inside and unsnap the hook attached to the mare's red nylon halter. That done, Jordana eased around the end and stood where the mare was tied. She attached a nylon halter lead and placed her hand on the horse's chest. "Back up," she told the mare.

Stormy obeyed. In a few moments, Jordana and her mare were standing outside the trailer.

"Bring your mare over here," Slade ordered. He walked away from the trailer into an area where the horse could be walked and trotted.

Jordana nodded and did as he asked. What a tough hombre he was! There were no articles that said anything about this man's personality. Maybe that's why, she thought. Anxious because Jordana wanted Stormy to be given the good seal of approval, she took the horse about a hundred feet away. McPherson stood with his arms across his chest, his face unreadable. The shade created by his tan Stetson emphasized the harsh lines gathered across his brow. What would he say about Stormy?

"Okay," Slade called, "trot your mare in a straight line toward me."

Clucking softly to Stormy, Jordana ran alongside her mare. She knew Slade was looking at how the horse's legs moved. She knew Stormy had a good set of legs. He would be checking out whether her hooves moved straight ahead or winged out or came into a pigeon-toed formation. If the horse's hooves winged outward, it was a sign of bad conformation. Stormy would never be able to take the hard, constant stress on her legs without breaking down and becoming injured.

Slade had one hell of a time keeping his eyes on the horse's movement. Jordana wore a bright yellow T-shirt, jeans and cowboy boots. She moved as fluidly as the mare. Slade cursed—he did *not* want to be drawn at all to this woman! He'd automatically looked at her left hand and found no wedding ring on it. That didn't mean much. Slade was sure she was hooked up in a relationship, anyway. Jordana was far too pretty, intelligent and professional to be alone out here in Wyoming. Just as well, he harshly told himself.

As Jordana drew her mustang to a halt about ten feet in front of him, Slade lifted his hand and growled, "Now walk away from me. Go the same distance and then turn around and walk back to me."

"Right," Jordana said, breathless. Stormy was feeling her oats, and she pranced as Jordana turned her around. Speaking softly to the mare, Jordana managed to get the mustang settled down and walking obediently at her side.

Slade groaned. He was watching the way Jordana swayed her hips. Her legs were long and firm. He'd been without a woman for some time now. And this one, for whatever reason, was fanning the flames of his monklike life. Forcing himself to watch the mare, he was pleased to see she was four square. That meant that at a walk, her rear hooves would land where her front hooves had previously been. That was a sign of the type of conformation Slade wanted to see in an endurance prospect. As the horse saying went: "No legs, no horse." And in endurance riding, legs either carried you through the challenging hill and mountain conditions, or they didn't.

As Jordana brought the steel-gray mare to a halt, he'd seen enough and changed his orders. "Take her over to that corral and put her on a longe line. I want to see you work her both ways at a trot and gallop." He turned on his heel and walked toward the corral.

What a terse person he was! Jordana patted Stormy's sleek gray neck, ruffled her thick black mane and said, "Come on, girl. Show-and-tell time."

Snorting, Stormy danced prettily for a few paces and then sedately walked beside her owner. Jordana saw the gate was open to the huge white painted pipe corral fence. There was a longe line hanging nearby. McPherson was already in the corral, arms across his chest, face expressionless, as if barely tolerating them being on his property. Anxious, Jordana knew, with this kind of person, the best way to defuse his coldness and bring down her armor was to do what he told her to do. Ordinarily, she wouldn't take this kind of rude behavior from anyone except a patient in shock, but today, she did. More than anything, she wanted to know if her mare had what it took to move to the national level.

Slade watched the mustang mare being worked, first clockwise on a thirty-foot longe line by Jordana, and then the opposite direction. The mare was thirteen and a half hands tall. Mustangs were very small in comparison to other light-breed horses. His own medicine-hat mustang stallion, Thor, was fifteen hands tall. He was the rare exception in the mustang world. Most were between thirteen and fourteen hands tall because of hundreds of years of lean food. Not enough food and the animals never fully developed their height. In the world of endurance riding, a leggy horse meant a long stride. And a long stride meant the horse ate up more ground which was important. Mere seconds could declare a winner and loser in an endurance race. Length of stride meant everything.

For the next ten minutes, Slade critically studied the gray mare. First, he needed to see if the mustang closely listened to her owner. That was a crucial piece of information because if the horse disregarded the owner's voice, it could put them in grave danger out on the trail.

"All right," Slade called. "Enough. Get her saddled up and bring her back into the arena." He needed to see how the horse responded to its rider. Was there teamwork? Or not? In an endurance contest, they would have to work like a well-oiled machine. Climbing rocky hills, jumping over fallen logs, making their way through water hazards or managing muddy trails were all required of them. If the horse didn't listen or was fighting the rider, it could place them into a dangerous situation where injury would be the outcome.

Jordana quickly took her mare back to the trailer and tied her on an outside metal loop. She wasn't sure what McPherson thought. He was one of the few people she couldn't read. Wondering as she saddled Stormy if Slade ever dropped that harsh mask he wore, Jordana was shocked by her sudden interest in this man. The fact he was almost a dead ringer for Dr. Paul Edwin turned her stomach. And yet, Jordana felt a calm come over her every time she looked into Slade's rugged face. His eyes, those gray shards of ice, never gave away how he really felt about her horse. And she knew as she mounted Stormy and walked her toward the corral, he was going to be judging both of them now. Taking a deep breath, Jordana tried to calm her anxiety. She wanted so badly to have McPherson's help to go to the top of the endurance world.

Slade watched from the fence as Jordana walked her horse around the large, sandy arena. Then, she urged Stormy to a trot and then a canter. She was an excellent rider. Jordana's hands were quiet on the hackamore reins as she guided Stormy. A hackamore was a bridle without a bit. It meant Stormy was very capable of wanting to work and listen to her owner. Most horses could not go without a bit in their mouth, so this spoke highly of Stormy's desire to work with her owner.

Jordana's long, beautiful legs were quiet and rested firmly against the mare's barrel. Never once did Slade see her use her heels to ask the horse to move from a walk to a trot or a walk to a canter. He knew then that the doctor was utilizing dressage techniques, the highest art form of riding in the horse world.

As he watched them move around the arena, Slade scowled. His ex-wife had been a dressage rider, too. It was easy to recognize how quietly Jordana sat, her shoulders back, spine straight, her hands low in front of the saddle. She had the exact same posture. Yet, Slade couldn't draw a comparison between her and his ex-wife. Isabel had been a petulant child who'd used pouting and throwing temper tantrums in order to get what she wanted out of him. Jordana didn't seem fazed by his cold, hard manner. She took it in stride, listened to his orders and then seamlessly executed them. That made him curious about her. The last thing he needed, however, was to be drawn to a woman. He'd been successful these last four years of ignoring the opposite sex. His focus was trying to hold his beleaguered ranch together one month at a time.

"That's good enough," Slade called to her. "Come on in."

Jordana slowed Stormy down and guided her mare over to where Slade was standing. His face looked like stone. What did he think? Was Stormy's conformation good enough? And why was she so drawn to this glacial cowboy? Dismounting, she took the reins over Stormy's head.

"Unsaddle her."

Jordana nodded, dropped the reins and went to lift the stirrup to reach the cinch around the horse's sweaty barrel. She lifted off the saddle and the blanket, settling them across one of the rails of the pipe fence.

"Lead her out to the center of the arena."

Picking up the reins, Jordana walked, and Stormy followed her like a dog at her heels. Jordana turned and stood beside her mare's head. She watched as Slade approached. His gray eyes were narrowed, and she knew he was now critically assessing Stormy. Crouching beside her, he spoke softly to the mustang before gently laying his hands on the top of her front right leg.

Stormy's ears twitched back and forth to the softened male sounds. She stood perfectly still as Slade ran his hands knowingly down the length of her leg. He also examined the health of her hoof.

Shocked at the change in his demeanor, Jordana could only stand there keeping her mouth from dropping open. She watched as Slade's large, scarred hands moved with knowing skill down Stormy's sweaty leg. Hands that moved with such ease that Jordana swore she could feel them caressing her at the same time. Shaking herself out of the shock that Slade wasn't a coldhearted bastard like Paul Edwin had been, she allowed herself to take a deep breath of relief. Slade had a soft side to him after all! Even if he only unveiled and utilized it with horses, that was fine with Jordana. She could take his military-like demeanor if only he treated her horse with loving care. And he was doing just that.

Slade moved quietly around to the other side of the mare. He placed his hands on her other front leg. One never squatted down at the side of a horse's rear. If something spooked them, they could kick out in a semicircle arc and nail the person. Slade had seen people kicked in the head for doing just that. Straightening up, he walked toward her rear legs. He placed his left hand on the animal's rump and then, with his right hand, leaned down and stood close to the mare so she couldn't kick and injure him. In this way, it was safe, and he could continue to perform a thorough examination.

Jordana watched in silence. Slade's calloused hands were sun-darkened from being outside most of his life. Stormy stood quietly. She trusted the large cowboy. More relief filtered through Jordana. After Slade had examined Stormy's legs, he then came to her face and gently moved his fingers around her ears and her poll, the top of her head. Jordana knew he was looking for bumps, scars or cuts. Once more she felt his hands flowing across her. It was a crazy sensation! *What* was it about this hardened cowboy that unstrung her as a woman?

Gulping, Jordana forced herself to remain silent. She knew Slade was tactically memorizing every part of Stormy's conformation. He was building an anatomical picture of her body in his mind. And once he was done, he would have his decision for her. She saw him slide his fingers across the black dorsal stripe down the center of Stormy's back. Mustangs often possessed this stripe. Plus, Stormy had horizontal curved black bars on the back of her lower legs. It made her look somewhat like a long-lost relative from the zebra species. But she wasn't. These were genetic markers mustangs carried strongly throughout the breed.

Slade rounded the mare and then stood about six feet away from Dr. Lawton. She looked concerned and serious. He understood why. Seesawing back and forth inwardly, Slade didn't know what to do. Lawton was pretty in a natural kind of way. She had an oval face with a stubborn chin that spoke to her ability to finish what she started. There was no extra flesh on her body that he could see. That meant she was riding daily. Endurance riders put in ten to fifteen miles a day on their horse to keep it in shape for the fifty- and hundred-mile contests. She was a woman, and Slade tried to avoid the opposite sex like a plague. His other students were men. And that's the way he liked it.

"Your mare has a problem," he stated bluntly, drilling her with a hard look. Instantly, her eyes opened wider, and a stunned expression came to her features. He pointed down at the horse's front left leg. "There's scar tissue on her pastern that indicates she's suffered a serious cut in that area at one time."

"But," Jordana said, "that shouldn't stop her from being an endurance horse."

Scowling, Slade said, "That cut was deep. What do you know about it?"

"I've owned Stormy for two years, Mr. McPherson. She had that cut there long before that." Watching his expression, Jordana felt frustrated. All she could see was the glittering shards in his gray eyes. It was obvious he was going to turn her down.

Not if she could help it! "Stormy was captured out in Nevada in a government roundup. She was sold to Bud Hutchinson, who lives here in Jackson Hole. He told me when I bought his house that the mare came with the deal. When I had the vet check her, he noted that scar on her pastern. Bud said the mare came to him with it. The vet thought she probably cut her pastern a year earlier, so no one really knows the extent of that injury."

Grunting, Slade said, "Well, it's her Achilles' heel, Dr. Lawton."

"What about the rest of her conformation?"

"She's sound and she has good legs. But that scar makes her questionable. If she cut a tendon as a yearling out in the wilds, and it healed, that tendon is always going to be weak and suspect of breaking down."

"But you don't *know* if it was a cut tendon," Jordana countered strongly. She wasn't going to let this cowboy run over her.

Shrugging, Slade muttered, "That's true."

"And her legs are fine otherwise?"

"Yes, they're good."

"What else?" Jordana prodded. She saw him scowl,

his thick, dark brown brows moving downward in a slash because of her needling. Maybe he was the type of trainer who wanted to see his students have courage to confront him. Maybe he wasn't. She wasn't sure. All Jordana did know is she wanted a chance to train her mare with this man, no matter how sour and antisocial he appeared to be. At least he was gentle with Stormy. Jordana had gone through residency and taken plenty of blows from men who were threatened by her presence as a woman and a doctor. She'd weather Slade McPherson, too.

Surprised at Lawton's sudden backbone and fearlessness to confront him, Slade growled, "The worst strike against her is your horse is a mare."

Mouth dropping open, Jordana snapped it shut. Her hand tightened on the rope. Stormy's ears flicked back and forth as she read her mistress's reaction. "A *mare*? Oh, don't tell me you're one of those people? Mares compete in endurance against geldings and stallions and *win*!"

The power and force of her tempered anger hit Slade directly. Eyes narrowing, he saw the blue fire in her eyes. "Mares are fickle, just like women. They're made up of unstable hormones."

Real anger fired through Jordana. How dare this man! Mouth tightening, she lowered her husky voice. "That's an old saw and it doesn't work anymore, Mr. McPherson. If you're going to turn me down because my horse is a mare, that's a lousy excuse."

Squirming inwardly, Slade realized Dr. Lawton wasn't going to take no for an answer. If he said, "you're a woman and I don't like training women," then she'd explode into rage for sure. "Mares are just more difficult," he snarled. "But it's your choice. I don't really care." And he didn't. His students had gone on to win major endurance rides over the years.

Brows moving up, Jordana said, "Then, you'll accept us for training?"

"You aren't going to get far," Slade warned. "Your mare has a weak pastern due to that old injury. She'll break down before she ever gets to an endurance contest."

Angry, Jordana said, "And I disagree with you."

"Just because you're a doctor of humans doesn't mean you know animal anatomy," Slade reminded her. She really got under his skin, and he recalled Isabel had exhibited that same capability. Grudgingly, Slade admired Jordana because she had fire, passion and wasn't afraid to fight for what she thought was right. Isabel always sneaked around behind him, manipulated him and then pounced. Lawton wasn't like that. In fact, he admired her fearlessness because even men didn't take him on. Slade had one hell of a reputation of winning any argument he chose to defend. And he was losing this one to this banty rooster of a woman with fiery blue eyes and a stubborn chin.

Stormy moved restlessly, and Jordana placed her hand on the mare's damp neck. Instantly, the mustang quieted. "You're correct about that, Mr. McPherson. There is no test that can conclusively show that Stormy partially cut a tendon in her pastern or not. I'm willing to go on faith that she didn't."

"Okay, it's your money and time," he drawled.

"Then, you'll train us?" Hope rose in Jordana's voice. She knew McPherson was going to be a hard, demanding trainer, but she'd endured the toughest job in the world as a resident and made it. She'd make this a success, too.

"I'll take you on, Dr. Lawton. It'll cost you plenty of money. And I don't put up with anyone who's late. You show up on time or I'll send you packing."

"I'll be on time from now on," Jordana gritted, glaring up at him. His rugged features were shadowed by his tan Stetson. There was nothing forgiving about Slade McPherson. In the back of her mind, Jordana wondered what course in life had molded him into such a hard person.

"We'll see," Slade said. "Shorty, my wrangler, will show you to the training barn. You'll be writing me a check today for two thousand dollars. One thousand a month for the box stall, hay, special feed and one thousand for training you ten times a month out here at the ranch."

Two thousand dollars. Jordana blanched inwardly. Two years ago she'd settled the lawsuit against Dr. Paul Edwin. The settlement had been four hundred thousand dollars. Part of the agreement had been that she had to leave her position at the New York City hospital. Then, the recession occurred, and she'd lost all her stock savings in the crash of the stock market. Jordana had ended up broke and out of a job when it was all over. The settlement money had bought her a home here in Jackson Hole.

Slade watched her waffle, her eyes downcast. He had doubled the cost of his services in hopes of getting rid of her. If he couldn't argue her out of it, then he'd raise his price so high she couldn't afford it. He stood there feeling badly, but he really didn't want to have to teach a woman. They were nothing but trouble.

Mind whirling, Jordana lifted her head and said, "That's fine."

Stunned, Slade kept his face carefully arranged. Two thousand dollars more a month would be a godsend. "Good." He pointed to Shorty who was walking toward them. "Go with my wrangler. He'll assign your mare to a box stall."

Jordana felt dizzy. What had she just done? Two thousand dollars was a lot of money! At what price did she want her dream? And with a man who obviously disliked the fact she was a woman and her horse a mare.

CHAPTER THREE

"THIS WAY, MISS," Shorty said, coming up and doffing his head respectfully toward Jordana.

Slade walked away. If he stayed, he'd be staring at Lawton like a lovesick puppy. Her face was arresting. And what drew him, dammit, was her fire and gutsiness. He wondered if that would translate into her endurance riding or not.

Smiling, Jordana held out her hand. "Hi, Shorty, I'm Jordana Lawton. Nice to meet you." She saw Slade walk away as soundlessly as a cougar on the prowl. Disappointed he wouldn't stay around so she could talk more to him about the training, she pulled her attention back to the bowlegged wrangler.

"Howdy, ma'am. Come with me. The Boss has one box stall left in his endurance-training facility and your purty steel-gray mare gets it." He turned and walked quickly to a pole barn painted the same color of red as the massive barn that sat next to it.

Excited despite the gruff manner of McPherson, Jordana felt a weight lift off from her shoulder. The trainer had tried to get rid of her. *Why?* Stormy was an excellent endurance prospect, in her opinion. Was it because he disliked mares? Or worse, women? She saw no wedding band on Slade's hand. Stormy walked at her side and Jordana decided to find out.

"Shorty, is Mr. McPherson married?"

Chortling, Shorty gave her a sly grin. "No, ma'am, he's not. I'm afraid he had a run-in with a filly a while back. He's divorced four years ago and likes to keep it that way."

They walked up the slight gravel slope that led up to the pole barn. Both doors had been slid open to allow maximum air circulation throughout the building. Jordana worked to keep up with the fast walking and talking wrangler. "How long have you been working here, Shorty?"

"Too long," he laughed. Then, getting more serious, he said, "I worked for Mr. McPherson until he was killed by Red Downing, another rancher, in an auto accident. At that time, Slade and Griff, who are fraternal twins, inherited this ranch. But they were too young to take over as six-years-olds. Slade was adopted by his uncle Paul McPherson and Griff went with uncle Robert McPherson, who was a Wall Street broker in New York City. When Slade was ten, his adopted mother died of cancer. Then, Paul drank himself to death and he died when Slade was seventeen." Shorty halted at the concrete floor opening to the pole barn. His voice lowered. "At seventeen Slade had to take over this ranch. His brother didn't want anything to do with it. So, he struggled by himself to keep it going."

"That's a lot to ask of any seventeen-year-old," Jordana murmured.

Motioning, Shorty said, "Follow me down the breezeway here. Your mare's stall is the last one on the right," and he pointed toward the other end of the long, clean barn.

Digesting the information about Slade, Jordana set it

aside for later. Right now, as Stormy clip-clopped down the concrete aisle, horses on either side nickered in a friendly fashion to her. Jordana counted ten box stalls. She was the last student. Feeling lucky and happy, she followed Shorty.

Each roomy box stall had iron bars across the top half of it and sturdy oak below. Shorty slid the door open. Jordana was pleased to see that not only did the floor have thick black rubber matting to make it easy on a horse's legs, but also fresh cedar shavings were strewn over it. She brought Stormy to the opening and allowed the mare to look around, study and sniff it first. Mustangs were wild, and Jordana knew that Stormy had to check out her new surroundings before she'd ever step into the well-lit box stall. To try and force the mare into it, without giving her time to inspect it, would have been a mistake. Stormy would have balked and fought her instead.

"She's a mighty alert horse," Shorty noted, standing and assessing Stormy.

"Pure mustang," Jordana murmured.

"I can see." Shorty nodded toward her legs. "Got the zebra stripes on her legs. Good sign she's got seriously good mustang genes."

"I agree," Jordana said with a smile. "And her name is Stormy." The mustang stepped into the stall on her own. Following her mare, Jordana slid the door shut and unlatched the rope attached to the mare's red nylon halter. "You want me to leave her halter on, don't you?" she called to the wrangler.

"Yes, ma'am."

Stormy moved around sniffing and checking out the shavings. She touched noses with the curious big black horse next door and then went straight for the huge water dispenser located at the front of the stall. The mustang drank deeply and then smacked her wet lips afterward. Laughing, Jordana patted her mare. "You like your new digs, girl."

Shorty slid the door open for Jordana. "She looks purty happy in there. She a beaver?" He shut the door after the owner stepped into the passageway.

A beaver in horse language was a horse that chewed on wood areas of the stall when it was bored. And that could cause wind colic or worse. Jordana knew that in those cases, they would paint the wood with a foul taste that discouraged such a bad habit. "Nope, she has no stall problems."

"Well," Shorty said, "we don't have bored horses around here. The Boss works them every day, and by the time they're done, they're tuckered out and glad for a rest. On the days the students come out to ride their horses, they get a solid workout." He smiled a little and studied the rows of stalls. "Nope, none of these horses have much time to become bored."

"That's good," Jordana said. "Can you tell me the training schedule, Shorty?"

"The Boss didn't?" he asked, surprised.

Shaking her head, Jordana pulled out a small notebook from the back pocket of her jeans and opened it up. "No. And I'd like to know."

"Why, sure you do, ma'am. Let's amble down to the tack room at the other end of the pole barn. You'll be putting your saddle, bridle and tack box in there."

Jordana followed. The wrangler was so different from the owner it was stunning. Shorty was jovial, kind and open. All the things Slade McPherson was not.

"Starting tomorrow, the Boss will have me put Stormy on the hot walker for half an hour."

Mechanical walkers were a must in training. Jordana saw the machine in another nearby corral. It had four long metal arms sticking upward with a thick rope and snap on the end of each one. She knew four horses at a time would be snapped on to each rope and then the speed would be set by the operator. The circular walker looked more like a space vehicle to anyone who didn't know what it was used for. The covered motor was located in the center. The operator could make the horses walk or trot.

"He's not trotting them on it, is he?" Jordana wondered.

"Oh, no, ma'am. It's a fast walk to warm 'em up before they're worked. And he also uses it to cool 'em out after their training. Any fool who thinks they can trot a horse in that tight circle is lookin' for leg problems to develop real fast."

"Yes," she murmured, "I just wanted to make sure, was all."

Shorty slowed and opened the thick oak door. "Endurance horses have the best legs in the world. The Boss isn't interested in harming those legs, only makin' them stronger."

"Good to hear," Jordana said. The tack room was huge, roomy, spotlessly clean and smelled of leather. She loved the scent and inhaled it deeply. There was one hook for a bridle and an aluminum saddle rack suspended just below it. Shorty gestured to it.

"This will be for Stormy's gear." He pointed to a large wooden tack box below it. "Anything your horse needs insofar as brushes, combs, hoof pick and such, goes in here. I'll be puttin' Stormy's name on this box so you can identify it among all the others."

Jordana was impressed with Slade's management abilities. The box stalls had fresh shavings and were obviously cleaned daily. The waterers were automatic and filled as the horse drank it down. In the tack room, there were no cobwebs in the corners, no dust on the thick rubber mats across the floor. All the leather gear was clean, the bits shining, the saddles contained no dust anywhere upon them.

"Now," Shorty said, a bit of warning in his voice, "the Boss don't like dirt. He's a real nitpicker about it." Shorty went over to a specially made endurance saddle that had no horn on it. He lifted up a leather flap on the rear of it. "He expects you to keep your gear in tip-top shape. No dirt, crud or oil between the skirts here. And he'll be inspecting you every day you come out for training. Equally important is the cinch." Shorty picked up the white cotton girth that spanned the horse's belly and kept the saddle in place on its back. "He expects you to not only minutely look at each twisted strand of the girth for dirt or weeds, but also wash it once a week. He *hates* dirty cinches. That dirt can work into the horse's belly and create a sore and inflammation. Something this simple can take an endurance horse out of a contest. Don't disappoint him on this."

"I'm beginning to like him," Jordana said, impressed. She knew a dirty cinch was only asking for trouble. A horse had hair, but any sawing motion could pull it out and leave the horse's tender flesh open to being rubbed raw. And as a doctor, she was always aware of possible infection starting at such a site.

"Oh, he's a stickler," Shorty promised with a lopsided

grin. "You'll be spending a lot of time either in here or just outside the door cleaning your gear afterward. He don't want you leaving the premises until you've bathed your horse over at the shower area and then cleaned your leather. Oh, and make *sure* your horse's hooves are clean. If he finds any mud, manure or, worse, a stone lodged in the frog area of the hoof, he'll give you one warning. The second time, he'll release you as a student."

"Got it," Jordana said.

"Crud in the hoof can make a horse lame in a heart-beat."

"Yes, it can. I'm a stickler on that, too."

"Good to hear, ma'am." Shorty scratched his chin. "Okay, let's go over to the bathing area."

Just outside the pole barn and to the left stood another enclosed area. It was painted red and made of an aluminum roof and wooden sides. Shorty led her down a thickly graveled path. He slid the door open. "Now, this is where you will bathe your horse after your training is done. It's got solid rubber matting on the floor so the horse don't slide or skid. We've got panic snaps on the cross ties that will be attached to both sides of your mare's halter."

"I like panic snaps," Jordana agreed, stepping into the shower shed. It, too, was well lit. If a horse ever got scared or bolted while in the cross ties, all the owner had to do was jerk the panic snap open, and it instantly released the horse so it didn't choke itself to death in the ropes. These hardy steel snaps had saved many a horse from such an awful and completely preventable death. Yes, panic snaps cost a lot more, and some horse people didn't purchase them because of that. But what was the horse worth to them? For a little more money, they could protect their animal from such a fate. Jordana liked that Slade thought of all the details. It was obvious that he cared for the horse in every way possible. Would he care equally about the rider? That remained to be seen.

"Here's the showerhead and hose," Shorty told her, pointing up to the gear hanging on a hook on the right side of the shed. "The Boss doesn't believe in hitting a hot, sweaty horse with shockingly cold water. You'll find the water tepid, instead. He doesn't want them traumatized with a cold temperature."

"That's impressive," she murmured, deciding that Slade's earlier demeanor didn't carry through in his training philosophy. Maybe he just didn't like her? Jordana frowned and hoped not. Still, he'd been this side of testy and rude to her. Maybe he was having a bad day, she thought.

Shorty gestured for her to follow him out. "The Boss treats his horses like himself."

Jordana liked the warmth of the early July sun overhead. Having spent two winters in Jackson Hole, she had come to welcome the summer as never before. There was snow on the ground eight months out of the year. That was the part she didn't like. When spring came, however, there was no place on earth as beautiful as this valley and the dragon's teeth of the Tetons thrusting up out of the prairie.

"Now," Shorty said, walking toward the huge rectangular corral, "the Boss will be riding your mare daily in here. It's got two feet of fine sand as a base. That keeps your horse from pulling a muscle or, worse, a ligament or tendon. He's going to be seeing what her strengths and weaknesses are this next week."

"You mean he does all the riding?" Jordana was

surprised. That meant ten horses a day were ridden. "I thought he had help."

"No, ma'am, he does it all himself."

"No wonder he was upset with me arriving late."

Shorty grinned. "Time's money."

Nodding, Jordana now understood his frosty stance. "How long does he ride the horse?"

"Depends. At first, he's not going to push your mare. He's gonna see how she does at a walk, trot and canter. Might be on her for thirty minutes at the most, depending upon how built up she is or not."

"I've been riding Stormy ten to fifteen miles every third day. He will want to know that."

"Yep, he will. But when you come out the next time, he'll cover all that with you. The Boss can tell how in shape or not your horse is by merely examining it and watching it work."

That was true, Jordana decided. And Slade's gray eyes had missed nothing. He was handsome in a rugged kind of way. She liked his full mouth even though it had been thinned with displeasure talking to her. His nose was strong-looking and had a bump at the root of it, telling her he'd broken it some time earlier in his life. She'd liked his broad, square face, his skin burned brown by being out in the sun so much, the creases at the corners of his eyes deep. Was that from squinting in the bright, white snow or sun? Or were they laughter lines? Jordana highly doubted Slade had any humor in his bones. Not once had he cracked even a slight smile toward her. No, he wasn't Mr. Social, that was for sure.

"Oh," Shorty said, "you need to know that the Boss will *not* allow a rider to wear spurs or carry a whip."

"Not a problem. I don't do either."

"That's good because the Boss believes that if the horse and rider have a good rapport with one another, you can get all the speed out of the animal because it trusts you. Don't *ever* be seen carrying a crop. He'll kick you out of here so fast it'll make your head spin."

Laughing, Jordana held up her hands. "Not to worry. Stormy *hates* crops. In fact, when I bought her from Bud two years ago, he told me she was combative if she even *saw* a crop. He thinks the BLM cowboys used whips to get her into a corral. No, Stormy hates crops."

"The Boss will want to know that."

"Good."

Shorty walked her back to the truck. "I'll help you bring in all your gear to the tack room and then you can leave."

"Thanks for the help," she said, appreciating the wrangler. Looking around the large operation, Jordana didn't see McPherson. The robins were singing in the oak and maple trees that surrounded the one-story ranch house in the distance. There was no lawn, and it looked pretty shabby in comparison to the spotless pole barn and showering shed. Maybe being a single male was the reason. Jordana would have put in a small lawn, flower boxes on the front windows and a small white picket fence around it. A woman's touch. But this hard cowboy wasn't much for decoration. At least he cared for his endurance horses. And that was all that counted in her book.

"Now, you need to write out a check for the first month's rent and training," Shorty reminded her.

"As soon as I get the tack put away, I will," Jordana promised him, opening up the trailer door to remove the saddle and bridle.

DRIVING AWAY FROM Tetons Ranch, Jordana felt happier than she had in two years. Hands firmly on the steering wheel of her three-quarter-ton truck that hauled the empty horse trailer, she drove out just as slowly as she had come in. Maybe McPherson had a tractor stowed away somewhere and would get Shorty out here to flatten it once more.

The sky was a bright blue. The sunlight made the Tetons mountain range west of her look tall, rugged and beautiful. By early July, the last of the snow was almost gone until September, when it would once more become a white cloak around each of the sharp, pointed peaks. Her mind ranged over the price of the training. As a physician, she made good money. Her savings was now gone. She'd spent it buying a house at the edge of town. Two thousand dollars a month for training was going to stretch her in a way she hadn't counted on. Jordana wanted to put money back into savings, but this training fee wouldn't allow it.

Grimacing, she slowed at the stop sign that would take her to the highway. Turning left, she drove back toward Jackson Hole. If she'd gone right, she'd be heading into Yellowstone National Park about forty miles away.

Between her clinic and working part-time at the hospital, Jordana made ends meet. Now, with two thousand going out a month, she was hamstrung. Yet, all her life she'd loved horses, and endurance riding had always been her outlet. Could she give that up? Was it too expensive to follow her dream of having the best trainer in the United States train her and Stormy? Jordana waffled, unsure.

Slade McPherson was challenging, to say the least to her. But he'd been gentle with Stormy. How would he treat her? A horse trainer didn't always transition well from animal to human. She'd had some bad experiences with horse trainers before. Yet, if Jordana was honest with herself, she'd been *drawn* to the iconic cowboy. That made *no* sense at all to her! Yet, she couldn't help but look at his mouth and wonder what it would be like to be kissed by this hard man who braved nature without a second thought. And as he'd run his hands lightly and gently down Stormy's legs, Jordana swore she could feel those rough, callused hands exploring her at the same time.

"Phew!" she muttered. "This is crazy!"

Was it? What adventures waited for her two days from now when she began her first lesson on Stormy with tough Slade McPherson?

CHAPTER FOUR

JORDANA TRIED TO calm her nerves as she rode Stormy out into the huge rectangular arena where Slade McPherson stood. Her heart wouldn't settle down. It was July 3, the late afternoon sky filled with threatening clouds. As she looked toward the ragged-edge Tetons, she saw a massive thunderstorm over their sharp peaks. It might come their way if it was strong enough. The wind was up, and Stormy was more alert.

Today was the first day of her training with the implacable McPherson. Why had she had two dreams in a row about this hard-looking cowboy? As Jordana pressed her calf into Stormy's side to make the turn into the sandy arena, she had mixed feelings. Wasn't it enough she was working twelve hours a day either at her clinic or the hospital? Since the settling of the lawsuit, she had no desire to get entangled with a man. She was still too raw from the experience, the trauma of the move west and trying to get some sanity back into her life.

"Take her at a walk around the arena to the left," Slade ordered, his voice carrying across the distance.

Nodding, Jordana took in a deep breath and tried to relax. She knew that Slade was going to be damn tough on her. Stormy had already had two daily workouts. The mustang mare seemed completely oblivious to her anxious state, just plodding along on a loose rein.

"Quit slouching," he called. "Straighten up."

Instantly, Jordana took the bow out of her back, squared her shoulders and lifted her chin slightly. Quirking her mouth, she wondered if McPherson was going to always yell at what she did wrong, but offer no praise for what she had done right. Many trainers were like that, she'd discovered. If she didn't have confidence built up over years of being a resident, she might wither away under such an unfair training system. At two thousand dollars a month, Jordana wasn't going to let his snappish orders scare her away.

Slade eyed the pair as they walked around the arena in a relaxed fashion. He tried to keep his eyes off Jordana, but that was impossible. His job was to see how she rode, how she sat in the saddle and how she handled her horse. He'd been dreading this moment for days. Having a woman among his male students was like a thorn in his side. He didn't want her or her runt of a mare, but he needed her money. Guilt niggled at him. Jordana was sincere in contrast to his greediness. Slade didn't like that about himself. She had come to him honestly. So what did that make him?

Not looking at the answer too closely, he enjoyed watching her lower body move in sync with the horse. Wearing jeans, boots and a dark green T-shirt, she was all woman. Curvy in all the right places, Jordana was a fit athlete. "How long you been riding in endurance events?" he asked.

"Two years," she called.

Grunting, Slade nodded. "Slow trot," he ordered.

Pressing her calves to Stormy, Jordana felt the mustang mare instantly obey. Although a small horse, Stormy had long legs. Jordana posted, which meant

she lifted her butt off the saddle with every other stride
of the animal. That resulted in less pounding on her
mare's back. She knew it was the English way of riding
a horse. The Western style was to sit the trot and flow
with the horse.

"Sit the trot," he called.

Grimacing, Jordana did. She hated not being able to
post. After going halfway around the arena, she called,
"I'd rather post. It's easier on the horse's back."

"Sit the trot."

Growling to herself, Jordana complied. It took a lot of
work to keep her legs against Stormy, her thighs strong
and clamped solidly to the saddle and horse. If she hadn't
done so, she'd be bouncing and flying all over the place.
Was he testing her strength? Was that what this was all
about? The wind sang through her hair. Lifting her hand,
she pulled the black baseball cap a little lower over her
brow. The wind would pull it off if she didn't.

"Do a series of figure eights at a sitting trot."

Jordana knew without a doubt he was seeing just how
much strength and control she had over Stormy. A figure eight required her to do a circle over one half of the
arena and, once they trotted down the center of it, to turn
the other way and complete the second circle. This was
easy stuff for her. Stormy wasn't breathing hard at all,
her ears flicking back and forth. When her ears moved
back, she was listening to Jordana's silent leg, weight
or hand signals.

"Canter the figure eight," Slade ordered, his deep
voice carrying strongly across the wide expanse.
Whether he wanted to admit it or not, Jordana had a lot
of good riding habits. It grated that she was using dressage, but that was only because Isabel had been a dres-

sage rider. A well-trained horse became fine tuned with dressage training, and it wasn't a bad thing to have in an endurance horse. There would be times that Jordana would have to use her weight or legs in tight places. Why the hell was he aching to kiss this woman? Slade hadn't liked his dreams of the past two nights. Both involved kissing this doctor, who exuded quiet confidence. *No way. Just no way. Keep it impersonal*, he ordered himself.

"Go the other direction now," he called.

By the time he ordered her into the center of the arena to rest, Jordana was feeling the intense workout. She halted Stormy in front of him and dropped the reins to allow her mare to lower her head and rest, too.

Slade studied Jordana's face. He had a tough time seeing her as a physician. She just didn't look like the type. Moving to the horse, he thrust two fingers beneath the horse's cinch. It was tight but not too tight. She was so close. He liked her long legs and the way her firm thighs curved against the horse.

"Why don't you let me post?" Jordana demanded. "It's easier on my horse's back and it also allows me to rest between beats."

Slade stared up into her narrowed blue eyes. She was tough, but then, in endurance riding, that was a good trait. "I wanted to see how your mare took to it."

Surprised, Jordana said, "Oh..." She hadn't thought about that.

"You can go back to posting. It's not a bad thing to do on fifty and hundred milers. It saves your horse's back and it also allows you to rest a bit between strides, too—like you said."

"Good," Jordana whispered, suddenly smiling with

relief. She leaned forward and threaded Stormy's thick black mane through her fingers. The mare's ears flicked.

Her hands were beautiful, Slade realized as he stood near the shoulder of the horse. Jordana's rhythmic movements reminded him of water flowing gracefully in and around rocks. There was a slight sheen of perspiration across her brow as she pushed the brim of the black baseball cap upward. And her smile melted him in a way he could never have fathomed. *What* was it about this woman that made him feel like putty?

"Several things," he growled. "All mustangs came from Spaniards' horses who escaped from them when they came up here in the 1500s. The conquistador leaders had part-Arabian mounts bred with local horses in Spain. They were known as Spanish barbs and that's what your mare is." Slade studied Stormy's fine head. "She even has the slightly dished face of an Arabian."

Jordana nodded. "And she possesses that long, elastic trot of an Arab, too, but I'm sure you already saw that." After all, he'd ridden Stormy two days in a row.

Nodding, Slade found himself enjoying Jordana's knowledge. She knew her mustang well. "Yes, and that's what will make your mare a potential winner. Arabians are the only breed with the extended trot where they naturally float, all four feet off the ground." He held his hands up to demonstrate. "All other breeds have an extended trot, too, but they don't float a foot or two farther with each stride when all four hooves are off the ground, like an Arab or mustang can. And it's that one to two feet of float above the ground that gives Stormy a stride advantage. She can take on horses that are fifteen and sixteen hands high and still match their stride. The taller horses have longer legs, therefore, a longer stride. Mustangs and Arabians, however, compensate with this genetic gift only they have."

"And that's why," Jordana told him, "so many Arabian and part-Arabians win the major endurance contests."

Nodding, he said, "Right."

"And Thor, your mustang stud, has the same type of stride. I've seen video on the internet of him when you've got him in the extended trot. He's magnificent."

Pleased by the sudden passion in her husky voice and the enthusiasm burning in her eyes, Slade privately arched a little over her praise. It struck him in that moment that he really had missed the soft warmth of a woman around him. There had been times when Isabel had been like that with him, but not very often. Scowling, Slade said, "Thor has won every major endurance event."

Relaxing in the saddle, Jordana brought her leg up and over the saddle. "You and Curt Downing, who owns that black Arabian stallion, are always trading for first or second. I can't tell you how many times you gave us an exciting finish."

Mouth tightening, Slade snarled, "Downing is a son of a bitch and I don't want to talk about him." He held on to his simmering anger. Seeing the shock register on Jordana's face, he added, "Whether you know it or not, Downing is a cheat and up to no good out on the trail when judges and spectators don't see him."

"What do you mean?" Jordana asked, confused. She saw anger come to his narrow eyes. This time, Slade was real easy to read. She was beginning to realize when his full mouth was thinned, he was upset about something. And the way his brown brows slashed downward, it was easy to see he was furious. With her? Jordana hoped not.

"Downing has no honor out on the trail," Slade gritted out. "We've got the fifty mile Tetons Endurance ride coming up on September 1st. He'll be there and so will I."

"What do you mean no honor?"

Studying her innocent face, Slade said, "You've been in endurance races?"

"Sure, many, but they were fifty milers was all, and I was small stuff compared to the pros who rode their horses."

"Did you ever see anyone strike a horse and rider with a crop? Crowd them off a narrow trail?"

"Why…no," she admitted. "Is that what Downing does?"

Giving her a sour look, Slade said, "Oh, yeah, and worse."

"You know this from personal experience?"

"I do," he said in a clipped voice. "And so do a lot of the other pros who ride the top endurance circuit."

"If Downing is as bad as you say he is, how come he's never been caught doing these things?" she demanded. Jordana knew that the ranch next to Slade's was owned by the Downing family. Was this a local dust-up? Two arrogant endurance champions who couldn't stand one another from a competitive sense?

"Believe me, there's plenty of endurance riders just waiting to catch him in the act. Once it gets beyond the 'he said-she said' and we've got cell-phone photo proof, he'll be booted out once and for all. Until that happens, it's one person's word against another and the judges can't move on that. Downing does his dirty work in areas where there are no prying eyes of spectators or judges."

Jordana felt the anger in Slade. "I never realized that

went on. All the contests I've ridden on, the riders were respectful and followed the rules."

Giving her a quirked grin, Slade said, "There's *always* a bad apple in every group. Downing is it. And you might as well know it because if you're going to ride on the national circuit, you'll be meeting him at every one of those endurance events."

Shivering, Jordana ran her hand down her arm feeling the goose bumps Slade's harsh words created. "I just can't believe it."

Whipping his gaze upward, Slade met and held her innocent-looking blue eyes. "You won't have much to worry about. Your mare will never be able to keep up with his black stud or Thor."

"We'll see about that," Jordana said, keeping her voice light. She saw the steel glint in Slade's eyes. God help her, but she thought he was the most handsome man she'd ever seen. He wasn't pretty-boy handsome. He was a man's man from the rugged cut of his sunburned features to the way he stood, walked and held himself. Despite his constant grumpiness toward her, Jordana allowed herself to at least appreciate him on purely a woman's level. The words "eye candy" came to mind. Despite his outer armored toughness, she'd seen him deal gently with her horse. There was good somewhere deep down in this Wyoming cowboy. And inwardly, Jordana promised herself she'd find it. Not sure how, she kept that secret to herself.

"Enough talking," Slade muttered. "Let's repeat the gaits and figure eight in the other direction."

"May I post this time?" she asked, smiling down at him. She saw his face thaw for an instant. And just as quickly become hardened. So, a warm smile got to him?

Well, that was good to know. Maybe just being friendly was all she had to do around him. Jordana wanted a less acerbic teaching relationship with Slade. She saw enough irritable and angry people in the emergency room of the hospital. She didn't need it out here, too.

"Post," he agreed, gesturing for her to get out in the arena once more.

Later, after an hour's worth of working Stormy in the arena, Jordana walked at Slade's side as she led her mare back to the stall area to be unsaddled. The sun's light was more westerly now, the thunderclouds approaching the valley beneath the slopes of the Tetons. The wind was picking up, too. "Looks like we're going to get that thunderstorm," she said, wanting to see if he would make small talk.

Grunting, Slade gave her a brisk nod.

Ouch. Undaunted, Jordana said, "When I was in residency at a New York City hospital, I always loved the storms that came during the summer. It cooled the city down for a little bit."

Staring at her, Slade almost stopped. "You're from New York City?"

She heard the stunned disbelief in his tone. Why was he looking at her suddenly as if she was an alien from another planet? "Yes, I was born and raised there. Why?"

Clamping down on an expletive, Slade said instead, "You're a city slicker."

"That sounds like a curse," Jordana teased lightly, taken aback by his scowl. Slowing up, she dropped Stormy's reins just outside the tack room. Stormy had been taught to ground tie. When the reins dropped to the ground, she was to stand and not move. Jordana eased the flap of her saddle upward to reach the cinch.

Slade stood uncertainly, his mind whirling. Isabel
had been from that same damned city, a spoiled brat
pouting all the time when she didn't get her way. She
would throw a temper tantrum like a young horse who
was saddled for the first time. And yet, as he watched
Jordana release the cinch and unbuckle the breastplate
around Stormy's chest, he couldn't help but stop the
comparison. This woman was confident, mature and
had a quick, easy smile that automatically felt as if her
hands were smoothing down his irritable nature just as
he'd touch a horse to calm it.

"Well?" Jordana prodded, smiling as she walked past
him with the saddle in her arms, "am I a damned city
clod in your eyes?"

Bristling, Slade opened the tack-room door for her.
"It explains why you post. East Coast riders are taught
English riding and not Western-style riding." It wasn't
a lie. He just didn't want to get into the painful and private parts of his divorce with Jordana. Oddly, as Slade
watched her put the saddle over the aluminum rack on
the oak wall, he thought Jordana might not only understand, but be sympathetic toward him. Isabel had taken
him for everything. He'd lost so much in the divorce.

Jordana would clean her gear later. Right now, Stormy
was wet and sweaty and needed to be bathed over at the
shower barn. "Guilty on all counts," she said, walking
past him.

"Were you always around horses?" he wondered,
walking with her to the shower barn.

"My father is a cardiac surgeon and my mother was
an Olympic dressage champion. I feel like I got the best
genes from both of them," she told him, a warm feeling
in her heart for her parents.

"They still live in New York City?" Slade liked talking with her a lot more than he thought he would. He saw her smile dissolve and her features become sad.

"They died in an airplane crash five years ago."

"I'm sorry," Slade muttered, meaning it.

"So am I," Jordana said quietly. She halted at the showering area. Dropping the halter lead, she slid the door open. Mustering a slight smile, she picked up the lead and asked Slade, "What about your parents? Do they live nearby? I've never seen anyone but you and Shorty here at the ranch."

As Slade watched her lead Stormy into the shower stall and put the cross ties on her mare's halter, he found himself wanting to tell her the truth. Walking around the horse and staying far enough away from getting splattered with water, he said, "Red Downing, who was Curt Downing's father, crashed into my parents' truck. They died instantly. He was drunker than a skunk."

Jordana froze when she heard his words hesitantly tear out of him. She recalled Shorty telling her about his parents but decided to hear his version of it. Looking over, she saw pain in Slade's face. For the first time, he'd unveiled his armor and she got to see the human in him. There was such grief in his eyes it tore at her heart.

"I'm so sorry, Slade. I really am. How tragic…"

"Yeah, it was. In more ways than one," he muttered, crossing his arms. Leaning against the wall as she began to use the shower hose to wet Stormy down, he added, "Me and my fraternal twin brother, Griff, were orphaned at six years old. My parents had left us the ranch in their will, but we were too young to run it. My dad had two older brothers, Paul and Robert. Griff moved back East with Uncle Robert. I stayed out here with Uncle Paul and Aunt Patty. Together, they took over the running of our ranch."

Jordana took a plastic brush and began gently scrubbing Stormy's neck. She stood quietly, appreciating the tepid water. Looking over her back, Jordana realized that Slade was this way because of the early loss of his parents. She tried to put herself in his place. Wouldn't she toughen up, too? Would the world look scary and uncertain to Slade and his brother? *Very.* Gently, she asked, "Is your brother Griff also an endurance rider?" She had never seen him on the circuit.

Giving her a jaded look, Slade felt helpless to stop from telling her about his painful past. "No. Griff went back to New York City with Uncle Robert and his wife. He's never cared about the ranch."

"Ah, this is where city slicker comes in?" she teased softly and added a smile. Slade's face went dark, and he refused to meet her gaze. *Oops.* She'd said the wrong thing. Scrubbing Stormy's withers with a soft rubber brush where the saddle sat, Jordana made sure to get all the grit and dust washed off her because it could cause inflammation and create a saddle sore if she didn't.

Battling his sudden emotions that rose unexpectedly within him, Slade muttered, "My younger brother is a Wall Street broker. He got sent to Harvard and has an MBA. He followed in my Uncle Robert's footsteps."

"I see," Jordana said, moving the brush and the water down the center of Stormy's gray back. "Does he visit often?"

Shaking his head, Slade said, "Griff likes New York. He likes the East, the big money he makes, the power he has, the women who like to follow the money trail. He doesn't have time for our family's ranch."

The hurt was so evident that Jordana couldn't shield herself from his sadness. All of a sudden, she wanted to drop the brush and shower wand, run over to Slade and throw her arms around him. In that split second, he looked like the grief-stricken six-year-old who had had his family suddenly torn away from him. Privileged to see the real man, Jordana stood there unable to say or do anything. She couldn't run over and embrace him. What Slade needed was to be held, rocked, nurtured and kept safe. Now, she was seeing a little of how he saw life. It was a hard life. It took those he loved away from him. And speaking about his brother tore away a new scab that hadn't really healed at all. Moistening her lips, Jordana said, "Sometimes, life is harsh."

He snorted, allowed his arms to fall to his side and glared at her. Scared that he'd opened up to this woman, who was really a stranger to him, had him feeling uneasy. "That's right. It *always* is. I'll see you in three days."

Watching Slade leave, Jordana saw how quickly he closed up once more. His eyes, however, couldn't lie. She saw such anguish in them that it made her want to cry. And he would *never* allow her close to him. Like the hurt animal he was, he'd bite anyone's hand offering help. Sighing, she continued to scrub Stormy free of sweat and dust. The first clap of thunder rolled across the land. Looking up, she saw the churning gray and black clouds racing down upon the valley. Soon, it would pour rain in buckets. Was the sky already crying for the pain that Slade McPherson carried daily within him? No parents were here to love and guide him. No one to help him grow up safe and nurtured. No wonder he was a loner...

CHAPTER FIVE

As JORDANA DROVE into the training facility, her heart leaped with surprise. There stood the most famous endurance rider and horse in the country—Slade and Thor. She wasn't sure who was more masculine, proud and aloof: the stud or the man. Smiling with excitement, she forgot about the stress of hurrying out to Tetons Ranch to arrive on time. As a physician she had unexpected emergencies that she had to attend to before anything else. Jordana lived in continued anxiety that one day, she might be late. Slade wouldn't tolerate tardiness.

Climbing out of her truck, she grinned. "Hey, seeing Thor in person, instead of in a photo, is astounding!" Thor had a "cap" of chestnut color splotched across his head and ears. That was known as a medicine-hat pattern. Native Americans considered such a horse as powerful, protective and lucky. Thor had sky-blue eyes, and Jordana knew it made him even more rare and beautiful. His white hair covered part of his face along with chestnut markings down to his pink-colored muzzle and wide, flaring nostrils.

Pride flowed through Slade. His stallion snorted, his chestnut-colored ears flicking as Jordana approached. The hot July sun beat down on them. "Get Stormy saddled up," he ordered. "We're going on a fifteen-mile run."

Shocked, Jordana halted. "Really?"

Giving her a sliver of a one-sided smile, Slade said, "You brought your mare to me in top shape. Shorty said you were riding her fifteen miles twice a week. She's ready for this."

Swallowing her shock and pleasure, Jordana said, "I'll be right there!" She trotted up to the training barn, her heart soaring with joy. Stormy greeted her with a friendly nicker as she walked down to the end box stall. As she placed her mare in the cross ties to be brushed and saddled, Jordana felt hopeful. Ever since meeting Slade, her days had taken on a new brightness and hope. Not wanting to look at that aspect too closely, Jordana told herself she was drawn to the cowboy because of his rugged good looks and that was all. Clearly, Slade had no women around here.

As she hurried to the tack room and picked up the thick pad and saddle, Jordana recalled talking to one of her patients who knew Slade. Tracy Border, a thirty-year-old mother of two who was trying to lose weight, had said Slade was called The Loner. That his wreck of a divorce had all but put his ranch into teetering foreclosure with the local bank. Further, Slade had been married to a brat of a woman who had no maturity. With that information, Jordana could understand why Slade was anti-female. He had to have time to get over a divorce.

The sweet smell of alfalfa hay wafted through the barn. Inhaling the scent, Jordana often wished that some perfume company would make the fragrance. She'd wear it for sure!

Releasing Stormy from the ties, she quickly placed the hackamore on her mare, clucked to her to follow and hurried out of the facility. Slade was already mounted on

the restive, powerful-looking Thor. Jordana knew that
the Native Americans felt the medicine-hat pattern, that
was sometimes found on paint or pinto mustangs, was
powerful. In fact, war chiefs often coveted such beautifully marked mustangs because they were considered
the ultimate, courageous warhorses. Thor was pawing
the ground, anxious to get on with the ride. He stood fifteen hands tall, which was rare for a mustang. Most were
very small in comparison. His white body was splattered
with chestnut markings that made her think of an artist
carelessly throwing paint here and there across his athletic body. She liked the mixing of white and chestnut
on his long, flowing mane and tail.

"I'm ready," she called, grinning.

Warmth flowed through Slade as he sat relaxed on
his stallion. "Mount up," he told her. For a stolen moment, Slade watched like a starving wolf as Jordana easily vaulted up into her specially made endurance saddle.
Today she wore a bright pink T-shirt, a beat-up black
baseball cap and jeans. Her curves called to him, and
Slade had to tear his gaze from her small breasts. Jordana's cheeks were red, and he'd come to realize when
she was excited, they colored to mirror her happiness.

Squeezing her calves against Stormy's sleek gray barrel, she rode up and paralleled Slade. "What now?"

Lifting his hand, he said, "We'll take the path between the pastures. At the end of it, we'll go left and then
we'll be on Elkhorn Ranch property. Iris Mason gave
me permission years ago to utilize her large ranch land
to train my endurance horses. I only have fifty acres,
which isn't enough to toughen up an endurance prospect. On her property, there's hills, slopes of mountains,

as well as flat areas. We need all those to challenge the horse and get him...her...up to speed."

"What a wonderful gift Iris gave to you!"

He nodded and brought the brim of his Stetson down more securely on his head. "She's the matriarch of this valley and has a good heart. When I went to her and asked for her permission, she gave it right away. And she didn't ask for any money. That's the kind of person she is." Slade was grateful that Iris hadn't demanded money for the use of her land. She could have but knew, as every other rancher did in this valley, he was nearly penniless. Iris helped out those who had less, and he was thankful for her kindness.

"I hear Iris is marrying Professor Timothy Varden from Harvard," she said.

Nodding, Slade thought of the invite he'd just received to the event. "Yes, she's in her eighties but she fell hard for the guy." And secretly, Slade was happy for Iris. She was one of the stalwart leaders in the valley.

"One of my patients told me about her yesterday. I don't think anyone dislikes Iris."

"She's special."

"I heard that Senator Peyton was convicted and going to prison. I met Clarissa Peyton the other day over at Gwen Garner's quilt shop. After Gwen told me what had happened, I felt very sorry for the woman."

"Yeah, it's been rough on Clarissa. Matt Sinclaire was his target. This year it's been a mix of good, sad and bad news."

"I met Casey Cantrell at a luncheon," Jordana said with a wispy smile. "She and Matt just got engaged. They're going to get married at Christmas. Matt felt that his daughter, Megan, would have the terrible memory of her mother killed in that arson fire erased by the happy one."

"Matt has gone through hell," Slade agreed, grim. The firefighter had lost Bev, his wife and almost lost his daughter Megan to Senator Peyton's attempt to kill them. "I like Casey a lot. And Megan is speaking up a storm now. After the fire, she went mute. And it wasn't until of late she started talking again."

"I think it was due to Casey," she confided. Slade's face had softened and he was reflective. Jordana knew that this valley's people were very close, and all had connections with one another like a larger family.

"I do, too. Megan calls her Mommy now and I think they'll have a happy ending. Matt certainly deserves a break after all this hell he's gone through."

Nodding, she added, "I suppose you hear most of the town gossip? That Zach Mason, Iris's grandson, has been caught driving drugs to and from Cheyenne with a gang? I'll bet Iris is heartbroken."

"There's not much I don't hear," Slade drawled. "And Zach's mother, Allison Mason, was just convicted of trying to murder her stepdaughter. Good thing she didn't succeed, but her son Zach, swore vengeance."

"I heard from another patient that Zach has been in drugs for a long time."

"That's true," Slade said, running his fingers through Thor's silky white-and-chestnut mane. "I'm more worried about the sister, Reagan. She had a real career ahead of her in movie directing but she's sat tight here after the conviction. Word's out that she's going to get even with Kam Trayhern, the woman her mother tried to murder."

Sighing, Jordana said, "That's what Gwen Garner said. My heart breaks for those two kids. Why didn't

Allison Mason think about them before she tried this harebrained scheme to kill Kam Trayhern?"

Shrugging, Slade said, "People do funny things when they're threatened." Hadn't he? After Isabel had left him, he'd turned into an angry bull, much like Diablo. Human feelings were tough to control sometimes. Slade lifted out of his thoughts and said, "I want you to take off in front of me. Walk Stormy to warm her up until we hit that left turn. Then, I want you to do a slow trot. At all times, I'll be behind you. I want to size up your mare on the different geological areas and see how she reacts."

"Okay," Jordana said, feeling her heart swell with a fierce affection for the taciturn cowboy. "I was doing the same type of riding in the south Jackson Hole area."

"I'm familiar with where you worked her," Slade said. "But this has more altitude, is rockier and is far more challenging. If you want Stormy to compete in the top tier, she has to not only take this type of terrain on, but excel at it. Today is a test run. We'll see how she does." He didn't say he'd also be watching how Jordana rode and negotiated the coming demands. As on every endurance ride, the rider never knew what was coming next. He'd get to see how Jordana "talked" to her mare and how the horse responded.

Nodding, Jordana smiled and said, "Okay, we're off on our first adventure with you!" She walked Stormy past the impatient Thor. The stallion was in magnificent shape. Jordana knew that Thor was the past winner of the Tetons Fifty-mile endurance ride. And he was signed up to run it in early September.

Stormy was hard-pressed to just walk. Like any well-trained athlete, she found walking boring. She pranced and danced sideways as they made their way between the two huge cattle pastures. On her right she saw the massive one-ton bull, Diablo, who was alone and looking forlornly across to the other pasture where his ladies were. In the other pasture, the calves had been separated from their mamas, and they were now fattening up on the lush Wyoming grass.

Slade liked the power of Thor as he rode. The stallion was competitive just like him, and he didn't like walking behind Stormy. Chomping at the bit, the stallion tossed his head, his long, thick mane flying like a banner in the breeze. At the corner, he watched Jordana give Stormy a leg signal to make the turn. And then, the gray mare broke into a slow trot. Thor lunged, partly reared and fought the bit.

"Easy," Slade murmured, sliding his gloved hand down the stallion's tightly arched neck. "You'll get to run here shortly."

Snorting violently, Thor pranced as he made the turn. Slade was pleased to see that Jordana was keeping Stormy at a slow trot instead of a fast one. It was so important to warm up an endurance horse the right way. Humans had to do stretches in order to limber up and get more blood into their bodies to face the demanding tasks that would be asked of them. Horses were no different. However, a highly trained and competitive endurance horse *hated* walking. They would much rather move into a ground eating trot. A horse could pull a muscle, ligament or tendon if not warmed up properly for the coming demanding distances.

Once they rode past the gate and shut it behind them, Slade told her, "See this trail? It leads up to two steep hills about five miles away. I want you to ride at an extended trot. Float her if you can. Tactics in top competition are to get your horse into any flat area where they can hit maximum stride. This is where riders can make up lost time that they'll encounter in hills or mountainous or steep areas."

Jordana rode next to the impatient Thor. "And then I'll be at those twin hills. What then?"

"There's a path up the first one. Follow it up and down to the second hill. Go up and over the second hill, then, turn left. The trail is flat for two miles. Open her up to a controlled canter. Nothing out of control. I need to see how winded she's become."

Patting Stormy's neck, Jordana said, "I think she'll sail through these challenges without a problem."

Grunting, Slade muttered, "We'll see."

Taking the gauntlet being thrown down at her, Jordana grinned. "Competition is my middle name."

Giving her a sour grin in return, Slade liked the blue fire dancing in her eyes. Her shoulder-length black hair was mussed around her face and neck. The urge to reach out and tame some of those reddish strands mixed with black ones nearly overwhelmed him. He couldn't touch Jordana. He didn't *dare*. Her winsome smile, the joy in her expression all served to make Slade happy. For the first time in so many years, he'd forgotten what that emotion felt like. What *was* it about this feisty upstart of a woman that took him on? Slade realized Jordana had never flirted with him. No, she was all business and professional. *Arm's length*. Sadness rolled through him. Maybe it was just as well, Slade acknowledged. He was in no position to think about a relationship. His whole focus was on saving his ranch from foreclosure.

Taking out a stopwatch from the leather vest he wore

over his white cowboy shirt, he said, "Okay, take off. I'll be timing you."

Jordana gave him an evil grin. "Okay, we're off! Watch us fly!" and she asked Stormy to move into an immediate trot.

Slade smiled reluctantly as she moved her small mustang down the trail. In moments, Jordana had the horse in that elastic, floating trot that only Arabians could manage for miles on end. Giving his restive stallion a nudge with his heels, Slade let Thor eagerly take off in pursuit. He did not like being second to anyone and fought the bit.

Jordana moved in sync with her mare as she continued for five miles at a floating trot. It was a hard trot to ride well. Lucky for her, her thighs had been molded by fifty-mile rides for the past year, so it wasn't much of an effort for her. Just knowing Slade was behind her made her smile for no reason. Her focus was on the terrain up in front of them. When they hit the first steep, forested hill, Stormy lunged easily up the dirt path. She moved into a walk to a regular trot when the landscape allowed it. The area was strewn with fallen logs and branches from the surrounding trees. Stormy easily leaped over them. Never once did she balk, skid to a stop and refuse to jump. Jordana knew that the top endurance horses were fearless and would attempt to jump without balking. She patted Stormy's wet, gleaming neck as they trotted down and across to the next hill.

As she leaned back in the saddle as Stormy skidded down the second steep slope, Jordana laughed out loud. The warmth of the July day, the strong scent of pine in the air, the wind moving past her face all conspired to give her a sense of freedom she loved so much. At the

base of the hill, she leaned forward, and Stormy immediately broke into a controlled canter. For the next two
miles, they were on flat but uneven ground. Ahead of
her, she saw the slope of another mountain. This one
would be different. Jordana knew that trees that had
been cut down, their stumps thrusting warningly above
ground, were a special hazard to a fast-moving horse
and rider.

She had expected Slade to stop her at the slope, but
he remained behind her. *Okay, no problem.* She urged
Stormy up the steep, twisting trail. Rocks were here and
there, and the mustang expertly stepped over and around
them. Stumps were always a special danger. Forest rangers or timber companies had come in and cut the pines
down and left the stumps sticking up like spears ready
to dig into her horse's fine, thin legs. Stormy was at a
trot, lunging upward, always alert, but Jordana had to
be, too. She couldn't just rely on her mare to see these
dangerous obstacles coming up.

Giving Stormy her head, laying the reins on the
horse's neck, Jordana leaned forward over the withers
to keep her mustang balanced as she negotiated the ever-
curving, twisting, uphill trail. Stormy was breathing
hard as they moved from sixty-five hundred feet in altitude to nearly nine thousand feet.

The trail was tricky, challenging and dangerous. Jordana forgot that Slade was behind and timing her. She'd
traversed this type of terrain in other rides but not often.
Stormy was proving more adept at it than she was. Her
legs were strong and more than anything else, Jordana
wanted to stay in balance as they hit the nine-thousand-
foot level. The trail then dipped downward at a precarious angle. Jordana clamped her legs to the horse and

leaned back, giving her full head, the reins lying down on her neck.

By the time they had hit the plain once more, Jordana urged Stormy into a canter toward the two hills. This was a rugged trail and as the mustang moved along, she realized the difference between level one and two endurance competition. This was brutal stuff. It asked everything of horse and rider.

At the gate that led to Slade's ranch, Jordana pulled up. She looked around to see Thor at a gallop not far behind. The stallion was powerful, and he looked rested and as if he were just starting this competition. Slade rode like the master horseman he was. His lower body moved in perfect rhythm with the stallion while his upper body was completely quiet. Thor slowed to a trot and then a walk, snorting and tossing his head. He had beautiful light blue eyes, his forelock of mane long and covering them from time to time.

"Well? How did we do?" she asked, patting Stormy. The mare's gray hair was wet and sleek.

He held up the time. "Not bad for a first run. You made it in one hour." Giving Jordana a look of pride, he added, "And you did well, too."

Glowing beneath his unexpected praise, Jordana dismounted and opened up the gate. "That's a good time?"

Riding Thor, Slade moved through the opened gate. "It's good for a first time."

Jordana shut and locked the gate. "I'm happy with it, then. That's quite a test riding range you have," she said as she remounted Stormy. They rode side by side at a walk.

"Your mare is typical mustang," Slade said as they

rode. "She's used to negotiating all kinds of obstacles and doesn't bat an eye at them."

"I know," Jordana said, running her fingers through her mare's thick black mane. "She's fearless."

"So is her owner."

Jordana felt as if Slade had lightly touched her. Praise didn't come from him very often. "Thanks."

"Maybe because you're an emergency-room doc? You're used to chaos and don't get rattled?"

"I like your observations, Slade. You're right, I'm a cool head when things get out of control around me."

"You took those hills like a champ. Maybe I need to revise my opinion of you and that runt of a mustang you ride." His mouth barely tipped into a smile.

Jordana laughed fully and reached out. She rested her fingers on his darkly haired arm for just an instant. When her fingers grazed his sunburned flesh, she felt his muscles leap instantly in response beneath her touch. Oh, she hadn't meant to reach out like that. But she had. Jerking her hand back, she saw surprise and then sudden darkness come to his narrowing gray eyes. Her flesh prickled with a delicious sense that he was stripping her with his intense gaze. Gulping unsteadily, Jordana knew what she'd read in those intense, large eyes of his. What had just happened? There was no room in her life for a man right now. She was working twelve to fourteen hours a day trying to make ends meet.

Slade was surprised at Jordana's warm, graceful fingers wrapping momentarily around his forearm. It had been completely unexpected. He felt helpless to remain immune to her spontaneity and childlike innocence. And that was how he saw Jordana. Oh, Slade knew she was thirty years old and life had erased the innocence from her, but somehow, she had kept some of it. He hadn't, he realized. He was so dark and glum in comparison to her light, sunny smiles she shared with him. And every time Jordana's mouth curved upward, Slade's heart pumped a little harder. Right now, he felt boiling heat building in his lower body; a sure sign of pleasure and more…

"A horse can trot anywhere from ten to seventeen miles per hour," he said, becoming taciturn. No way did he want Jordana to touch him again. If she did, Slade wasn't sure he could control his reaction to her the next time around. "Your mare at her float trot was doing seventeen, which is good." He picked up his timer and showed it to her. "Your canter was about twenty miles an hour and that's excellent."

"Heck," Jordana said, making sure she kept her hands on the reins, "Stormy has never been timed like this before. I know thoroughbreds can race at forty miles per hour. And quarter horses can run fifty in a quarter of a mile race."

"Yes," Slade said, "they can. But in endurance contests, you want to save up that burst of speed for the finish line. This is all about understanding the speeds of your horse and then rating her such that you have something left in her tank for the finish line." He reached down and patted Thor. "Here in the Tetons Fifty race in September, after you get off the mountains, you have a flat, five-mile run to the finish."

"That's a long ways," Jordana said, sobering over that information. "I know if you let the horse run hard in the steep areas, then they will likely have little gas left for that last run to the finish. Usually, it's one or two miles, isn't it?"

"Yes," Slade said. He'd silently enjoyed when their

legs had brushed against one another on the narrow trail between the pastures. It hadn't been often, but he'd liked it. Maybe a little too much. Forcing himself to stay on topic, he added, "The Tetons Fifty has one of the longest finishes in the business. If you don't rate your horse's energy in the mountain climbs, you won't have anything left on the final run."

Giving Thor an admiring look, Jordana said wistfully, "Your stallion is *such* an incredible animal! He barely looked damp from that fifteen-mile run. Look at Stormy." She ran her fingers down the mare's wet, glistening neck.

"I ride Thor fifty miles once a week," Slade told her. "So this fifteen miles is like a warm-up to him."

Shaking her head, Jordana said, "He's in magnificent condition." And so was his master. But she kept that comment to herself. Both man and animal were hard-muscled, brimming with explosive energy and power. Perhaps, Jordana surmised, that is what drew her to Slade. His masculine power. She could not remember one time when she'd *ever* met a man like him. Confidence oozed from Slade like honey she wanted to taste. Body hardened by living in the harsh Wyoming climate, he exuded energy like the sun itself. She loved being drenched by that invisible sunlight that pulsed around him. It made her feel ultrafeminine. And now, she'd actually touched him. His arm was like finely honed steel, the muscles leaping to life as she'd grazed him. Her fingertips still tingled from that contact.

"So, how many times a week do I take this circuit?" she asked.

"Twice a week," Slade said. "And you'll take a stopwatch with you. I'll write down the gait and time. Then, we'll see where we need to refine and improve Stormy's performance."

"But Stormy did okay for a first time?"

Slade held her gaze. He focused on her soft, full lips. Jordana never wore makeup that he could see. Her cheeks were ruddy with health and vibrancy. She was strong, confident and truly fearless. "Yes, she did okay."

Mustering her courage, Jordana said, "Slade, if we work hard, could we be ready for the Tetons Fifty? I'd *really* like to enter her in it if you think we'd be ready for it." Jordana saw the surprise come to his eyes. His mouth thinned for a moment. Brows slashed downward. *Oops.* Had she spoken too soon? Were her dreams too high? Impossible to reach so soon? Or did he think she was talking hot air?

"She could be ready, providing the pastern with the scar on it doesn't give you trouble." He held up his gloved hand. "But don't go where I see you going, Jordana. Your mare is new to this. You'll be lucky to finish in the top fifty of the hundred riders that are coming. And if Stormy does that, it will be enough for a first time."

"Phew, I thought you were going to tear into me because I asked."

Shaking his head, Slade managed a sour smile. "You have a horse who can do it. And your riding skills are solid. There's no reason to think that you can't compete. Just don't expect to win, is all."

CHAPTER SIX

CURT DOWNING HAPPENED to glance up from where he was standing in the aisle of Andy's Horse Emporium. He was in here to buy some Absorbine liniment for his endurance stallion, Shah. A woman with shoulder-length black hair and incredibly beautiful turquoise blue eyes entered. The pink T-shirt and jeans outlined her athletic body. She had the warmest smile on her face for Andy, the owner, who greeted her at the counter.

Who is she? Curious, Curt was always looking for a woman who liked horses. Setting the bottle on the shelf, he eavesdropped on their conversation.

"Andy, how are you?"

"Long time, no see, Dr. Lawton. I'm fine." Andy patted his protruding girth with his hand. "You'll probably see high cholesterol."

Chuckling, Jordana said, "Hey, I'm just here to pick up a few items, not diagnose you or your patrons."

Andy nodded his balding head. "Good to know," he said, laughing in return. "Anything I can help you with?"

Jordana looked around the large store. Andy had cowboy clothing for men and women, saddles for sale and anything else a horse person might need for themselves or their mount. "No, this is like a candy store for me. You know that. Just got to get a few items that need replacing."

"Hey, I heard through the pipeline you're in training with Slade McPherson. True?"

Sighing, Jordana leaned against the old, well-worn oak counter that Andy sat behind. "There's no secrets in this town, is there?" she said with a smile. "Let me guess…Gwen Garner told you?"

"Yes, she did." Andy smiled a little. "Actually, my wife, Belinda, was over buying some fabric at Gwen's store and she heard about it."

Jordana's grin widened. "Ah…the rest of the story. Gwen is careful with the info she hands out. I'm in good hands and don't mind her spreading the word that Mr. McPherson is my teacher."

Andy nodded. "Gwen is never wrong." And then he learned forward and whispered, "You know McPherson is an ornery cuss?"

Shrugging, Jordana said, "I manage to get along with him."

"You taking that gray mustang mare you bought to him?"

"I did. He gave her a thumbs-up on her ability to be a top endurance horse and I'm jazzed."

"Nobody knows endurance horses better than Slade," Andy agreed.

Jordana was about to speak when a shadow of a man came over her. She glanced to her left. A man in his mid-thirties with short, carrot-red hair and pale blue eyes studied her. It wasn't a pleasant sensation, either. His eyes were almost a colorless blue. It made his black pupils even more intense-looking. There was nothing weak about the man's face. He was dressed in a white cowboy shirt, jeans and wore a black Stetson on his head.

"I'm Curt Downing, Dr. Lawton," he said and held

out his large, callused hand toward her. "I couldn't help but overhear your conversation that you're an endurance rider."

Out of social habit, Jordana forced herself to shake the man's hand. He had copper freckles all over his face. What bothered her was his small-set eyes. In fact, to Jordana, Downing's features sent further alarm through her. In the horse world, a horse with small, close-set eyes was considered mean and unpredictable. She recalled Slade had mentioned Downing in unpleasant terms. As she released his hand, she remembered that Curt's father had been drunk and killed Slade's parents.

"I'm an endurance rider in the making," she told Downing. She saw his eyes narrow speculatively upon her. Downing stood about six feet tall and probably weighed around one hundred and seventy pounds. He was lean and athletic. Maybe her negative feelings toward him were because Slade disliked him.

"How long you been here, Doctor?"

"Two years," Jordana said. She moved a few feet away from Downing. He was hovering over her like a proverbial vulture ready to clean the bones of some dead animal. Indeed, there was a fierce, hawklike look in Downing's eyes, and it unsettled her.

"And you're just starting endurance riding?"

"No, I've been competitive for two years."

"Ah, I see," Downing murmured. He appraised her body with a sharpness honed from knowing horse conformation. Hills and valleys in all the right places, Curt liked what he saw. "Pity you went to McPherson. Did you know I also run a championship-training facility? I'm the national endurance champion." He lifted his head a little more proudly than before.

Disliking his ego, Jordana said, "Yes, I knew about you, Mr. Downing."

"Please, call me Curt," he pleaded with a smile.

"I prefer to call you Mr. Downing, if you don't mind." Jordana added a slight smile to take the sting out of her decision. She saw him frown. Downing was handsome but in a twisted way as far as Jordana was concerned. She glanced over to see Andy scowling, too. What else did Andy know about Downing? That he played dirty tricks out on the endurance rides against other riders and their horses? Jordana knew the gossip pipeline in this cow town was very, very efficient.

"Listen," Curt said, ignoring her coolness toward him, "if you get a chance and would like to see my Arabian stallion, Shah, I'd be more than happy to show him to you. No one beats my stud."

Andy coughed.

Jordana eyed Curt and held his arrogant gaze. "Oh, he's been beaten by Thor, Mr. McPherson's medicine-hat mustang stallion."

"Not often," Curt laughed. "Arabians *always* win the endurance contests."

Jordana admitted that was true up to a point. "Half Arabians have won them, too, and so have mustangs which have Spanish barb blood in them."

Nodding, Curt enjoyed the woman's unexpected pluck. "Right you are, Dr. Lawton." She didn't melt before him. Did she know how rich he was? When women came into his orbit, they were usually attracted by his money. But something told him that Lawton wasn't like that. He knew doctors were rich in their own right but not a millionaire like he was. A sense of power flowed through him as he absorbed her natural beauty.

"If you'll excuse me," Jordana said, starting to move away because she really didn't like talking to this arrogant man. She took a step toward the aisle.

"Hey," Downing said, grabbing her wrist.

Instantly, Jordana shook off his hand. "I'm done speaking with you, Mr. Downing," she said coldly, glaring at him for his aggressive action. Her wrist smarted where his strong fingers had wrapped around it. His grip had been hard. Controlling. Jordana was alarmed by his boldness. Suddenly, she could see the competitiveness in his eyes. And now, she understood a little better what Slade had said about this man. She didn't like him. At all.

"Oh." Curt laughed. "Sorry. I just find you fascinating. It isn't often I meet another endurance rider. We're a pretty rare breed."

Ignoring him, Jordana left the area and headed down the aisle looking for a new comb and brush for Stormy. She heard Downing talking amiably with Andy as his purchases were rung up and placed into a bag. *Good riddance!* She moved down to the endcap as far away as she could get from the rancher. Downing's ego burned into her. How unlike Slade he was! Watching warily until Downing marched out of the emporium, Jordana gave a sigh of relief. Now, she could relax and shop. This was a treat to come to Andy's place.

Andy came shuffling up to her. "Jordana, I'm awful sorry about Mr. Downing's behavior. He shouldn't have laid a hand on you."

She saw the worry in the man's eyes. "No problem, Andy. I can handle myself around men like him."

"Downing thinks every woman is for sale," Andy muttered apologetically. "I shouldn't say much more than that. I just wanted to make sure you weren't upset."

Smiling, Jordana said, "Not at all."

"You know," Andy said, a gleam in his brown eyes, "you might go over to the Quilter's Haven. The owner, Gwen Garner, knows everything about everyone here in Jackson Hole. You should get the rest of the scoop on Downing."

"I'd heard Gwen was the go-to gal for honest information on anyone in Jackson Hole," she admitted.

"Well, you might amble over there after you leave here."

Jordana nodded. "I will. Thanks, Andy."

Andy gave a relieved sigh. "Good. I'm glad you'll do that…"

JORDANA ENTERED QUILTER'S HAVEN on Friday afternoon. At the counter, she asked for Gwen Garner. The clerk pointed to a section at the rear of the fabric store. For years, she had heard that Gwen, whose son, Cade Garner, was a deputy sheriff for the county, was the person who had the goods on everyone in the town. Andy's relief that she would talk with Gwen had prompted Jordana to carry through on his advice. She knew the older man who owned the emporium wasn't given to such reactions, but Downing had certainly triggered something in him.

"Gwen?" she called, seeing a gray-haired woman with a clipboard in hand. "I'm Dr. Jordana Lawton. Do you have a moment?"

Gwen looked up to see the young, confident woman walking around the end of the fabric aisle. "Sure," she said, holding out her hand to her. "Dr. Lawton. I've heard plenty of good things about you. It's nice to finally meet you in person! Are you here for fabric? Quilting patterns? Or something else?"

Jordana smiled, shook the sixty-year-old woman's hand and lowered her tone. "Actually, Andy from the Horse Emporium, suggested I come over here to talk with you."

Gwen put her pen on the clipboard. "Oh?"

Jordana told her what had happened at the store. She saw Gwen's face pinch and her eyes go hard. When she got done telling her the experience, Gwen moved a little closer and lowered her voice.

"Red Downing owned the Lazy D Ranch that butts up against the McPherson ranch. He was an alcoholic. Sally Downing, his wife, was constantly abused by her husband. And so was the son, Curt. When Red plowed into Bob and Dolly McPherson's car and killed them, he died, too. That left the ranch to Sally, who had the battered wife's syndrome. Fellow ranchers gathered around her and her young son to help her. Red had controlled everything and Sally was useless, but she was a victim of violence. Eventually, Sally got the ranch on better financial ground. In the meantime, Curt fell in love with endurance riding and it was his only passion. When Sally died of a heart attack in 1996, Curt was willed the ranch."

Gwen looked up to ensure no one was nearby to eavesdrop. The store was pretty much empty, and the few patrons who were shopping were at the front of her store. "Curt Downing won a lot of races, bought a good stallion named Shah and, through smart marketing, made millions. His ranch is now solvent, he owns an endurance-training facility and he also breeds his

Arabian stallion to other endurance mares from around the country."

"That sounds like a rags-to-riches story," Jordana said. "As a physician I've seen plenty of abused women and children in my E.R. back in New York City, so I know what abuse does to people."

Gwen moved to the corner of the store. "Abuse is wrong. But it's *how* the person handles it that counts. And that's why Andy got protective of you today. Curt Downing is known to play rough and dirty on endurance contests. No one has caught him at it—yet. He will do *anything* to win. When he whips a rider or their horse, or pushes them off a trail and endangers them, these people file complaints to the judges. But without a third witness as proof, or a camera photo, they can't do anything. So, he continues to get away with it."

Nodding, Jordana said in a low tone, "I'm in training with Slade McPherson. He said the same thing about Downing."

"Yes, I know you are." Gwen smiled a little. "We hear everything that goes on in this town."

Smiling faintly, Jordana said, "I feel like Downing is stalking me. It's my gut feeling. When he put his hand on me like that, I wanted to run away."

"And run you should," Gwen said. "He goes through women like water from a faucet. And he carries on his abuse. He's beat up his other women and they've all left sooner or later. And he made a move on you at the Horse Emporium. My advice is stay clear of this guy. He's no good. Further, there's plenty of his students that come in here and talk about how he uses the whip and spurs on the endurance horses they own. They don't like it. He might have a state-of-the-art facility, but he continually loses students who don't abide using those instruments to make their horses run faster to win a race."

"He sounds amoral," Jordana said. Sighing, she said, "Slade doesn't like him. Now, I see why."

"Oh," Gwen said, "it goes a lot deeper than that. Slade hates Curt Downing for Red killing his parents. It wasn't Curt's fault, but he's done nothing to heal that wound between them, either. These men are the top two champions in the U.S. when it comes to endurance riding. Curt wants to win to pat his ego. Slade has to win to keep his ranch from falling into foreclosure."

Eyes narrowing, Jordana said, "I didn't know that."

"Slade's a proud man. He busts his butt to make ends meet. The bank isn't working with him." She shook her head. "The banker, Frank Halbert, is in bed with Curt Downing. Slade went several times to get his loan readjusted, but Halbert, I think, has been paid off by Downing not to do it."

"Why?"

"Five years ago, when Slade was making his mark as an endurance champion, Curt was threatened. He offered Slade ten million for his ranch. The way Curt figured it, if he could get the Tetons Ranch, then he'd have a much larger ranch and he could expand his training facility. Of course, Slade turned him down and that's when everything went to hell in a handbasket. Curt has made sure the bank won't remortgage Slade's ranch."

"But can't Slade go to another bank?"

"No. Money is so tight now and they won't loan hardly anyone anything. We're in a depression, pure and simple. Everyone is belt tightening. Slade teeters between foreclosure and keeping his family ranch every month. It's that bad."

Jordana sighed. "I didn't know that, Gwen. That's *awful*. He's such a good person. And he's a wonderful trainer for me and Stormy."

"The man's got a heart of gold, but few can see it. He's a loner. He sticks to himself. And he's got just as much pride as any Wyoming rancher. All he does is buckle down and work harder and longer hours to make ends meet."

Jordana said, "I hurt for him. He's wonderful with horses."

"Oh," Gwen said, "no question there. Slade is known as the horse whisperer here in the valley. And Curt hates him for that. Plus, Slade beats him in the endurance contests."

"Bad blood," Jordana agreed. "I knew some of the past history between them."

Wagging her finger at Jordana, Gwen warned, "You watch Downing. Chances are he already knew you were a student of Slade's. I wouldn't put it past him to squeeze information out of you about Slade and his ranch. If he tries, clam up."

"Not to worry," Jordana promised. "I disliked Downing the moment I saw him. He has small, close-set eyes. That was enough to put me on guard."

Chuckling, Gwen nodded. "And he's just like a small-eyed horse—meaner than the dickens. You'd do well to stay as far away from him as you can. My sense tells me he's up to no good. No one will talk about Slade to him. He's angry at everyone because we protect Slade from him."

"He must think the town is against him."

Laughing softly, Gwen said, "We are. Downing has no morals or values. We know he plays dirty tricks on other endurance riders. And the locals around here who sign up to ride the Tetons endurance contest know him too well. The judges might not have the proof that he's using his whip on another rider or horse or that he's shoved a rider off a horse, but we know he's done it."

Shaking her head, Jordana said, "Slade's a hero, then."

"Oh, he is. And ranchers stick together like fleas on a dog. They help one another out. And Slade has done the same for others. He's a good man in a bad position. He's got to win the Tetons ride this September. There's a ten-thousand-dollar award for the winner. With that win, Slade can give the mortgage a breather."

"If he doesn't win it?" Jordana asked, feeling worry for Slade.

Shrugging, Gwen said, "Then he's probably going to lose his ranch sooner rather than later. And that would be a pity."

"Curt is riding in the same race?"

"Yep. And you can bet those two will go at it like they always do…out of sight of the judges. Curt has had his crown taken away from him by Slade. And truth be told, Slade is a far better endurance rider and has a better horse under him. But Downing is competitive and he'll be out to win that race by hook or crook. It will turn dangerous for Slade and Thor. We all worry about them and there's nothing we can do."

Feeling helpless, Jordana quirked her lips. "I'm glad I'm contributing to Slade's ranch, then."

"He never advertises his training facility. Sometimes, he's as dumb as a box of rocks."

Laughing, Jordana said, "He's an anachronistic kind of man. He has a cell phone and a computer, but he says he hates both of them. The nineteenth century instead of a modern-day man. Most ranchers use ATVs to round up their cattle, but Slade still uses his horses. Old-fashioned, but he also has those old values, too. He's a man of integrity. His word is his bond. If he shakes your hand, he means it and will carry through with whatever was agreed upon."

"I hear he's divorced." The words popped out of Jordana's mouth, unbidden.

"Yes, Slade is. He was married for four years to an immature New York City socialite. Isabel was a pre-Olympic dressage champion. She came out here on a vacation, met Slade and in a week, they were married. Stupidest thing I've ever seen that man do," she muttered, shaking her head. "It was hell for Slade. Isabel had millions and he was a pauper in comparison. She had temper tantrums and pouted and sulked when she didn't get her way. Eventually, Slade divorced her, but it's left a real bad taste in his mouth for women ever since."

"I see," Jordana said. "It explains why he feels armored up and unreachable to me."

"Slade can be a knight on his horse, but no one can reach him and how he really feels. You just have to accept him as is. I'm hoping that over time, he'll drop his walls and be more friendly and social. He's ashamed of his whirlwind marriage to Isabel and the divorce. Slade hides as much as he can."

Smiling a little, Jordana said, "You nailed him, Gwen. Truly, he's boarded up and no one can get to his soft parts except the horses he cares for and trains."

"Well, if I were you, I'd hold out hope that one day, he would become human and join the rest of the world again," Gwen murmured with a smile.

Jordana agreed. Her heart opened wider now as she

had a much more clear picture of Slade and why he was a loner. Life had been hard on him, and it hadn't let up. "Thanks for the info, Gwen. I really appreciate your help and warning about Downing."

Picking up her pen from the clipboard, Gwen nodded. "Anytime, Jordana. If you got questions, bring them to me. I'll probably be able to give you some truth and background to 'em."

As Jordana left the shop to drive out to Slade's ranch, she reran his sad, hard life through her mind. He was a good man in a bad place. And she knew a ranch was often handed down to the next generation. He was battling to keep the memory of his beloved parents alive. Because it was his life, too, with or without them around. As she drove her Ford truck through the town, Jordana wondered if life was going to finally give him a reward instead of more punishment.

CHAPTER SEVEN

"IS SOMETHING BOTHERING YOU?" Slade asked as Jordana walked Stormy back to the barn. She'd arrived and rode the fifteen-mile circuit and hadn't said much. Which wasn't like her. The July sun was hot, and it felt good to him. Slade knew he wasn't the most sensitive person on earth, but even he could see a murkiness in Jordana's glorious blue eyes.

"Oh, it's nothing," she protested as he walked with Stormy to the cross ties located in the center of the barn. Jordana didn't want to tell him about meeting Downing. She knew there was bad blood between them now, thanks to Gwen Garner's information, and she didn't want to stir the pot. What bothered her was Slade had seen she was upset. Slipping off the hackamore from Stormy, she pulled on the nylon halter and then put her horse between the cross ties. Slade had taken off Stormy's saddle and took it into the tack room. Jordana had seen him become less icy and unavailable the past week. Maybe he was getting used to having her around?

When Slade returned from the tack room, there was a nice breeze through the center passageway of the barn. It felt good against the eighty-degree heat. Jordana was busy brushing Stormy down. Slade liked to watch her move around the mustang. There was such natural grace to Jordana. As he leaned against the wall of a box stall, his arms across his chest, Slade absorbed the pleasurable moment. Every time he saw Jordana, he wanted to be around her even more. Slade fought the inexplicable desire. Acidly, he told himself he was a pauper and getting tangled up with another woman just wasn't in his cards.

"Stormy seemed upset today, too," he drawled, watching her expression.

"She has her days like I do," Jordana joked, hoping her smile would stop him from digging any further. It was unlike Slade to be concerned about her. Why now? Did he have a sixth sense for smelling trouble? Or for Downing, in particular? Brushing Stormy, she worked to get out the sweat and dirt along her back. They were now doing fifteen-mile rides three times a week. She'd changed her schedule to compensate for this new training demand. Next week, Slade was going to up her to thirty miles in preparation for the fifty-mile Tetons contest.

Compressing his lips, Slade murmured, "You're unhappy."

Straightening, Jordana looked across her mare's back at him. His hat was tipped down, shading his gray eyes that felt like X-rays moving through her. He was incredibly handsome, shaped by the elements. She broke down and told him about the incident at the Horse Emporium. Jordana knew instantly by Slade standing, his arms coming to his sides, that he had hate for Downing. When she finished, she didn't tell him that she'd went to Gwen Garner. More than anything, as he stood there bristling with rage, his eyes hard and gleaming, Jordana simply wanted to throw her arms around Slade and hold him. He'd been without love and nurturing for so long. In her imagination, she saw him as a lonely, grieving six-year-old boy who had just had his parents torn from him.

"You can't trust him. *Ever*," Slade gritted. His fist curved. For the longest time, he'd wanted to punch the arrogant and rich bastard in the face. Red Downing had taken everything from his family. Curt had grown up to be hard and mean and did anything he had to do in order to win, just as his father had.

"I know that," Jordana said in a soothing tone. Now, Slade was upset. His entire tall, powerful body was tense, fists knotted at his sides. "I handled it and there won't be another confrontation. Trust me, Downing got the message."

Pacing, Slade wasn't so sure. "You've lived here two years and never ran into him. Gossip in the town is everywhere. He knew you'd come here to train with me."

"It's jealousy on his part," Jordana said, using an aluminum blade to shed the excess sweat off Stormy's body. "Nothing more."

"Damn him," he ground out to no one in particular.

"Frankly, I'm more worried for you, Slade." She held his startled look. "You're competing against him in the Tetons ride."

"Nothing new there. Don't worry about me. I've handled him before and I know his tricks." Still, Slade felt his chest expand with an unfamiliar emotion. Jordana's eyes were warm and anxious-looking. She cared for him. She really did. Slade hadn't been born yesterday. He knew that look. And it made him go soft inside for a moment. What would it be like to relax and be himself around Jordana? Something told Slade she was utterly trustworthy, unlike Isabel. Still, the past screamed at him, and he tucked that warmth away like a stolen moment within his heart.

Sighing, Jordana said, "Getting to meet Curt face-to-face makes me worry *more*, Slade." Unhooking the panic snaps on both sides of Stormy's halter, she led her tired mare down the concourse to be washed. She heard a man's voice boom from the other end of the barn.

"Slade! I'm back!"

Turning, Jordana saw a man who was almost as tall as Slade standing at the opened door. He wore a dark brown suit, tie and white shirt. Blinking, she thought he looked an awful lot like Slade. And then, it hit her. Could this be Griff McPherson? Slade's younger fraternal twin brother? If it was, Slade had not said anything about his visit. Glancing toward Slade, she saw him freeze for a moment. And then, his face darkened with an unknown emotion. Sudden tension crackled in the barn. Confused, Jordana stayed where she was as this meeting played out.

"Slade, good to see you again," Griff said, striding forward, his hand outstretched toward his older brother.

"What the hell are you doing here?" Slade growled, refusing to shake his brother's hand.

"I've come home for good," he told Slade.

"You're an Easterner. An Easterner. And you have a job on Wall Street. Since when have you said this ranch was your home?" Old anger stirred through Slade. Griff had black hair and green eyes, like his mother. Slade's younger brother was an inch shorter than him, more slightly built than he was. Griff looked painfully out of the norm by wearing his Wall Street suit. Few people wore suits around here.

Griff grimaced and held his ground. "Hey, brother,

I own half this ranch. And I was born here in Jackson Hole." Giving him a grin, he added, "Besides, I'm done with Wall Street. I wanted to come home."

"Damn nice of you to let me know you were coming," Slade said, glaring at Griff. His younger twin had always been spontaneous and gave no second thought to how his decisions might affect others. He was very immature compared to Slade.

"Sorry, but I wanted to surprise you. I thought you'd be happy to see me."

Snorting, Slade growled, "What? You visit once every five years? Stay for a day and can't stand being out in the middle of nowhere? Pining away for your exciting, nonstop life back in New York City? Give me a break."

Unfazed by his older brother's snarling disposition, Griff said in a lower tone, "Look, I've lost everything, Slade. My company went belly up and I don't have a job. I've tried getting another one, but no one is hiring." Opening his hands, he added, "I was in stock derivatives. I lost *everything*, Slade. I lost twenty million dollars in a blink of an eye. I should have diversified my portfolio, but I didn't."

Staring into Griff's tormented green eyes, Slade snarled, "And so you come crawling home to the ranch I've kept going without *any* help from you?"

"I have half ownership of this ranch," Griff reminded him more strongly. "The will decreed we'd each own half."

"Not that you've *ever* dropped a dime to help keep it afloat. Hell, you wouldn't even give me a loan six years ago when I asked for it."

Grimacing, Griff fearlessly met him on this comment. "In my opinion as a Wall Street banker, you were a bad risk, Slade. I wasn't going to throw my money away. When you loan money, you expect interest and payback. I just didn't feel at that time you could do that."

Glaring at him, Slade barely tolerated his sibling. "I'll never forget that day. I'll go to my grave remembering you wouldn't loan your brother money." Snorting, Slade added, "And now you're broke. Well, if you think you can come back here and leech off me, you have another think coming." He held up his hands. "I *work* for a living. Not like you living in some posh skyscraper playing with computers and enjoying the good life."

Wincing, Griff said, "I'm staying here. I'll take one of the spare bedrooms in the main house. My old bedroom."

Helpless to stop him, Slade said, "You're worthless to me and this ranch, Griff. You don't know how to ride, brand a calf, put up fence posts or string barbed wire."

Mouth tightening, Griff held his brother's rage. "I'll learn."

"This is insane," Slade growled. "And how long before you leave and go back to your precious Wall Street? When the first person offers you a job, you'll be out of here in a heartbeat. You won't care a tinker's dam about this ranch once more." Slade wanted to add, *or me*, but didn't.

"I can work hard," Griff said stubbornly. "You show me what has to be done and I'll do it. I'm not lazy."

Shaking his head, Slade muttered, "You're useless as tits on a bull, Griff. Look at your hands." He jabbed his index finger down at them. "They're white, soft and pretty." He thrust his hand into his brother's face. "Look at *mine*."

Griff didn't blink. He saw the sunburned quality of Slade's large hand. It had small white scars here and there, plus thick calluses on each palm showing the hard physical work performed daily. "We're brothers," he reminded him in a tight tone. "And I'm not unlike you. I can't help it if we got split up after our parents were killed. I had no choice when the court decided to send me to Uncle Robert's part of the world any more than you did when you got to stay here."

Bristling, Slade hated to be reminded of that painful time in the past. In his opinion, Griff was like a butterfly compared to his anvil hammer. They didn't see each other very often at all, the brotherly ties broken a long time ago. "Drop the excuses. There's no way I'm taking you on as an employee. I don't have the money to pay you a dime."

Shrugging, Griff said, "I'm not an employee, Slade. I'm half owner. And I expect to work. I have a lot of good ideas for the ranch—"

"Another time," Slade growled. He saw two bags of luggage at the opening of the barn. "You know the layout of the house."

"Good," Griff murmured, giving his upset older brother a smile. "I'll make myself at home." He turned and walked with his shoulders back, head tipped at a proud angle.

Slade put his hands on his hips, glaring after Griff. Spinning emotionally from his unexpected arrival, he hung his head and wrestled with the snakes writhing violently in his gut.

"Slade?" Jordana walked down the passageway with her horse. She hesitantly put her hand on his broad shoulder. "Are you okay?"

Her softened words were like ice water to his boiling anger and shock. Lifting his head, he absorbed her ten-

tative touch like the starving animal he was. "Yeah…
yeah, I'm fine."

Removing her hand, Jordana stood there seeing a
host of emotions pass across his face. This was the first
time she'd seen Slade without that hardened expression.
Seeing desperation, grief and anger in his eyes, she said
gently, "No, you're not fine. What did Griff want?"

Taking off his Stetson, he wiped his brow with the
back of his hand and then settled it back on his head.
Slade had no intention of spilling out the painful past but
somehow, Jordana was able to wring it out of him. His
voice turned steely as he said, "And Griff took to Wall
Street and New York City like ticks on a dog. He was
filthy rich. I once asked him for a loan, but he turned
me down. He didn't care if I lost the ranch to the bank.
Even though he supposedly owns half of it by our parents' will, he didn't give me a dime."

The bitterness in Slade's tone tore at Jordana. She
stood quietly. He was obviously in shock. And sometimes, when a person was able to just talk out the trauma,
it blunted the shock and they felt more emotionally stable. Her job was to ask questions. "What will Griff do
now that he's penniless? I know a number of big name
stock-brokerage firms went under."

"I don't know," Slade admitted, some of the venom
dissolving in his tone. Jordana's quiet, calming presence
was what he needed, he realized. She had a soft touch
and asked the right questions to defuse him. "He's just
like my ex-wife, Isabel. She was lazy. She screamed if
she got some dirt under her painted fingernails. And
she refused to clean out box stalls with me. She said it
was a man's work."

Catching his gaze, Jordana smiled a little. "Box stalls are gender neutral."

"Yes," Slade sighed. He looked up and then around the quiet barn. "Griff is going to be a burr under my saddle. He's useless. He doesn't know the first thing about running a ranch." And then he gave her an apologetic look. "I shouldn't be washing my family's dirty laundry in front of you."

Reaching out, she slid her fingers along his slumped shoulder. Each muscle leaped where she'd grazed his dark blue cowboy shirt. "It's all right, Slade. I consider you not only my trainer, but a friend, as well. I want to be here for you."

More than Isabel ever was for him, he thought. His skin felt as if it was on fire where she'd grazed his shoulder. Jordana's touch was calming. Slade felt his anger beginning to recede. "You not only have a quieting touch with a horse, but with me, too," he said wryly, giving her a quizzical look. Drowning in her warm blue gaze, Slade suddenly wanted to pull her roughly into his arms and kiss that soft, haunting mouth of hers. That jolted him. He couldn't ignore the building ache in his lower body, either. His whole reaction was loco!

Jordana felt a shift within Slade. Suddenly, she saw raw hunger burning in his eyes—for her. It was so unexpected, she took a step back. Blinking, she managed, "Blame it on my doctor's demeanor."

It was much more than that, Slade realized, feeling suddenly dizzy beneath her gaze. *Much more.* For the first time in four years he ached for a woman. But not just any woman. Jordana made him feel alive as never before. And Slade knew her touch was meant to calm and soothe, not incite flaming desire within him. But it had.

Feeling nakedly vulnerable, he said gruffly, "You've got to get Stormy washed. I'll see you in two days. We'll start Stormy on a thirty-mile route at that time." Turning, he left her standing in the middle of the barn.

Jordana swallowed hard. It was a good thing Slade had abruptly left or she wasn't sure what she'd have done next. The man was unpredictable! Yet, so were her yearning emotions, too. Something had happened between them, and she couldn't think clearly enough to understand what had gone down. She watched his long, striding form as he headed back to his ranch house. Feeling suddenly alone without his masculine presence, Jordana sighed.

Leading Stormy out of the barn, Jordana headed for the shower facility. Afterward, she went to the tack room and cleaned all the leather. The fragrance of oiled leather was always a perfume to be inhaled deeply. Her mind raced as she sat there with the oil and a cloth, the saddle nearby. What was Slade going to do now that Griff had dropped into his life? She had no idea what the siblings were like together. Maybe talking to Gwen Garner might give her a clearer picture of Griff. He certainly looked a lot like Slade, but there were differences, too. And he was just as handsome as Slade. Yet, his face was not deeply lined, but pale because in his job as a Wall Street broker, he didn't see the sun that often, never mind braving the elements.

The day had been one of lightning bolts, Jordana thought, as she scrubbed down Stormy in the bathing facility. First, Curt Downing was stalking her like a cougar would follow his intended prey. But she was no prey. Jordana could see why Slade disliked Downing. She felt as if some invisible stickiness was left behind after he'd grabbed her wrist. Wanting to take a hot shower to feel clean once more, Jordana moved the rubber brush across Stormy's gleaming back. As if Slade didn't have enough to worry about with Downing in the coming race, he was now saddled with his twin brother.

Feeling sorry for Slade, Jordana wished she could do more. But what? He'd finally broke through his armored barriers and shared with her. Those moments were sweet and Jordana began to realize their relationship had changed because of that. Slade was no longer iconic and distant. When he'd dumped his frustration out about his brother to her, he'd been vulnerable and emotional. Was it possible not to love a sibling? Jordana had seen this happen in other families. Hadn't Slade been dealt a hard enough hand without Griff barging in unannounced? Clearly, Slade didn't want him here.

Jordana saw Shorty on his paint mustang herding in a group of growing calves. They would have to be vaccinated and branded. She raised her hand in hello to the wrangler, and he did the same. Looking around, Jordana did not see Slade or Griff. What was going on inside that house? Were they arguing? Coming to physical blows? Frowning, she thought it wasn't her business. She was a student here, not Slade's lover.

Chores completed, Jordana drove slowly out of the parking area. She tried to appreciate the clear blue sky, the high cirrus clouds that reminded her of a horse's mane blowing in the wind. Her heart was still back there at the ranch as she drove the two miles to the highway that would take her back into town. In the distance, the Tetons, now nearly bare of any snow, showed their deep, rugged blue granite slopes. Their flanks were covered with thick green forest of pine below the ten-thousand-foot level. And one day soon, she and Stormy would be hidden beneath those pines on a rocky trail competing in her first big endurance ride.

Her excitement was cooled by her worry for Slade. Driving down the highway, the valley lushly green and the mountains silhouetted against the sky, Jordana wanted to turn around and go back. But what good would that do? Slade had trusted her enough to open up and speak about something deeply personal with her. Jordana knew she had to wait it out. Slade was so distrustful of women because of his bad marriage to Isabel. Further, she knew he didn't like Easterners. There were so many hurdles to jump!

Somber, Jordana paid attention to her driving as she sped down a long, gently sloped hill that would take her into downtown Jackson Hole. And why was she so anxious to have some kind of personal relationship with Slade? Right now, Jordana knew she couldn't afford to get into anything like that. She was working long, hard hours. And every penny had to be accounted for. Until she was past her endurance training, she had no savings, and that bothered her. Her parents had drilled into her that savings were always important. Symbolically, she felt rich in a personal way, but in reality, she wasn't financially. That was okay for now. She'd weathered storms in her life before, and she'd get through this one.

As she slowly moved through downtown traffic, tourist season in high gear, Jordana appreciated the plaza of the main part of town. Elk horns were bundled together to form a massive arch that was twenty feet high. Tourists stood, marveled and took photos of it. Her heart lifted. Every time she pictured Slade's hard, weathered features, she felt her insides becoming as soft as a marsh-mallow. No man had ever had that effect on her.

Turning off to a side street that would take her to the southern end of town where her home was located, Jordana wondered what the next two days would be like for Slade and his unwelcome brother.

CHAPTER EIGHT

SLADE HELD ON to his shock and rage as he strode into his ranch house. Inside was a brother he'd rarely seen since they had been separated. Griff had conveniently forgotten about him and the ranch. There was the occasional Christmas card, but that was it. And Slade could count on one hand how many times Griff had bothered to come out for a visit.

"Dammit," he seethed under his breath, jerking open the screen door and stepping inside. Halting in the mudroom, he took off his hat and hung it on a nearby elk-antler hook. His boots thunked hollowly down the pine hall. Heading for Griff's old bedroom, he heard a noise to his left in the kitchen. Turning on his heel, he strode into it. Griff was making coffee and he had changed out of his suit for a pair of jeans and a white long-sleeved shirt. He *almost* looked like a cowboy.

"We need to talk," Slade told him gruffly without preamble.

Griff glanced over at his older twin. "Sure." He smiled a little. "I think I should have warned you I was coming home. I'm sorry I didn't."

Resting his hands on his hips, Slade said, "Yes, you should have, but then, that's your way, isn't it? Did you learn that on Wall Street? Just traipse in and think people are going to be okay with that kind of city-slicker attitude and rudeness?"

Switching on the coffeemaker, Griff turned and rested his hips against the kitchen counter. The anger was leaping in Slade's narrowed eyes. "I don't see it that way," he countered strongly. Looking around, Griff murmured, "Not much has changed here, has it?" The light over the table was the same one he recalled as a young child. Their mother had loved yellow, and the kitchen was still painted that bright color.

Slade walked over and brought two cups down from the cabinet. "*Nothing* has changed. Our parents struggled every month to pay the mortgage on this place. And now, so do I."

Griff frowned. "You still aren't solvent?"

Stung, Slade snarled, "No, thanks to you. I came to you years back for a loan. If you'd have loaned me the money, it would have gone toward stabilizing the mortgage. But you couldn't see your way clear to do that for whatever your stupid reasons."

"You weren't a good loan applicant," Griff said coolly. "And if you're still in deep trouble with the mortgage, that proves my original assumption that you weren't a trustworthy loan applicant."

Cursing to himself, Slade wanted to strangle his younger twin. Griff looked smug and self-assured. Oh, he might be wearing Western clothing, but the look on his face told a different story. "And that's why I don't want you here. You've paid nothing into this place except to write it off."

Shrugging, Griff said lightly, "Legally speaking, I'm half owner. I'm not going anywhere." He grinned. "Besides, I have a host of ideas that can turn this ranch around so we can get it onto solid financial footing."

"Bull," Slade muttered. "You don't have a clue as to how to keep a ranch solvent." The coffee was done, and he poured himself a cup and put a splash of cream into it. Sitting down at the pine table with chairs hewn from the same wood, he watched Griff pour his own coffee. His twin wandered over, far less tense-looking than he felt.

Sitting down, Griff sipped his black coffee and said, "Before you throw the baby out with the bathwater, Slade, I *do* have some good ideas for our ranch."

The word *our* grated across Slade like a file rasp running across his exposed flesh. It wasn't morally right that Griff suddenly dropped in out of the blue to claim his half of the ranch. "You've done *nothing* to earn half this ranch." Slade glared at his unperturbed brother. Griff's black hair was military short. He hadn't been toughened up by the harsh elements of Wyoming.

"I know that, but now," Griff said lightly, "but now, I intend to rectify the situation."

"Only because you can't find another job on Wall Street," Slade acidly pointed out. "And I'll bet my last, bottom dollar that as soon as someone you know in your network has a job offer, you'll leave this place in a heartbeat and fly East again. Out of sight, out of mind with you, Griff."

"I do miss my job. I miss the money I made. And had," he admitted. "Right now, we're in a depression and there's no doubt about it. A lot of people are going back to their parents' homes right now because they've lost their jobs. I'm coming back here because I have a legal right to do so. I know you're not happy about it, but I'm staying."

"Until things improve on Wall Street."

Nodding, Griff said, "Most likely that is so." He swept his hand around the kitchen. "You can't make money ranching. You've proven that. And frankly, I like *big* money. I like living in a three-million-dollar penthouse in the upper east side of Manhattan. I like being able to buy the best of wines, throwing big parties for the rich and famous."

Shaking his head, Slade stared down at his coffee cup. "Your heart isn't here in Wyoming, Griff. It never has been."

"I don't know that," he countered strongly. "We were *born* here, Slade. Until our family was killed by Red Downing, we were happy."

"Yeah, well, life is hard," Slade uttered, sipping his coffee and nearly scalding his tongue. Setting the mug down he added, "And your heart and soul are in Wall Street, making millions and not sharing it with anyone else in the family."

"You're my only family," Griff said. "And you're a bad loan risk. I can't help that."

Slade jadedly eyed him. "You're an Easterner by heart." He jabbed a finger at Griff's hands that were enclosed around the coffee mug. "Your hands are lily-white and soft like a little baby's would be. You're out of shape. You could no more sink a fence-post hole than a ten-year-old girl. You don't ride. You don't know how to herd cattle, vaccinate or care for them. And you don't get to stay where it's warm when there's a blizzard going on. You have to care for ten horses, clean out box stalls and get to the Horse Emporium for hay, feed and other supplies."

"I've got skill sets in engine mechanics and construction. When I was at Harvard, I had a part-time job with a major construction company. I know how to use tools, and I'll apply my knowledge to the ranch," Griff said grimly, holding his twin's hard stare. "I had a gym membership in New York City, and I worked out regularly." He held out one of his hands. "It's true, I don't have sunburned skin and thick calluses on my hands, but that doesn't mean I can't use them to work with. That's what leather gloves are for."

"You know *nothing* about endurance riding."

"No," Griff said steadily, trying to hold on to his rising temper, "you're right. I don't know a thing. But I don't think I have to remind you, I'm the one with a Harvard MBA, not you. I'm a fast learner."

Stung, Slade knew he had only a high-school education compared to his brother. "No, I don't have a diploma from an uppity Eastern school. Uncle Paul died just as I graduated from high school and I had no chance for college. If I hadn't decided to stay and fight to keep this ranch going, I could have walked away from it. I had planned to go to college, but it just didn't happen."

Nodding, Griff said, "So you're a hero, Slade, and I'm not. My MBA opens doors you could never open."

Grinning sourly, Slade muttered, "Seems like all those golden doors are closed to you from what I can see. That's why you came slinking home with your tail between your legs. No one *wants you*, Griff. And I don't, either."

"You don't have a choice," Griff said, anger in his deep voice. "Legally, I own *half* of this ranch. You can't kick me out."

"You're right about that. And I'll guarantee you, Griff, if you stay, you're going to work your butt off just

like Shorty and I do." He held up a finger and wagged it
in Griff's face. "And I'm the *boss* here, not you. In my
eyes, you're a green wrangler learning the trade. Nothing more."

"And do I get paid?"

Snorting, Slade said, "Hell, no! My budget allows
me to pay one wrangler and that's it. You work to keep
a roof over your head and eat, that's all."

"Why not get rid of Shorty? That way you can pay
me?"

"In a pig's eye," Slade growled, rising. "You're worthless, Griff. We work twelve hours a day around here during the summer. I don't have *time* to break you into our
business without a solid, reliable wrangler like Shorty
around to pick up your slack. You're wasting my valuable time trying to train you. All you get out of this gig
is room and board. You don't like that, you go into town
and hire a lawyer and we'll duke it out in court." Turning, Slade walked out of the kitchen. He was this close to
hitting his stubborn brother. Griff didn't have an ounce
of common sense, which ranchers had to have in order
to survive. He was worthless!

Griff sat there feeling his burning anger toward Slade.
The kitchen was quiet. He heard Slade slam the front
screen door. He was gone. Looking around, he felt frustrated. In his former life as a Wall Street broker, he
moved billions of dollars a day. Now, Slade was telling
him he got room and board. That was it. No money for
the work he'd be doing.

Mulling over the situation, Griff knew it would be
useless to sue Slade. First, he had no money to do it. And
he knew Slade probably didn't, either. It was a standoff.
Right now, Griff needed a place to land. He lamented

their parents had been killed. His father would have welcomed him back to the ranch, and he knew it. But Slade wanted no part of him. How to fit in? Or could he?

Studying his left hand, Griff knew he was soft in comparison to Slade. He made his money with his brain, not his physical body like his older twin. Grudgingly, Griff felt his heart break a little. There was no love lost between them. He'd had idealistic expectations that Slade would welcome him with open arms, but he hadn't. Instead, Griff was sure Slade saw him as an interloper who was nothing more than a pain in the ass who had to be babysat.

Rubbing his chin, Griff looked around the kitchen. He dimly recalled sitting at this very table with Slade and his parents. He had few memories from that time. After all, he'd been only six years old. Smiling fondly, he recalled his father had always sat at the head of the table and his mother at the other end. He and Slade had sat opposite each other. There had always been a radio playing in the background. His mother had loved what was now termed elevator music. His father had loved Nashville music. Griff could recall both types of music being played as they sat at this dinner table. Running his hand along the varnished grain of the reddish-gold surface, he felt a sense of returning home.

Getting up, Griff walked over to the kitchen sink and rinsed out his mug. Setting it in the dish drainer, he looked around. No dishwasher, either. Well, that meant he'd be washing dishes, too. What a comedown! The sky had fallen open and disgorged him from his place in the stock brokerage firm where he'd been a banker. In one week, he'd lost everything. Being in derivatives, he'd amassed nearly twenty million dollars. And in the blink of an eye, it had disappeared in a poof. And the next day, he'd found out his firm was going under. Everyone had scrambled to call other brokerage firms for a new job, but no one was hiring.

Looking out the yellow-curtained windows, Griff saw Slade walking toward the big red barn. He saw Shorty, his only wrangler, coming up and speaking to him. Ego smarting over Slade's harsh judgment of him, Griff had to figure out a way to show he was an important part of this ranch. One way or another…

SLADE'S DAY WENT from bad to worse. He was at Andy's Horse Emporium that afternoon to pick up some skid boots. And as he walked down one of the aisles, he saw Curt Downing come in. Instantly, he went on internal guard. Downing saw him and grinned like a wolf ready to bite him. Slade knew he would.

"Hey, Slade, good to see you," Curt hailed, raising his hand.

Glaring, Slade said nothing. As he walked up to the cash register, he saw Andy grow nervous.

Curt continued to grin as he stood at the opposite end of the counter. Slade was dark and angry-looking. Prodding him, he said, "You looking forward to meeting me on the field of battle on September 1st?"

Pulling his wallet out of the back pocket, Slade muttered, "To you, every endurance contest is a war, Downing."

Laughing heartily, Curt said, "Isn't it?"

"No," Slade snapped at him. "But you don't get that, do you?" He itched to put his fist into Downing's arrogant face.

"Oh," Curt drawled, relaxing, "it *is* war. Every endurance race is a war against all the other horses and riders. That's the way it is."

Andy's hand shook as he took the bills from Slade's hand. He didn't want a fight breaking out in his store.

Smiling tightly, Slade murmured, "I hear you're losing your students, Downing. Could it be because of your war mentality?"

Scowling, Curt retorted, "I am not! Is Gwen Garner spreading lies around?"

Slade knew how much Downing bragged all over town about how many students he had. His grin turned sour as he held Downing's angry stare. "I don't have to go to Gwen. All I have to do is read the newspaper where you have ads in every week trying to snare some students." Snickering to himself, Slade saw Downing's smiling mouth turn down into a snarl. "Besides," he added, putting salt into Downing's wound, "most people don't like the idea of hitting other riders with a whip or shoving them off the trail."

Andy rolled his eyes and said nothing.

Curt stared hard at Slade. "Those are all lies! Just because Shah and I are damn good at what we do, there's no reason to believe a bunch of whiners who are sore losers!"

Taking the change from Andy, Slade said, "In my experience, Downing, endurance riders are somewhat like knights of old: *most* of them have high morals and values, except for a few, like you. They aren't whiners. They're in those rides because they've put in a lot of hours and days of training with their horses."

Downing could feel his face flushing. His anger flared, and he wanted to strike Slade. "Are you accusing me of *not* being moral out on the trail? I've *never* stopped anyone from going around me."

A grin leaked from Slade's tightened mouth as he pocketed his change and thanked Andy, who was sweating profusely. "Oh? Seems that just last year when me and my stud caught up to pass you, you had that whip of yours ready." Slade had seen him pull it out to strike Thor. Slade had lifted his boot out of the stirrup and slammed it into Downing's body. He'd shot off his startled mount like a bullet. And Slade had passed him safely and gone on to win the race. Downing had eventually caught his mount and come in fourth in the race. He'd never spoken a word about the incident to anyone. And Slade knew why. The judges might not take action on riders in general, but he had national standing. If he'd turned Downing in for his dirty tricks, the judges would have listened, and there would have been a convening of all involved. Slade knew no one liked Downing and would have sided with him on this charge. Downing's career would have taken a big hit. Without proof, nothing could be done, but Slade's word would have destroyed him in the endurance riding world. And Downing knew it.

Curt glared at McPherson. "We'll settle this out there on the trail in September," he ground out.

Slade halted at the door, turned and rasped, "You can *count* on it, Downing."

Jerking the door open, Slade left. The late-afternoon sunlight was delicious compared to the air-conditioning within the Emporium. Anger lapped at him. How badly he wanted to expose Downing. This year, he was riding with a small camera around his neck. No one would see it until he brought it out from beneath the shirt he wore.

Once and for all, Slade intended to prove the bastard was committing fouls out of sight of the judges. He smiled a little as he sauntered down the weathered wooden steps to his green Chevrolet pickup.

For a moment, he had a spontaneous urge to go see Jordana, whom he knew would be on duty at the E.R. of the hospital. She worked twelve hours at night so she could ride and get Stormy in shape during the day. Would she be surprised if he showed up? Pleased? Or not? Slade didn't know as he opened the door to his truck. Getting in and pulling the seat belt across his body, he waffled over the idea. It was unlike him to be spontaneous. He'd had such a hellish day he ached to be with Jordana. Starting the engine, he decided to hell with it. He'd surprise her.

JORDANA'S MOUTH FELL OPEN. She was just coming out of a cubical where she'd attended a new patient when she saw Slade walking into the E.R. What was he doing here? Worried, she gave the nurse her orders and then pushed the door open to the entrance area.

"Slade?" she called.

Turning, Slade saw Jordana. He'd never seen her in her hospital clothing. She wore dark green scrubs with a white coat over them. The stethoscope hung around her slender neck and her name was sewn onto the lab coat. This time, her hair was tied up on her head, a far different look than he'd seen before. His heart pounded briefly as he managed a twisted smile.

"I was just passing by and I thought I'd come and see the world you live in."

How tall, handsome and powerful he was as he stood in the waiting room. All around her, there were sick and suffering people waiting to receive help. Slade was like magnificent sunlight in the room. Grinning, she said, "What a nice surprise. Listen, I have about ten minutes' worth of paperwork to finish before I get my dinner."

Slade looked at his watch. "It's only 4:00 p.m."

Laughing a little because she suddenly felt like a giddy teenager, Jordana said, "I have the midnight shift. Dinner comes early. Can you meet me in the cafeteria? I'll be there shortly."

Tipping his hat, Slade said, "Like a cup of coffee waiting for you?" She always had a coffee thermos with her at his ranch.

Giving his arm a squeeze, she said, "Absolutely. See you in a few…"

The coffee was waiting for her when Jordana hurried into the quiet cafeteria later. She waved to Slade, who had chosen a large table near the window. Grabbing a tray, she went through the line choosing dinner items. After paying the cashier, she walked over to the table. Slade had laid his hat down on the chair next to him. Her cup of coffee sat opposite him. A sense of happiness threaded through her. Slade stood as she approached and pulled the chair out for her. She thanked him and sat down.

"That's quite a tray of food," Slade observed as he sat.

Chuckling, Jordana said, "It's a full moon tonight. I know we're going to get super busy. I tank up and top off for these times with a lot of protein." She picked up the coffee and lifted it up to him in a toast. "Thank you for the surprise visit."

"My pleasure," Slade murmured. Just sitting here in her calming presence made the whole miserable day dissolve. How was that possible? What was happening? Slade didn't know. He folded his large hands in front of him. "What happens when it gets busy for you around here?"

"I go into super doc mode." She laughed. Cutting her beef steak, she gave him a shy look. Slade's face was utterly relaxed for the first time. She was actually seeing the man, not his armor. It was an amazing gift for Jordana and her heart opened wide because he smiled just a little bit. It made Slade look even more handsome in her eyes.

"Super Doc. Is that what they call you around here?"

"You hit the nail on the head. I'm the manager calling the shots to my team of nurses."

"I'll bet you don't yell."

She salted her spinach and squeezed some lemon juice across it. "Yelling gets you nowhere."

"You never lift your voice to Stormy. I've found that people who treat animals well usually treat humans pretty good, too."

His observations were simple and yet profound. "I like the way you look at the world, Slade." Jordana ate and simply absorbed his demeanor. Slade might be sitting quietly at the table, but there was such strength and sunlight exuding off him, it made Jordana feel dizzied by his utter maleness.

"How has your day gone?" she asked.

"You don't want to know."

Hearing the sudden heaviness in his voice and a darkness come to his eyes, Jordana realized she was watching him shift into a more protective mode. Would he ever open up and remain that way with her? She found herself desperately wanting that. "Is that why you dropped by?"

The softness of her voice opened him up. "Yeah, it was a bad day and when I see you, it doesn't seem so bad after all…"

CHAPTER NINE

THE COOLNESS OF the early morning was dissipating as the sun rose higher in the sky. Slade took a deep breath and got ready to enter the corral where Diablo, the short-horn bull, was standing.

"Boss, be real careful. He's been pissy since the sun rose," Shorty called, standing outside the pipe corral.

Grunting, Slade nodded. Yesterday Shorty had seen the bull limping out in his pasture. Now he'd herded the testy one-ton animal into the small corral where they could get a closer look at his left rear leg. After coming home yesterday, it had been one more thing that had gone wrong. The only thing good about it was having the impromptu visit with Jordana at her hospital. That had lifted his troubled spirits.

Diablo tossed his head, his short, thick horns sticking out of the top of his massive brown-and-white head. His dark eyes were ringed with white; a sign that the bull was highly unpredictable. As Slade opened the gate and quietly stepped into the small, rectangular corral, the bull's ears twitched. Not a good sign. Closing the gate and locking it, Slade never took his attention off Diablo.

Shorty moved opposite of where Slade was, his face filled with tension. The bull snapped his attention to the wrangler.

Perfect. Slade moved closer, within five feet of the

massive animal so he could get a good look at that bloody rear leg. Shorty was keeping the bull's attention. Diablo would never allow a human this close under ordinary circumstances. Leaning down, Slade had trouble seeing the leg clearly. He saw dried blood on the inside of bull's pastern. The flesh had been peeled back.

"Look out!" Shorty yelled.

Too late!

Diablo whirled around, throwing his massive one-ton body straight at Slade, who was caught in a crouched position.

One second, Slade was leaping to his full height, and the next, he felt the bull's powerful impact against his body. White-hot heat and pain roared through his right thigh. In seconds, the bull had hooked him with his deadly horns and tossed him upward in the air like a puppet.

Slade heard the bellowing of the enraged bull. He landed close to the gate, crashing into the ground with an oomph!

Shorty was screaming to get the bull's attention. For a second, Diablo broke his charge and whipped toward the frantic wrangler.

Those seconds enabled Slade to scramble to his feet and lunge for the gate.

Diablo whirled around and charged, his bellowing echoing around the area.

Slade slammed and locked the iron gate. The bull hit it full force, sending him flying backward several feet into the dirt.

Safe! He was safe! Dazed, Slade sat up, breathing hard. Diablo eyed him through the pipe rails, huffing and snorting. He angrily pawed the dirt and lowered his head once more, wanting to get to Slade. But he couldn't. That iron-railed gate had withstood his massive charge. It would hold.

"Boss! Boss!" Shorty scrambled around the corral and ran toward him.

Slade shook his head. He'd screwed up. *Damn it!* As he tried to get up, his right leg collapsed beneath him. Slade fell to the ground.

Shorty breathed in gulps as he knelt down next to where he sat. "Boss, you're hurt. Oh, my God, you're bleeding bad!"

In shock, Slade looked down at his right high. Diablo's horn had ripped his Levis open and gored him. Blood was pumping and purling quickly out of a very deep wound. Mind numb and wrestling with the shock of the attack, Slade pressed his hand hard against the heavily bleeding wound.

"Get Jordana on the phone," he rasped.

Shorty's hands were shaking as he pulled his cell phone out of his back pocket. He dialed.

Slade sat there, knowing he shouldn't move. He wasn't a medic, but he knew there was a huge artery in his leg, and it appeared to him that Diablo had struck it. That accounted for the heavy bleeding. Cursing softly, he saw Shorty's face grow hopeful as he connected with Jordana.

"Give it to me," Slade ordered, holding up his other hand.

Shorty did as he was told.

"Jordana," Slade grunted.

"Hi, Slade. What's up?"

"I just got gored by my bull. It's my right thigh.

Where are you at?" He knew on three days a week she had her clinic in town.

"You're gored?"

"Yes. I need your help."

"It is bleeding badly?"

"Yes." He heard her suck in a breath.

"Listen, I'm just next door to you. I've just finished a house call with Iris Mason. I'll be right over. Whatever you do, keep pressure on that wound."

"I will, thanks," Slade said. Blood was oozing through his fingers no matter how hard he pressed down on the wound.

Handing the cell back to Shorty, he said, "Give me your belt."

Without blinking, Shorty quickly pulled off his well-worn leather belt. He knew what Slade was doing. In ranching, knowing first aid was a must. "Okay, Boss, you just keep pressure on it. I'll slide the belt around your leg above it and we'll see if we can slow the bleeding."

Slade was glad his brother was asleep in the house. He'd be useless in this kind of emergency, anyway. Pain was beginning to drift up his leg and into his torso. Diablo had nailed him but good. Shorty quickly slid the leather belt around his thick thigh, and then he hauled hard on it to tighten it. Grunting with pain, Slade clamped down, gritting his teeth.

"It's working, Boss," Shorty said, out of breath. He pulled again and locked the belt down. The bleeding was slowing.

"Good," Slade said, his voice sounding far away to him. He'd lost a lot of blood. Maybe too much.

"You want me to help you stand?"

"No. Just leave me here. Jordana will be here any

minute. Get some towels, a bucket of water and bring it to me."

Shorty leaped to his feet and ran for the ranch house. Slade sighed. Damn, this was bad luck. He felt that the world was caving in on him. First Griff showed up. Now this. Even worse, Slade knew it would be impossible for him to ride Thor in the endurance race. A deep puncture wound like this would take a minimum of six to eight weeks to heal up properly. And if he tried to ride a horse while it was healing, it would simply tear it open and make things worse.

As Shorty came running out with the pail of water in one hand and a bunch of towels in another, Jordana drove in. She slammed on the brakes, dust rising all around the truck. In her hand she had her black physician's bag. Running toward Slade, her face set with concern, she met up with Shorty as she got to Slade.

"Slade?" Jordana asked, kneeling next to him. "Tell me what happened." She quickly donned protective gloves and pulled his bloodied hand away from the wound site.

"Damn bull hooked me," he muttered.

Getting out a pair of scissors, Jordana quickly cut away the material to get a better look at the wound. She gently probed the area. She felt Slade tense. "Okay, this is serious, Slade. Call 911. You need to get to the hospital right away. I can't fix this out here."

"I'm *not* going to the hospital," he growled. He felt faint and fought it.

"You've lost a lot of blood," Jordana whispered. "That bull has hit a major artery in your leg, Slade. That belt is stopping most of the flow, but you need immediate surgery to repair this. What blood type are you?"

"Son of a bitch," Slade whispered. "I'm O positive." Of all things, he was going to have to go to the hospital. He glared up at her. Jordana was incredibly calm and centered. She saw things like this all the time, he reminded himself. "Are you sure? I don't want to go to the hospital."

Shaking her head, Jordana quickly wrapped it with a dressing. "You're going, Slade."

"I don't want a damned ambulance out here."

He was so stubborn! Compressing her lips, Jordana finished protecting the wound. "All right, then I'll take you in myself." She twisted a look up at the wrangler. "Shorty, get the passenger side door of my truck open and come back and help me get Slade to his feet. He's lost a lot of blood and he's going to be weak."

"How can you tell?" Slade wondered, watching the red blood quickly soak through the thick dressing she'd placed over the injury.

"You're white as a sheet, Slade," she said tensely, closing her bag and standing nearby. "You're going to need a transfusion. Has Diablo had all his shots?"

"Yeah," Slade said. "So have I."

"Tetanus?"

"Yes, two months ago. I'm fine."

He wasn't fine. Jordana saw how murky his eyes were looking. He was frighteningly pale, which told her he needed a blood transfusion pronto. Worse, he'd torn that major artery. If it wasn't repaired quickly, he could bleed to death. She didn't want to tell him the details. Pulling out her cell phone, she connected with the E.R. of the hospital, telling them to be ready to receive Slade. She ordered two pints of O positive blood to be on standby for him. Dr. Jonas Powers was the surgeon who was on duty. She ordered them to prepare the O.R. to accept Slade as soon as she could get him there. Everything was in motion.

Shorty came running back, his face filled with anxiety.

Jordana hooked her arm beneath Slade and Shorty took the other side. Together, they hoisted Slade to his feet. He was none too steady and walked with a heavy limp toward her truck.

"I hate hospitals," Slade growled unhappily as Jordana strapped him in and got inside the truck.

Shorty closed the passenger door after putting the seat belt across him.

Starting the truck, Jordana said, "It can't be helped, Slade. That's not a puncture wound you want to argue with. If we don't get that artery repaired pronto, you'll bleed out. I don't think you want to die." She gunned the engine as she turned the truck around. Luckily, Slade had had the road bladed by now, and it was smooth, graveled and flat. Forcing herself to pay attention to her driving, Jordana would occasionally glance over at Slade. His dusty cowboy hat was in his lap, his bloodied hand holding it in place. He had leaned back, eyes closed, his face pasty-looking. Heart pounding, Jordana knew the seriousness of his injury. He didn't seem to, but she knew he was in shock and going deeper.

"Are you in pain?" she demanded, turning the truck onto the highway and speeding toward the town.

"Not much," Slade muttered. It felt good to close his eyes. Suddenly, he felt sapped of all his mighty strength. He didn't like it. Feeling the movement of the truck, hearing the engine roaring, he asked, "How fast are you going?"

"Fast enough for the police to give me a ticket," she answered grimly. Both hands on the wheel, Jordana sorted out options of the quickest way to get to the E.R. Back roads were best because this was high tourist season with heavy traffic on major streets. Worriedly, she looked at his thigh. Blood was now leaking down his hairy leg below the wound. Even with the belt closing off a lot of the blood supply to that leg, it wasn't enough pressure.

By the time Jordana pulled her truck into the E.R., Slade was slipping in and out of consciousness. Two young, strong orderlies helped him out of the truck and placed him on a gurney. Together, they quickly wheeled him inside while Jordana parked the truck.

Running into the E.R., Jordana was pleased to see Jonas was already attending to Slade. There were seven nurses and orderlies waiting for his next orders. Breathing hard, Jordana saw they'd put an oxygen mask on Slade. His eyes were closed. She quickly looked up at the monitors they'd hooked him up to. His blood pressure was down. Way down. Too far because he'd lost so much blood.

"Let's prep him," Jonas ordered his team. "He's going into O.R. one."

Jordana saw that he'd probed the wound. It was still glistening with bright red blood, indicative of an arterial bleed. Slade lifted his hand and gripped her fingers.

"I don't want surgery. I don't want to be knocked out."

His eyes were dark and confused. Jordana leaned over him and whispered, "Everything's going to be okay, Slade. I'll be in the operating room with Dr. Powers. He's the best. He'll get that bleeding stopped."

They was the last words Slade heard. He felt himself

spiraling down, down, down. The only shred of consciousness he could retain was Jordana's warm, strong fingers gripping his. Eventually, he felt movement. It must have been the gurney moving. Voices were all around him, but he could no longer make out what they were saying. He didn't want to be in the hospital. And he never wanted to be in here for surgery. Unable to open his lids, he homed in on Jordana's comforting hand gripping his. In a moment of need, she had been there for him. It was the only good thing to happen in this sordid mess. His whole world crashed down upon him at that moment, and Slade lost consciousness.

VOICES. SLADE HEARD VOICES. But one he recognized as he slowly emerged from the anesthesia. It was Jordana's calm, husky voice. It took every bit of strength he had to just crack open his lids enough to see where he was. Jordana was at his side wearing green scrubs. There was a man next to her. His mind wouldn't work. His mouth felt like cotton balls were stuffed inside it. There was a dull ache in his right thigh.

"He's coming around," Jordana said. She leaned over Slade and laid her hand on his gowned shoulder. "You're in the Jackson Hole hospital, Slade. Dr. Powers just repaired that artery tear. How are you feeling?"

She was so close. Slade clung to her warm blue gaze and hungrily absorbed her hand on his shoulder. "Like hell…" he managed to say thickly, words not easy.

She smiled a little. Slade was no longer pasty-looking. His deep tan was back once more. "Are you in pain?"

"A little," he managed. "No big deal. Just give me… some aspirin."

Jonas grinned. "Mr. McPherson, I'm your surgeon,

Jonas Powers. We'll put a pain med in your IV. We repaired that artery. That bull of yours did a good job and ripped it open."

The information was too much for Slade to digest. He continued to drown in Jordana's blue eyes that were warm with an emotion he couldn't decipher. It was her hand on his shoulder that helped him orient back to the here and now. "Dr. Powers did a good job on you, Slade. Are you thirsty?"

Nodding, Slade closed his eyes. The anesthesia was wearing off but it was hell trying to think two words, much less put a sentence together.

Powers ordered the nurse to bring in another IV. that would help manage his post-surgery pain. He then patted Jordana's shoulder and said, "I think you can handle it from here on out."

"Yes," she said, giving Jonas a quick smile. "Thanks for all your help."

"He'll live despite himself," Jonas added with a grin. "Tougher than nails."

Jordana agreed. The nurse moved with quiet, quick efficiency, and in no time, she had the pain medication flowing into the main IV. Jordana could see almost an instant relief on Slade's face. She thanked the nurse. Now they were alone in the private room.

Picking up the glass of water, Jordana put a straw into it. "I'm going to raise your bed, Slade. You'll hear a whirring sound. I have to get your bed up enough so you can sip this water out of a straw." Jordana knew that people were groggy and confused as they came out of anesthesia. Pressing the button, Slade's bed moved up so that he was placed in a partial sitting position.

Opening his eyes, he saw Jordana holding the water glass. She slid the straw between his cracked, dry lips.

"Drink all you want. Most people are thirsty after surgery."

The water was cold and delicious. Slade found himself gulping the water like a thirsty horse after a fifty-mile endurance ride. The fluid served to wake him up more. After he finished the glass, she pulled the straw from between his lips. Everything about Jordana was gentle. He looked forward to every contact with her.

Pouring a second glass, Jordana watched Slade finish it off in short order. "Your eyes are looking a little less dark. Are you feeling more here than there?" she asked with a teasing smile. It was sheer delight to touch Slade, to help him. And he seemed to respond powerfully to her voice and touch. Yes, there was something between them, no doubt. Jordana hadn't had time to think about it.

Swallowing the last of the water, Slade held up his hand and whispered, "Thanks, that's all I want..." Truth be known, Slade wanted *her*. Each time Jordana touched him, his heart pounded. It made him feel better. Truly, she was a healer.

"Anything else?" she wanted to know, standing beside him, her hands on the bed.

Looking around, Slade slowly absorbed his surroundings. Feeling more like himself, he asked, "What happened?"

"You were in surgery for two hours. Dr. Powers opened up the wound and repaired the artery. I was there beside you all the time, Slade." She smiled a little, lifted her hand and pushed several dark strands of his hair off his wrinkled brow. There was such pleasure in getting to touch this hard, tough cowboy. Even now, lying in a bed and wearing a white cotton gown, he couldn't hide his powerful masculinity. There was nothing weak about Slade.

Scowling, Slade muttered, "Did you call Shorty and let him know I survived?"

Nodding, Jordana smiled and said, "Yes, I did." She'd asked Shorty to tell Griff because she knew his brother would be worried. She didn't tell Slade that, however.

"And how long will I be laid up?"

"At least six to eight weeks," she told him. Seeing his brows slash down, Jordana understood his reaction. "You won't be able to ride at *all*, Slade. That artery must heal completely before you can throw your leg over a horse."

His mind whirled with anger and frustration. "The Tetons ride is coming up."

Placing her hand gently on his upper arm, Jordana said, "I know…. I'm sorry." She didn't let on what Gwen Garner had told her earlier, that Slade was counting on that ten-thousand-dollar prize to push away the bank foreclosure that was looming over his family ranch. "I wish…I wish this hadn't happened," she added softly. How badly she wanted to touch Slade. His face was drawn in a different kind of pain. All Jordana wanted to do was hold him tight and protect him against harsh reality. Moving her fingers up and down his upper arm, she had nothing else to say because it couldn't change the facts.

Her fingers created warmth throughout his arm. Slade lay there, eyes closed, simply soaking in her grazing touch. Terror overrode it, however. Terror of losing his ranch. If he couldn't ride Thor in the race, he couldn't get an opportunity to win that ten thousand dollars. And he knew Frank Halbert at the bank was just waiting like a vulture to swoop down and take his family ranch away from him once and for all. Up to this moment, Slade had managed to stave off the bank. Now…oh, hell, he was going to lose his ranch. A ranch his father and grandfather had carved out of the wilderness and made bloom. He tasted the ashes of defeat in his mouth. Slade knew no bank would loan him money. His credit was worthless. Struggling with the enormity of what his injury had just done, Slade felt hot tears jamming into his closed eyes. Fighting them, he refused to give into his emotions.

"Excuse me, Dr. Lawton, but Mr. McPherson's brother Griff is downstairs and asking to see him," a nurse called from the door.

Jordana saw Slade's eyes snap open. She saw tears mingled with anger. Automatically, her hand tightened a bit more on Slade's shoulder.

"I don't want to see him," Slade ground out, lifting his head and glaring at the blonde nurse.

"Yes, sir, Mr. McPherson," she murmured, "I'll let him know."

The door closed.

Slade's gut felt like a nest of writhing, angry snakes. Only Jordana's quiet presence helped him calm down enough to think clearly. He looked over at her.

"Get me out of here, Jordana. I don't want to stay."

"But," she said, stunned, "you have to, Slade. You need to be here at least two days."

Forcing himself up into a sitting position, the blue blanket falling away, he growled, "No. Either you help me leave or I'll do it on my own."

Jordana saw he meant it. "Okay, hold on, Slade." She

lifted her hands to stop him from climbing out of bed. "Let's compromise."

Scowling, he said, "What do you mean?"

"I know you want out of here. And it won't do you a bit of good to be around your brother at your ranch right now. You need some quiet and rest, not agitation." Jordana lowered her voice and said urgently, "You can't move around much. That artery was just sewn up. What if I took you over to my house? I have a second bedroom. And I have the next two days at my clinic, so I could come home and check on you from time to time."

Startled by the idea, Slade nodded. "I appreciate this, Jordana. I'll go home with you."

CHAPTER TEN

JUST AS JORDANA was wheeling Slade out in a wheelchair to the front door of the hospital, his brother Griff met them. He was obviously concerned, and she saw anxiety in his green eyes.

Slade glared up at him. "I told you I didn't want to see you," he growled.

"I wanted to see if you were okay." Griff nodded respectfully toward Jordana. "Doctor, thank you for saving his life."

"You're welcome," Jordana murmured as she pushed the wheelchair down a wide hall. "You are Griff? His twin brother?" She saw how agitated Slade was becoming. It had taken her fifteen minutes to persuade him to sit down in a wheelchair. If he'd tried to walk, it would have torn the artery open again. He'd angrily sat in the wheelchair. Pride was evident even now in his ashen face. And his eyes were black with rage that his twin had come for a visit.

"Yes, I am. May I push the wheelchair for you?"

"No," Slade snarled at him. "Go back where you came from, Griff. You have *no* business out here."

For a moment, Griff was hurt by his brother's angry behavior. Shoring himself up from the unexpected attack, he said, "Are you coming home?"

"No, thank God, I'm not," Slade said bitterly.

Giving Jordana a searching look, Griff stumbled. "Then…where?"

"My home," she explained. Jordana didn't want to get into any more of a discussion. Slade was enraged, and, she was sure, embarrassed that his brother had seen him in a wheelchair, of all things. Giving Griff a sad look, she said, "I'm taking him to my home for the next few days. If you can have Shorty, his wrangler, bring him some clean clothes, I'd appreciate it." Giving Griff something to do would help Griff deal with this situation. She saw his face lighten.

"I can do that," Griff said, managing a slight smile. He looked down at Slade. "I hope you get better. If there's anything I can do—"

"There isn't," Slade snapped flatly. He saw hurt come to Griff's eyes and tried to protect himself from his twin's reaction.

Jordana knew how helpless Griff felt. Slade was going to have it his way or no way. And she knew he was not going back to the ranch because he didn't want to rely on his brother to help him out in such a tight spot. "We'll see you later," she murmured, giving Griff an understanding look. Griff perked up beneath her softened tone. Nodding, he turned and strode out of the sliding glass doors.

"Good riddance," Slade muttered. Feeling ashamed and weak in the wheelchair, Slade wished to hell this was all over. His leg was aching. So was his heart. He hadn't expected Griff to show up. "I wonder how long he's been waiting around outside my room?"

Keeping her voice light and without judgment, Jordana slowed the wheelchair and waited for the huge glass doors to automatically slide open. "I don't know. It's not important right now, Slade. You're looking very pale, and we need to get you to my house. How is your leg feeling?"

It had taken every ounce of Slade's energy to dress himself. He'd refused Jordana's help. And he'd told the nurse to leave. The struggle had drained him. "A little ache, but it's not bleeding."

Nodding, Jordana pulled a huge breath of fresh air into her lungs as she pushed Slade down the wide sidewalk. "If you'd let me help you dress, you probably wouldn't be feeling so exhausted," she said. There was no sense in making Slade feel more angry and upset than he already was. He looked shaken by Griff's unexpected appearance. Slade was having to deal with a lot right now, and she touched his shoulder gently. "Things will work out, Slade. I just have that feeling."

Shaking his head, his Stetson on his lap, he muttered, "They can't get any worse."

Wheeling him out to the asphalt parking lot, she laughed. "Well," she said wryly, leaning down and catching his stormy gaze, "yes, they could. You could be dead."

Grunting, Slade said nothing. He saw Jordana's pickup. A sense of freedom flowed through him. "Thanks for letting me stay with you a couple of days. I realize this isn't what you need, either. You work all the time. You're riding thirty miles twice a week..."

"Hush, Slade," she murmured, parking and braking the wheelchair beside her truck. "Don't you try and carry my loads for me, too." Jordana patted his shoulder to try and give him solace. "Right now, I know things look dark to you. We all have those times in our life." She unlocked the truck and opened the passenger-side door.

"But we get through them because other people support and care for us. Life is never lived in a vacuum."

Nodding, some of Slade's anger dissolved. Being around Jordana was heavenly, but he couldn't tell her that. Even the ache in his leg receded when she grazed his shoulder. She was a healer, he realized. And inwardly, right now, he was starved for every smile, every touch, she would bestow on the likes of him.

"Okay, cowboy," Jordana murmured, holding out her hand, "let's get you into my truck."

Slade didn't refuse her hand this time. Being stubborn or prideful could get his leg artery torn open again and he bitterly swallowed his pride. Reaching out, he grasped her opened hand. Her skin was cool and soft. Slade could feel the strength in it and her as she helped to bring him to his feet.

"Dizzy?" Jordana asked, concerned as she gripped Slade's elbow. He'd put out his other hand on the truck to steady himself. Often after transfusions, there could be some dizziness when suddenly standing after being in a sitting position for a long time.

"Yeah," he admitted hesitantly. One step at a time, he made it to the truck and carefully eased himself into the passenger-side seat.

"It's because of the loss of blood," Jordana murmured. Leaning across him, she pulled the seat belt in place. He was a powerful man even though he was injured. His barrel chest was well sprung. There was nothing to dislike about Slade as a man. Jordana felt herself trembling inwardly as she worked so closely to Slade for those few moments. Her dreams had become more and more sensual regarding Slade. And she was so close to his face and that wonderful mouth of his, that she could have turned and kissed him.

Shaken by her own neediness that was growing for Slade, Jordana eased away and shut the door. The sunshine was warming, and she looked up to appreciate the deep blue sky. A hawk was flying high above the area, its rust-colored red tail bright for a moment as it turned. She took the wheelchair, closed it up and placed it in the back of the truck. Struggling to contain her own emotions because being around Slade automatically stirred her up, Jordana opened the truck door and climbed in.

On the way through traffic to her home on the outskirts of Jackson Hole, Jordana kept an eye on Slade. He'd leaned his head back and rested it against the seat, eyes closed. His pallor was unchanged. She knew the confrontation with Griff had take anything he'd had left out of him. How badly Jordana wanted to simply put her arms around this prideful man and give him a moment's ease from his world that had just crashed down upon him. Understanding that Slade felt safe enough to be with her made her heart sing with unexpected joy.

"When we get home," Jordana told him softly, so as not to speak too loud and disturb him, "I'll take you through the garage to the inner door. I have a second bedroom nearby. And there's a ramp so it will be easy to push your wheelchair up and into my house."

Slade barely opened his eyes. It felt good to just be alone with Jordana. "Sounds good," he murmured. "I need to thank you for doing this. I know it's putting a hell of a burden on you."

She smiled a little, reached over and touched his hand that rested over his Stetson in his lap. "I'm happy to do it."

"I can't go back to my ranch," he uttered tiredly. "Not

right now. I have to get strong enough to do the work around there. I don't want Griff in the way. He knows *nothing* about ranching."

"You're injured, Slade. You need to be somewhere safe so you can heal up. Maybe being here for a few days will help you sort everything out and you'll come up with a plan."

"Are you always this hopeful?" he wondered, feeling a desperate need to sleep. The surgery and anesthesia had taken even his powerful energy and sucked it out of him.

"Always," Jordana said with a soft laugh. Slowing down, she said, "We're here."

Opening his eyes and sitting up, Slade saw a white single-story ranch house with dark brown trim. The lawn was small and rectangular. The bushes were trimmed, and flowers were on either side of the concrete walk leading up to the front door. "Nice place," he said, meaning it. Jordana pressed the garage-door opener. Easing the truck up and into it, Jordana turned off the engine. She gave him a gentle look. Slade looked exhausted. "I'll bet you're ready for a nap."

"How did you know?"

"Your eyes are dark-looking, Slade. And you can barely keep them open," she said with a full smile. "What you need is a bed and some good, uninterrupted sleep. Come on, let's get you inside…"

SLADE GROANED AS he lay down on top of the queen-size bed in Jordana's guest bedroom. If he hadn't been so exhausted, he'd have appreciated all her efforts to make the room look as if it came straight out of the nineteenth century. Instead, as she guided him to lie down, all he could do was slur, "I need to sleep…" and that was the last thing Slade remembered.

Jordana saw Slade's pale face relax. His beard needed to be shaved and it gave him a dangerous look. The house was cooled by central air conditioning, and she took a blanket from the closet and put it over him. He was too tired to get undressed and slip beneath the covers. Tucking him in, she saw for the first time the real Slade as he sank into a deep, untroubled sleep. Standing there, Jordana felt guilty for looking upon him without his knowledge.

Slade's face was utterly free of strain. She saw the fullness of his mouth for the first time. The wrinkles that were always on his brow had dissolved. The slash marks on either side of his mouth lessened. As she stood there, Jordana tried to imagine what Slade would be like without the awful weight of his ranch balancing on the edge of foreclosure. Or the fact he couldn't take part in the Tetons endurance ride to save his ranch from the bank. Jordana knew from personal experience that financial woes were the most stressful of all.

Moving quietly, Jordana pulled the dark burgundy curtains closed. Slade would probably sleep for six to eight hours. She knew what the stress of surgery did to people. Forcing herself to leave, Jordana quietly shut the door. Slade felt safe enough to sleep, and that made her feel good. Looking at her watch, she saw it was nearly five o'clock in the evening. Her stomach growled. She had taken a few hours off from her shift to help Slade. Luckily, another doctor had agreed to come in and take her place so she could take Slade home.

Humming softly, Jordana walked into the kitchen. It

was painted a soft yellow with white curtains on either side of the long rectangular windows across the twin sinks. From where she lived, she couldn't see the Tetons. Instead, large hills loomed out of the valley floor. Tinkering with the coffeepot, she was grateful to have the next twelve hours off. That meant she could stay with Slade and be here as a nurse of sorts. The phone on the wall rang.

"Hello?"

"Jordana, this is Shorty, out at the ranch."

"Hi, Shorty."

"Is the Boss okay? His brother, Griff, came back here and was lookin' worried."

"He's fine," Jordana soothed, hearing the anxiety in the wrangler's tone. "Right now, he's in the guest bedroom sleeping off the stress of the surgery and the anesthesia."

"And his leg? I tried to ask Griff about it, but he didn't know nothing."

"Slade refused to see him, that's why," Jordana explained.

"Oh, there's plenty of bad blood between those two," Shorty agreed heavily. "But what about the Boss? Is he gonna be okay?"

Jordana gave Shorty all the information.

"When can he come back to the ranch?"

"Probably in two or three days," she told him. "Right now, he needs no distractions, Shorty. That artery has to heal up so when he puts weight on that leg, it doesn't tear it open again."

"I see, I see," he murmured. "Well, you tell the Boss

to get well. Tell him he has no worries. I can manage here by myself."

"What about Griff?" she wondered. "Can't he pitch in?"

Shorty laughed a little. "Him? Oh, Dr. Lawton, he don't know the right end from the sharp end of a pitchfork. You know how they are?"

"Indeed, I do. But it looked like Griff *wanted* to be of help. Maybe if you could assign him some easy jobs around the ranch?" She was hoping Shorty wouldn't be as hard on Griff as Slade was. All he needed, she thought, was a chance. And he'd looked as if he'd wanted to be of help to Slade but really hadn't known how.

"That's an idea," Shorty said. "He's following me around like a lost calf. I think I'll hand him the tools to go start cleaning out the box stalls. That should keep him outta my hair."

Laughing softly, Jordana said, "Don't be too hard on him, Shorty. He loves Slade and he wants to help. Griff may not know how, exactly, but my bet is you'll come up with chores he can do around the ranch."

"Yes, ma'am, I know I can. Are you coming out here tomorrow morning to ride Stormy thirty miles? Tomorrow is your day to ride. Or are you staying there with the Boss?"

"I'll be out," she promised. Jordana didn't want to say anything right now, but she thought they might have a chance to try for the big money of the Tetons endurance ride. Oh, it was true she was a greenhorn when it came to the top level of competition, but she wanted to win the money for Slade and his ranch. But that was her secret. She wasn't sure she could pull it off, but she was going to give it one heck of a try.

"See you at 7:00 a.m., then," Shorty said, his voice lighter and sounding almost happy.

"See you then," Jordana promised. Hanging up the phone, she stood there for a moment digesting her newly hatched plan. There was no doubt in her mind that her sturdy, small mustang mare could win that race. The only real question was her. She lacked the competitive knowledge of a ride like this. And she recalled that Slade was very worried about Curt Downing. Shrugging, Jordana compartmentalized the daunting idea and put it aside. What she would do was cook Slade dinner. She was sure when he awakened, he'd be a starving cow brute.

SLADE HAD JUST sat up, leaning against the headboard, when the bedroom door opened. He wiped the sleep from his eyes. Jordana looked beautiful wearing a red-checked apron around her waist. He saw a smudge of white flour on her left cheek. "What time is it?" he asked in a sleep-thickened voice. He didn't have his watch back, and he missed it.

"8:00 p.m. You slept three hours," Jordana murmured, walking over to the bed and peering down at him. Only the light from the hall was spilling into the room. Jordana thought he looked stronger. "How are you feeling?" she asked, picking up his thick, hairy wrist to take his pulse.

"Like I'll live," he told her. Her touch was electrifying to him. Slade almost lifted his other arm to pull her down beside him. Jordana no longer looked like a doctor. She had changed out of her scrubs and white lab coat into a soft orange T-shirt with three-quarter sleeves and a set of figure-revealing jeans. Her fingers

LINDSAY McKENNA   139

were cool and soft. Another ache began in him, and this time it wasn't at his injury site. He wanted to reach up and thread his fingers through her mussed hair. Jordana looked vulnerable.

"Good, your pulse is normal," she said with a smile. Reluctantly, Jordana released his wrist. "And you look less pale. Ready for a light on in the room?"

"I'm ready to get up," Slade said. He threw off the blue blanket.

"Not so fast," she cautioned, going to the wall and flipping on the overhead light. "You need to move around with that wheelchair for at least forty-eight hours."

Groaning, Slade said, "I hate that thing."

Laughing, Jordana brought the wheelchair beside his bed. "I know you do, but it can help you heal faster."

Slade was strong enough to bring his legs over the bed and sit up. It felt good to simply move. "I don't want anyone seeing me in that contraption."

"Cowboy pride," she laughed softly, leaning down to put the brakes on the wheels so it wouldn't move when he stood up.

"I guess so," Slade admitted, frowning. Jordana stood back and allowed him to stand on his own.

"Dizzy?"

Shaking his head, Slade moved carefully into the wheelchair. "Not so far."

"Good, your body is adjusting. Bathroom?"

"Yes," he said. In moments, Jordana was pushing him down the pine-floored hall to a huge bathroom that had plenty of room for his wheelchair.

"I'll leave you here," she said lightly. "When you're ready to come out, just open the door."

Slade nodded. "I'll be out in a bit."

A few minutes later, Slade sat at a large, rectangular pine table in the dining room, the home filled with delicious odors. He wasn't prepared for the meal that Jordana had made for him. It struck him that she'd gone to a lot of trouble. There were fresh rolls, and now he understood where that bit of flour on her cheek had come from. A small beef roast surrounded with potatoes, carrots and celery sat in front of him. And best of all, thick, dark brown gravy was in a bowl next to it. *Homemade gravy.* How long had it been since he'd tasted good gravy? Slade could remember his mother making the best gravy in the world.

"Are you hungry?" she teased, smiling as she untied the apron and placed it on the counter.

"I am," Slade admitted. As she sat down near his left elbow, he added, "This is a mighty fine-looking meal, Jordana. You shouldn't have gone to all this trouble." Slade didn't want to add that at his ranch, he ate a lot of frozen dinners, pizza or canned goods. This meal was a feast, and his mouth watered in anticipation.

"It's nothing," she assured him, placing a dark blue linen napkin across her lap. She picked up a large spoon and said, "Give me your plate. I'll put what you want on it."

Slade was starving. By the time Jordana handed the plate to him, it was piled high with food. He saw a slight, sparkling smile in her eyes, but she said nothing about the amount of food.

"I feel like an interloper," Slade confided, spooning the gravy over his beef and potatoes.

"Oh?" Jordana took the gravy boat from him. When their fingers touched, she inwardly sighed. Any reason to touch Slade was a good one. Did he know how much she loved these moments? Jordana didn't think so.

"Yeah," Slade said, digging hungrily into the food. "My mother used to make the best gravy in the world. And yours tastes just as good."

It hurt Jordana to see him wolfing down the food as if he'd never had a home-cooked meal in his life. As she sat there eating with Slade, she realized that he probably cooked for himself. "You don't make gravy?" she wondered.

Embarrassed, Slade murmured, "No. I don't know how."

Grieving for Slade, for the loss of his mother at such an early age, she saw how much he appreciated the gravy she'd made. "It's something that's easy to make," she assured him. "If you're interested, I can show you how some time."

"I'd like that," Slade said, meaning it. How beautiful Jordana looked in that moment. Her cheeks were pink, her blue eyes sparkling with joy. As Slade's gaze slid down to her mouth he felt his lower body suddenly go hot with longing. For her. There was such grace in every movement she made, whether it was spooning out gravy on his potatoes or the simple act of eating her food.

Uncomfortable with his neediness of her, Slade found himself helpless in the wake of his epiphany. Her shoulder-length hair had been tamed into a ponytail at the nape of her neck. A few long, black strands of hair dipped across her unmarred brow. Slade fought the need to slide his fingers across those strands and tame them back into place behind her delicate ear. Why hadn't he truly seen her beauty before this? Had the surgery and anesthesia done it? Shaking himself internally, Slade felt confused. His whole world had been upended with Diablo goring his thigh.

"How soon can I get back to the ranch?"

"Probably in two or three days."

"Not any earlier?"

"No. That artery has to heal up to a certain point."

Slade scowled. He continued to eat as if he were starved. Really, he hadn't realized how he'd hungered for a good home-cooked meal. "Are you going out tomorrow to ride Stormy?"

"Yes," she said. "Thirty miles. Why?"

"I was just thinking I could hitch a ride back with you, was all."

Giving him a merry look, Jordana said, "Bed rest means exactly that, Slade. You don't get to go home right now. You need complete rest."

The look he gave her melted her heart. Despite his condition, Slade was a powerful, masculine cowboy. Jordana thought that he was the perfect iconic cowboy of the nineteenth century. Strong, silent and enduring. *The last cowboy.* She saw the worry in his gray eyes, the anxiety about his ranch on the brink of foreclosure. It was easy to read Slade's face right now. Jordana was grateful that his armored mask wasn't in place. It probably had to do with his surgery. Trauma and surgery were a powerful combination to strip anyone of their normal personality traits.

"Well," he murmured, a catch in his deep voice, "this feels like home to me."

CHAPTER ELEVEN

HOME! THE WORD held such power for Jordana. After dinner Slade had reluctantly agreed to sit in his hated wheelchair and watch some TV in the living room. She placed the dishes in the dishwasher. Afterward, she went to her office at the other end of her home and answered calls from her patients. She was never without her pager, and although her clinic was involved only in a Functional Medicine specialty, her patients had questions that needed to be answered. That took an hour of her time.

Slade heard Jordana's phone ring just as she walked through the living room and into the kitchen. She was a model of efficiency, and he reminded himself she was a physician. In some ways, her life wasn't her own; it belonged to her patients. And he was intensely jealous of them right now. Inwardly, he wanted that time with her. Watching television was something Slade rarely did. He was simply too busy out at the ranch with things that were far more important and that needed to be handled on a daily, ongoing basis.

Trying not to eavesdrop on the phone call, he realized it was something serious. Jordana hung up.

She popped into the living room. "Slade, I've got to go to the hospital."

"Okay," he said, frowning. "Do you ever get any time off?"

Jordana smiled a little and picked up her purse from a table in the corner. "I'm out riding Stormy every time you said I needed to, don't I?" She saw he was looking weary. "Do you want to go back to bed? I could wheel you in there before I leave."

Shaking his head, Slade said, "No, I'll stay up. Will you be back soon?"

"I don't know," she said, lifting her hand to tell him goodbye as she headed for the front door.

The door closed with finality. Slade felt suddenly and inexplicably abandoned. He knew it was silly to feel that way. For so long he'd wanted quality time with Jordana. And now, this. Running his fingers through his short hair, Slade realized he was emotionally raw from the surgery. Jordana had warned him about that. Looking around the warm apricot-colored living room that had several living plants sitting here and there, he realized just how much he missed having a woman in his life.

It wasn't a pretty picture, Slade decided. This injury had set him back in uncounted ways. And being here in Jordana's home simply reminded him of something else he didn't have. Unwillingly, he continued to absorb the room from where he sat. There were dark green drapes at the huge picture window. The evening sunlight was making the sky a paler blue. The overstuffed velveteen green and brown chairs made the golden pine floor prominent. There wasn't a bit of dirt or dust anywhere. If he didn't know better, he would have thought he was in a nineteenth-century home.

The furniture was made of blond oak, and it was old and stained from probably a hundred years of use or more, Slade guessed. The stained-glass floor lamp and table lamps reminded him of Tiffany's work. On one wall was a series of photos, and he pushed his wheelchair in that direction to get a better look at them. They were all family photos. He saw a baby photo and thought it might be Jordana. Next to that, she was six years old, her parents on either side of her as she sat on a black-and-white pinto Shetland pony. At six, Jordana had a cute little red cowboy hat, a leather vest and red bandanna around her neck. A smile cracked his tense veneer.

For the next fifteen minutes, Slade hungrily absorbed Jordana's life. He saw photos of her riding in dressage classes, in another, holding a trophy and smiling with relief that she'd won. There was always a horse in her life, Slade realized. He'd taken her for little more than a greenhorn who rode English and did a little bit of dressage. But these photos told a whole different story. An impressive one.

As he moved down a few feet and observed her college years, she was still riding in dressage and endurance contests. And he saw her in a white lab coat during her residency years. Another photo showed her holding up her stethoscope and smiling triumphantly. Slade guessed that's when her seven-year residency was over and she was now free to be an E.R. physician. Moving his wheelchair back to the center of the room, his mind spun. The television was on, but he didn't hear it.

By the time Jordana arrived home, it was dark. Slade had had plenty of time to digest her life and how badly he'd erred regarding it and her. When the door opened, his heart leaped. As Jordana walked into the living room, she smiled a little tiredly over at him.

"How are you doing? Bored to death?" she teased. Slade looked thoughtful, not tense as before. His mouth softened and was no longer a thinned line. "The pain meds must be working. You look relaxed."

Slade watched her progress to the table and said, "Do you ever take care of yourself?"

Startled, Jordana suddenly laughed. "Of course I do, Slade." She came up to him and peered down at his recently washed jeans. Barely touching the area where the dressing over the wound was, she murmured, "This looks good. I don't see any seepage." Looking up, mere inches from his face, she asked, "No pain?" Jordana was sorely tempted to lean just a little bit forward and kiss that masculine mouth of his! Shaken by that need, she straightened and removed her hand from his thigh.

"I'm fine," Slade said. His whole leg burned white-hot from her unexpected touch. Oh, he knew it was a doctor's touch, a medical examination, nothing more, but his body didn't know that. And neither did his galloping heart. She stood there smiling down at him and taking off her bright red-yellow-and-orange scarf from around her slender neck. Her hair was softly mussed, and Slade ached to slide his fingers through it.

"Good. I'm ready for a cup off coffee. How about you?"

Nodding, his spirits soared as he was now beneath the spotlight of her warmth and care. She wheeled him into the brightly lit kitchen and placed him at the pine table so he could see what she was doing at the counter. Suddenly, Slade realized he felt a strange, new emotion. It was happiness. Shocked by it, he watched Jordana move around the spotless kitchen as she made them a pot of fresh coffee.

"What happened at the hospital?" he asked. Her hands were long, her fingers beautifully tapered. Hands that performed surgery on people who had gotten into traumatic accidents. Hands that healed. Hands that he wanted touching him everywhere.

"A rollover truck accident," she said over her shoulder as she put the coffee grounds into the coffeemaker. "The kid was sixteen, going too fast and the sheriff's deputy found him at the bottom of a hill."

"Did the kid live?"

Jordana turned after she finished getting the coffee ready to perk. "Yes."

"Did you perform surgery on him?"

"Yep, I did. But I had another specialist in there with me. He was an orthopedist. This kid shattered his left leg. He wasn't wearing a seat belt, and as he was thrown from the cab, his left leg smashed through the front windshield and struck the side of the cab as he flew out of it." Shaking her head, Jordana added more softly, "I don't think he's going to keep that leg. It's too shattered. The bone surgeon did all he could, but he's doubtful, too."

"Sixteen," Slade muttered, his brows falling. "Messing up your life that young by losing a leg? That's bitter medicine."

Sighing, Jordana felt her sadness lift as she sat down opposite Slade at the table. "I know. The parents are taking it hard."

"Who is the kid?"

"Randy Bateman."

Cursing softly, Slade said, "I know them. They're a local cattle-ranching family south of Jackson Hole. That's a real shame."

She settled her elbows on the table and absorbed Slade's quiet, strong presence. Even if he was crippled for a while, he was still so powerful that it rocked her emotionally as a woman. "That's the hard part of my job, Slade. I love being a surgeon and I love helping people mend. What I don't like—" and she clasped her hands in front of her "—are days like this. Randy is only sixteen. One stupid mistake of driving too fast around a curve is going to change his whole life, forever."

Frowning, Slade touched his injured leg. "I guess I have nothing to bitch about, do I? I might be laid up and crippled for a little while, but that kid might lose his leg."

"Right," Jordana said, giving him a soft smile. "Hey," she said teasingly, "I like this sensitive side to you, Slade. How come I never see it when I'm out at your ranch?"

Giving her a shy grin, he melted beneath her sunny smile. "I'm your teacher out there. You're my student. It's a different relationship than what we share here."

Chuckling, Jordana stood up and went to the counter. "That's true, but I like seeing this other side to you. It's a pleasant surprise."

"Don't get used to it," Slade teased back with a slight chuckle. His heart opened powerfully as he sat there watching her take down two orange ceramic mugs and pour the coffee into them. How slender and firm she looked in her jeans and T-shirt. Her hips were flared, her legs long and coltish looking. The T-shirt outlined her small breasts and waist. She wasn't voluptuous, but that didn't matter to Slade.

Sitting down after she'd delivered the coffee, Jordana said, "I'll need to open that dressing before you go to bed tonight. It has to be changed twice daily."

The thought of her hands on him like that made Slade almost burn his tongue as he sipped the dark brew. She'd said it matter-of-factly, not like a woman who wanted to intimately touch him. Slade warned himself to be careful with how he was overreacting to Jordana in such close, intimate quarters. "I appreciate it. Thank you."

"After forty-eight hours, you will be able to do it for yourself."

"After forty-eight hours I'm going to be back at my ranch," he warned her. Although, Slade wistfully found himself wishing he could stay here with Jordana, instead. When she walked in that door, the whole place lit up with sunlight. When she was gone, it felt cold and lifeless. Slade didn't know a woman could affect him so powerfully in such a positive way. He'd never experienced this with Isabel. And really, all Jordana had done was a generous offer to keep him here because he hated hospitals.

Chuckling, Jordana said, "Yes, as your physician, I'll write a script for you to go home." She grinned over at him, and she liked his boyish reactions. This was a side to Slade that she'd never encountered. And she liked it maybe a little too much.

"That's big of you," he said. Seeing the merriment sparkle in her blue eyes, Slade liked the fact he could make her smile. Teasing wasn't something he did a lot, but with her, it came naturally, and it was playful and harmless. It made her laugh, and that sent a keening ache through him. Isabel had never made him laugh. Her contact was nothing like Jordana's hand upon him. Their touches were so different, it made Slade realize how bad a choice he'd made when he'd impulsively married Isabel. His wife had been flirty, always grazing his hand or shoulder and giving him that sultry, come-on look. Jordana was the exact opposite. There was so much Slade wanted time to sort out. But time wasn't on his side.

"Uh-oh," Jordana said, giving him a slight smile, "what were you just thinking? You went from being open to closing up like an iron book."

Startled, Slade realized he had allowed her to see his emotions. "Uh," he stammered, "just thinking about the past was all." He didn't want to lie to Jordana. She was too kind and loving to have that done to her. And Slade wasn't the type to lie, anyway. His blunt, unvarnished truth usually got him into more trouble than not. Lies weren't a part of his makeup.

Jordana had to tread carefully. She knew Slade's house-related finances were in ruins, but he'd never let on about it to her. She surmised he was worried about not being able to ride Thor and winning the Tetons endurance race. "I don't know about you, but my past put me in a financial hole the size of the Arizona meteor crater," she said lightly. When Slade's demeanor changed, and he looked interested, she added, "When I was at a New York City hospital earning my spurs as a resident, my boss made it impossible for me to continue working there. And when it was all over, I was just about penniless."

Frowning, Slade recalled the photos on the living-room wall. "You lost the suit?"

"No, I won it, but as that happened, the stock market plunged and I lost my entire savings. I won the suit, left my job at that hospital and came out here. For the last two years, everything has been stressful for me insofar as finances went. I had to start all over. I didn't want to put my money back into the stock market ever again."

Stunned, Slade digested her story. "I guess I never thought doctors were poor."

She smiled a little, her hands sliding around the mug.

"Normally, you're right. But I had to pay hundreds of thousands of dollars to my attorney. When we settled the case, there was four hundred thousand dollars given to me. I bought this house with it."

"I'm sorry to hear this. I didn't know…" And he didn't. Conscience eating at him, Slade said, "I want to reduce your monthly training bill to one thousand dollars."

Shocked, Jordana sat up. She had paid him two thousand dollars. "What? Are you serious?"

As badly as Slade needed that money, he could not go on with his scheme to milk her for extra money. Even though it could hold off the wolves from the bank, he couldn't do this to Jordana. She was the soul of kindness, and he'd rooked her because he hadn't wanted to train a woman. "I'm very serious. I'll write you a check when I get back to the ranch for that extra thousand. You need it worse than I do."

Alarmed, Jordana didn't think so. "But Gwen Garner said you were on the brink of foreclosure, Slade."

Oops! She didn't mean to blurt it out! Slade had already told her, too. She knew the topic was painful for him. Pressing her hand against her mouth, her eyes went huge, and Jordana saw the impact the words had on Slade. His gaze narrowed and his gray eyes darkened with pain.

"Yeah, that's right," he said, his voice suddenly dull and bitter. The cat was out of the bag, so Slade didn't tell Jordana that he'd tried to milk her out of an extra thousand a month because he'd thought she was a filthy rich doctor.

She reached across the table and gripped his hand. "You've had such a hard life, Slade. Everyone who knows you tells me that you're one of the hardest working ranchers in the valley." She saw his eyes widen for a moment as she touched his hand that was curled in a fist upon the table. It felt so good to touch him. She could feel the latent power in that hairy hand. A hand she wanted exploring her. Surprised by her thoughts, Jordana quickly pulled her fingers away.

"You need that extra money from me, then," she said stubbornly. "I *want* to pay you that two grand a month, Slade."

"You can't afford it, either, Jordana."

Hearing the frustration in his tone, she shook her head. "If I don't put a thousand dollars into my savings a month, I'm not losing this house." She gestured around the kitchen. "You, on the other hand, can use it to stop bank foreclosure."

Giving her a look of impatience, Slade growled, "You don't understand, dammit. I charged you *twice* the amount of my other students because I didn't want to have to train a woman for endurance!" There, the truth was out.

Jordana's brows flew up. "Oh," was all she could choke out.

Slade reached over and placed his hand over hers. "Listen, I was wrong about you, Jordana. Dead wrong. My own past with my ex-wife, who was from New York City, made me do this. I'm sorry. I really am. And I want to make things right between us because you don't deserve this kind of trickery." And she didn't. Slade moved his fingers across her hand and watched her eyes turn soft and hungry. It was then he realized that not only was he attracted to her, but she was to him, too. Slade removed his hand. He'd hurt Jordana. Basically, he'd defrauded her. And Slade was ready to accept her censure, even if it meant she'd leave him and go train with Curt Downing.

Sitting there, Jordana felt the wild tingles moving up from her hand, arm and encircling her pounding heart. Oh! Slade was dangerous-looking, his beard darkening his face, emphasizing his high cheekbones and those icy gray eyes of his. Her gaze kept returning to his mouth. A mouth she wanted to cherish and kiss and then she wanted to make hot, untrammeled love to this man. Swallowing hard, Jordana whispered tautly, "Slade, you had good reasons for your choices. I can forgive you for them."

Staring at her, Slade shook his head. "If I were you, I'd be damned angry."

Shrugging, Jordana finished her coffee. "You told me the truth, Slade. You're willing to give me the money back. We all make mistakes. It's what we learn from them that's important."

How different Jordana was from Isabel! Her maturity was like a warm blanket surrounding him. "I'm learning to stop comparing you to my ex-wife, Isabel. It's not fair to you. You're nothing like her."

"After hearing your story about her," Jordana said with a pained smiled, "you're right about that." She got up, feeling suddenly exhausted. It had been an intense one-hour discussion. "I don't know about you, but I'm ready for bed. I need to change your dressing, but would you like to get a shower first?"

Slade nodded. He saw the dark circles starting to appear beneath her eyes. "Is the dressing waterproof?" he wondered.

"Yep, sure is. Come on, I'll take you to the master

bathroom because it's very large and easy for you to maneuver around in."

"I can stand and take a shower on this leg?"

"Yes," she assured him, wheeling him out of the kitchen. Her master bedroom was on the opposite side of the house from the guest bedroom. "Do you need help undressing?"

The thought was hot and provocative. Slade put a lid on it. "No, I'll be fine. Just get me my hospital robe and I'll call you when I'm done?"

Nodding, Jordana wheeled him into the tan-tiled bathroom. It had a shower at one end and a Jacuzzi-style bathtub at the other. "I can do that." Putting the parking brakes on the wheelchair, she called, "I'll be right back with your robe."

Slade sat there appreciating the huge master bathroom. The tile floor allowed easy movement of his wheelchair. There were metal handholds outside the shower and inside, as well, so he could hold on to something if he felt dizzy or weak. Hearing her footsteps down the pine hall, he twisted his head. Jordana smiled and placed his bathrobe across one of the two basins.

"Holler if you need help, okay?"

"I'll be fine. You just take care of yourself," he told her gruffly. When she smiled a little, his heart raced. How could he ever have deceived this woman? Jordana was kind and generous. Reeling from how he'd treated her initially, Slade swore he'd right that wrong.

Jordana closed the door. Her heart felt like singing. Almost giddy from the intimate and personal talk with Slade, she felt as if she were floating down the hall toward the kitchen. Although Slade had pride, he could swallow it when the chips were down. As she puttered

in the kitchen cleaning up for the night, Jordana knew
he didn't have to tell her about the thousand dollars extra
he'd hit her up for. She understood on a deeper level that
Slade needed it to keep the bank at bay.

Where was their relationship going? Jordana wasn't
sure. Had it been a mistake to bring Slade over here for
two nights? She knew if he'd gone to his ranch, the ran-
cor and bitterness he held against his twin, Griff, would
have interfered with his healing process. Jordana knew
this instinctively and breathed a sigh of relief for Slade.
This was the first patient of hers that she'd ever allowed
in her home. So what *else* was going on? As she stood
at the sink staring out the curtained windows into the
night, her heart whispered to her. She was powerfully
drawn to Slade. But what were the consequences?

CHAPTER TWELVE

THE MORNING WAS clear and cool as Jordana trotted Stormy down between the cow pastures. The sun was barely tipping above the Rocky Mountains to the east of her. Stormy was prancing and dancing beneath her hand, eager to get on with the thirty-mile training ride. Happiness thrummed through Jordana. Just having Slade in her home was working miracles for both of them, she realized. The intimacy was powerful, like an aphrodisiac. She hadn't made love to a man in over two years. Now, she wanted to.

Stormy snorted and tossed her head, her black mane flying. Laughing softly, Jordana leaned down and whispered, "Easy, girl. You have to warm up before we start."

Another snort and Stormy danced sideways.

Jordana laughed out loud and pressed her left calf against the barrel of the horse. Stormy righted immediately and was impatient at being kept to such a slow trot. Jordana knew that if her horse was not properly warmed up, she could pull a tendon and that would take her out of the competition for a year. Tendon pulls or tears were an endurance rider's worst nightmare. It could easily sideline a horse for six months. And sometimes, if the tendon didn't heal properly, they could never resume that level of athletic challenge again.

Up ahead, Jordana saw that Diablo, the Hereford bull

who had gored Slade, was tossing his head. He, too, felt
the coolness and was frisky. She knew he was being
taken over to the cows for breeding, and it was obvious
he was ready to take on that role today. Shorty would
be coming out in an hour to herd the feisty bull over to
a smaller pasture where his girls awaited him. She saw
the white jets of steam shooting out of his large nostrils.

Joy filtered through Jordana. Yes, the day was young.
Full of promise. She felt the movement of Stormy between her strong legs and smiled. Riding a horse was
like being rocked in a cradle by a mother, she thought. It
was a rhythm and movement she couldn't live without.

Suddenly, Diablo bellowed. Startled, Jordana saw the
bull charging toward them! Stormy reacted first. As the
bull hit the pipe railing with all his weight, the mustang
leaped away to avoid the oncoming attack. Jordana followed through with her mare's defensive movement.
Diablo had never charged them before! She watched
the metal-pipe railing tremble beneath the bull's unexpected charge. He bellowed again. Leaping forward,
his eyes rolling and spittle drooling out of his opened
mouth, he charged.

Jordana was about to ask Stormy to gallop in order
to get away from the angry bull. Just as she pressed her
calves into the horse, she felt Stormy falter. *Oh, no!* In
seconds, the mare, who was trying to avoid the next as-
sault by the angry bull, had slipped into a newly made
gopher hole at the edge of the trail. Jordana threw the
reins away to give Stormy her head in order to try and
regain her balance. Stormy grunted. Jordana felt her left
rear leg suddenly crumple beneath her. They were going
down! Instinctively, Jordana jerked her feet out of the
stirrups and lifted them upward. It felt as if she were in

slow motion as the stalwart mare tumbled sideways and fell toward the ground.

Pushing off the saddle with her right foot, Jordana sailed out of the saddle. Stormy hit the grassy ditch next to the cow pasture with a grunt. Jordana hit the ground on her back, and she curled into a ball to absorb the fall. Air whooshed out of her lungs. Jordana rolled several feet before coming to a stop. Anxiously, she leaped to her feet, alarmed for Stormy. Jordana ignored the bruises to herself. Diablo galloped down the fence line away from them.

Stormy clawed with her four legs momentarily up in the air after she rolled into the ditch. The mustang righted herself and tucked her legs beneath her body. Jordana ran to her and Stormy lurched to her feet.

"Oh, no…" Jordana whispered, more alarmed as the mare stood, holding up her left rear hoof off the ground.

Speaking softly to her, she pulled the reins over Stormy's head. On the other side, Diablo bawled and continued to run down the fence line away from them. Jordana knew the fence would hold the angry bull and devoted her full attention to Stormy. The mare's nostrils were flared, and she was breathing hard.

"Easy, girl, easy," Jordana crooned as she slid her hand over the mare's steel-gray rump and ran her hand down the lifted rear leg. Jordana's fears ballooned as she felt the lower leg where the tendon was located. It had a mushy feeling, and already she could see swelling. Moaning to herself, Jordana realized Stormy had fallen into a gopher hole, twisted her rear leg and either tore or sprained the tendon as a result.

Grief avalanched Jordana as she gently felt the entire length of that tendon. Stormy stood quietly, her ears flicking back and forth. Jordana could tell the mare was in pain. Straightening, she looked toward the ranch area. She had to get hold of Shorty and pulled out her cell phone. With shaking fingers, she punched in the numbers. When he answered, relief shot through her.

"Shorty, call the vet. I think Stormy has pulled a tendon. And then, drive out here and bring me some elastic wraps. I've got to wrap her leg and walk her slowly back to the barn."

SLADE HEARD THE front door open. He'd just finished taking a shower, shaving and getting into his jeans and shirt when he heard the door. Moving out of the master bathroom, he pushed the wheelchair down the hall. Jordana appeared out of the foyer looking grim. Instantly, his heart accelerated. He saw her face was smudged with dirt, her hair loose and messy. As he looked closer, he saw mud on the left side of her jeans.

"What's wrong?" he demanded, meeting her in the kitchen.

Tearing up, Jordana halted and said in a choked tone, "Slade, I have awful news. I was trotting Stormy between the pastures when Diablo charged us." She sniffed and wiped the tears from her eyes. "Stormy jumped sideways, her left rear hoof falling down into a gopher hole at the side of the path. We went down. She's got a torn tendon."

"No…" Slade rasped. Of all things! He saw the tears continuing to stream from her eyes. He knew how much Jordana had wanted to race in the Tetons ride. "How bad is it?"

Sniffing, Jordana said, "The vet said it was a small tear but that Stormy was going to have to rest for a minimum of six months." She tried to shrug her shoulders, the bruising pain flowing through her shoulder and back where she'd hit the ground. "That ends my endurance career for a year."

Reaching out, Slade cursed his own weakness. If he'd been whole, he'd have pulled Jordana into his arms and held her and let her cry. He gripped her dirty hand. "Are you all right?"

"I—I'm fine," she rattled. "I'm sorry for crying…"

"Don't be," Slade rasped. Her hand was cool in his. How badly he wanted to console her, but he couldn't. She continued to wipe the tears from her face. "You're okay, that's all that counts."

Managing a grimace, Jordana whispered brokenly, "I wish I had the torn tendon and not Stormy. This is bad, Slade."

He watched the dream she had for Stormy die in her blue eyes. His heart contracted with anguish for her. Jordana didn't deserve this. She just didn't. Slade squeezed her hand gently. "Stormy is a mustang. They're as tough as they come, honey. So don't give up on her. Mustangs have an unbreakable spirit. They overcome odds other horses can't. It's in their genes, their breeding."

Nodding, Jordana couldn't be consoled. "For years, I've dreamed of this, Slade. Years… And when I found Stormy, I knew she was the one that could carry me on these endurance rides. She was my outlet, my dreams…" She choked back a sob. Embarrassed, Jordana whispered, "I've got to get cleaned up. I'll see you in a little bit…"

Slade nodded and grimly watched her move into the master bathroom. The door shut. He felt pain over the incident. Wheeling toward the counter, he made coffee. Jordana was probably crying in earnest now, and he couldn't be there to hold her. That hurt him more than anything else. Feeling weakened and angry, Slade hated his breeding bull for a moment. There was nothing he could do about it. Coffee and talk after her shower were in order. But Slade wasn't so sure he could do anything to lift her crushed spirits. Shaking his head, Slade cursed softly under his breath. He hated when dreams died.

JORDANA TOOK IN a deep breath and opened the door to her bedroom. Her hair was washed and combed, and she had changed into a fresh pair of jeans and a yellow T-shirt and put on her leather shoes instead of her cowboy boots. Running her fingers through her damp hair, she reluctantly headed to the kitchen. The scent of freshly perked coffee filled the air, and she managed a wobbly smile of thanks as Slade sat at the pine table, two cups of freshly brewed coffee sitting on it.

"That's nice," Jordana whispered, holding his dark stare. "Thank you."

"I imagine you want something stronger than coffee right now," Slade offered in a rasp. He watched as she sat down next to him, her long fingers curving around the orange ceramic mug.

"Yes," Jordana admitted sheepishly, lifting the cup to her lips, "if I were a drinker, I'd be drinking now."

Watching how the damp hair framed her face, Slade ached to kiss her. Normally, Jordana's cheeks were flushed with good health and vibrance. Right now, she was pale, and her blue eyes looked like wounded holes of grief. Reaching out, he squeezed her hand gently and said, "It's a bad break for you, but it doesn't mean Stormy can't come back for next year's ride."

Gripping his strong, callused fingers, she set the mug aside. "Thanks for being optimistic." Jordana could see the burning care in his dark gray eyes, the way his mouth was thinned. Slade cared, she realized dully. He cared for *her*. And her fingers tingled after he released her hand. Giving him a slight smile, she added hoarsely, "I cried my eyes out in the shower. I guess I never realized how important this was to me, Slade. I'd just come out of a nightmare lawsuit, left a job I loved and moved out here on blind faith to start all over. I always wanted to compete at the top level of endurance riding. And when Stormy suddenly dropped into my life when I bought this house, I couldn't believe my good luck."

Nodding, Slade knew to just let her talk it out. Women were like that, he'd discovered. Talk was like opening an infected wound and letting it discharge the toxic stuff. Talk was healing for them. He sipped his coffee and simply listened. Jordana's face was always readable. There was never any hiding how she felt, at least around him. He knew in the hospital, however, she had to mask her real feelings in order to help the traumatized patient under her care. He stared down at her fingers. They were long and graceful. Hands that healed the wounds of others. Did she know that she was healing him?

"I'm a very competitive person," Jordana continued in a whisper. "I like to win. I've devoted my life to being the best at everything I ever undertook. Even with the doctor who I worked under in New York, I made the decision that I wasn't going to let him stop me from being a damned good trauma surgeon. And I didn't." Jordana frowned and sipped her coffee. "I paid a price for it, Slade, but I won. I won back my integrity after he shredded it, and I graduated at the top of my class at that hospital despite him."

He nodded and pursed his lips. "You're the kind of competition rider that someone like me dreams about having. You have heart, guts and a can-do spirit."

"Well," she said bitterly, giving him a sad look, "it's all for naught. I don't have a horse to ride, Slade. I'm grounded. And we both know it takes a year of working with the right horse to get him or her up to that point where you can potentially win an endurance competition."

"I'm sorry, Jordana." And he was. "I'd do anything to make this right," he told her in a deep tone. *Anything*. Slade wanted to hold her because that's what she needed right now. Her proud shoulders were slumped, and her eyes held nothing but grief. It hurt him to sit here and not be able to fix this situation.

"Wait!" Jordana came out of her seat. She stared down at Slade. "I got it!"

Sitting up, he said, "Got what?" He saw her face come alive, her cheeks flush with sudden excitement. The grief in her eyes disappeared in a heartbeat and was replaced with unparalleled excitement.

"Slade, let me ride Thor in the competition! I know I can do it! He's the right horse. I'm not you, but I know I could potentially ride him and win the money you need to save your ranch!" She leaped for joy and clapped her hands. "Slade, I can do this!"

His eyes widened. She stood before him, hands clasped, her eyes suddenly filled with hope. He sat back, stunned over the idea.

"Slade," Jordana whispered, leaning over and gripping his shoulder, "I can *do this*! I know I can! If you'll just trust me with Thor, I know we have a chance to win this competition! Think about this. I would give you any money we earned. All I want is my dream to ride in a level-one competition. I don't want the money. If you could just see your way clear to let me try? Please?" Never had Jordana wanted something as much as this. She knew Thor was the optimum endurance mount. He was mustang, he was tall, his stride long, and he had a built-in toughness that always put him in top position to win. But would Slade entrust his valuable mount to her? That was the real question.

Feeling her hand gripping his shoulder, seeing the hope suddenly glinting in her eyes, Slade was at a loss for words. He saw the excitement dancing in her blue eyes, the soft parting of her lips begging him to say yes. Mind spinning, he remembered those photos in her living room. He'd underestimated Jordana's riding ability, her experience over the years with horses. Yes, it had been in dressage and lower-level endurance riding competitions, but she'd been a winner at both. And more than anything, Slade wanted to make Jordana happy. He didn't know why, and that didn't matter. All he did know is he couldn't stand to see her crying and so sad. And there was something he could do about it.

He lifted her hand off his shoulder. "Sit down," he told her.

Jordana sat, her heart beating so hard she could hear it in her ears. Slade looked thoughtful, and she knew he was mulling over her impromptu idea. Squirming, she forced herself to remain silent as Slade chewed over the idea. Would he entrust Thor to her? That was the crux of the request. Plus, Jordana knew how desperately he needed the money to put his ranch between foreclosure with the bank and surviving. Biting down on her lower lip, Jordana silently prayed that Slade would trust her enough to give her permission.

Giving her a hard look, Slade demanded, "Have you ever ridden a stallion?"

Some of her hope died. "No, I haven't," Jordana admitted. "But I can. I know I can!"

Mouth quirking, Slade kept her gaze. "Studs are different. You get a mare in heat on that endurance ride, and he's going to want to breed. Studs are powerful, Jordana. They aren't your sedate gelding or mare. They're testosterone on legs times ten."

"I *know* I can manage Thor," she told him strongly. "I've had all kinds of horses throughout my life, Slade. I know how to handle a horse that wants to run away or do something I don't want it to do." She held up her hands. "I might look weak, but I'm not."

"You've never been weak," Slade agreed. "But a stallion is a whole other proposition. They're headstrong, and they think they know what's best. When a stallion is passing another horse, he's in the heat of competition and he wants to win. A stallion can bite another horse so damn fast that you have to know it's coming. In endurance riding, a stud can't kick or bite another competitor's horse. It's against the rules. Stallions see every horse as competition to beat. He doesn't think about being nice when he wants to win. He'll do things instinctively to do that. And biting is one of them."

"I won't let Thor bite or kick at anyone," Jordana promised breathlessly. "I won't. I'm strong and I can handle him."

Slade wasn't so sure. "It's one thing to be around horses all your life, Jordana, and it's a helluva another to ride a stud. All that's on his mind is breeding and winning. That's it."

"You need the money, Slade. What if I could ride Thor well enough to win that ten thousand dollars? The money means nothing to me. All I'd like to do is have a chance at riding at this level."

She wanted to fulfill a dream. He desperately needed the cash to stave off foreclosure. The look in her eyes, the pleading, tore at him. "What if you can't control Thor? I'm risking my stud, his breeding fees and his good name. You could fall off, be knocked off by a low-hanging branch, or be unable to control him."

Nodding, Jordana sat down, her voice urgent. "I know all that, Slade. I would do everything in my power to keep Thor safe and sound."

He wasn't convinced.

Jordana saw him open his mouth. "Wait!" she pleaded, holding up her hands. "What if we go out to your ranch and you let me ride Thor in the corral? You could then see if I have what it takes to handle him." Anxiously, she drilled her gaze into his. Slade closed his mouth and scowled.

Feeling the shift in energy, Jordana leaned forward, gripped his hand and whispered, "Let me *try*, Slade! Just give me *one* chance?"

Slade knew Thor hadn't been ridden for two days now. Ordinarily he took the stallion out on a thirty-mile training run every three days. Thor would be so full of himself that he'd be tearing through his bit to run. The stallion loved to compete. Slade really didn't think Jordana could control his mustang. And by putting her on him in a corral, there was little chance that Thor would hurt himself. On the other hand, Jordana could easily be bucked off by the vital stallion and hurt herself.

"If you can't control him, Jordana, you could be thrown off and injured."

Shrugging, she released his hand and sat up. "Slade, I've lost count of how many times I've been thrown or fell off a horse. That doesn't scare me."

"You'll wear a helmet," he warned, not wanting her hurt.

"Of course. I'll wear one." Excitement roared through Jordana. She could see Slade considering the idea. "Slade, if I could win…"

"You'll *never* win it, Jordana."

"But I've got the horse!"

"You've *never* competed at this level," he said heavily. "And even if I let you ride Thor, that's no promise you'll finish. Horses break down on these rides. Quirky, unexpected things happen."

"We'll be okay," she promised him. She wanted to sound confident because she could see the worry in Slade's gray eyes. "Let me *try*, Slade. Tomorrow I'll take you back to your ranch. That forty-eight-hour period for your surgery will be over. You can call Shorty and ask him to have Thor saddled and ready to go. I can ride him in the large arena. You can use your cane and walk out there and watch us. Please?"

Her voice was husky with joy. How could he tell her no? Slade lowered his gaze and stared at the table for a moment. Did Jordana know how much he was coming to like her? Even with Isabel in the back of his mind screaming at him not to trust her, he was beginning to do just that. Mouth thinning, he muttered, "All right, we'll *try* it." He lifted his gaze to hers. Happiness was written all over Jordana's expression. Best of all, he saw the soft mouth of hers lift, and it sent his heart racing with need of her.

"Great!" Jordana whooped, clapping her hands together. "I *know* this can work, Slade! I just know it!"

"I don't," he warned her in a worried tone. "And don't go getting your hopes too high, Jordana. Thor's a handful even for me. You'll be like a fly on his back to him."

"My weight is much less than yours," she agreed excitedly. "And that should help Thor even more in the race!"

Slade grunted. That was true, and he hadn't thought of that angle. He weighed over two hundred pounds, and she was barely one hundred and thirty-five pounds. Thor could conserve his energy even more with a flyweight like her riding him. "We'll see," was all he'd agree to. "We'll see…"

CHAPTER THIRTEEN

JORDANA HAD TO hide her excitement. As Slade eased out of the passenger side of her truck, Griff came out the back door of the ranch house. He looked concerned as he walked toward them. Inwardly tensing, Jordana knew Slade wanted nothing to do with his twin brother. Compressing her lips, she lifted her hand in greeting to Griff as he approached. He smiled a little and nodded in her direction.

"Hey, I'm glad to see you home," Griff said to his brother as he rounded the front of the truck.

Glaring at Griff, Slade leaned heavily on the aluminum cane. He hated looking weak. "I'm fine. Now why don't you leave me alone?" He saw his twin's eyes widen with shock. Right now, Slade did not want his brother around.

Halting, Griff said, "I've been working with Shorty while you've been in the hospital."

Limping toward the barn, Slade said, "It's about time."

Jordana came up. "Good morning, Griff."

"Hi, Dr. Lawton," he said, tipping his hat to her.

She looked into his eyes and saw pain in them. Slade had rebuffed him without a second thought. "We're going to try me out on Thor over in that corral," she said, pointing toward it.

"Oh?" Griff said, falling in step with her.

"With Slade's wound, he can't ride his stallion in the competition," she explained. Slowing down to let Slade keep the lead up to the training barn, Jordana added, "And Stormy pulled a tendon yesterday and I can't ride her."

"I heard from Shorty about that. I'm really sorry," Griff murmured.

She could see that New York City Wall Street broker Griff didn't really grasp the enormity of the situation. Jordana said gently, "It's more than that, Griff. Slade needed that ten-thousand-dollar first-place prize in this coming competition to stave off bank foreclosure of your ranch. Did you realize that?"

"Why," Griff said, halting and stunned, "no...no, I didn't. Slade said nothing about that. I knew the ranch was precarious, but not in *that* much trouble." His brows fell and he looked at his older twin and then back to Jordana. "He doesn't share much with me," he added quickly under his breath.

Nodding, Jordana said, "Don't feel bad. He doesn't share much with anyone." She reached out and squeezed his upper arm. "Give him time and space, Griff. If you prove yourself worthy in his eyes by hard work around here, he'll soften toward you over time."

Griff nodded, grateful. "Thanks, Dr. Lawton, I'll keep that in mind. I appreciate you taking the time to talk with me. Is Slade going to be okay?"

Releasing his arm, Jordana said, "Yes, in the long run. Slade isn't going to be able to ride for six weeks, well past the time to get in shape for the endurance competition. He'll need to use that cane for the next week and then he can get on with getting back to ranching a little more. He won't be able to lift heavy stuff, either, so you might be there to help him in that way."

Relieved, Griff murmured, "I can do that."

Nodding, Jordana gestured toward the training barn where Slade had just arrived. "Let's go see Thor." Keeping her voice businesslike, Jordana didn't want Griff to know just how badly she wanted to show Slade that she could handle Thor. They walked together up to the training facility.

Slade was needled by Griff's presence. He noted that Griff had a pair of leather gloves tucked into his belt. Maybe he really was listening to Shorty and working odd jobs around here. Still, Slade felt as if his twin was imposing himself on them, and he didn't like it at all.

"Thor's ready," he told Jordana, hooking a thumb over his shoulder.

Shorty waved hello to Jordana as she walked down the airy passageway. She returned the wave. In the cross ties stood tall, powerful Thor. Her heart pounded because she'd seen the stallion when Slade had ridden him. But now, it was different. She could feel the heat of Slade's gaze on her back as she approached the saddled stallion.

Thor's small, fine ears twitched back and forth as Jordana approached. His large nostrils opened to pull in her scent as she halted at his left side.

"He's rarin' to go." Shorty chuckled, getting the saddle stirrups changed for her leg length. "Too many days of not being exercised."

Jordana held out her hand for Thor to smell. "Yes, he is." Smiling over at the wrangler, she added, "But so am I." She knew a stallion who wasn't well mannered would sometimes bite the hand, and so she was on guard.

Thor's nostrils flared, showing red deep inside as he took in her womanly scent. His blue eyes were pinned on her. Jordana kept her hand outstretched while he picked up on her scent. She knew how important it was the for the stallion to know her long before she threw a leg over him. "That's it," she crooned to the stud, "this is a handshake, isn't it, fella?"

Ears moving forward to pick up the sound of her soothing, husky tone, Thor shook his head, the cross ties jingling.

Laughing softly, Jordana allowed her fingers to slide firmly along Thor's massive jaw. His white-and-chestnut coat gleamed. He felt like smooth velvet beneath her touch. The stallion pawed his right hoof against the concrete.

"He's ready to go," Slade agreed, coming up alongside her. He nodded to Shorty who was coming around the front of the stud.

"Does he always paw like this?" she asked.

"Always. He's born to run."

Nodding, she asked, "Do you walk him out of here?"

"Yes." Slade saw his twin standing well off to the side. It was obvious Griff was unsettled by the powerful stallion. "I take the reins and walk on the right side of him."

"Okay," Jordana said, "I can do that."

"No," Slade said, waving for Shorty to come over. "Go to the arena. We'll meet you there."

Trying to hide her disappointment, Jordana nodded and turned away. Slade didn't trust her to even walk his stallion to the corral! Heart sinking, Jordana realized that Slade probably wasn't going to let her ride Thor in the competition. A fifteenhand-high horse was tall, and she was diminutive against Thor. Or, was he just taking extra precautions? Walking out of the training barn, Griff hurried to her side.

"What now?" he asked.

"Slade is going to test ride me on Thor down in the arena," was all she said.

"Can you ride that stud?"

Nodding, Jordana saw Griff's expression told her different—he didn't believe her. "Yes, I can."

"He's a big horse."

"*Every* horse is, Griff. Not just Thor."

"He's mean," Griff muttered, turning to see Shorty leading the dancing, prancing stallion out of the barn.

Jordana heard the growl in his tone. "What do you mean?"

"Shorty was having me feed the horses in the training barn two days ago. When I tried to slide open Thor's box-stall door, he attacked me."

"What?" Surprised, she almost stopped.

"Yes," Griff said, unhappy. "He bared his teeth and charged me as I started to open the door."

"That's not good," Jordana murmured.

"It scared the hell out of me. I've never been around horses at all, and he was the last horse on that side of the barn to be fed. The other horses whinnied or nickered and welcomed me into their box stall when I brought in the hay. Not him." He turned and glared at the medicine-hat stallion who was prancing and tossing his head.

Jordana got to the arena and pulled open the long pipe-rail gate. Griff followed her in, and they stood holding it open for Shorty. Thor danced into the large arena, snorting and continuing to impatiently toss his head. Slade limped in at a slower pace, a scowl locked into his expression. Jordana waited until he moved into the corral before pushing the gate shut and locking it. Climbing between the pipe rails, she walked out to where Slade stood next to his stud. Griff remained outside the corral, hands on the fence and watching from a safe distance.

"I'm ready," she told Slade as she halted beside him. Shorty was walking the stud around the arena. The sand flew beneath his small, sharp hooves as he danced from side to side. Shorty was calm and quiet and just maintained a steady walk.

Slade looked down at her. "Are you *sure* about this? He's full of himself today. More than usual."

"More than ready," she said with a grin. "Just because he's full of himself doesn't mean he's intractable."

Grunting, Slade said, "Come on…"

Following him, Jordana took a deep breath to quell her excitement. She wasn't afraid of the stallion. She knew Slade was afraid for her. He obviously didn't believe she could even mount Thor, much less handle him.

"Shorty, give her the reins and step away."

"Sure, Boss," he murmured, smiling at Jordana as she opened her hands to receive the reins. He stepped over to Slade's side.

Now for the test. Jordana saw the stallion's eyes flick toward her. His ears were pointed in her direction. Good, he was listening. Talking softly to him as she did to any horse she was going to ride, she slowly moved the reins over Thor's head. The stallion snorted and started to step away.

"Whoa," Jordana murmured in a firm tone. "Stand."

Instantly, the stallion stopped moving. A well-trained horse knew "whoa," "stand" and a whole bunch of other English words. Pleased that Thor obeyed her, she kept

her full attention on the stallion. He whipped his chest-
nut-and-white tail, which was long and flowing, from
side to side. That was okay. If the stud had moved his
tail up and down, it was a sign of anger. Thor was curious about her. And that's exactly where Jordana wanted
the stallion to be.

Gathering the reins in her hand, she gripped a piece
of his long mane and inserted her left boot into the stirrup. Thor was tall, so Jordana had to draw on all her
strength to pull upward and lift her right leg over the
horse's back. She had a good pull on the horse's mouth
so he couldn't step forward while she was mounting.

Like a gentleman, Thor stood quietly as she mounted.
Slipping her boot into the right stirrup and settling down
in the specially made saddle, Jordana quickly gripped
the horse's barrel. Thor's ears were flicking restlessly.
Snorting, he tossed his head.

Jordana didn't look toward Slade or Shorty. She
clucked and squeezed Thor's barrel. Instantly, the stud
jumped forward. Not surprised, Jordana flowed forward
with him. She used both hands on the reins. The stallion wanted to run. She wanted him to walk. The battle
was joined.

Slade stood there, eyes narrowed speculatively, as
he watched the featherweight deal with over a thousand
pounds of raw stallion energy. At first, Thor tried to take
over, but Slade saw Jordana sit the saddle and play with
the reins so that Thor had to curve his long neck and
bring his head perpendicular to the ground. He knew
enough about dressage to realize that Jordana's legs and
hands were asking the stallion to collect himself in a
highly balanced way. Thor wasn't used to dressage, so
Slade wondered what his stud was going to do about it.

Would he fight Jordana? Or submit? Slade wasn't sure as she got the horse to do a dancing walk around the corral.

Tension thrummed through Jordana. She kept her shoulders squared, her spine supple and legs taut and firm against Thor. The power of this animal was exciting to her. He was ten years old and in excellent shape for an endurance horse. His white-and-chestnut coat gleamed in the sunlight, his mane fine and feathery as it moved like ripples of water across his deeply arched neck. She felt as if she were sitting on top of a keg of dynamite that was ready to explode at any second. Yet as she asked Thor to flex his neck and collect himself, he did just that. Exhilaration swept through Jordana. She knew this horse had not been trained for dressage, yet, with her light, constant touch on his bit to keep it from sawing on his mouth, Jordana had secured the horse's surrender.

"I'll be darned, Boss," Shorty whispered, impressed. "Lookie at that stud. He's mighty tame under her direction."

Grunting, Slade didn't say anything. As Jordana worked with her strong legs and light hands, she was getting his stud to do things he'd never seen him do before. Looking like a tiny jockey on the massive stallion, Jordana impressed Slade. But he kept those thoughts to himself.

Jordana felt the stallion respond quickly to her leg pressure. She had him moving diagonally across the arena, neck flexed, his body in balance. When she arrived at the other side, she moved him the other way in the arena with a simple pressure of her other calf against his barrel. Her joy soared. Not only was Thor listening, but he was trying to please her! Allowing the reins to ease, she asked a slow trot of Thor.

Thor wanted to run. He snorted and lunged forward, wanting to gallop. Instantly, Jordana countered and pulled on the reins just enough to let him know he couldn't do what he wanted. He had to do what she asked of him, and that was all. Headstrong, Thor snorted violently, humped his back and tried to throw her off. Instantly, Jordana gripped his barrel hard with her legs and rode out the two hopscotching jumps.

Shorty snickered. "Hey, Boss, she's got his number!"

Grinning a little, Slade nodded. It wasn't unusual for Thor to do what they termed "crow hopping." It was a series of bucks and jumps designed to throw off an incompetent rider. But Jordana had stuck like proverbial glue to the stallion's back when he'd tried those antics with her. "Yes, I think she might," he admitted in a gravelly tone.

Jordana worked with Thor. It was important the stallion do exactly as she wanted, when she wanted. He was chomping on his bit, foam gathering on the sides of his opened mouth. She could feel the power of each of his long strides as she kept him at a sedate trot. Literally, she could feel the stallion puffing up and trying his best to run, but she kept him under control. With every stride, he grunted and snorted, as if to scare her. But she wasn't scared. Riding Thor was like riding a lightning bolt.

When she finally allowed him into what was called an extended trot, she felt Thor begin to release some of that stored power. Amazed at the speed and stride of the stud, she posted in the saddle. Jordana was sure that Slade never posted in the saddle, and the horse seemed confused by the motion on his back. Talking soothingly to Thor, his ears flicking, Jordana understood the stud's sudden wariness. His long legs struck out, and as she continued to keep a firm, guiding hand on him, Thor eventually adjusted to her posting.

Now, Jordana wanted to see if Thor had the floating trot of Stormy. She knew not all mustangs possessed this very Arabian trait. Did he? Squeezing her legs more, and yet holding the reins where they were, she asked that of Thor.

"I'll be darned, Boss. Look it!" Shorty crowed.

Eyes slitted, Slade watched his powerful stallion move into a strong, flowing trot. Thor's tall legs snapped out with military precision as he moved into that distance-eating floating trot. He knew to ride that kind of a trot was the hardest on the rider. Yet, Jordana was flowing like a ribbon in the wind as he moved with effortless ease around the arena. Some of his anxiety abated.

"She's doin' it!" Shorty said, smiling.

"So far…" Slade muttered. "Let's wait and see what happens when he gallops." Slade knew from long experience that the stud's favorite gait was an all-out gallop. He lived to run. It was bred into his blood and bone. Jordana might think she had control over Thor, but until she had ridden him at that all-out gallop, she wouldn't realize his raw, competitive power.

Jordana slowed Thor back down to a sedate trot and then asked him to stop. The stallion fought her, moving his head and trying to take control of the reins. *No way!* Jordana glanced for the first time toward the center of the arena. Was Slade unhappy with her? Or did he trust her? She saw his face dark and unreadable and those gray eyes narrowed like those of a predator.

"Okay," she told Thor, "he still doesn't think we can get along."

Thor snorted and finally halted. He switched his tail from side to side, his ears back and mouth opening and closing. All signs that he didn't like what was being asked of him.

Jordana knew enough about the stallion to now ask him to canter. The canter was a slow, controlled run. In a gallop, the horse was asked for all his speed and stride. They were very different gaits. She collected Thor with her hands and legs. And then, she gave the stallion the signal to canter.

Thor exploded beneath her, nearly unseating Jordana. Caught off guard by the powerful leap forward, she quickly seated herself and got him back beneath her control. Thor fought the bit, shaking his head from side to side. He was grunting and snorting with every cantering stride. How badly he wanted to run! Jordana felt the unequaled power of the stallion she was riding. Never had she felt this kind of massive energy in any horse. Now, as she flew around the arena fighting Thor with every stride to get him to canter, Jordana saw why he was the top endurance champion. The wind tore past her even at a canter. Jordana's whole focus was on being ahead of this feisty stallion and guiding him where she wanted him to go. Her hands ached and sweated on the slick leather reins. She couldn't afford to let Thor get the best of her now. Would he buck and crow hop at this gait? She didn't know, and she wasn't about to be caught off guard again.

After warming Thor up in the arena at a canter, she glanced over at Slade.

"Let him run!" he called out.

Okay, a full gallop. Sucking in a breath, Jordana got ready for the ride of her life. Thor heard his master and lunged. For a split second, Jordana was behind the horse's change of gait. Settling down, she released the reins. Thor dug into the deep sand, grunted and stuck out his long neck. His hooves plunged into the soil, the sand flying in veils all around him as he sailed forward at high speed. His tail lifted up like a flag, a very Arabian characteristic. Jordana's attention narrowed to the quick striding stallion who was finally off the leash and running as hard as he could. They flew around the arena in a blur. For a bit, Jordana simply let the stallion get it out of his system. She was a mere jockey on the hard-running stud. But at a certain point, she needed to re-establish control.

When she pulled in on the reins, Thor snorted and fought her hard. The reins slipped through her fingers. He lunged forward, ears pinned against his neck. It was his way or no way! Quickly gathering the reins through her aching fingers, Jordana leaned forward and hauled him in. Again, Thor fought her. Again, she reestablished her superiority. The stallion reluctantly slowed down, his legs high and long.

Slade watched the battle between woman and stallion. Jordana's face was intense, her mouth thinned, her eyes ahead of the horse to ensure he was going where she wanted him to go. An unwilling sliver of a smile tipped the corners of his mouth.

"I'll be darned," Shorty crowed, "she's handling him, Boss! How about *that*? I never thought another man except yourself could handle Thor." Taking off his hat and shaking his head, Shorty added, "Much less a *woman* to ride that machine!"

And Thor was a machine, Slade knew. There had been times when he'd had trouble handling the competitive stallion. He watched as Jordana worked and wrestled with Thor. The stallion didn't want to surrender his will over to her. But he didn't like surrendering over to Slade, either. It was always a fight, a part of his makeup as a stallion. But handle Thor, she did. Pride for her flowed through Slade. He found himself watching Jordana move the stud around and move him in the other direction. Thor hated giving over his freedom to any rider. He constantly tossed his head, chomped aggressively down on the bit and flattened his ears against his neck. Yet, Jordana was controlling him. His heart opened to this woman who looked as light as a postage stamp on the back of his stallion. She was small but mighty.

Jordana took Thor in the other direction, forcing him to canter for several minutes before she opened him up again. This time, she was ready for that explosion. And explosion it was! Thor grunted, crow hopped twice and leaped forward. Jordana moved with him this time. She didn't allow him to run full speed. Instead, she kept him between a canter and a gallop. The stallion had to do as she wanted every moment or this wouldn't work at all, and Jordana knew it.

Pleased, Slade watched his stallion succumb to Jordana's more stubborn spirit. Shorty was cackling and pointing at them and constantly making remarks about Jordana's amazing riding skills. Yes, she had guts and savvy to ride that beast of his. Thor had never known another rider but him, and for this small woman to come and ride Thor and force him to obey her was simply stunning to Slade. It made him want Jordana even more than before. He saw the muscles of her arms leaping as the stallion constantly challenged her. The set look on her face, her eyes narrowed and mouth thinned, told him she was fighting him every second. Yet, she was winning.

"Okay," Slade called, "bring him in."

Thor snorted and squealed as Jordana brought him down to a trot. The stud crow hopped some more, but she stayed with him and remained quiet in the saddle, her hands firm and guiding. Giving up for a moment, the stallion broke down into a trot. And as she guided him to the center, she asked him to walk. Tossing his head in protest, Thor settled into a prancing, dancing walk.

Finally, Thor stood still. Jordana smiled down at Slade. She was breathing hard, sweat running off her. "Well? What do you think?"

"I think he damned near tossed you off."

Shorty came up and gripped the reins. Jordana eased them and laid the reins against Thor's neck. She grinned and patted the stallion's sweaty neck. "Yes, he's a horse that wants to run. Hates walking and trotting."

Nodding, Slade came up alongside her. Jordana's face was flushed, her eyes sparkling with joy and those lips, he found he couldn't stop staring at, in a wide, joyous smile. As Slade patted Thor's neck, he wondered what it would be like to see her smiling like that as they made love to one another. The thought slammed into him, and it took Slade's breath away for a moment. Stunned, he stood there speechless until he felt Jordana's hand coming to rest on his shoulder.

"Slade, he's marvelous! I've never had such a ride in my life! Thor is incredible!"

Just her hand on his shoulder for that brief moment made Slade start aching from his heart down to his lower body. He turned and looked up at her. Jordana's hair, once in a ponytail, had been mussed by the wind and the wild ride on Thor. Her eyes were sparkling, and he felt heat flow through him, lifting his dour look on life. "He is incredible."

"I mean," Jordana said, sighing, "I knew he has been a great breeding stallion and passed on his endurance traits to others, but getting to ride him…" She rolled her eyes and laughter flowed out of her. "Thor is amazing, Slade." She leaned forward and patted the stud's neck once more. "Just amazing."

"He is," Slade agreed. "Dismount."

Doing as he ordered, Jordana walked to Thor's head and spoke quietly to him. Rubbing his face, which was beaded with sweat, she smiled at him. "You're one hell of a horse, Thor. But I think you and I can get along. Don't you, boy?"

Snorting, Thor's ears twitched. He nuzzled into her hand and tried to rub his sweaty head against her shoulder.

Laughing softly, Jordana stepped back, keeping her hand on Thor's jaw. "I'll give you a bath, but you're not using me as your towel to wipe off that sweat," she told him with a grin.

"Shorty, take Thor to the bath," Slade ordered.

"Yes, Boss."

Jordana stepped out of the way as Shorty took the reins and led the stallion toward the gate. Griff was there and opened it for them. She looked up at Slade's set face. "Well? What do you think?"

"I think you rode a wild stallion that likes his way or no way," he told her. He stopped himself from reaching out and taming those strands of hair around her face.

"He's a handful," she agreed. Searching his light-colored gray eyes, Jordana said, "But I controlled him."

Nodding, Slade turned and began to limp back toward the opened gate. He saw Griff accompanying Shorty at a healthy distance from the dancing stallion. His twin was afraid of horses, no question. He felt Jordana come to his side as they walked down the center of the arena. "You weren't afraid of Thor," he said.

Shaking her head, Jordana grinned. "Like I said before, Slade, I've been tossed and bucked off by horses much worse than Thor. He was crow hopping because he wanted to run." She met his gaze and thought he saw respect for her in them. "The other horses were trying to get rid of me because they didn't want to be ridden. That's a huge difference."

"Yes," Slade murmured, pleased with her insight, "it is."

"So," Jordana said as she turned and stood in front of him. "Will you let me ride Thor in the endurance competition?" She held her breath, never wanting anything more. Would Slade say yes? Or no?

CHAPTER FOURTEEN

SLADE LIMPED INTO his ranch home. Griff was sitting at the kitchen table having a cup of coffee. For a moment, he felt sorry for his younger brother. But not for long.

"Take your coffee and go out and help Shorty," he muttered, gesturing toward the front door.

Griff stood. He took the mug and nodded deferentially to Jordana as they passed one another in the foyer.

Slade felt his leg throbbing. He needed to sit down.

"Can I make us some coffee?" Jordana asked as she walked into the kitchen, noticing the pot was now empty. She saw Slade's face had turned pasty; it was a sign of pain.

"Yes," he said, scowling. Looking around at the kitchen, it was a mess. Dirty dishes abounded. Nothing was cleaned up, nor was it neat. He saw the red-tile floor was dirty, too. "Damn brother of mine doesn't know how to use a vacuum cleaner, dust, mop or wash dishes."

"Mmm," Jordana agreed. "It's not like I've seen your place before," she said getting down two mugs. Griff had used the coffeemaker but had neglected to turn it off when it was empty. She quickly shut it off and rinsed out the glass container with hot water so it wouldn't suddenly crack from the drastic temperature change. The bottom was black with boiled coffee, indicating Griff had done this many times before.

Slade sighed. "I'm gone two days and he lets this place go. What the *hell* did his uncle and aunt teach him? All he has eyes for is making millions in the stock market. He probably had a maid he hired to keep his million-dollar penthouse clean."

Hearing the bitterness in Slade's gravelly tone, Jordana scrubbed out the container and then set to work making fresh coffee for them. She desperately wanted to know if Slade would allow her to ride Thor in the coming endurance event but knew this was the wrong time to broach it again. He was very upset over the dirtiness of his normally clean ranch home. She didn't blame him but didn't know enough details of his relationship with Griff to make comments one way or another.

Slade absently rubbed his thigh where the operation had taken place.

"Are you in pain?" she wanted to know, coming over and standing near him.

"Yeah," Slade admitted sourly.

"You stood on it too long out there."

"I had no choice."

Smiling a little, Jordana placed her hand on his shoulder for a moment. "You're a big mama hen in disguise, Slade."

The warmth of her hand on his shoulder neutralized the ache in his leg. It was an amazing experience for Slade. How could her hand *stop* the throbbing of his leg wound? Twisting a look up at her, his heart briefly pounded. Her black hair was now hanging around her shoulders and framed her flushed oval face. She was beautiful, Slade realized, in such a natural way. Jordana rarely wore makeup. Hungrily absorbing her lingering touch on his shoulder, he managed a lopsided smile. "Maybe a rooster, but never a hen."

Laughing, Jordana wanted to lean down and kiss those lips of his. But it would be impossible to do. He might take such an act as manipulation. And she knew enough about his ex-wife, Isabel, to know she was a premier manipulator. Jordana had no desire to be compared to this woman. "Okay, you can be Big Daddy Rooster." Lifting her hand, she walked back to the counter where the coffee was gurgling away. Looking out the window, she saw Griff walking up toward the training barn. Thor had been unsaddled and washed, and Shorty was taking him back to his stall in the barn.

Slade enjoyed absorbing her curvy figure as she stood at the drain board, hands resting on the tiled surface of the sink. The room just seemed to light up with sunshine when she was present. What was so different about Jordana? Was it because she was a professional woman? Unlike spoiled, rich Isabel? He made a mental comparison of the two and had more questions than answers.

Jordana poured two mugs of coffee and brought them over to the table. There had been crumbs on the pine surface, and Slade had absently corralled all of them into one group near one corner. She took a dishcloth hanging across the spigot and wiped the table clean. It gleamed once more with golden and reddish colors across its surface. Griff was definitely not housebroken, she decided.

"Thanks," Slade murmured, appreciative of her sensitivity to him not liking dust and dirt around.

Coming back, Jordana smiled and sat down at his elbow. "I can't stand a dirty place, either," she confided.

"My brother is lost. He's lost his job, lost all his mil-

lions, lost his self-esteem, and now he's here on my doorstep telling me he owns half this ranch."

Sipping the coffee, Jordana nodded. She could see
the anger and frustration in Slade's look.

"Now he's trying his hand at ranching. And he's no
good at it."

"Maybe with time he might be?" Jordana said. She
saw Slade's thick brown brows move downward.

"He came back here because he had nowhere else to
go. All his 'friends' wanted nothing to do with him after
he lost his money. Some friends they were…"

"What did he want from you, Slade?"

"He wanted me to take care of him until he could
get back on his feet." His laugh was short and harsh.
"Money! Hell, I'm scrambling every month to find
enough just to pay the ranch mortgage. He didn't believe me that I didn't have the money. He said I was
holding a grudge against him because he'd refused to
loan me money about six years ago."

"What will you do about it?"

Shaking his head, he rasped, "He's a spoiled greenhorn. And when his world collapsed, he came crawling
back here to try to figure out what his next entrepre-
neurial idea would be." Snorting, Slade met her eyes as
she withdrew her hand from his. "Griff doesn't get what
hard work and earning your way in this world is really
all about. Griff learned about money, how to make it,
and his world was about millions of greenbacks."

She saw Slade's face go grim, his mouth thinning. "A
lot of people have been hit hard in this recession," she
agreed in a soft tone. Jordana didn't see Griff as bad;
merely out of touch with the reality of the middle class
that was the backbone of this country. He'd had it easy

for too long and didn't know how to settle into the reality of having to earn a daily living.

Sighing roughly, Slade slid her a glance. "You're always gentle with people. How did you get that way?" And when he saw her soft mouth curve upward, Slade instantly wanted her. In every possible way. His hands tightened around the mug in front of him. He was finding that just sharing time and space with her was like a delicious and unexpected dessert.

Shrugging, Jordana said, "It's just me, Slade. When I was in residency in New York City, I saw too many of my friends and the doctors who were our bosses be short, hard and disconnected from a suffering patient. I didn't want that kind of connection with sick people. I know a smile and a touch can give someone a world of hope to cling to. I've seen the way my way of working with a person works miracles. I took what I've learned from that arena and applied it everywhere."

Slade held her sparkling blue gaze. "And why do you think Thor responded to you?"

Her heart beat hard, once. Losing her smile, she said in a low tone, "Slade, I know horses. It's true I've never ridden a stallion before this, but they all have personalities. I've handled some spoiled and wounded horses when I was younger. I treat them like people, and ask myself how would I respond best? It's a mind game with each horse to feel him or her out. What will make the horse *want* to work with me instead of working against me?"

Nodding, Slade said with some admiration in his tone, "Well, you sure as hell got Thor's number."

Chuckling a little, Jordana leaned back in the chair and held his stare. "I believe I did, but that's for you to ultimately decide." Would Slade allow her to ride Thor? How badly she wanted to know his answer!

"He's never had another rider but me," Slade said, staring down at his nearly empty coffee mug. "I broke him gently and we grew up together. I know his every quirk and eccentricity. You didn't. And you handled him firmly but gently. Because of that, he responded to you."

"Well," Jordana insisted with a grin, "Thor responded when he *wanted* to, not when I wanted him to."

"Yes, I saw him fighting you from time to time, but that's his nature." He swallowed more of the coffee and set the mug aside. Giving her a look, Slade said in a low tone, "I believe that the more you ride him, the more he'll fall in line and respect you. Thor likes to get away with his antics, but you stopped him every time he tried one of them."

Nodding, Jordana wondered if Slade was going to let her ride Thor. "Every horse has quirks, Slade. We both know that."

"What I didn't know until I was over at your home was how extensive your riding credentials really were. You told me your mother had been a dressage rider but you said little about your own accomplishments. I was out in your living room one time and saw all the photos, the trophies and newspaper clippings you had hanging on your wall. You never let on that you've been riding since you were young, or that you were a pre-Olympic rider in dressage." He held her startled gaze. "I may be a Westerner and pooh-pooh English saddles in lieu of Western gear, but I do understand dressage. And when you were out there riding Thor, you were using your knowledge of dressage to haul him into line. And he responded."

"Dressage is a riding art form that *any* horse will respond to," Jordana told him in a serious voice. "Thor is an exceptionally intelligent horse, Slade, but I don't think I need to tell you that."

"He's smart and clever," Slade agreed. "But he isn't going to agree to work *with* you unless you're damn good at what you do. Mustangs originally came from Arabian stock. And Arabians are the most intelligent of all breeds. You can't bull them around, you can't beat it into them with a two-by-four. You have to know horse psychology and plenty of it for them to respond and want to work willingly with you."

"I'm in total agreement," Jordana said. Nervously, she gulped down the rest of her coffee. Slade seemed ready to give her his final decision. Never had Jordana wanted something more than this. Thor was an exceptional mustang in every way. She now understood why he was the top endurance breeding stallion in the country. Just having the privilege of riding him once was enough to make her appreciate Thor on so many more levels.

"If I let you ride him in the endurance contest, Jordana, you have to agree to take the prize money *if* you win it."

Stunned, she sat up and pushed her mug aside, holding his flat, stubborn gray stare. "No, that's not what we agreed to do. You *need* that prize money, Slade. I'll do my darnedest to win it for you, but I don't want it."

"You're not in good financial straits, either," he pointed out.

"That's true," Jordana murmured, "but I'm not as bad off as you are."

Slade winced over her words. Jordana was right. "Out

here in the West, a man's word is exactly that. If Thor wins, you win the money. That's it."

Frustrated, Jordana sat up, her eyes blazing. "No way, Slade! I love this ranch!" and she jammed her index finger down at the tile floor. "You're such a wonderful teacher and I've learned so much from you in such a little time. This ranch and you *deserve* to not only survive but thrive. I know I lack experience riding at this level, but I think you can see that I can handle Thor and he's responsive to me. That," she whispered rawly, "is what gives us a chance to win that money for you. You *must* see that!"

Slade sat back as Jordana's passionate argument struck him. Her cheeks were flushed red, her eyes blazed with righteousness, and, God help him, she was incredibly beautiful in that moment. Jordana lived in the world of her heart, he realized, unlike him who was locked up tighter than Fort Knox. That is what touched Slade: her unbridled passion for life, for living with her sense of morals and values. The competitiveness was in her eyes, and he liked what he saw. "I do see all of that," he countered. Opening his large, callused hands, he said, "But there's no way I'm taking free money from you."

"Then," Jordana exploded with frustration, "look at it this way. You're *paying* me to ride Thor! If I win that ten grand, it's yours. You can set out a training program for me here at the ranch so I can continue to learn from you, Slade. I don't care what money you assign to it, either. Don't you understand that I feel more than paid by getting to ride Thor in that competition? Some things," Jordana said, her voice dropping, "can't be bought with money. If you give me permission to ride Thor, that's all I want. This isn't a money issue for me. What endurance rider wouldn't give his or her right arm to ride your remarkable stallion?"

He sat back, digesting her emotionally fueled arguments. Staring at her, Slade smiled a little. "You're a regular bantam rooster when you get your feathers all riled up. You know that?"

Chuckling a little, the tension flowing out of her because she saw the warmth and care burning in Slade's eyes for the first time, Jordana said, "Funny that you said that. My mother raised banties and sold their eggs. My dad always called me 'Banty Rooster,' because I would fly into a tantrum when I didn't get my way as a four- and five-year-old."

Slade could see that. Her black hair was mussed. Without thinking, he reached over and pushed some of the errant strands away from her face. He saw her eyes grow large with shock over his gesture. Removing his hand, he saw her soft mouth part. Wanting to kiss her, but knowing it wasn't right under the circumstances, Slade muttered, "I can believe it."

"Will you let me ride Thor, Slade? And if I get lucky and win any of the prize money, it goes to you. And then you can arrange repayment in the form of riding lessons for me and Stormy once she gets well."

"That's fair," he nodded. "Only Stormy isn't going to be ready for a year."

"I realize that," Jordana said. "I know you have other endurance prospects in your training stable. Maybe you can let me ride one of them instead until Stormy is ready?" She understood the importance to Slade of being fair about this. Slade could have the money. She wanted the advance training only he could give her. That was worth everything to Jordana.

Mulling it over, Slade said, "Okay, you got a deal." He thrust out his hand toward her. "Out here, we live by our word and a handshake."

Giving a whoop of unfettered joy, Jordana stood up and gripped his hand. "You got a deal, Slade!" And then, she released his hand and followed her heart. Swiftly leaning over, Jordana pressed a chaste kiss to his cheek.

Startled by Jordana's unexpected enthusiasm, his flesh tingled wildly where her soft lips had grazed his cheek. Before he could react, Jordana had slid her arms around him, hugged him hard and immediately released him. Slade's mouth opened, but nothing would come out of it. Jordana stood there, her blue eyes glinting with joy, her hands clasped between her breasts.

"Slade," she promised breathlessly, "you won't regret this! I *promise* you!" Her heart pounded to underscore his decision. And she had kissed him. And hugged him! What was Slade drawing out of her?

Sitting back in the chair, Slade soaked in her happiness that trickled through him like hot lava awakening his heart and lower body. What was there not to like about this small, feisty woman? His cheek still tingled. Slade was in shock over her warmth and unexpected kiss. Was this Jordana, the doctor who hugged her sick patients? He thought so. She was just letting him see more of who she really was. Inwardly, Slade wished her kiss and hug had been more personal, more private… woman to his man. Harshly, he warned himself that was a crazy whim at best. No woman wanted a man with a ranch floundering on the edge of foreclosure. Further, Jordana was a physician. He was merely a horse wrangler and trainer. Their two worlds were so different, just like Isabel and himself had been. Isabel had been rich and well-off. She hadn't known what it took for Slade to keep his ranch above water and then had pouted when he didn't spend his time with her instead.

"I won't disappoint you, Slade," she went on quickly. "If you'll set out a training schedule, I'll work my other jobs around it. I really want to be ready for this ride. I know you can help me get there." Jordana wanted to hug him again but thought better of it. Oh, how she'd wanted to kiss that masculine, powerful mouth of his, but she didn't dare. And the shocking look in his gray eyes told her he hadn't expected her warmth and enthusiasm. But this was who she really was, and Jordana couldn't apologize for her childlike reaction to getting to ride Thor. Would Slade hold it against her? Jordana didn't know.

"Sit down," he ordered her.

Jordana sat, barely able to stop from squirming with joy. She tried to put on a serious expression to match Slade's somber look. Shocked by her own spontaneity, Jordana wondered if her two-year hiatus without a serious relationship had made her kiss and hug Slade. Unsure how he took her enthusiasm, Jordana knew she couldn't be the playful puppy that she really was. "What now?" she asked in a solemn tone. Slade *had* to know she was not only serious about this but equally responsible. Those qualities were important to him—and to her.

Running his fingers through his hair, he scowled and thought. "Thor's used to thirty-mile runs twice a week." He looked up and out the windows where he could see the beautiful, jagged Tetons in the distance. Turning, he held her gaze. "You've never ridden the fifty-mile contest here."

"No, I haven't."

"Then we need to get you on that trail so you memorize it in every way. There's places to run Thor, there's others where a fast trot will be all you can get because of the rockiness of the area. There's places where it's high meadow water and you can't plunge him through that muck and mud or you'll pull a tendon on him."

Nodding, Jordana hung on his every word. "Draw me a map?"

"I wish to hell I could ride it with you," Slade muttered, frowning. "Then I could show you the hazards and challenges, but I can't."

Jordana forced herself to remain quiet. "You draw me a map," she told him quietly. "And I'll do the fifty miles at half pace. I have a small camera I carry around my neck. I can take photos. I can memorize these situations, Slade."

"You only have a month," he said in a heavy tone. "Only a month. The people you're up against know this trail like the back of their hand. They know how to gauge their mount, themselves and throwing themselves against this harsh land. You don't. You're on a new horse and had never traversed this trail."

"Horses memorize," Jordana pointed out. "I'm *sure* Thor knows these places."

"He does, but you have to *trust* him if he slows down or speeds up. That's where you two are not in sync."

Nodding, Jordana said, "But if I can take the trail once a week as a tune up with Thor? Could we make up the difference, Slade?"

Hearing the low-key excitement in her husky voice, he said, "I don't know. That's the unknown." Sitting back, his brows slashed downward. "And then there's Curt Downing…"

"Oh," Jordana murmured, "I forgot about him."

"Yeah, he's going to be a real burr under your saddle. And once he finds out you're riding Thor, his gloves will come off. He'll do *everything* in his power to unseat you from Thor, Jordana. He's a son of a bitch with a crop. Thor hates crops, and if Downing gets near enough to use it on my stud, I don't know what he'll do in reaction to it." Slade shook his head. "Worse, I worry for you."

Reaching out, her fingers wrapping around his lower arm resting on the pine table, Jordana whispered, "Slade, don't worry about me. I'll have a helmet on and I'll be wearing a Kevlar vest. I know how to fall off a horse. I'll be all right, so don't worry about me. My focus is on Thor and keeping him sound and out of trouble. That's where my focus should be." Hesitantly, Jordana lifted her hand away. She saw a glint of hunger in Slade's expression as she'd spontaneously touched him once more. Her womanly core stirred hotly to life. She recognized that look: a man starving for his woman. He wanted to kiss her. Or? Make wildly passionate love to her? Here and now? Shocked by what she saw, Jordana avoided his fiery look. Her world rocked, suddenly unstable and dangerous. Slade wanted her. In *every* way.

Jordana tried to quell her need for him. Yes, Slade was ruggedly handsome. And he stirred the fires of her sensual womanhood, too. No question about it. Gulping, Jordana tried to push her own desires for Slade away. Now was not the time to get into a tangled relationship with him. She knew he was still hurting over what Isabel had done to him. And he had his problems with Griff, too. She couldn't see her way clear to embrace Slade on that level as badly as she wanted to. Yet, as Jordana lifted her eyes and met his stormy gray gaze, all the reasons melted hotly and disappeared. What was she going to do?

CHAPTER FIFTEEN

CURT DOWNING COULDN'T believe his ears. He was having hundred-pound gunnysacks of sweet feed carried out to his Chevy pickup when he overheard the two workers talking to each other. Standing on the wooden dock of the loading area, the truck parked up against it, Curt gestured to red-haired Sandy Jenkins, a twenty-year-old who worked at the store.

"Hey," he called, "what did you just say?"

Sandy threw the last gunnysack of feed into Downing's truck and straightened.

"I heard from my boss this morning that Dr. Jordana Lawton is riding Thor in the endurance race." He wiped his brow with the back of his sleeve.

Stunned, Curt growled, "That's crap, Sandy. No one rides Thor except McPherson."

Grinning, Sandy sauntered over, his body lean like a whippet. "Where have you been, Mr. Downing? Three days ago Slade got gored by his bull, Diablo. It knocked him out of the competition. My boss said he talked to Dr. Lawton about the rider change this morning."

"I've been out of town," Downing snarled. Mind spinning, he couldn't believe his good luck. "So, McPherson can't ride?"

"Yes, sir, that's what the doctor said. He tore a major artery in his thigh and had to have emergency surgery.

Dr. Lawton said he was grounded from riding for six to eight weeks."

A slow grin of delight crawled across Curt's face. "Well, now, isn't that too bad?"

Shrugging, Sandy said, "I thought you might like that news."

"And Dr. Lawton is going to ride Thor instead?" Curt demanded.

"Yes, sir," he murmured, running his sweaty hands down the sides of his Levis.

Snorting, Downing muttered, "She's *never* ridden in a level-one endurance ride. She'll finish dead last." And his mind churned around Slade losing his ranch to foreclosure. He was that much closer, then, to buying it from the bank.

"I dunno," Sandy said, watching as he leaped off the lip to the ground. "She's got pretty good endurance-riding credentials."

Laughing, Curt moved to the front of his truck and opened the door. "Thanks, Sandy. See you around." He slid into his truck and decided to go visit his good friend, Frank Halbert, the head of Wyoming Bank. Glee filled Curt as he drove slowly out of the feed-lot area. The sky was cloudy with a mix of white and gray clouds. It might rain, which was a good thing for this hot summer.

"I WANT YOU to put the screws to McPherson," Curt told Frank Halbert in a low tone. They sat in his large office on the third floor of the bank. During the recession, Wyoming Bank had been not only bailed out, but had received a flush of money from the government. Right now, Halbert, in his fifties, balding and wearing silver-rimmed bifocals, was richer than hell. And Curt knew the wheedling, manipulative bastard could sink McPherson once and for all.

"Well, Curt, he's up to date on his mortgage payments."

Downing gave the fat banker a cutting smile. He didn't like Halbert. The banker was easily led by his money. Curt had used him many times in the past. He was slowly buying up ranches going into foreclosure. He also had his eye on the Bar H south of town, as well. It, too, was in dire straits. He needed the hundred acres of the Bar H as a place to establish a larger breeding facility. By getting McPherson's fifty acres next to him, he was able to enlarge his training program. The fact that he bought half a million dollars into Halbert's bank meant if he wanted something done, the banker would do it, no questions asked. "So? Change the rate on him."

Studying the computer screen that had Slade McPherson's data on it, Frank murmured, "He does have a floating loan percentage."

"Then," Curt said, "make it go up."

Nodding, Frank said, "I can, but I have to justify it." He wiped his brow with his linen handkerchief.

Halbert reminded him of a pig. He had close-set brown eyes and a pug nose. His round face only emphasized his chubbiness in Curt's eyes. His patience thinned as Halbert kept clicking the keyboard looking at various elements of McPherson's long-term loan on the Tetons Ranch. Hands moving slowly into fists on the arms of the overstuffed brown leather wingback chair, Curt barely held his impatience in check.

"Well," Frank murmured, looking up from his computer, "it's done! I've raised it a quarter of a percent. We'll send out a letter today to him notifying him of his new mortgage payment."

Rising, Curt said, "Excellent. Thank you, Frank," and he turned on his heel and strode across the wooden floor to the door. A frisson of joy flowed through Curt as he walked to the elevator and pressed the down button. Mentally, he was rubbing his hands. If McPherson had the added pressure of a new, higher mortgage payment due October first, it would put him in a helluva bind. Unable to ride Thor and putting a greenhorn on the stud instead would be enough stress. The elevator door whooshed open and he stepped inside and pressed the button. The doors closed.

By the time he'd left the bank and headed for the parking lot behind the three-story building, Curt was walking on air. There were plenty of ranchers in the area who were hanging on by a thread because of the deep recession. Curt knew that McPherson was counting on winning that ten grand, but now, he wouldn't. There was no way Dr. Lawton could win on Thor. She simply didn't have the experience necessary.

Approaching his truck, he gave a short, sharp laugh. Curt now saw that not only was he going to win, he'd do it easily with McPherson removed from the competition. There was no one at the top of the endurance riders who could beat his Arabian stallion, Shah. Thor had been his only worry, and now, he could breathe and relax. Sliding into the truck, Curt pulled the door shut. He snickered to himself as he drove out of the parking lot. Raindrops began splattering across the windshield. The sky had turned dark above the cow town. He turned on the wipers. Right now, he'd give *anything* to see McPherson's face when he received that letter from the bank and the higher monthly mortgage bill.

"WHAT THE HELL," Slade muttered as he stared at the bank letter. He was sitting at the kitchen table. Shorty had just brought in the mail from the box sitting on a post near the highway.

Jordana was at the sink washing dishes. She had just come in from a thirty-mile ride on Thor. It was the second of the week. Slade's leg was still bothering him, and she knew he liked to keep a clean, neat house. Her hands in suds, she turned and saw the dark look on his face. "What is it?" she asked. Feeling energized and hopeful because of the second ride on the stallion, Jordana felt them beginning to get used to each other.

"My floating mortgage rate just went up a quarter of a point," he muttered unhappily.

"Does that mean you owe more monthly?"

"Exactly. Five hundred dollars more." Where was he going to get it? Slade charged a high price for each endurance student. They helped cover his mortgage. But now…

Jordana wiped her hands on a towel and walked over to the table. Little by little, Slade was letting her into his world. And it was a stress-filled one from what she could see. She saw his broad shoulders slump and defeat come to his face. "Five hundred a month is a lot," she murmured.

Griff came through the door into the kitchen. "Slade, we got that hay moved to the main barn," he said, walking to the coffeemaker and pouring himself a cup of coffee.

Irritated by his brother's lighthearted mood, Slade snarled, "Fine."

Turning, Griff frowned. He looked at Jordana silently, asking why his twin was in such a funk. She barely shook her head and moved her gaze toward the front door. Okay, he got the message. Nevermind that his hands had blisters on the palms even with the protective leather gloves. Or that they burned like fire. Griff had tried putting Band-Aids on them before the work started, but it did no good. Shorty had laughed when he'd bitched about his hands having blisters. The wrangler had no pity for him. Griff thought telling Slade what he'd accomplished might make him feel better. But Slade was obviously in no mood to hear it. Feeling proud of himself that he'd actually done some physical labor and done it well, Griff turned and left.

The door shut. Slade lifted his head and glared toward the foyer. "I wish to hell he'd leave," he told her.

Jordana saw and felt the tension in Slade's face. Every time Griff came in, she saw his armor come up and his face go expressionless. That didn't mean he wasn't feeling anything because by now, she knew he felt plenty. The twin was a burr under his saddle. Griff was not motivated like Slade. If Slade didn't kick his butt and give him orders to do something specific, Griff was on the computer looking for Wall Street jobs for hours on end. Griff was not earning his keep, and she knew Slade was in a constant angry stew over the situation.

Moving closer, she placed her hand on Slade's slumped shoulder. "If we win the ten thousand dollars, will that get you over that extra monthly hurdle?"

Slade sat back, relishing her soft touch. There was such calmness and clarity about Jordana. More and more, he found himself wanting her around. He counted the days until she'd be out for half a day at his ranch. They were his only time-outs from the present financial situation threatening to overwhelm him and his ranch. "Yes, it would give me the breathing room I need." He felt like crying. His whole world was crumbling before him. Slade knew in his heart that Jordana would never win the race. He was going to lose the ranch. *Oh, God...*

"Slade," she whispered, coming around and sitting down at his elbow, "don't give up!" Jordana gripped his hand that was curled into a fist. "Listen to me, will you? I *know* I can win this for you!" She clung to his dark, hopeless gaze. His mouth was thinned, the corners drawn in because he was in pain. Fingers tightening on his fist, she said urgently, "Slade? You have to have faith."

He cut a glance toward Jordana. Her hand soothed some of his pain, but not all of it. She was the pinnacle of faith and hope. "Listen, I've been in such bad straits with this ranch for so many years that this feels like the last bombshell that is going to destroy it." There, he'd said it. Slade didn't ever confide his real fears to anyone, but Jordana's hand on his triggered his admittance.

"No, it won't destroy it, Slade," she said solemnly, holding his dark gaze. He looked as if he were going to cry. Slade swallowed several times as if choking back the tears. Her heart burst open with such pain for him. "You've done everything right," Jordana whispered. "And I can't believe the cosmos is going to take this ranch away from you."

Slade didn't have the heart to tell her she didn't stand

a chance of winning. Hell, she'd be lucky to finish the race at all because it was such a wicked and challenging one. Instead, he rasped, "I can."

Shaking her head, Jordana said, "I wish I had the money, Slade. I'd give it to you. This ranch is beautiful and you've worked hard to keep it in good condition." She couldn't imagine what he would do if he lost it. Yet, it looked as if he would. Her heart tore more for him. Slade was suffering so much, struggling to keep how he really felt away from her.

"You're as poor as I am," he reminded her. Slade knew she was living from paycheck to paycheck. Yes, he'd lowered her training rate to one thousand dollars a month, but that put him into an even worse financial hole.

"I can loan you that extra thousand dollars a month," she told him, a fierceness in her husky tone. She gripped his hand hard. "Slade, for once, take some gifts from someone else. You're not alone in this fight!"

He grunted and pulled his hand away from hers. Because if he didn't, he was going to kiss her until she melted into him. It was driving him hard, and Slade was too anxious about the loss of his ranch staring him in the face to divide his energies right now. "I've been alone since my parents died in that damned car accident, Jordana. Every day is a fight. You're around here enough to see that." His nostrils flared as the shock of losing his ranch was imminent. Nothing had hurt so bad as this. He wadded up the bill in his right hand and threw it on the pine table.

"Oh, Slade," Jordana whispered, "this isn't over! I can loan you the money. I have a thousand dollars a month. I won't charge you interest—"

"Dammit, Jordana, I can't do that!" he exploded. Slade shoved the chair away and stood, fighting back a real need to sob. He swallowed hard, the lump in his throat being pushed down once again.

Standing, Jordana heard the cry of anguish in his growling tone. No longer was she afraid of his irritable and snarling disposition. She'd come to realize that when Slade was under pressure, he was that way. But she'd seen him when he wasn't, and he was a man that any woman would desire. Without thinking, she threw her arms around his shoulders and pressed herself to him. The startled look in his eyes told her he wasn't expecting this. Well, that was fine because she was being driven to pull him out of the throes of his anguish.

Leaning up, Jordana pressed her lips against the hard, flat line of his mouth. Instantly, Slade groaned, and he rocked her hard against him; his arms moving like steel bands around her slender torso. The breath was crushed out of her. Jordana kept her eyes closed, her arms tight around Slade, and rocked his lips open. There was a tremble that rolled through him as her soft mouth pleaded with his to open and allow her entrance. Something primal and raw pushed Jordana. Her world melted into a fiery heat as his mouth turned mobile and hungry, and he took her with savage intensity.

An explosion of incredible heat tunneled through Slade. Kissing Jordana was the last thing on his mind in his crumbling world. Yet, the soft insistence of her mouth, the movement of her full lips gliding teasingly against his dragged a volcanic and animal response from him. It had been years since he'd kissed a woman. Her breath was moist and caressed his cheek. He'd shaved this morning, but already his beard was growing back.

Her face was like velvet, and he was starved for her touch. Slade's mind melted, and all he focused on was her breasts pressed against his massive chest, her mouth wet and hungry against his, her breath moist and the scent of pine in her silky hair.

Moaning, Jordana surrendered fully to Slade as a man. His arms were powerful, his mouth ravenous against hers. The texture of his beard against her cheek was proof of his masculinity. He swept his hand down her back, his fingers memorizing the curve of her spine. Sliding his hand over her hip, Slade pressed her insistently against him. Jordana became aware of just how much he wanted her. She relished the incredible virility of him. Slade's mouth was hungry, and so was hers. She couldn't get enough of him, enough of his mouth ravishing hers with an animal-like need. Wasn't she needy? Oh, yes, it had been too long without a man who stirred her heart and her body. Slade did both. As his hand ranged up her spine, Jordana trembled inwardly. He was strong, and yet he didn't hurt her. He was monitoring the strength of his touch. When his hand moved across her back to graze the curve of her breast, she moaned. The sound echoed between them.

What was happening? Slade felt drugged, his mind turning into useless mush, his body throbbing with white-hot need of Jordana in every way. He wanted to lock himself into her willing body, feel every curve and valley, drawn in by the throbbing heat as he plunged into her welcoming depths. If he didn't stop, he'd haul her into his arms and carry her off to his bedroom. And he'd love her until she moaned with utter pleasure. As Slade tore his mouth from hers, he opened his eyes to mere slits. His breathing was harsh and ragged, but so was hers.

Jordana moaned as the kiss abruptly ended. Lips throbbing from the power of his searching kiss, she wanted more. No...she wanted Slade...all of him. Her mind whirled, and she felt as if she were floating in a way she never had with a man. Slade was incredibly masculine in a way she'd never experienced. And the boiling tension in her lower body ached to pull him deeply into her and consummate something Jordana felt was inevitable. As she forced her lids open, she burned beneath Slade's predatory look. Here was a man who was as raw and untamed as the wilderness he lived within. She felt his hands roaming across her back and hips, as if remembering her and burning every curve of hers into his mind.

Slade pulled away. He didn't want to, but he had to. Jordana was too willing, too beautiful and he was in such a hell of a mess with his ranch and life right now that he couldn't take this on, too. His mouth tasted of hers. She liked to chew peppermint gum when riding, and he could taste it now. "We can't do this," he growled unsteadily. "Not now, Jordana." *Not ever.* All Slade saw was another Isabel Stephens debacle. "There's too much at stake," he managed in a raw whisper. "I don't want to lose my ranch. I have to focus on that...not...us."

Hurting for Slade and knowing her spontaneous kiss was healing to him on one level, Jordana understood. She touched the strands of hair against her cheek and pulled them aside. "Sure, Slade. I understand."

The quaver in her husky voice tore at him as nothing else ever had. He saw disappointment and hurt in her large blue eyes. She was guileless, Slade realized as he stood before her, tense and unmoving. His heart told him Jordana was not another Isabel Stephens. His mind shouted at him that she was. Every woman was a temptation because he'd gone so long without real nurturing from one. Raking his fingers through his hair, he said, "I appreciate your care, but right now, I need to focus on a way to keep my ranch."

Her whole body was burning and throbbing like a flame flickering in the wind. How badly Jordana wanted to consummate their relationship. She saw the raw need and anguish in Slade's narrowed gaze that never left hers. "It's tough to balance off financial stuff against a new relationship," she acknowledged in a hoarse tone. "I do understand, Slade." Jordana lifted her chin and held his stare. "But I'm not sorry I kissed you."

She had such guts, Slade decided in that moment. Jordana was a fierce warrior, afraid of nothing. "I'm not, either," he confided more gently. Opening his hand, he offered, "But right now, I can't, Jordana. I'm sorry." And he was. God, how sorry he was. How could he explain that he distrusted her because of Isabel? That he saw all women as waiting to steal his family ranch from under him? Yet, Jordana had offered him a thousand dollars a month to make up that difference. Pride wouldn't let Slade accept that offer.

CHAPTER SIXTEEN

"ARE YOU READY?"

Jordana nodded. She was holding the reins on Thor tightly because he was pawing and ready to get on with the fifty-mile run. Slade stood next to her. They were at the beginning of the actual endurance starting line. His hand was on the slope of the stallion's shoulder. It was barely dawn; and she could just see the trail ahead. "I am."

Worried, Slade knew his stallion was more than ready to do a test run across the entire course. This was the first time Jordana would take the route. "You got your iPhone with the maps?" They had worked a week to input the information into her Apple iPhone so that it would be on her, and she could use it during the ride.

Patting the iPhone strung around her neck and hidden beneath her sweater and Kevlar vest, she said, "Got it."

"Okay, take it easy. Don't let him run full-out. I'll time you, but don't try and push him."

"Right," Jordana said, excitement thrumming through her. She smiled down at Slade. Since the unexpected kiss, they'd danced around each other, never really mentioning it. The past two weeks, she'd ridden three times a week on the thirty-mile circuit on the Elkhorn ranch, fine-tuning Thor's endurance and preparing him for the race. How badly she wanted to speak to Slade about their

kiss, but he'd withdrawn since then. Jordana tried not to
be hurt by it. After all, neither had expected it.

Patting Thor's taut, arched neck, Slade murmured,
"Okay. We'll be in constant contact by radio," and he
pointed to the one hooked on his belt. "At every five
miles when you hit a point, you call. If you don't call,
I'll know you're in trouble."

Nodding, Jordana knew he was nervous for her and
his horse. "I'll do it, Slade. And I'll be okay." She wanted
to reach out as she had done before the kiss, but after
it, he'd really retreated, and Jordana had forced herself
to stop touching him from time to time. The race and
learning the trail and handling Thor was paramount right
now. Jordana wanted to win that money for Slade. And
nothing else mattered at this point. They could talk about
their kiss after the race.

"Okay," he said, holding up the stop watch, "take
off…"

Thor heard his master's voice and reared, fighting
the bit.

Jordana laughed and eased the reins. Instantly, the
stallion dug in with his hind legs, dirt and rock flying as he hurtled down the path strewn with rocks and
grass. The wind sailed past her as she settled into a fast
trot with Thor. Very quickly, they were swallowed up
by the thick stands of evergreens across the slope of
the mountain. The trail started at six thousand feet and
quickly climbed to ten thousand. Thor snorted violently,
continuing to fight the reins, but Jordana held him at a
ground-eating trot.

Slade watched as the pair disappeared up the winding, twisting trail. The last two weeks had been hell on
him in so many ways. As he walked back to his truck at

the trailhead, he was glad to be rid of the damned cane. Climbing in, he felt his leg that was still tender and sore. He'd never realized that a puncture wound of this size could cause so much havoc. Cursing Diablo under his breath, Slade started his truck. He would drive to the first checkpoint twenty miles into the ride. It was a high meadow at nine thousand feet and was accessible by vehicle. It would be there that the first vet station check would occur for all riders.

Even though he wasn't a vet, Slade knew what to look for. Thor would come into the station, and Jordana would dismount. The vet and assistant would check Thor's pulse, his blood pressure and look over each leg very carefully for any signs of injury or swelling. Shorty would walk Thor for twenty minutes, cooling him down. Thor would then be checked again by the vet team. He would be given water to drink. If Thor's pulse and blood pressure had settled to a normal rate and his legs passed inspection, Jordana would be given permission to continue on for the next twenty-mile leg. This time, Slade would be doing the checking.

As Slade drove slowly out of the huge, oval gravel parking lot, he knew he had to have Jordana run the fifty miles at least three times before the actual race. There were plenty of other horse trailers and pickup trucks around, signs that other endurance riders were familiarizing themselves with the challenging trail. What he didn't like was seeing the bright red trailer owned by Curt Downing. He was already on the trail ahead of Jordana, but Slade didn't know how far ahead. Worried, he hoped they wouldn't meet. And Slade knew that every one of these riders would have assistants waiting at the first checkpoint.

As he drove down the long, flat graveled road within the Tetons National Park, Slade's mind and, if he were honest, his heart, centered on Jordana. He'd dreamt every night about that unexpected kiss that had exploded between them. And then, his torrid dream would melt into the nightmare of his past with Isabel. The last year of their marriage had been a daily donnybrook. She would scream, curse him and call him a loser. Slade had taken it all, and he'd felt relief when Isabel had finally had enough, packed her bags and flown back to her rich parents' penthouse. He'd felt even more relief when the divorce papers had been served on him. Cutting Isabel out of his life had been like getting out of prison to Slade. Rubbing his unshaven chin, Slade braked at the stop sign. At 5:00 a.m. on this August summer morning, few tourist cars were on the highway. Turning left, he kept the truck at the twenty-five mile an hour limit. It would be no time before he was at the vet-check meadow.

The sky was turning pink as the sun rose in the east. Herds of elk were here and there near the highway. One thing about the Tetons, the wildlife was not afraid of park visitors. And one had to be careful about driving this time of morning because all the deer, elk and moose were grabbing their last grass meal before settling down to sleep during the daylight hours. Often, they were near the road. Too many crashes at dawn had occurred because of this situation.

What was he going to do about Jordana? Clearly, she liked him. Hell, he liked her. Slade knew he was in no position to start a relationship as bad as his body and heart keened for it. Isabel had just done too much damage to him. His brows fell. Finally, Slade admitted he was afraid. Afraid of another failure. Oh, no question there was a chasm of difference between Isabel and Jordana, but his mind balked anyway.

Soon enough, the exit came up for the twenty-mile stop. Slade turned and drove slowly down the six-mile gravel road that would end at the trailhead parking area. When he arrived, he saw about fifteen teams waiting for their riders to come in. Parking, Slade knew every one of them. Some waved to him. He waved back. His gaze moved across the large, oval meadow. It had been mowed, so it was easy to work with incoming endurance riders and their sweaty mounts. Wearing a red T-shirt, Chuck Merced, Curt Downing's assistant, stood away from the other endurance crews, his wrist held up as he looked at his stopwatch.

Climbing out of the truck, Slade knew that twenty miles at a trot would bring Jordana and Thor in at a certain time. He was content to lean against the front of his truck and watch because she'd been the last of all these riders to start the trail. When had Curt Downing started? That worried him to no end. What if Jordana came upon him and that black Arabian stud of his? Stallions, when together, automatically wanted to fight one another. He'd repeatedly warned Jordana about this. She'd never seen two studs go at it, but he had. It was visceral, primal and brutal. Stallions fought to win, and their intent was to inflict as much damage upon their competitor as they could.

"Hey," a male voice called, "Slade! How are you?"

Turning to his right, Slade recognized red-haired Bart Peters. He was the husband of Bernadette, a champion endurance rider.

"Hey, Bart," he said, greeting the forty-year-old man

with thick glasses with a smile. "What time did Bernadette start the course?"

Walking over and smiling, Bart looked at his stopwatch. "She started off at the trailhead thirty minutes ago."

Nodding, Slade said, "And how's her mount?" He knew her Arabian gelding, Smithy, had been retired last year. They had bought one of Thor's offspring from him, a part mustang and part Arabian gelding called Checkers.

Leaning against the truck front with Slade, Bart said, "Checkers is doing great. You know he placed fifth in the Tevis Cup?"

"Yes, I heard. That's damn good for a first timer." And it was. Thor's stamina and endurance being passed on to his offspring was well known. People brought their Arabian mares to be bred to him. The resulting offspring had shown consistently in the past ten years that Thor's genes were winners.

Bart grinned. "It sure was. Bernadette was surprised. So was I." His green eyes danced as he held Slade's gaze. "Your stud is remarkable. We'd always heard how good he was, but Checkers is just blowing us away. He's six years old and just starting his career. It's hard to believe he took fifth place in the Tevis."

"That was a combination of Bernadette's riding skills and her horse," Slade murmured. One could have a great horse, but if the rider wasn't up to snuff, there would be no winning anything.

Smiling fully, Bart agreed. "Hey, we were really sorry to hear you aren't competing this year. We heard on the circuit one of your students, a woman, is riding Thor instead? We never thought you'd let anyone ride that stud of yours. What changed your mind?"

"Dr. Jordana Lawton is riding him," Slade said. He didn't want to tell anyone.

"This is the first female student you've had, isn't it?"

Uncomfortable with the fact that his business as a teacher and competitor was public knowledge, Slade frowned. "Yes, it is."

"She must be exceptional," Bart said, watching the other teams going out to the meadow with buckets, brushes, stethoscopes and towels in hand.

"She is," Slade agreed.

"Is she new? Bernadette and I haven't heard of her being on the circuit before."

"She's competed at the lower levels for many years and is moving up."

Red brows raising on his long, narrow face, Bart murmured, "Wow, she must be a heck of a rider, then. We know how much of a handful Thor is." And he laughed.

Grinning, Slade said, "Dr. Lawton has a strong dressage background coupled with two years of endurance riding under her belt."

"Ah," Bart said, nodding his head. "Dressage. Well, we all know a good dressage rider is pretty capable. How's Thor getting along with her?"

"Actually, very good," Slade told him. He enjoyed Bart's company. There were many times that Bernadette would be in the first ten riders on this particular endurance ride. They were a husband and wife team, and it was their love of the sport that kept them trailering around the United States on the national-circuit rides.

"Amazing. We all thought that feisty stud of yours was a one-man horse only."

"Well," Slade said with a smile, "he's got more facets to him than I thought. I didn't think Dr. Lawton could handle him, either, but he's completely surrendered over to her." And then Slade wanted to add, *just like I have.* Thinking better of it, he remained silent.

"Wise horse," Bart laughed.

"Hey, did you see when Downing left the trailhead?" Slade kept his voice nonchalant and the worry out of it.

"Yeah, he was driving in his trailer just as I was leaving. Bernadette started the trail at 4:30 a.m."

"I see," Slade murmured. In his head he was calculating the difference. "He probably took off at 4:45 a.m., then." The horse had to be saddled and bridled, and that took a few minutes.

"Yeah, I'd guess about there. I'm worried he and that black devil of his are going to catch up to Bernadette." Shaking his head, Bart lowered his voice and muttered, "I always worry about her when Downing is around. He's known for his tricks."

"I know," Slade said in a low tone. Everyone on the circuit knew Downing's maneuvers could harm other horses and riders.

Looking at his stopwatch, Bart said, "I'd better get out there. Bernadette should be coming in any minute. I'll look forward to seeing Dr. Lawton on Thor. That has to be a sight to behold." He eased away from the truck.

"Later," Slade murmured, watching his friend carry the water bucket and sponges toward the meadow. Every team had to do a lot of things when a rider and horse came into a vet-check station. Bart had several white towels draped over his left shoulder. In another bucket he had liniment, dressings, bandages and medications. There was a long garden hose strung from the parking

lot out to the check area where teams could fill and re-
fill their buckets with water for the horses. After twenty
miles, every horse was thirsty. The animals would gulp
down one to three buckets at one stop.

If Downing was fifteen minutes ahead of Jordana,
Slade mentally calculated that they would not meet. But
if Jordana wasn't pacing Thor correctly, letting him run
when he should be trotting, it was possible the two might
encounter each other. He hoped to hell they didn't. Jordana had no way to counter Downing's deceit out there
away from prying eyes. Did Downing know that she
was riding Thor? Most likely—because it was common
knowledge between the top endurance riders. It wasn't a
secret. Worry ate at Slade. He rubbed his jaw. The sun
was just starting to peek over the mountains in the east.
The sky was a light blue and cloudless. It was a perfect
day for a test run on the course.

THOR WAS GALLOPING along on the part of the trail where
Slade had wanted him to trot. Jordana's hands and arms
ached from holding in the athletic stallion. She reasoned
on this trial run, on one of the few flat areas that was a
mile long, it was all right to open him up a little. Thor
was bursting with such robust energy that it shocked her.
It seemed that every upward, winding mile along the dirt
and rock trail within the tree line made him stronger, not
weaker. His coat was gleaming with sweat, foam around
his mouth from chomping constantly on the bit because
he wanted to be let go to gallop at full speed.

She saw no other riders ahead of her, although they
had passed three already. What harm was there in letting
him run a little? Jordana knew on this section that Slade
had wanted him at a trot. But Thor was so full of himself

and she'd been fighting him so hard, she needed the rest. Leaning forward, she knew her weight would signal to the stallion that he could run. She loosened the reins just a little. Instantly, Thor surged out of the trot and into a ground-eating gallop. This one-mile run was across a high altitude meadow filled with dried yellowed grass.

The wind whistled past her. Jordana wore the helmet and Kevlar vest. Her thin leather gloves were soaked with sweat. Thor thundered down across the meadow with such fierce strides it took her breath away. Jordana knew from the map on her iPhone, that the trail suddenly turned wicked at the other end as it disappeared once more into the evergreens. Checking Thor at a half mile, she fought him back down to a trot by the time they hit that twisting, winding trail upward.

Shaking his head, angry, Thor fought her as he easily climbed up the switchbacks. They were at nine thousand feet. In no time, they broke out of the evergreens that stopped at the ten-thousand-foot level. Jordana saw the radiant slats of sun just cresting the eastern horizon. She didn't have time to enjoy the beauty of it. The trail turned very narrow, and they climbed more. Thor was breathing evenly, snorting and still wanting to run.

As they crested the last switchback to the trail that now lay between millions of boulders and loose rock at ten thousand five hundred feet, Jordana saw another rider just ahead of them. It was Curt Downing and his black Arabian stallion! Surprised, Jordana automatically felt her gut clench. Slade had warned her so many times about this rider. What should she do? Pull Thor up and bring down his stride to not meet up with them? Her mind ranged over the options. This trail went on for five miles and then curved down through the forest to nine thousand feet where it emptied out on the vet-check meadow.

Gripping the reins hard, Jordana watched the pair flying across the rocky expanse. There was no question the black stallion was powerful and fast. But Thor was equally swift. She also knew that there was no possibility of passing on this narrow trail. There was no way for another rider to move over so she could pass. If anyone got off this trail, it would be disaster. This trail had been carved out of the scree that lay on the slope of the mountain. To get off would be to invite injury of both horse and rider.

Her intuition told her to rein Thor in. She couldn't expose him to possible injury. This was just a test run, not the actual race. And once they got off this high altitude trail, she didn't know if the thousand-foot drop provided a place wide enough to pass, either. This was why she was riding; to understand the lay of the land and where she could and could not safely pass another rider.

She saw Downing look back. She was close enough to see his surprise and then rage cross his face. He knew Thor when he saw him. Continuing to rate Thor's pace and slow him down so that he didn't run up on the other stallion, Jordana focused on keeping the distance between them. *Damn. Of all things.* She had passed three other riders, and they had easily moved aside to allow her transit. Slade had warned her that Curt wouldn't move. More than one rider had been forced to stay behind because he bent and broke the rules where judges couldn't see him do it.

"Easy," she whispered to Thor, "just take it easy, big boy," and she watched his ears flick back and forth over her crooning voice. With her arms, legs and hands, she slowed the mustang even more. Slade wouldn't be happy to see them arriving in the meadow one after another, Jordana thought.

SLADE'S EYES WIDENED as he stood out in the meadow. He saw Downing burst out of the tree line, his black Arab stallion surging at a wild gallop toward the center of the meadow. It was a mile-long run. And right behind him came Thor and Jordana. The mustang wanted to run, he saw, but Jordana was fighting to keep him at a floating trot instead. Realizing what was going on, he waited for Jordana to pull up the horse.

"Whoa," Jordana told the stud. Thor came to a halt, shaking his head. She saw Slade's frowning face as he walked up to her and took the reins.

Dismounting, Jordana took the reins back.

"What the hell happened?" Slade demanded. He put the stethoscope to Thor's sweaty chest and listened. Once he got the information, he went and took the horse's pulse. Writing down all the statistics, he timed the horse's breaths for fifteen seconds and then multiplied it by four.

Jordana waited until he'd finished writing down the information. "I came up to the rocky trail at ten-five and saw Downing ahead of me."

Scowling, Slade gestured for her to take Thor over to the waiting pail of water. "You must have been pushing faster than you should have. Downing left the trailhead at 4:45 a.m. You left fifteen minutes later."

Grimacing, Jordana heard the anger in Slade's growling tone. "I was fighting him so much, Slade, that I let him move out faster." She held up her leather-gloved hand. "My fingers, wrist and arms ache from holding him in." She slipped the halter around the stud's neck and removed the bridle. Bringing the blue nylon halter over his head, she led him to the water.

"Doesn't matter. You *have* to rate him properly or he won't have any gas left for that five-mile run at the last." Slade took the bridle from her and hung it on the saddle horn. As the horse drank in great, gulping drafts, he unsaddled the stallion. For the next ten to fifteen minutes, Thor would be walked around. When his resting heartbeat was reached, the vet would give the signal for the rider to resaddle the horse and take off.

Chastened, Jordana brought over a second pail of water to the thirsty stud. "I never expected him to fight me like that." She was amazed that anyone could force Thor to keep up a steady, ground-eating pace. Slade had. Her respect for him rose even more than before.

"He's a competitor," Slade warned. He looked ahead to where Downing and his crew were. Anger stirred in him. He returned his gaze to Jordana. She was flushed, her eyes bright and filled with joy, despite the rugged ride on Thor. And God help him, he longed to be in her company. Gaze automatically moving to her mouth, Slade swore he could taste Jordana on his lips once more. His lower body throbbed to life, much to his chagrin.

"What do you want me to do tactically now that Downing is here with us?" she asked. Lifting a third pail to Thor's water-dripping nose, she watched him thrust his muzzle into it.

Slade moved to her, his voice low. "Let's see whose horse leaves first. Knowing Downing, because this isn't an official vet check, my experience tells me he isn't going to wait for his stud to get to his resting heart rate.

He'll take off a lot sooner because he knows Thor is here."

Eyes widening, Jordana said, "But that hurts his horse if he does that."

Shrugging, Slade said, "Downing doesn't care. He thinks that stud of his can make up the difference. He won't want you moving out ahead of him."

Sure enough, as Jordana continued to walk Thor in a large circle to cool down, she saw Downing resaddling his stud five minutes later. Shaking her head, she saw Slade watching the pair. Who would harm their horse like that? Endurance riders prided themselves on horses first, contest second. She lifted her hand and patted Thor's neck. The horse was a lot less feisty right now. He was more tractable. Twenty miles was a lot for any horse. And she hoped that when she resaddled him and took off for the next twenty, that he would be less of a handful.

The meadow was filled with horses and riders coming and going. It was always exciting for Jordana. Slade's leg had healed up enough so that he could walk on the other side of his horse with her. She walked ahead of Thor and said, "How are *you* doing?"

Heat surged through Slade. Jordana's care extended to him even during the competition. Maybe it was the E.R. doctor in her. He didn't know. "I'm fine," he groused. Watching Downing galloping out of the meadow, he felt some relief. "My leg is fine, if that's what you're asking."

Nodding, she smiled a little. Slade had on what she termed the "bad cowboy look" of the perpetual scowl. He hadn't shaved this morning, and the beard made him look primal. It appealed to her as a woman. Did he know how handsome he really was? She didn't think so. "That's good," Jordana said. "Let's go over things I need to remember on this next twenty-mile stint." Because if she didn't, Jordana knew she'd start thinking of that hot, ravishing kiss all over again. Oh, for sure, she wasn't going to confide in Slade her nightly amorous dreams in which they made wild love with each other. Jordana blushed just thinking about it. Still, he made her feel good. She was always happy when she was around Slade. What kind of relationship was maturing between them? Where would it lead?

CHAPTER SEVENTEEN

IT WAS LATE afternoon when they arrived back at Slade's ranch. Shorty had unloaded Thor and was taking him to the bathing facility. Jordana was helping by unloading the saddle, bridle and other items to be placed in the tack room. As Slade entered the ranch house, the phone rang.

"Slade here," he answered. His leg was aching. Grabbing a chair in the foyer, he sat down.

"Slade, this is Charley."

Brows raising, Slade's heart made a little skip. "Hey Charley, do you have good news for me?" Two weeks ago he'd put in a bid with the U.S. Forest Service at the Tetons Headquarters to supply them several packhorses. It was an open bid system and Slade had always gotten these contracts from Charley, who was the head ranger of the Tetons district. He hoped he had, because every source of money was vital to keeping the ranch above financial disaster. This particular bid was for ten horses, and that wasn't a small amount of money. It could mean close to eight thousand dollars for him. Unconsciously, he held his breath. Whoever the winner of the bid was, they received a phone call from Charley to seal the deal.

"I'm afraid not, Slade. Listen, your brother Griff was over here yesterday."

Scowling, Slade muttered, "My brother? What the hell was he doing over there?" His mind whirled. Slade

recalled filling out the contract bid one morning when
Griff was sitting and having his breakfast with him.
Slade had explained the system and how important it was
to put in the lowest bid so that that individual would be
chosen and, therefore, hired or paid for their services.

"Yes," Charley said gruffly. "I'm hard-pressed not to
report this, Slade."

"What are you talking about?"

"You didn't send him over here to talk with me?"

Frustration came out in his tone. "Charley, I don't
have a *clue* as to what you're referring to. I never told
Griff to go over to your office."

"Griff came over, out of the blue, and demanded an
appointment to see me. Lucky or unlucky, I happened
to be here and told him to come on in."

Slade heard the tense tone in Charley's voice. He'd
been supervisor of the Tetons for five years. "What did
he come to see you about?"

"Your bid," Charley warned heavily.

"*My* bid?" Slade sat up, his brows moving upward in
complete surprise. "How can that be? I didn't send him
over to talk to you."

"Well, he alluded that you did, Slade, and that's why
I'm calling you direct. Your brother sat here and told me
that if I would choose your bid over all the others, that
you would throw in another horse for free."

Rage exploded through Slade. Instantly, he was on
his feet. Pain shot through his injured thigh as he did so.
"What?" He nearly shouted the word. His hand tightened around the phone, his other hand curled into a fist.
Slade knew that no one could do something like this. His
heart sank. His brother had just scuttled his chances of
getting that badly needed contract!

"It was a bribe, Slade. Your brother seemed to think that by throwing in an extra packhorse for free that it was obvious that I should choose your bid over the others."

"I *never* sent him to do that, Charley." Breathing hard, rage filling him, Slade tried to fight down his anger enough to think clearly. His entire connection with Charley and the U.S. Forest Service was now in jeopardy. Griff had stupidly blundered in, and now Slade knew that Charley could report him. And then, because this was clearly a violation, Charley could bar him from ever bidding again on a U.S. Forest Service contract. *Son of a bitch!*

"That's why I'm calling you, Slade. We've worked together for five years, and you've never tried to influence a bid before."

"I'm sorry, Charley. My brother is from New York City and a Wall Street type. He's stupid for trying to do this behind my back. He's got the morals and values of a sidewinder. That stuff might sell in the East, but it don't out here."

"That's what I thought. Your brother appeared to be completely clueless about the bid system. I had a good talk with him, and it became clear he was ignorant."

Closing his eyes, Slade felt sweat pop out on his brow. "What are you going to do about it?" he asked in a rasping tone. Slade knew he could be turned in and blacklisted from future bids—forever. The Tetons put out three to four bids a year, and Slade would lose a valuable source of income. Money was hard to come by in ranching, and Slade counted heavily on winning at least one or two bid contracts a year from Charley.

"I could turn Griff in for bribery."

"Yes," he said tightly, "you could."

"But if I did that, the only person it would hurt would be you, Slade. I know from experience that you are trying to keep your ranch out of foreclosure. You've never attempted to influence a bid with me—ever."

Rolling his eyes, Slade knew that if Charley turned in Griff, there would be an arrest and charges against him. His stupid brother didn't realize the damage he'd just done. "No, I would *never* do that, Charley."

"Right," he said. "I know that from dealing with you for five years now, you're a man of your word."

"What is going to happen? Are you calling the sheriff to pick Griff up and charge him with bribery?"

"No, I don't want to do that, Slade. I think if you talk to him and make him understand what he did, that will be sufficient." Charley hesitated, his voice lowering, "But I can't allow your bid to be chosen, Slade. You had won the bid, and I was getting ready to call you. Your brother screwed you royal. Now, I have to pick the next lowest bidder, and he will be awarded the money instead. I can't, in all good conscience, let your bid win. Griff came in here and destroyed that chance. I'm sorry. I know you were counting on this money."

Hanging his head, gripping the receiver, Slade rasped, "I understand, Charley. Thank you for being fair-minded about this."

"I wish I could overlook Griff's bribe, but I can't."

"No, you shouldn't." Slade smarted because it was his good name that was being dragged through the mud. Sucking in a breath of air, Slade finally asked, "Are you barring me from further bid lists, Charley?"

"No, I'm not. And I'm basing that on your good name,

Slade. But don't *ever* let that brother of yours come in here again and try to bribe me. Okay?"

"Thanks, Charley. I'll take care of him when he gets home."

"Good. Again, I'm sorry I can't award you this bid, Slade. You were the lowest."

Mouth tightening, he rasped, "It's just deserts under the circumstances, Charley. Thanks for not tarring and feathering me with the same brush as my younger brother."

Jordana walked into the ranch house as Slade hung up the phone. He felt a wall of rage boiling inside of him. As he turned to look at her, she looked tired from the grueling fifty-mile test run on Thor. Choking it all down, he said, "Everything taken care of?"

For a moment, Jordana hesitated. Slade's eyes were black with rage. Who had been on the phone with him? "Yes, I just brushed Thor down and he's in his paddock rolling." Tilting her head, she reached out and said, "Slade? What's wrong? You look really upset."

The touch of her cool fingers on his lower arm nearly unleashed his rage. Shaking his head, Slade pulled his arm away from her. "It's nothing. Why don't you get going? It's been a long day for you."

Just then, Griff entered the ranch home.

"Hey, you're back," he hailed, taking off his tan Stetson and hanging it on a wooden wall hook near the door.

Jordana felt rage explode around Slade as he snapped his head up and glared at Griff. She stood between them, feeling the blast of anger leaping from Slade toward his twin brother. *What* was going on?

"You," Slade ground out, and he took three steps around Jordana, grabbed Griff by the collar of his shirt

and shoved him hard against the wall. "Son of a bitch, you just cost me a bid!" he snarled into Griff's shocked features.

Automatically, Griff threw up his arms and broke Slade's hold on him. "What the hell has gotten into you?" he yelled, backing toward the door.

Jordana opened her mouth and then shut it. Slade looked like a volcano ready to spew out lava as he strode toward Griff. She felt as if she were in a corral with Diablo. But Slade was the enraged bull this time.

Griff dodged Slade's outstretched hand and moved into the living room. He hunched over, waiting for another attack. "What the hell is the matter with you?" he shouted. Why was his brother looking as if he was going to kill him? Griff simply didn't understand his sour brother at all. What had he done?

Moving swiftly to the living room, Slade roared, "You stupid bastard! You just cost me an eight-thousand-dollar bid contract with the U.S. Forest Service. *That* is what you've done!" He punched his index finger into Griff's chest.

Peddling backward, Griff kept the pine coffee table between them. "What are you talking about?"

Slade stood there, breathing hard, his breath rasping. "You went to Charley at the Tetons headquarters and tried to *bribe* him. *That's what you did!*" Slade rounded the coffee table, wanting to punch his twin in the face.

Moving quickly, Griff avoided Slade and kept the coffee table between them. "Bribe? You're insane! I didn't bribe Charley! I just went in to make a deal with him."

Jordana entered the room. Both men were roaring at each other. She stood there, helpless to interfere. Griff's expression was one of confusion and then surprise. Slade looked as if he wanted to kill Griff.

"A deal?" Slade roared. "Don't you know *anything* about bids? Once they're entered into the system, you don't contact the party about it! You went sallying into Charley's office today and offered him a bribe."

Nostrils flaring, Griff yelled, "Like hell, I did! I was just sweetening the pot was all. One extra horse would seal the deal!"

Shaking his head, Slade snarled, "You might wheel and deal on Wall Street like that, but that kind of crap doesn't fly out here in the West. You got me deleted from this bid." Slade held up his hand. "I had the bid, dammit! Charley was going to call me tomorrow morning and tell me I had it."

"That's good," Griff muttered. "So I don't see why you're so pissed off at me."

"Because," Slade thundered, "Charley saw your little visit as a bribe and I got removed from the list because of it." Slade's face reddened with rage. "Damn you, Griff, you just cost me eight thousand dollars I needed to pay on the ranch mortgage. You interfered and screwed me and my ranch." He jammed his finger down at the pine floor. "You stupid jerk, you just put this ranch in a financial hole! What you did is a *bribe*! Do you get it?"

Breathing hard, Griff glared at his enraged brother, who was hunkered over him like a bull ready to gore him. "It was not a bribe! We do deals like this on Wall Street all the time! It's not a bribe. It's just part of what we do. No one calls it a bribe. Damn, you're crazy, Slade!"

Jordana saw Slade start to move. She knew he was going to grab a hold of Griff and beat him. Racing forward, she gripped his left arm with both hands. "Slade! Calm down! You need to take a walk." She tugged insistently on his arm. He didn't budge, his focus on his white-faced brother across the coffee table. Using all her strength, digging in her heels, Jordana jerked Slade hard.

Snapping his head to the left, Slade saw Jordana's grim face. Her full lips were tight, her eyes hard and insistent. Trembling with fury, he felt the strength of her small hands around his thick upper arm. The look in her eyes told him that she meant business. For a second, his rage cooled. He wasn't angry at her. But he sure as hell wanted to beat Griff to a pulp.

"Come *on*," Jordana insisted, tugging on his arm again. "Walk with me outside, Slade. *Now!*"

Hesitantly, Slade nodded. He glared over at Griff. "You son of a bitch, you get the hell off this ranch. *Now.* I don't care where you go, but don't *ever* step foot back here. You understand?"

Glaring back, Griff snarled, "This is my ranch, too! You can't kick me out of here!"

"Watch me." Slade made a move to go toward Griff.

Instantly, Griff leaped away, ran to the door, jerked it open and left.

Jordana sighed and released Slade. "You can't hit him, Slade. Calm down, please." She used her best soothing tone, the one she'd use with a traumatized patient at the hospital. She saw the anger leave and, in its place, anguish return. "Let's go to the kitchen. I'll make us some coffee. Come on…" She tugged at his hand that was still folded in a fist.

His rage began to dissolve by degrees as Slade opened his hand and entwined it within Jordana's fingers. She might be small, but she was gutsy coming between him and his brother. "Okay, coffee," he whispered, defeated. He walked her to the kitchen.

"Here, sit down, Slade. Your leg has to be hurting you."

It was, he realized. "Yeah, it's throbbing a little."

Nodding, Jordana went to the counter and made coffee. "You've been on it all day. It's bound to be achy." Her hands flew knowingly over the counter to get the coffee beans and the other items she'd need. "Can you tell me what happened?" she asked, turning and giving him a gentle look.

Slade sighed, rubbed his face with his hands and told her the whole conversation with Charley. He ended it by saying, "I can't believe Griff doesn't know what the hell a bribe consists of. Charley and I sure know what one is."

Placing two heavy ceramic mugs on the table, Jordana said, "Maybe things are different on Wall Street, Slade. He looked confused when you charged him with bribery."

Shaking his head, he pulled the empty mug over to him. "That's a load of crap, Jordana. Bribery is bribery. Why this nation is in shambles is because of the very mindset my brother has. He no longer knows right from wrong. To him, this was just another deal-making session. But in the West, a man's word is his bond." He looked over at the counter where Jordana was plugging in the coffeemaker. Just having her around was like a wet blanket to the fire he felt. His rage was rapidly receding in her quiet, calming presence. She had that kind of effect on him.

"Griff grew up in the East," Jordana offered. She sat down at his elbow. "I can't believe he'd purposely go to

Charley to sandbag your bid. Do you?" She looked him squarely in the eyes.

Shrugging, Slade muttered, "I don't know Griff. We rarely saw one another. He's from a different planet, Jordana. His world is a world of no morals and values. He doesn't *care* what effect his decisions have on others." And then, he closed his eyes. "Damn, I was counting on winning that bid. I knew I was low enough to get it."

Placing her hand on Slade's arm, she whispered, "What does this mean?"

Opening his eyes, Slade looked blankly at the wall of the kitchen. His hands tightened around the mug. "Charley usually has four bids a year for services at the national park. I have been winning two of them every year for the last five years he's been the supervisor. I provide packhorses and mules to him for his construction crews. I also provide good horses for the rangers to ride, too. It was enough money to help keep me out of foreclosure." His mouth moved downward. "This bid was the one I was really counting on."

Frowning, Jordana said, "Can the bank do that?"

Snorting, Slade growled, "A bank can do anything it damn well wants. The president doesn't like me. I was informed that my bill is going up with the October payment."

Nodding, Jordana knew that homes across America were in what was termed an upside down mortgage, thanks to the antics of Wall Street destroying the finances of millions of people. Because Slade's ranch was right on the border of foreclosure, she had read that banks were now forcing such owners to either pay up or lose their home. In this case, Slade stood a very real chance of losing his family ranch; a ranch that was his lifeblood. Moving her fingers in a grazing motion across his forearm, she asked, "What can I do to help?"

He gave a harsh laugh and sat up. "Win the endurance race. But that's not going to happen, Jordana. That ten-thousand-dollar award could mean all the difference right now." The anger went out of him, and Slade rested his elbows on the table. Head falling forward, he muttered, "I'm screwed. Griff just put this ranch into foreclosure. The bastard…"

Tears gathered in Jordana's eyes. She whispered, "I know you don't think I can win this race, Slade, but I can. I just rode Thor for fifty miles. I know the trail better. If I ride it one more time before the actual race, I *know* I can win! There's never going to be another horse like Thor. He's one of a kind, Slade." Gripping his hand, she forced him to look into her eyes and whispered fiercely, "Slade, I can do this! I know you don't think I can, but you don't really know me!"

Jordana released his arm. "I'm made out of titanium steel inside, Slade." She poked at her chest. "But you don't know that yet. How do you think I made it through medical school and seven years as an intern? Trust me," she said, lowering her husky voice, "that really separates the men from the boys. I made it to become a doctor because I *wanted* it. I have terrific focus and drive. You'll see it come out in that race. I will win that money for you."

Shaking his head, Slade said in a dull tone, "Jordana, I appreciate everything about you, but you won't win. Curt Downing is going to take it. He knows this trail inside out, like the back of his hand. You don't."

"Well," Jordana said, allowing some anger into her

voice, "your horse sure does! Thor will make up the difference. I'll let him guide me."

"I want to believe you," Slade told her gently. Reaching over, he gripped her hand. Slade saw the feisty quality in her blue eyes and the way her mouth was set. "You're already a champion to me, Jordana. I know you mean well and want this for me, but the truth is, you're going up against Downing. You're not used to his dirty tricks and he'll sandbag you. I know he will."

Sitting up, Jordana gripped his hand. "Now, you listen to me, Slade McPherson! I'm not going down without a fight! I'm not a quitter and neither are you! Stop looking like you've already lost, because you haven't!" She released his hand, got up and brought over the coffee. Pouring the steaming liquid into each of their mugs, Jordana added, "You have never seen me in action, Slade. And because of that, you don't know my capabilities in the saddle. I've won plenty of second-level endurance races and I win them consistently. Put a little faith in me?"

Jordana placed the coffee on the counter. Turning, she held his sad gray eyes. How badly she wanted to wrap her arms around Slade, hold him and tell him to have hope. Sitting down, she added cream and sugar to her coffee and stirred it.

The silence was thick and strained. Slade sipped his coffee. It burned his tongue. Frowning, he set it down and wrapped his large hands around it. Jordana looked fierce right now; something he'd never seen in her before. Admiring her spirit, he found nothing else to say. The kitchen hung with pregnant silence.

"I'll do it, Slade. I promise," she said grimly, holding his stare.

CHAPTER EIGHTEEN

CURT DOWNING SMILED as he watched his groom, Brodie Myers, brush his black Arabian stallion, Shah, until he gleamed. He watched the quick, sure motions of the fifty-year-old man who had always taken care of his horses. Shah snorted in the ties, defiantly lifting his head as he impatiently pawed the concrete. The horse had large dark brown eyes, small, refined ears and a dished face, typical of the Arabian breed.

Hearing a car pull up, he saw it was Frank Halbert, the president of the bank. "Finish him up, Brodie," he ordered the groom, "and then wrap his legs."

"Yes, sir," Brodie sang out, brushing the stallion's long, flowing black tail.

Moving down the breezeway, Curt wondered why the banker was coming here. Usually, he saw Halbert in town. The man looked happy as he emerged from his black Mercedes-Benz. Walking down the slope, his curiosity piqued, Curt saw Halbert smile when he caught sight of him.

"I have good news," Halbert said without preamble as they met down on the flat.

"Oh?" Curt said, lifting his hands and placing them on his hips.

Grinning, Halbert said, "I just heard something today you need to know about."

"Go on," Curt said. He saw a number of his wranglers herding a group of horses into one of the many pipe-rail corrals.

"I was out at the Tetons headquarters working with Charley, the U.S. Forest Service supervisor. He'd left the room and I saw all the bids on his latest packhorse contract." He could hardly keep the joy out of his tone as he continued in a whisper, "You're getting the bid, Curt!"

Brows raising, Curt said, "Really?" He knew that Slade McPherson usually won two out of the four yearly contracts. His bid wasn't the lowest, and therefore, he hadn't expected to get it.

"Yes." Frank looked around to ensure no one was listening. "I saw a hand-scribbled note on McPherson's bid." He grinned a little. "Griff McPherson, his twin brother, had called and tried to bribe Charley."

"What?" Curt frowned. "A bribe? Are you kidding me?"

"No, no, I'm not kidding!" Frank raised his hands and smiled fully. "Charley had a note on the bid saying it was declined due to Griff's interference. How about *that*? Slade's brother is an ace in the hole for you."

Shaking his head, Curt muttered in disbelief, "A bribe? Charley wouldn't put up with that. What's this twin doing that for?"

"He was a Wall Street banker who lost his job when his company went broke," Halbert explained.

"I'd heard rumors of McPherson having a twin in town, but I hadn't ever seen him myself."

"Yes, he's around, and you do realize what all this means?"

The gleam in Halbert's eyes reminded him of a coyote getting ready to pounce on his victim. "It means," Curt drawled, "that I'm not an idiot. He's lost out on money he could have sunk into that ranch of his. It puts him closer to foreclosure."

"Exactly!" Frank said excitedly.

"And McPherson knows his monthly mortgage has gone up?"

"Oh, yes," Frank said, satisfied. "I raised it another five hundred dollars."

"Damn, so the only thing between him and foreclosure is this endurance ride," Curt murmured.

"Exactly," Frank said with enthusiasm. "And then, when it goes into foreclosure, you can snap it up. I'll make damn sure no one gets a bid in on it before you. I know you want the land so you can expand your operations."

Nodding, Curt said, "I'm desperate for more land," he agreed. And it wouldn't hurt that this new land gotten by the foreclosure would butt up against the biggest ranch in the valley, the Elkhorn Ranch. "I've *got* to expand my breeding facility. I got more people wanting to breed to my stud than I have room to accommodate them. I'm losing a helluva lot of money because of this situation. I've been looking at the Bar H south of town. They're about ready to go belly-up. That's a hundred acres where I could move my entire breeding facility down there and keep this place for student training."

"I understand," Frank murmured. "But you know Gus Hunter, who's a pistol in her own right, isn't going to sell the Bar H family ranch to anyone."

Nodding, Curt muttered, "Old Gus is a firecracker. She's eighty-four. A tough old buzzard. I'm going to wage a war against her soon. She's alone and she's in poor health and can't continue to handle that ranch by herself."

"True," Frank said, "but I hear from Gwen Garner over at the quilting shop that her granddaughter, Valerie Hunter, is coming home to take up the reins of running the place."

Snorting, Curt muttered, "Buck Hunter was a mean bastard. He beat the hell out of his wife, Cheryl, and his daughter, Val. Cheryl's dead now. And Val left for good. She hated her father and hated the ranch. I have a hard time thinking she's leaving the Air Force to come back to the scene of the crime and try to save it."

Shrugging, Frank murmured, "That's what I heard. Gwen is never wrong."

"Well," Curt said with a frown, "I think I'll go visit Old Gus and see what I can persuade out of her."

Chuckling, Frank said, "You won't get anything out of Gus. She's a bona fide pioneer woman. Tough as they come."

"Maybe. But Valerie Hunter will be more than ready to dump that broken-down old ranch into my hands two months after arriving home. I'll just have to bide my time. In the meantime, my sights are set on Slade McPherson's ranch. It's mine. He just doesn't know it yet."

Looking around, the banker straightened and said, "It's just a matter of time, now, Curt. I'm sure you'll win this contest. You're taking McPherson's last chance to save his ranch away from him. You did hear that, because he got gored by his own bull, that Dr. Lawton is riding his stallion for him?"

"Yeah, I saw her out on the trail two weeks ago." He didn't add that Lawton was a helluva better rider than he thought. No sense in letting Halbert know anything. Curt didn't trust the banker any further than he could throw him. His thoughts about Lawton and Thor were known only to him.

"And?"

Shrugging, Downing muttered, "She was fighting that mustang stallion all the way."

Chuckling, Frank said, "I'm surprised McPherson let *anyone* on that mustang's back. That's a one-man horse."

"Yes, Thor is," Curt agreed. He switched topics. "Tell me more about Griff McPherson."

"He came in last week and filled out a résumé to work at our bank. Of course, I have no openings."

"Not for him you don't," Curt growled.

"I would never hire a McPherson," Frank told him in a confidential tone.

"So, he's looking for local work?"

"Yes. I interviewed him myself. He's lost everything. His job, his millions he had in derivatives, and he has nothing but a dwindling savings account."

"Really?" Curt said, his mind spinning. "Those two twins split up when my father killed their parents. I never did know where Griff went."

"Back East. His uncle was a big-time Wall Streeter. Griff grew up, went to Harvard and got an MBA. He worked for his uncle's company until it collapsed. Now, he's destitute like thousands of other Wall Street brokers."

"Too bad," Curt murmured. "But that's good for me. Griff can't loan Slade money to save his ranch."

Chuckling indulgently, Frank said, "You've got that right. When I interviewed him last week, he had two hundred dollars left to his name."

Grinning, Downing said, "I saw a help wanted ad at McDonald's. They're looking for help."

Joining in the laughter, Frank said, "Oh, I don't think he'll lower himself to that level. Too much pride."

"Pride goeth before a fall," Downing said, enjoying this piece of unexpected news.

"He's got a *lot* of pride," Halbert agreed. "You won't find him working at a burger joint. He tried to come in and sell me on the fact he's got an MBA from Harvard. And that he can make my bank a ton more of money. I told him if he was so good, why had he lost his entire job and livelihood?"

"Right on," Downing said. His brows fell. "One thing I *am* worried about is Dr. Lawton. What if she loans McPherson money?"

"Oh, that won't happen," Frank consoled him. "Her account is at my bank. She's got a thousand dollars in her savings and only two thousand in her checking."

"She's a doctor. I thought they were all rich."

"I spoke to her two weeks ago. She did come in to try and get a loan. I knew it was for McPherson, but she didn't say that. She said it was to build an addition on to her home." Snorting, Halbert said, "She's not a very good liar. You can read her face like a road map."

Laughing softly, Downing said, "You're full of all kinds of good news, Frank." He clapped the banker's rounded shoulder. "How much was she trying to get out of you?"

"Ten thousand."

"That's a lot. But that's exactly the amount McPherson needs to dig him out of potential foreclosure. It gives him breathing room."

"Correct," Frank murmured. "And I knew from that moment on, it wasn't for any house addition."

"Does she have a credit score to get such a loan from the other bank in town?" Curt asked, worried.

"No. She's had plenty of debt and lost everything two years ago. Right now, she's trying to rebuild, but it's slow. Don't forget, she's still paying off loans for her medical schooling."

Rubbing his hands together, Curt grinned. "You've really made my day, Frank. I thought those two were getting a little close. And I figured she might try to loan that bastard the money."

"She can't," he said with finality. "No bank right now, in this recession, will loan her a dime."

"Have you put out the word that Griff McPherson shouldn't be hired?"

Frank, who had loans on every business in town, smiled. "Not to worry. I've already done that. Griff won't find *any* job open to him except for a burger joint." He snickered.

Curt liked using Halbert. He was a fat slug of a man, but he was wily and knew where money power was at. "Well, under these circumstances, I'm going to buy more stock in your bank, Frank."

Eyes widening with pleasure, Frank mopped his perspiring brow with a white linen handkerchief. "Why, that's mighty good of you, Curt. I didn't expect that."

Mouth lifting into a slight smile, Curt murmured, "You're my eyes and ears on the McPhersons, Frank. And you're doing a good job. I'm just showing my appreciation."

Nodding, Frank stuffed the handkerchief in the back pocket of his gray pinstripe suit pants. "Good, good."

"Wish I could be a fly on the wall and watch Griff McPherson squirm."

"I heard that Slade kicked him off the ranch."

"That's even better. I like Slade in such a state. It will keep his mind off trying to win this endurance ride."

Shaking his head, Frank murmured, "Oh, I doubt Dr. Lawton can even come in among the top ten riders."

"I agree," Curt said. "She's never raced in a level-one event. I don't care how good Thor is, it's the rider who sets the pace and knows how far they can push their mount, and when."

"My money is on you," Frank chortled. "I'll be there at the finish line to see you and your black stud coming in first."

Downing's mind was elsewhere. If Griff McPherson was in town, kicked off the ranch, he wondered what he was going to do. This had to weigh on Slade. And that was good. Very good.

GRIFF SAT IN McDonald's nursing a cup of coffee. It was a busy place with plenty of tourists in town. Sitting alone, smarting under Slade's rage, he tried to think of a way to get a job. The sky was a bright blue, but white clouds over the top of the mountain rose above the town. It looked as if it might rain later in the day. As he sat watching families, hearing laughter and seeing the smiles, he felt even more depressed. They had money. They had a home. They had family who loved them…

The coffee, although hot, tasted bitter. He knew it was him, not the brew. Yeah, he was damned bitter. After he'd been sent to his Uncle Robert, life had turned out well for him. At first, he'd missed his parents and Slade terribly, but his aunt and uncle had taken over as his parents. They'd loved him. Maybe not as he remembered his own parents doing so, but he'd been loved. Slade had slowly disappeared from his life. Looking up, he saw a family of five sit down next to his table. All he could afford was a cup of coffee. With only two hundred dollars in his pocket, he had to be very careful how he spent what was left.

Would Slade let him back on the ranch or not? Smarting beneath the attack by his angry older brother, Griff turned the paper cup around and around between his long hands. What if he wouldn't? What next? Going into the county welfare office and asking for food stamps? God, he didn't want to do that! Shame flowed through Griff. He'd never thought he'd ever be poor. Not *ever*. Now here he was drinking a cup of coffee from McDonald's and not from Starbucks. He never came to such a place. No, he'd eaten at the best five-star restaurants that New York City had to offer. The maître d's had known him instantly and had always saved the best table for him.

Not now. What am I going to do? Had it been a mistake to come West? Griff had already tried to get at least twenty positions along the East coast, but no one wanted a Wall Street has-been. After all, many interviewers reminded him, *he* was the reason the economy had crashed worldwide. His greed. His lack of care for what derivatives might do to the middle class of America, nevermind the rest of the world.

Mouth turning downward, Griff stared blackly into the steaming cup of coffee. Right now, he was a pariah. He'd found it an error to tout his resume. People blackballed him and saw him as part of the reason why the economy was failing. It was *his* fault.

His gaze fell on a sign in the window: help wanted for night shift. Moving uncomfortably, Griff didn't want to try for a job that was so far below him. A hamburger turner? Was that the only job open to him? He opened his hand and looked at it. When he'd first arrived, he'd had soft palms. Now, there were a few calluses from working daily out at the ranch with Shorty. Ranch work, he'd discovered, was damned hard, always ongoing and never finished. Animals needed to be fed every twenty-four hours. There was no dispensing machine that could feed them. And he was exhausted after mucking out box stalls and hauling old hay and horse turds to the compost bins. Some of the horses, like Thor, hated him. The stallion would charge the box-stall door every time he walked past him. Shorty had to clean Thor's stall, instead. There was no way Griff was going to get bitten by that ornery stud.

Even horses hated him, Griff glumly decided, sipping the coffee and feeling sorry for himself. Slade certainly hated him. How was he to know that by offering to throw in an extra packhorse that Charley considered the gesture a bribe? In his business, they were always wheeling and dealing like this. It wasn't wrong; it was just the way things were.

Pulling over the local newspaper, Griff turned to the want ads. There were a pitiful few of them, as usual. And all of them were either for cleaning hotels, burger joints or janitorial work. There was nothing that appealed to him. Yet, as he sat there, he had no house to go to. Rents were high here, he'd discovered. Too high for the likes of him. So, where was he to go? At least at Slade's he'd had a room at the main ranch house. What could he do about this?

Angry, Griff dropped the paper on the table. This was all Slade's fault! He hadn't meant to bribe Charley. It was all a misunderstanding. Obviously, they didn't meet or agree on much of anything. How badly he missed his penthouse apartment. It was gone. Everything was gone. And his brother had kicked him off the property.

Just as he looked up, he saw Dr. Jordana Lawton enter. She saw him, waved and smiled.

Griff waved back, feeling at least she didn't think he was a bastard as Slade did. He watched as she stood in line. Would she avoid him, too?

"Hey," Jordana called as she got her salad and walked toward Griff, "can you use some company?" She felt sorry for the younger twin who looked terribly sad.

Griff stood and said, "Hi, Jordana. Come and sit down."

"Thanks," she said, smiling and sitting opposite him. "I didn't expect to see you here, Griff." Jordana unwrapped the plastic fork and poured the salad dressing across the salad. "How are you doing?"

Sitting down, he grimaced. "Not good, to tell you the truth. Is Slade still pissed at me?"

Jordan speared a slice of grilled chicken breast on top of her salad. "He didn't say anything about you this morning."

"I didn't mean what I did as a bribe," he said.

"I'm sure you didn't," Jordana said. "You don't strike me as a weasel, Griff."

Feeling a bit of relief, he tried to explain his actions to Jordana. She nodded, ate and looked sympathetic. Just encountering someone who was at least neutral about the situation helped Griff a lot. He wondered what she saw in his dark, over-responsible brother.

"I don't think Wall Street and the West can meet on similar ground," Jordana told him after the explanation. "I'm sure you meant well, Griff."

"Thanks, I needed to hear that." He stared down at his cup. "Do you think Slade meant it?"

"What?"

"That I can't come back to the ranch?"

Giving him a pained look, Jordana said, "I don't know, Griff. That's something you have to talk over with Slade."

"I was hoping you could put in a good word for me."

Jordana wiped her mouth with the paper napkin. "Slade and you have to settle this. I'm not getting between you."

"Actually, a smart, strategic choice," Griff told her, a slight smile hooking one corner of his mouth.

"He's under a lot of pressure right now," Jordana gently offered him. "I can't believe he really means it, Griff, but now is not the time to test the waters. If I can't win that ten-thousand-dollar purse on this endurance ride, he's going to lose the ranch."

"*Our* ranch."

"Okay," Jordana said, frowning, "but Slade doesn't see it that way and you know that." She felt sorry for Griff. He was literally like a fish out of water here in Jackson Hole.

"Yeah, yeah, I know," he muttered unhappily. "I've been trying to find a job ever since I got here. I've been on fifteen different interviews here in town. I never told Slade that because I know he's worried about our ranch. I can't seem to get a job," Griff said, frustrated. "If I could get a job, I could help Slade pay that mortgage."

Sympathetic to Griff, Jordana said, "Maybe you

should have kept Slade in the loop and told him you were interviewing for jobs. If you don't tell him what you're doing, Griff, how can he know any different?"

"I know, but I was hoping to surprise him. A good surprise, for once." His voice fell in disappointment.

Seeing the sadness in Griff's eyes, Jordana said, "Look, I think if you offered to come and help him at the race, he might look upon that favorably. Slade needs a team of people. He's got Shorty, but he's a person short. If you could run errands, fetch water, towels and brushes, I think Slade would jump at that. Right now, his leg is hurting him, and he's not as fast and nimble as he hoped to be."

"You think he'd go for that?" Griff knew he could run errands.

Shrugging, Jordana picked at her salad. "It's worth a try. But, Griff, I'd give him a few days to cool off. He desperately needed that bid contract."

Nodding, Griff said, "I get it—now. I just thought I was helping…"

"Easterners have a different mindset, I know, because I came from New York City myself. This is the first time I've been out West. And in the two years I've been here, I've seen remarkable differences. Stunning, sometimes."

"Yeah, it sucks. But I need a real job, Jordana. I'm really frustrated. No one wants me…"

Sipping her coffee, she offered, "Griff, I can go to our human-resources department and see if they need a medical orderly."

"I don't know anything about medicine," he protested.

"You don't need to. Nursing assistants do a lot of clean up. They mop, sweep and change bedcovers and such. It's a good wage, too."

Griff looked at working at a hospital as slightly above flipping burgers. "Could you? I'd really appreciate it. I'm not afraid of work, Jordana."

Hearing the hope in his voice she said, "My shift is tomorrow morning. I'll go see Cary and find out if she has any openings, Griff. If she does, I'll give you a call on your cell phone?"

Embarrassed, Griff admitted, "I'm losing my cell phone coverage in a month. I don't have the money to pay for it any longer." It hurt to admit that to anyone. He saw Jordana's blue eyes go soft with understanding. No wonder Slade was in love with her. Jordana was special.

"Okay," she murmured, giving him a slight smile, "I'll do what I can. In a hospital, people are always coming and going. And assistants are always needed."

Relief started to trickle down through him. Griff whispered, "Thanks a lot, Jordana. This means a lot to me."

"I know it does. Let me see what I can do."

CHAPTER NINETEEN

THE ENDURANCE CONTEST was only one day away. Slade felt a twinge in his thigh where Diablo had gored him. Watching Jordana as she walked out of the training barn after putting Thor away, he felt his heart open. Her hair was mussed, and she looked beautiful in her jeans and yellow tank top. He ached to hold her, kiss her and most of all, make slow, exploratory love to her. Such were his dreams that were mixed in with nightmares of losing his family homestead.

Jordana smiled and tucked her damp, thin leather gloves into her belt as she approached Slade. The sun was starting to set. Tomorrow was the big day. Her heart raced as Slade's eyes revealed raw desire for her. When had their relationship changed? She wasn't sure. All Jordana knew is that she wanted to get past this race and see where the chips would fall. Her desire for Slade was visceral.

The last rays of the sun slanted across the wide, oval valley, the peaks of the Tetons turning pink.

"I have a surprise for you," Slade told her as she came to a halt.

"Oh?" Jordana grinned and saw a slow smile work its way across his mouth. What a mouth! To kiss Slade again would be as close to heaven as Jordana thought she might ever get. And she warmed to his dropping

that mask and being human with her. As the month had
worn on toward the race, Slade was no longer the man
behind the armor. Now he was allowing her to see him
as he really was, and it was breathtaking.

"I'm taking you out to dinner tonight," he said. "You
want to get a shower and into some clean clothes?"

Surprised, Jordana said, "Really?" Was this a date?
Or, more than likely, Slade's way of thanking her for
riding Thor tomorrow. Looking deeply into his eyes,
Jordana saw happiness gleaming in them. That wasn't
something she saw often in Slade with the pressures
haunting him.

"I'm trying to be more social," Slade admitted wryly
as he walked with her toward the ranch house. "So be
kind to me on my first try?"

Laughing, Jordana asked, "And did someone put a
bee in your bonnet about this?" She loved the way Slade
walked with a boneless kind of grace. He was a man in
his prime in every way.

Chuckling a little, Slade slid her a glance. "Guilty as
charged. I was in Gwen Garner's quilt shop the other
day. I was buying some soft fabric to wrap your knees
in for the ride. She gave me an earful."

Slade opened the back door for Jordana, and she
walked into the mudroom. He enjoyed simply absorbing her small, athletic form. She sat down on a wooden
bench and pulled off her boots.

"So, Gwen suggested this?"

"Yes," he admitted with some hesitancy. Taking off
his Stetson, Slade hung it on a wooden peg near the door.
"She asked me how I was repaying you for all the hard
work you're putting into this race. I told her about our

agreement that if you picked up any of the prize money that it would go toward future training for you."

Sitting there, hands in her lap, Jordana laughed. "I'll bet that went over like a lead balloon."

He sank into her soft, wide smile. Jordana's blue eyes danced with deviltry. Slade had to stop himself from reaching out and tunneling his fingers through her soft, mussed black hair that lay about her shoulders. "Yes. She wagged her finger in my face and you know how short she is."

Getting up, Jordana padded in her sock feet toward the door to the kitchen. "Gwen's my height," she laughed, opening it and stepping inside.

Slade followed and closed the door. The kitchen was neat and clean. Ever since Griff had gone, the ranch had settled down to a fixed routine that Slade needed. "Yes, she is."

"And she said?"

"I should take you out and wine and dine you. It was the least I could do, and I agreed with her."

Jordana stopped and looked up into his weather-beaten face. Heart warm with the unspoken care she held for Slade, she reached out and touched his arm. She knew that he was saving every penny he could for the coming mortgage payment that was due a week after the race. "Listen, you don't have to do this, Slade. Just the fact you'd do it is plenty good enough for me."

Her fingers were strong and caressing on his upper arm. Slade wished things were different. But the pressure of the coming race tomorrow morning took his attention. "No, I'm taking you out to dinner. We're going to Red's Steakhouse on the southern end of town. You ever been there?"

Allowing her hand to drop back to her side, Jordana
shook her head. "No, but I've heard they have great
steaks."

"Yes, and I'm buying you one," he promised firmly.
"Now, go get cleaned up and put on that other set of
clothes you brought with you."

How badly she wanted to step into Slade's massive
arms. He looked handsome in the dark blue long-sleeved
cowboy shirt and Levis. His chest was broad, and she
ached to explore what was beneath that material. "Okay,
I'll be out in about thirty minutes," she promised, turning and heading out of the kitchen.

Slade stood there after Jordana was gone. The kitchen
suddenly seemed sterile as if the life had gone out of it.
Such was the sunshine nature of Jordana, he thought.
Looking down at his dirty Levis, he walked toward his
bedroom. He had to get cleaned up, too. As his boots
thunked hollowly down the hall to the master bedroom,
his heart sang. Grateful to Gwen Garner, Slade realized
he had to learn to get involved with people and society
once more. He couldn't keep hiding out like a polecat.
But life had made him that way. Now, Jordana bright-
ened his life and was changing it in a good way. And
that was something Slade wanted equally as much as he
wanted to keep his ranch.

JORDANA SAT IN a black leather booth with Slade. Red's
Steakhouse wasn't loud and raucous as she had thought
it would be. Instead, Nashville music drifted softly in
the background while waiters and waitresses zipped
smoothly between the many tables. The booth was hidden in a darkened corner, and it felt intimate to her. Slade
sat opposite her looking handsome in a clean white cow-

boy shirt and Levis. He wore a red bandanna around his throat, his hair recently washed and gleaming beneath the lamplight suspended above the table.

"I like the fact we can be here in working clothes," she admitted. The waitress who was serving them was an older woman in her fifties. She set down two glasses of water and a basket of freshly baked bread and corn-meal muffins.

Slade thanked the waitress who smiled and left. "Gwen suggested this place because I didn't want to go anywhere that demanded a suit and tie."

"Oh," Jordana teased, picking up a warm cornmeal muffin, "that would be The Aspens. It's a five-star res-taurant."

Nodding, Slade watched her long, graceful fingers as she buttered the cornmeal muffin. What would her fingers feel like moving across his body? He squelched the thought for now. "I've never been there," Slade ad-mitted. It was too pricey, for starters.

"I've been there," Jordana admitted, setting the but-tered muffin on the small white porcelain plate near her dinner plate. "The Aspens is nice, but stuffy. The senator's wife, Clarissa Peyton, goes there all the time."

"She's a good person," Slade murmured, picking up a piece of sourdough bread from the basket and butter-ing it. "The senator is in prison in Washington, D.C., on murder charges. I felt sorry for Clarissa throughout that godawful public trial of Carter Peyton. She was the in-nocent in that mess."

Sad, Jordana said, "Yes, she was."

"Have you ever had lunch with her?" Slade wondered. Nibbling on the muffin, Jordana said, "I have. Clarissa has brought in a lot of donations to our hospital. She's a national charity organizer and very good at it."

"Clarissa has a big heart. I don't blame her for divorcing Senator Peyton and taking back her maiden name, Renard, after the trial was over."

Nodding, Jordana added, "Clarissa got the house here in Jackson Hole as part of her divorce settlement. Right now, her little sister, Nicky, is living with her. Her son, Bradley, just went off to college this year."

"She looks happier than I can recall," Slade said. "She's raised money to protect the mustangs out in Nevada. I liked working with her because she's the real deal."

"A Wyoming native like yourself," Jordana pointed out.

Smiling a little, Slade murmured, "Wyoming bred and Wyoming tough. Clarissa is beautiful, talented and intelligent. But she doesn't suffer fools for long." He chuckled.

Laughing with him, Jordana said, "That's so true. And I'm glad to see her getting back her life now that the trial is done and her divorce is final. She deserves a break." And, Jordana thought, so did Slade.

Slade chewed on the warm sourdough bread. Red's knew how to make it right. He gazed over at Jordana. Her black hair was still damp from the recent shower, the strands curling around the collar of her pink blouse. Jordana always brought along a clean pair of clothes after riding thirty miles. It was hot, dusty work. He liked the cream-colored slacks she wore because they showed off her long, beautifully tapered legs.

"I think this dinner is a pre-celebration, Slade. I *know* that Thor and I can win."

Shaking his head, Slade smiled at her passion. "I wish I had your faith, Jordana. I'll feel good that you and Thor will complete the ride without injury." And Slade knew there were plenty of places where she could fall off and injure herself. Even more, he worried about Thor's legs. Jordana was competitive but not foolish. He knew she'd take care of the mustang stud and not put him into a potentially injurious situation. The only fly in this ointment was Curt Downing. Slade had nightmares about the bastard.

"Ye of little faith," Jordana teased with a laugh. "We've gone over the fifty-mile trail twice. I've worked hard to memorize all of it."

"Especially the parts where you trot Thor or canter him?"

"Absolutely," Jordana said, seeing the worry creep back into his eyes. "I'm not a risk taker, Slade. I won't put Thor into a situation where he could be hurt. You know that."

Slade impulsively gripped her hand for a moment. "I could lose him, but I can't lose you, Jordana." Shocked over what he'd just blurted, Slade pulled his hand away from hers. He saw the sudden widening of her eyes and then her mouth going soft and kissable. Clearing his throat, he looked down at the table and muttered, "I've come to like you a lot, Jordana." Slade forced himself to meet her gaze. "You're unlike my ex-wife, Isabel. You might come from New York City, but you're a Westerner at heart. You love the land and the animals. You aren't afraid to get your hands dirty…"

The words came hard from Slade but they made her fast-beating heart melt like hot butter in a skillet. Jordana sat there savoring his admittance. How like Slade to be all bottled up and then suddenly explode with the truth. Gently, Jordana said, "I like you, too, Slade. I admire your honesty and work ethic. You always tell the truth, no matter how tough it is. When I first met you, you scared me to death." Jordana managed a sour smile. "You bluster a lot and I had to get past that. It was easy to do because of the way you treated Stormy. You might be a bit rough around the edges with people, but you have a kind heart."

Heat ran up from his neck and into his face. To Slade, who wasn't used to blushing, it felt as if he'd stepped into a patch of stinging nettles. It was Jordana's husky tone, the longing look in her blue eyes, that tore loose the rest of Slade's hidden truths. "I'm not one for fancy words," he managed awkwardly. Opening his hands, he added, "Isabel always called me stupid. I knew I wasn't stupid. Gwen would tell you I lack some social skills, but I'm far from dumb."

Digesting his painful admittance, Jordana saw a little six-year-old boy struggling to make sense of his parents' sudden deaths. And then, to be handed over to his aunt and uncle. She couldn't appreciate all that Slade had gone through. Losing his parents had put armor around his shredded, grieving heart. At eighteen, she knew Slade had taken over the ranch. He'd struggled ever since then. Nothing had come easy for him. He'd earned every bit of money he got. "Social skills," she murmured, "are something you can add to your repertoire as you see fit, Slade."

"They call me a loner," he finally admitted. It felt so right to just let all the poison out of his soul and share it with Jordana. He knew now that she could handle the worst-case scenarios and not flinch. "And I guess I have been. At least…until lately."

She saw the little boy in the man's eyes. He was so scared to admit all of this to her. Reaching over, Jordana grasped Slade's hand. She felt the toughness of his flesh, the hard calluses earned by unrelenting work in all kinds of weather conditions. "Slade, you lost everyone you loved. You did the best you could. I don't know of too many eighteen-year-olds who could walk into a ranch situation and keep it on its feet. You don't see yourself, but I do." Her fingers caressed the back of his hand. "Slade, you're an incredible person. I'm absolutely in awe of you. I know I couldn't have done what you did and kept your ranch solvent."

Her words were warmth to his wounds and scars. He saw the sincerity in her darkening eyes and the gentle expression across her face. "I've made some stupid decisions doing that," he admitted. "Isabel stepped into my life and I lost control of my world. I couldn't think straight, I couldn't be realistic. I guess I was lonely…"

Hearing the pain and personal censure for his actions in his gravelly tone, Jordana leaned forward and whispered, "Slade, stop gigging yourself. You *were* lonely. When did you have an opportunity to date women after the ranch got hung around your neck? All you did was focus on keeping the ranch viable. That doesn't leave a lot of time to date and be social."

He lifted his other hand and captured hers. Although her hand was small, her fingers were long and elegant looking. The warmth of Jordana's hand heated him up from his heart down to his throbbing lower body. Forcing himself to look deeply into her pleading gaze, Slade said, "Do you always give people a long length of rope to run around on instead of hanging them with it?"

A grin tipped her mouth. Holding Slade's hand and having him respond like that was salve for her soul. Somehow, Jordana had never seen who she might fall in love with, but Slade fit her dreams. "Always. People get stressed out, traumatized and in shock by what goes on in their lives, Slade. I see this all the time in the E.R. of the hospital. Life isn't easy on anyone. And it's been especially rough on you."

How badly Slade wanted to kiss her. Right now. Here. He didn't give a tinker's dam about who saw him do it, either. Unable to reach across the length of the table, he squeezed her hand gently between his own. "I want to think we have something to build on after this race?"

Nodding, Jordana whispered, "Yes, there's a lot there to work with, Slade."

The waitress arrived, and they released one another's hands. In no time, large oval platters filled with T-bone steak, baked potatoes with all the fixings and buttered peas sat before them. Slade thanked the waitress, and she left.

"Wow, this is a *lot* of food!" Jordana said, giddy over Slade's admittance. "I don't think I have a stomach big enough to hold all of this!"

Grinning, Slade picked up his knife and fork. "Listen, stuff yourself because tomorrow you won't be doing much eating, just guzzling water at the vet stops."

He was right, she realized. "It looks delicious, Slade."

So did Jordana, but Slade didn't dare say that. "Just enjoy it."

"I'm enjoying *us*," Jordana parried with a smile.

Again, that hot sensation moved to expand his heart,

which was beating double-time. Slade had never felt what he felt for Jordana. As he focused on cutting up his steak, he found himself hungry—for her. Where would this all lead? He was afraid to dream because of his less-than-glorious past.

"Have you ever been married?" he wondered.

Stunned, Jordana's fork halted halfway to her mouth. "Er...no."

"You never found someone? I find that hard to believe."

Jordana popped a piece of steak into her mouth. Slade's bluntness was, at times, unnerving. With a slight smile, she said, "Let's put it this way, Slade, when you're a resident, there's no time for anything. I would sometimes work twenty-four hours straight and stagger back to my apartment and sleep the sleep of the dead. I would put in a minimum of twelve hours a day at the hospital. I never had a day off. I found it hard to do all the other things that needed to get done, nevermind having a man in my life. There just wasn't room."

Slade tried to imagine her world as a doctor-in-training. "But you had time for riding. I know you rode in endurance contests."

"Yes, that was my only gift to myself," Jordana agreed. She spooned up some peas. After eating and swallowing them she added, "What you have to understand is that riding was my outlet. If I could throw my leg over a horse, no matter how bad my hospital life sucked, I was free for those hours. And it helped me deal with my boss, who was a sexual predator."

Brows raising, Slade set his hands on the table. "What are you talking about?"

Jordana confessed to him her six years with the phy-

sician she'd had to work under. When she finished the
sordid tale, the court drama and final judgment for her,
she said, "I was so burned out by the whole thing, Slade,
that I left the east coast to come out here and start a new
life. I didn't want to be known. I wanted to have a good
career as a physician and still be able to ride endurance
races." With a shrug, she said, "And the last two years, I
didn't have time for a relationship. Oh, there were some
guys, that's true, but I wasn't swept off my feet by any
of them."

Giving her a heated look, he asked, "Do I sweep you
off your feet?"

The question was thickly spoken and pregnant with
promise as it hung between them. Jordana stopped eating and looked up. She felt her heart expand powerfully
as she held his warm, gray gaze. "Yes, you do, Slade."

Nodding, he said, "I'm glad to hear that." His world
spinning and wobbling inwardly, Slade tried to tamp
down the sudden joy that sizzled through him. Jordana
liked him! And God knew, he liked her more than any
woman he'd ever met. Frowning, he glanced up and
asked, "Do you think it's possible that a doctor and a
cowboy can get along?"

Laughing softy, Jordana said, "Haven't we so far?"

"That's true," Slade admitted in a deep tone. All he
wanted to do now was bring Jordana home, take her to
his bed and make love to her until dawn rose. But none
of that could happen. Tomorrow, long before dawn, they
would be out at the beginning of the fifty-mile endurance ride. Reality crashed like cold ice upon Slade.

"I feel like Alice in Wonderland," he told her. "This
date with you is good, but when I look at my watch, I
know it's not going to last. At 4:30 a.m., we're going

to be out in that meadow and you're going to be riding Thor."

Hearing the disappointment in his voice and seeing it reflected in his sad-looking eyes, Jordana reached out and squeezed his hand. "Yes, and I'm going to ride him to win, Slade. That ten thousand dollars is yours."

Shaking his head, Slade couldn't believe her. He wanted to, but he knew the dangers, knew Downing and knew that she or his horse could be injured or killed tomorrow. Jordana simply refused to believe that she could be harmed. But she didn't know Downing and he would be gunning for her. The first thing he'd do is take her out one way or another. Thor was his only competition. Suddenly, the magic of their intimate dinner dissolved into sheer terror for Slade.

CHAPTER TWENTY

"ARE YOU READY?" Slade asked Jordana as he checked Thor's cinch one last time. Dawn was a thin, gray line on the eastern horizon. Bright lights had been set up around the huge staging area so horses and riders could see what they were doing.

Jordana nodded, pulling on the Kevlar vest that would protect her torso should she fall. Her heart was doing a slow pound. "I am," she told him. Around them were a hundred other horse trailers, riders and their nervous, frisky endurance charges. The meadow was a controlled bedlam of a sort. Jordana had seen this before, but not as a level-one endurance rider. Slade held Thor's reins. The stallion snorted and pawed, more than ready to get on with the race. Slade handed her the black, protective helmet she'd wear.

Slade looked around. The start line was about a hundred feet from where they were parked. Thor, because he'd won last year's endurance ride, would be the first to leave the starting gate. He'd get a five-minute head start, and then Curt Downing and his black Arab stallion would be next. Worried, he said, "Remember, let Thor gallop. Don't hold him back on this first mile. It's flat and even. This is where you want to make up time between you and Downing."

Strapping on the helmet, Jordana nodded. "I've memorized the trail, Slade. I'll do what you told me to do. Don't worry." And she gripped his hand and gave it a firm squeeze.

Slade saw Downing on his black stallion, Shah. In Arabic, shah meant "king." And indeed, the black stud who was rearing and pawing the air in anticipation was all of that. Shah was nearly equal to Thor. But there were subtle differences that would determine the winner and loser. Slade watched Jordana wrap an Ace bandage around each of her knees. The tape would stop the chaffing of rough material against her skin that always occurred over long-distance rides. It would stop the skin from being rubbed off. If it did happen, it made riding excruciatingly painful and sometimes took a rider out of the race because so much tissue damage occurred. She was quick and professional about it. Some of his anxiety dissolved. Everything about Jordana was confidence and focus. It entered Slade's mind that maybe, if she was lucky, she *might* finish in the money. Second place was five thousand, and third place was two thousand dollars. Any money would be better than none, but he knew she had her sites set on winning. His heart opened with such a rush of startling emotions, he blinked. He'd never felt this way before. What *was* it? Slade had no time to figure it out.

"I'm ready," Jordana announced. She looked up into Slade's dark and shadowed face. How handsome he was! How utterly rugged as the Tetons was this man that she felt such a powerful love for. Jordana no longer tried to explain how she felt toward Slade. She didn't know when she'd fallen in love with this iconic cowboy, but she had. It was her secret—for now. After the race was over, she'd have the time to speak of it to Slade. How would he react? Jordana wasn't sure. "And," she whispered, throwing her arms around Slade's broad shoulders, "I need a kiss for good luck!"

Taken aback by Jordana's bold move, Slade automatically curved his free arm around Jordana's slender form as she leaned up to kiss him. Startled by her assertiveness, he leaned down and captured her smiling lips. Her mouth was warm and inviting as she surged against him. Groaning softly, Slade melted into her lips, tasting the coffee she'd had earlier. She was all woman, all sensuality in that moment. The scent of her briefly dizzied him. And just as suddenly, she pulled away. The kiss was over far too soon.

"You're my luck," she told him in a husky tone. She saw Slade's narrowed eyes smoldered for her. Jordana felt every cell in her body tingle over that raw, hungry look. "Help me mount!" She turned and took Thor's reins from his hand.

In moments, Slade had boosted her up on the stallion. Thor moved sideways, full of himself, vital and like a powerhouse ready to explode. Slade grinned and settled his hands on his hips. Despite his stallion's aggressive nature, he immediately answered to Jordana's quiet hands and guiding leg pressure. "Okay, be careful out there."

Smiling down at him, Jordana heard the horn blast. That meant she had to get Thor up to the start line. "I will." She blew him a kiss. "And we have some important things to talk about after the race," she called, whirling the mustang around.

Standing there, Slade watched her move the sunbonnet stud in and around the horse trailers. The first ten riders were mounted. Every five minutes, one would be released in the order they'd earned from other races. Pride sifted through Slade. As he stood there watching Jordana guide Thor up to the start line where two judges and a timer stood, he smiled faintly. The feeling he had was one of intense love for her. Even in the semidarkness, the dawn barely crawling over the horizon, Slade felt the immense power of love avalanching through him for this feisty, petite woman. Thor was a huge, rangy stallion, and Jordana literally looked like a jockey on his broad, long back. He was chomping on the bit, tossing his head, his brown-and-white mane flying like spun candy around his neck and withers. Jordana was focused on a judge who came up to speak to her. He would ask her name, the name of her horse, double-check the number pinned on her back and the number spray painted onto the rump of the horse. Everything had to match and it did. He shifted his gaze to a woman with a red flag standing fifty feet inside the start line. When the male judge lifted his hand, she brought the flag down. That meant, "go!"

Jordana didn't need to do anything as Thor saw that flag whip downward. Instantly, he launched off his powerful back legs, dirt and rocks flying from beneath his hooves. He knew it was the signal to run! Hunching down on him, her face close to his neck, her hands steadying the thundering stallion as he surged forward for the one-mile run to the slope of the Tetons, Jordana felt a thrill unlike anything before. Thor knew he could run here. His legs stretched, and she felt him establish a ground-eating stride. All she had to do was look ahead for holes, branches or anything else that might make him stumble. As the rider, she was always looking ahead. The wind whipped past her, her eyes watering as the stallion gained even more speed. It was dizzying! The dawn light was there, but she still had to squint to see a few hundred feet ahead of the stallion.

By the time they reached the trail that would eventually twist upward toward ten thousand feet, Thor had gotten his initial burst of energy expended. Jordana didn't look back. She knew that Downing would be galloping as hard and fast as he could to catch up with them. As they entered the thick forest, the path well marked with red-orange flags every quarter of a mile, Jordana negotiated with Thor. The stallion still wanted to run, but it was impossible as the trail twisted upward. In some spots, there were tight, ninety-degree turns. In others, there were logs fallen across the path and they had to jump them. The best she could do now was throttle Thor's nuclear power down to a steady, hard trot. He hated it, snorted and tossed his head. Laughing, Jordana sang softly to him. Ears flicking back and forth, Thor stopped chewing on the bit and got down to the business of trotting.

It would be impossible to know how close Downing was to her. The trail was wicked, steep and she could barely see twenty feet behind her. Slade had told her to just keep Thor moving at a fast trot and negotiate all the tight, demanding turns. There were pullouts about every quarter of a mile on this narrow portion of the race, where a rider could move over to allow another to pass, but that was all. Jordana keyed her hearing behind her. Now that Thor was trotting, the wind wasn't tearing past her as it had out on the meadow run, and she could hear very well. The light grew as the dawn became stronger.

The path was tricky, full of rocks sticking out of the soil along with roots that grew across it. She wondered how close Downing was to her.

CURT CURSED SOFTLY as he took the whip he always carried and let it hang on his wrist. Shah was snorting hard, his black nostrils wide open and showing red deep within them as they hit the beginning of the trail. How far ahead was Jordana and that damn stud of McPherson's? Gouging his heels into his black Arabian, Curt forced the horse to canter up the path until he couldn't do it anymore. No horse could gallop around tight, ninety-degree turns. He cursed, trying to see ahead. It was impossible on this part of the trail. It was narrow, thickly wooded, and while it was a switchback trail that wove back and forth across the slope of the Tetons, it didn't allow him to catch sight of his competition. The only thing he could do is take advantage of every straight spot, which were few, and canter his horse. Every stride meant a second of time and Curt knew that. And sixty seconds made a minute. And one minute could determine the difference between winner and loser. He pushed Shah as much as he dared. Inwardly, Curt knew he could overtake the woman. Thor might know this trail, but she didn't. Women were conservative riders compared to a man. She would be slowing down on this weaving, narrow trail, not urging Thor as he should be pushed. Grinning, Curt took his whip and laid it against Shah's rump as a short, straight part in the trail popped up. The Arab grunted and lunged forward, hurtling up it at a dizzying speed.

SLADE DROVE HIS trailer and pickup to the first stop in the high mountain meadow. He found a parking spot, got out and saw that Shorty was already there and prepared for the vet check. Griff had volunteered to help. Slade had been surprised by the generous offer and told him to help Shorty. His wrangler had driven the other truck up earlier. When Jordana came galloping into the vet check, she'd have to dismount and have the saddle and bridle taken off so that the vet team could check Thor. Shorty would then walk the stud for the vet. After the check and figures were marked down by the team, he would then walk the stallion for twenty minutes. Slade would have time to give Jordana water and talk to her about the race.

Worriedly, Slade looked at his watch and then glanced at the opening into the meadow that was half a mile away. He knew this first section of the race was very challenging. Would Jordana still be in the lead? What if Downing tried to pass her? Would he push her out of the way? Slade knew that there was no cell-phone reception on this endurance ride. There was no way for Jordana to let him know what was happening to her and Thor. As he paced and kept glancing at the opening, Slade found himself far more worried over Jordana than her place-ment in the race. When had he fallen in love with her? Slade knew it was love. It was nothing like he'd felt for Isabel. No, this feeling was like a warm glowing light in his chest. He thrummed with joy he'd never experienced in his life. Jordana made him happy. Just her smiling face, those dancing blue eyes, fed his starving soul in a way Slade had never realized existed.

Thor and Jordana burst out of the forest. By now, the sun had risen. Long, bright slats of light filtered strongly across the flat, oval meadow. Slade breathed a sigh of relief. Jordana was in the lead! Thor looked good. So did she. Where was Downing? A million questions showered through Slade as he walked to where Shorty was standing. Thor was wet with sweat, but there was no foam on his neck or hindquarters, which was good. That would indicate nervousness, which would voraciously eat up a horse's energy and slow him down. Jordana had him at a full-out gallop because this was where she could get time against other riders following her. He enjoyed seeing them flying toward the awaiting vet group. She was so small bobbing on Thor's back. Clearly, Jordana had the stallion in hand, and he was fully listening to her commands. Pride for her abilities moved through Slade.

Jordana brought Thor to a halt. Quickly leaping off, she handed the reins to Shorty. She saw Slade grinning fully as he came around to uncinch the saddle.

"How are you?" he asked, quickly removing the saddle, blanket and breastplate.

Sweaty, Jordana smiled and said, "Fine."

The vet team moved in with a stethoscope and their clipboards that would list Thor's pulse, breathing and heartbeat. The stallion snorted, still full of himself even after twenty miles. Within moments, Shorty put the halter over Thor's head and then removed the bridle. Griff nodded to Jordana and helped the wrangler.

Jordana smiled at the twin. She was happy Slade invited him to come along and help.

Slade gripped Jordana's arm and guided her toward the truck. "You need water and food," he told her.

Laughing with relief, Jordana said, "I'm not hungry! We're doing fine, Slade. How's our time?" She walked close to him and he reached out and gripped her hand in his. Her heart soared with joy. She could still feel the power of his mouth against hers from their kiss earlier in the meadow.

Slade drew her to the rear of his pickup where he had pints of cold water and trail mix waiting for her. Releasing her hand, he picked up a bottle and twisted off the cap. "Drink. You're more dehydrated than you realize."

Nodding, Jordana dutifully took the water bottle from him. The moment their fingers met, she felt a wild and tingling feeling up her arm. Slade looked serious, his cowboy hat drawn down over his brow, his gray eyes narrowed upon her. It was a look she eagerly absorbed as she gulped down a pint of water. As soon as she was done drinking, she watched the vet people work with Thor. They had gotten their numbers, and now, Griff had to walk him for twenty minutes.

"How's Thor doing?" Slade asked, leaning against the tailgate as she munched on the granola and dried fruit.

"Good," she murmured between bites.

"Is he listening or fighting you?"

Grinning, she said, "A little of both, but when it got down to it, Slade, he did exactly as I asked him."

Nodding, Slade absorbed her sparkling blue gaze and the happy smile on her mouth. Strands of black hair had crept out on the sides of her helmet. Perspiration dotted her brow. Her cheeks were flushed a bright red. He knew how strenuous and demanding this part of the trail was. "How are *you* doing?"

"Great," she said.

"Your legs? Any chapping of the inner knees or cramping of your legs yet?"

Leaning down, Jordana checked the duct tape on her knees. "No, I'm fine so far. No burning sensation, no rubbing on my inner knee area. The duct tape is doing

its job." She straightened. "Is our time good?" She knew
Slade had all the times from past rides on the clipboard
setting on the tailgate.

Picking it up, he motioned for Jordana to sit on it
next to him. "Your time is actually one minute ahead of
what I did last year," he told her, pointing to the numbers. How badly Slade wanted to kiss her. But now was
not the time.

Studying the figures, Jordana said, "The next twenty
miles is from seven thousand to ten thousand feet. We
take that trail across the high, rocky slopes and then
come down to nine thousand into our next pit stop."

Nodding, Slade said, "Here comes Downing…"

Looking up, Jordana saw Downing running the
stallion full-out across the flat meadow toward the vet
check. The horse looked fit and his sweaty body gleaming like polished ebony. She frowned as she saw Downing whipping the horse's rump with that ever-present
whip that hung around his wrist. "He shouldn't beat his
horse," she muttered, frowning.

Slade looked at the time the horse flew across the
vet-check line. "No, he shouldn't, but Downing beats
everything he owns," he growled. "He's thirty seconds
later than his time last year," he added, smiling a little.
"And Shah looks good."

Jordana watched Downing's team race over and
quickly unsaddle and unbridle the black stallion. Downing was scowling and yelling at his team as the vet came
over. "He's pissed about something."

"He's always angry on a ride," Slade said. "He's competitive."

"He should relax while he's got a chance." Jordana
was happy to sit on the tailgate of the truck with Slade.

She continued to eat. Food and water were necessary for the rider, who was expending a tremendous amount of energy. She saw that Shorty took Thor over to the waiting pails of clean, cool water. The mustang eagerly thrust his muzzle into the first pail, gulping down the contents.

"Downing never relaxes," Slade warned. Sighing, he said, "If he's going to make a move to pass you, it will be on this next stretch. And you have to be ready for him. He'll try and run you off the trail. If you get into those rocks…"

Holding up her hand, Jordana said, "Stop worrying, Slade. I know what he's capable of doing. And I'm not going into the rocks with Thor." More grimly, she added, "We'll be okay. How are you doing?"

He smiled slightly. "Worried."

"That's to be expected. Thor's doing fine. He's an old hand at this. He remembers this trail and knows how to negotiate it."

Picking up her hand, Slade kissed the back of it. "I was worried for you, not my horse."

Touched, Jordana clung to his burning gray gaze. His hand was firm and strong around hers. Her flesh warmed instantly as his mouth settled on it, and he kissed it. "Oh," she whispered, suddenly touched by his unexpected gesture. "I'm okay, Slade. Really."

"Well, it's the second twenty miles that you'll start feeling the push and getting tired," he warned, releasing her hand. At that moment, he could have drowned in Jordana's eyes. Slade wanted nothing more than to bury himself into her, take her and love her until she fainted in his arms.

For a moment, Jordana's world swam around Slade. She ached to kiss him again. Tucking away that need, she slipped off the tailgate and gave him a warm look. "Time's almost up." She was ready for the next twenty miles.

DOWNING WHIPPED HIS stallion as they raced along the narrow dirt track across the rocky slopes at ten thousand feet. He pushed his Arabian hard to make up that minute of difference between him and Thor. What he hadn't expected was how well Jordana rode the horse. He'd miscalculated terribly, thinking she would never finish this grueling event. So far, he'd been dead wrong. She rode smart, and she rated Thor like a pro, much to his chagrin.

They were coming down from the rocks. Thor flew into the forest at nine thousand feet. He spurred Shah. The stallion grunted and pounded even faster down the trail, eating up the distance between them.

Jordana's full focus was forward. She didn't hear Downing coming up on them until it was too late. The path was wide enough for three horses in the forest. Thor was trotting at this point because a tight turn was rapidly coming up. She suddenly heard the pounding of hooves bearing down on her. Thor's ears laid back. He squealed a warning but it was too late.

In seconds, Jordana found Downing and his black Arabian alongside them. It happened so swiftly that she was caught off guard. Downing grinned savagely and threw his stud into hers. Instantly, Jordana hauled back on Thor, not wanting to be shoved off the trail and into the trees. Her reaction was wrong, but at the time, it was visceral. Downing flew past them. The Arabian took the sharp turn and disappeared. *Damn!*

"Come on!" she called to Thor. Angry at herself for

not dividing her attention between the front of the trail and who was coming up behind, Jordana leaned forward. Thor snorted and plunged forward, thundering down the trail in pursuit of the black Arabian not far ahead of them. Jordana focused on catching up with them. She knew in less than a mile, the trail ended and opened up into another meadow where the second vet check was located. She'd screwed up. Big time. Slade was going to be disappointed when he saw she wasn't in the lead at the next stop. *Damn!*

Slade's brows dropped as he saw Downing whipping his horse to high speed as they burst out of the trail and into the meadow. Worriedly, he stood, holding his breath. Where was Jordana? Had Downing hurt them? Rage warred with concern. When Thor galloped out of the woods, Jordana still on him, Slade's breath exploded from him. Without thinking, he ran toward where Shorty was waiting for her.

Jordana quickly dismounted, handing Shorty the reins to Thor. She saw Slade's dark face and worried look. Trotting toward him, she was angry and upset. "I screwed up, Slade. I let him get around me. I'm sorry."

Slade gripped her arm and brought her to a halt. "What did he do?" he demanded, quickly looking her over. She had no scratches, bruises or whip marks on her arms. Downing had done worse to other riders who challenged him out of sight of the judges. Her eyes were narrowed. The set of her mouth told him how upset she was. "Come on, you need to drink and eat," he coaxed as he led her to the truck.

Jordana told him what had happened as she drank the water. "I'm sorry, Slade. I wasn't paying attention like I should have…"

Soothing her, Slade said, "Don't worry about it. The last ten miles of this race is where Thor will excel." He pointed toward the other end of the busy meadow now milling with horses and riders galloping in. "You've got a five-mile steep trail down from eight thousand feet to the final leg at six thousand feet. And then you've got five miles of flat land to make your final run on him. Wait until you get out of the woods. When you're on the flat, open Thor up."

"There's no way to try and make up this thirty seconds on that five-mile trail?" Jordana demanded. How badly she wanted to win that money for Slade! It broke her heart to think that he'd lose the ranch without it.

Shaking his head, Slade muttered, "It's narrow, twisting and few places to pull over to let a horse and rider move past. It's too dangerous, Jordana."

Frustrated, she stared over at him. "But not impossible to do?"

Hesitating, Slade muttered, "No, not impossible…" Holding her angry glare, he added, "Listen, I want you to come out of this alive. You can't challenge Downing in that section. He'll eat you alive, Jordana. Don't try it. You'll be putting yourself and Thor at risk."

The grave tone of his voice along with the pleading look in his gray eyes made her contrite. "I won't risk Thor, Slade."

"He's second in importance to you, Jordana. Do you hear me?" He drilled a dark look into her startled gaze. Gripping her hand hard for a moment, he rasped, "Dammit, Jordana, you're important to me. I can lose the ranch. I can't lose you…"

Those words echoed within Jordana as she rode hard down the narrow, steep trail toward the flat plain. Thor didn't like being second, either. She loosened the reins and let the stallion eat up seconds as he inched closer and closer to the fleeing black Arabian. She saw Downing jerking a look back at them every time he could. They were gaining on him! Jordana wanted nothing more than to overtake them! And in the last mile before they hit the flat, she surged Thor forward to do just that.

Downing cursed and saw Jordana make her move. The trail was wide enough. But he was damned if he was going to politely move over! Grabbing his whip, as Thor thundered even with them, he raised it up to slash at the animal's face and force him to retreat.

Jordana saw Downing's face turn livid. As he raised the whip to strike at Thor, she jerked her leg out of the stirrup, leaned to the right and slammed her boot as hard as she could into Downing's leg.

With a scream of surprise, Downing felt her heel connect. It broke the momentum of his whip coming down to strike Thor. Shaken, the Arabian spun to the left. It nearly unseated Downing. Thor charged past. Cursing, Downing got a hold of his startled horse, and he whipped him unmercifully to catch up with them. *Damn her!* He hadn't expected the woman to fight back! Mouth tightening, Curt leaned down across his stallion and urged him to catch up.

Jordana hit the flat at an all-out gallop. Fifty feet behind came Downing. They had five miles to go! The dust tore up under the pistonlike surge of Thor's hind legs as he lunged forward. His nostrils were wide open. He was sucking up and blowing out explosive drafts of air. The wind screamed past Jordana's bobbing head. She looked back. Downing was gaining on her! He was unmercifully whipping his stallion. Leaning down, riding Thor for all he was worth, Jordana began to use her hands, legs and weight to push him just a little faster. The stallion gamely responded.

Out of the dust, Slade saw Thor and Jordana in the lead. Not more than twenty feet behind was Downing on his foaming black stallion. Cheers began from bystanders standing on either side of the course the last half mile, urging the riders on. Watching through his binoculars, Slade swelled with pride for the woman who rode his medicine-hat stallion. Jordana had proven so many times before that she was a champion in every way. He never, in a million years, thought that she could win this race. But there she was, riding Thor, the two of them flying across the sagebrush plain toward the finish line.

Jordana heard the hoofbeats of the black Arabian approaching from behind. Her eyes were tearing so much from the wild run that she could barely see. Thor was hitting the ground hard and swiftly, his mane constantly whipping and stinging her face. She had to win! Slade's ranch was at risk! Looking over, she saw Shah's black head slowly edging up toward her. She saw a maniacal look in Downing's eyes, his mouth lifted in a snarl at her. She knew he couldn't hit her or do anything at this part of the race. The judges would see it.

Her legs were tired, and she felt herself loosen the grip she needed. Understanding that the first forty miles had taken more of a toll on her than she'd first believed, Jordana dug deep. There was only a half mile to the finish line! They were now neck and neck!

Mouth thinning, Jordana moved her hands firmly against Thor's neck. She called out to him. Instantly, the stallion's ears went back. He stuck his nose out, grabbed the bit and surged ahead.

Slade couldn't believe his eyes as Thor pulled away from Downing in the last quarter mile. His stallion was literally flying, his mane and tail furling outward like a flag, Jordana was barely a bump on his back, her hands and arms pushing him forward with every massive, ground-eating stride. Cries of triumph erupted from the crowd as Thor and Jordana passed the line into first place. Shorty came over and leaped up and down, slamming Slade on the shoulder.

"She did it! She did it!" he screamed, throwing his hat into the air.

Stunned, Slade stood there watching as Jordana and Thor galloped across the finish line. His ranch would be saved! God help him, he loved her with a need that engulfed him. As he walked toward them, slightly dazed by the unexpected turn of events, a crooked grin of triumph began to spread across Slade's face.

CHAPTER TWENTY-ONE

"READY TO GO HOME?" Slade asked. Slade knew the winner would not be honored or the check given out until tomorrow morning at the awards ceremony. Riders would be coming in until dusk. The late afternoon sun slanted across the valley, the Tetons reflecting the light.

Jordana grinned, turned and threw her arms around Slade. Shorty gathered up Thor's reins, and Griff began to unsaddle him for the final vet check. "We did it!" she whispered against Slade's ear, feeling his strong arms slide around her. Closing her eyes, Jordana didn't care who was watching them as she leaned up and kissed Slade fully on his smiling mouth. She felt as if she were floating on a cloud of pure joy as he returned the swift, quick kiss.

Releasing her, Slade knew many were watching them. Some had shock written on their faces. No one had suspected there was a brewing relationship between them. Grinning down at her as she removed the Kevlar vest, he said, "You did it. You and Thor. I was wrong, Jordana. You're a champion through and through."

Feeling heat crawl into her face as she lifted the helmet off her head, her hair mussed, Jordana smiled up at him. "I knew you'd realize that sooner or later," she teased. When Slade smiled, it did something warm and wonderful in her heart. It was so good to see Slade smile!

A number of people came over to congratulate them. In the distance, Jordana saw a fuming, angry Curt Downing glaring at them. Both Thor and Shah were being walked to cool down after being vet checked. She wondered if he was going to charge her with a foul.

Turning to Slade, she whispered what had happened on the trail. His brows instantly fell, and his gray eyes turned angry.

"He won't say a word," Slade muttered, lifting his head and glaring at Downing in the distance. "I'm sure he was surprised you fought back."

Taking her vest and helmet to the pickup truck, Jordana tucked them into the area between the seats. She was hot, sweaty, dusty and in dire need of a shower. "He had a surprised look on his face," she told Slade with an elfish grin. She followed him to the rear of the trailer.

Slade saw Shorty bringing a tired Thor toward them. The stud had earned a nice, cooling bath when they got home. Opening up the one side of the trailer that Thor would be led into, he smiled a little over at Jordana. She looked beautiful, her face streaked with dust, her black hair gleaming beneath the late afternoon sun, the strands showing reddish highlights. His lower body tightened with screaming need of her. Jordana was such a brave, fierce warrior. Why hadn't he seen that in her before?

As Slade pulled down the ramp and placed the rubber mat over it so Thor wouldn't slip walking into the trailer, he knew why. Jordana was nothing like his ex-wife, Isabel. But he hadn't seen the difference until now because he'd allowed Isabel to color his view of all women.

Thor was damp and dusty as he obediently climbed into the trailer. Shorty tied the rope to the bar and gave the stallion a pat. "He did good, Boss. He won with five minutes to spare. That's a new, personal record for him."

"It is," Slade agreed. Shorty left the trailer, and they closed it up. Shorty and Griff would take the other truck after putting all the supplies in the back of it.

Jordana waited for Slade. Once he climbed in and started up the Chevy, he drove slowly down the dirt road toward home. Leaning back, she closed her eyes. "It's over. We did it, Slade. We won that ten thousand dollars for you."

He reached over and gripped her hand resting in her lap. "You've got a lot of lessons coming," he told her.

Opening her eyes, she met his warm gaze. "I'm looking forward to them, Slade. Stormy is slowly healing and by the time next year comes around, we'll bring her back to her original shape." She absorbed the strength of his hand around hers. He divided his attention between driving and her. She wanted Slade fully focused on driving and released his hand. What she had to say could wait until they got home. *Home...*

"Stormy has a good chance to fully recover," he agreed.

JORDANA WENT TO shower immediately upon arriving at the ranch. Shorty unloaded Thor and took him to his showering facility. The stallion would be bathed and then turned out into his own paddock with some well-earned sweet feed as dessert along with his hay for winning today. Slade went to the master bedroom. Everyone was dirty and sweaty from the endurance contest. Jordana scrubbed her hair with almond-and-spice shampoo from her favorite soap company, Herbaria. The scent of almond and cinnamon encircled her like a magical potion.

After drying off, Jordana tucked the fuzzy pink terry-cloth bath towel around her body. Today was the day. And she hoped Slade agreed. Padding down the pine hall, she saw Slade's bedroom door was ajar. Feeling a bit of anxiety, Jordana allowed her heart to do the talking.

"Slade?" She knocked lightly on the opened door.

Slade had just come out of the bathroom, a cream-colored towel wrapped low around his waist. When he heard Jordana's voice, he knew. "Come on in," he called, walking toward the door. Slade saw her round the door. Her hair was damp, uncombed and fell around her face. Seeing the shining love in her blue eyes, he reached out for her. Without a word, Slade drew her gently against him, rested his head on her damp hair and felt her arms twine around his waist.

"This is what I needed," Jordana whispered softly, lifting her face to meet his narrowing gray gaze. "I need *you*, Slade. I have for a long time. Maybe since I first met you." She moved her fingers down his powerful back, feeling his muscles leap, tense and respond to her grazing movement.

"You're a bold little thing," he told her, taking his hands and framing her upturned face.

Jordana grinned mischievously. His roughened hands were warm, and he smelled of the pine soap he always used. "I learned that in residency. He who doesn't move first, gets nothing." She lifted her hands and caressed his unshaven face. Her fingertips tingled as they flowed across his sandpapery flesh. "Slade, I love you. I don't know when it happened exactly, but it has."

The words flowed over him like a hot, beckoning shower. His heart flew open. "And how long have you been hiding this little secret?" he murmured, leaning down and brushing his lips against hers.

"Mmm," Jordana whispered against his mouth, "probably ever since I met you. Looking back on it, I was always wanting to come out here just to be near you. I loved the riding lessons, but I began to realize the highlight of my day was simply sharing time and space with you, Slade." She became serious and held his stormy-looking gray gaze. "I know what love is. I know what it means." She framed his face with her hands. "Do we want the same thing, Slade? Or is it one-sided?" Jordana held his suddenly serious look. His hands gently moved across her damp strands. Inwardly, Jordana shook. She'd waited a long time to feel that kind of loving caress.

A sensation of trembling began in Slade's core. Drowning in her blue eyes was like being given the keys to heaven. With great gentleness, Slade placed a series of kisses across her hairline and her brow and whispered near her delicate ear, "We want the same thing. I love you, Jordana. Like you, I don't know when I fell in love with you. I only know that I did..." Slade melded his mouth to hers. She tasted of toothpaste, the peppermint mingling with her sweetness as a woman. She pressed herself against him, her lips opening, allowing him deeper entrance into herself. Groaning, Slade leaned down, picked Jordana up in his arms as if she were nothing but a feather.

Slade placed her on the bed. Jordana opened her eyes and smiled up at him as he divested himself of the towel. He dropped it to the floor. Truly, he reminded her of a Greek god, his body solid, heavily muscled and athletic in every way. As her gaze drifted down in appreciation of him as a man, it was clear he wanted her. That sent a

white-hot need lancing through her lower body. Pulling
the towel off herself, Jordana felt the burn of his gaze as
he memorized every inch of her exposed body. Beneath
Slade's heated gaze, she felt her breasts grow taut, the
nipples hardening and her belly beginning to glow with
anticipation. He hadn't even touched her, and she was
responding to him! Such was the power of mutual love,
Jordana realized, as she reached up, gripped his fingers
and pulled them lightly across her body.

Slade moved slowly. He weighed enough that he
didn't want to crush Jordana beneath his body. As she
guided him over her, he turned on his side, slipped his
arm beneath her neck and with his other hand, placed it
on her hip. In one smooth, unbroken motion, he pulled
her against him. As he lay down, holding her liquid blue
gaze that had gone misty with what clearly was love
for him alone, Slade allowed himself to feel every inch
of her pressed against his hard body. Her breasts were
small but firm, teasingly moving against his dark haired
chest. Where her hips met his, he began to ache until he
thought he'd explode. When she wrapped her small, fine
legs around his thick, hairy ones, he closed his eyes and
gripped her. His lips pulled away from his gritted teeth,
and he sucked in a sharp breath as she moved suggestively against him.

When Jordana's mouth settled on his, Slade felt her
hips nestle against his. He took her mouth command-
ingly. She responded with hungry nips and her tongue
slipping into his mouth. There was nothing sedate or
conservative about Jordana now. Slade was getting a
taste, literally, of her as a strong and powerful woman.
Her hips ground demandingly into his. Slade smiled
beneath her lips. She was heat, softness and hunger all

wrapped into one. Without realizing it, Jordana had lifted and slipped herself over him. A tortured groan rolled out of him as her wet confines enveloped him. Stars exploded behind his tightly shut lids. Slade buried himself into her heated depths.

Every bit of Isabel and his doomed marriage dissolved beneath the heat of Jordana's lithe, athletic body. Any questions he had about comparing the two of them disappeared forever. Her mouth was wanton, searching and assertive. He liked Jordana's fierceness as a woman wanting her man. She made him feel as if he were the king of the world as she began to move sinuously against him.

Jordana shuddered as Slade moved his hands down from her damp shoulders, slowly exploring her long back and then covering her hips. He raised his and thrust hard into her, establishing a wild rhythm that made her moan with pleasure. In seconds, he had lifted Jordana so that her thighs straddled him. As he brought her fully against him, she cried out with joy, her back arching, her hands spread across his shoulders. The world tilted and spun into the boiling heat gathering deep within her. As Slade rose up, his lips feathering her taut nipples, she moaned and wanted more of him.

He lavished his attention to each of her throbbing breasts and puckered nipples. Jordana felt the boiling cauldron deep within her explode. She froze, cried out, her fingers digging deeply into the taut flesh of his shoulders. Slade ground his hips, rocking against hers, prolonging the delicious sensation and orgasm. Lightheaded, her eyes shut, Jordana whirled in light and heat in those precious moments as Slade guided and deepened the experience for her.

Slade could no longer withhold his own need of Jordana. As she collapsed against him, her lips parted in a whisper of pleasure, he took her fully. He released his love into her. Her hips moved in delicious rhythm with his, designed to pull every bit of energy out of him. Throwing his head back, teeth clenched, Slade sank into the throbbing fire. For molten, wonderful moments, he was spun out into a sensual, black world that enclosed him as her arms wrapped around his neck. As her mouth met his, Slade surrendered to her searing lips. The heat releasing in his lower body surged and melted within her.

Groaning and satiated, Slade relaxed. So did Jordana, resting her head in the crook of his neck. Both breathing raggedly, their hearts in pounding union as they lay against one another, Slade managed a sliver of a weak smile. He moved his fingers in a grazing motion against her damp flesh. Tracing the length of her strong, straight spine, he absorbed every delicious inch of her. Memorizing Jordana's firm body was easy. His mind had no other thoughts except to absorb her into him in those moments after they'd surrendered to one another. Inhaling her sweetness, the almond scent in her drying hair, Slade murmured, "I've died and gone to heaven..."

Barely opening her eyes, Jordana lifted herself just enough to meet Slade's gaze. She whispered, "We're heaven for one another, Slade."

Caressing her shoulders, Slade drowned in her barely opened eyes. They were a deeper blue, he realized, and she looked like a satiated mountain lion. Grazing her lips, he whispered, "I love you, sweetheart. You're all I want."

Warming to his nickname for her, Jordana moved off him and snuggled at his side. "You are surely a stallion among men, Slade," and she smiled into his stormy gray eyes, seeing pride flash in them over her whispered compliment. Leaning upward, Jordana kissed Slade once more, cherishing that strong mouth of his. She wasn't disappointed as Slade smiled his very male smile and returned her tender kiss.

Slade whispered, "Marry me?"

Jordana sighed and relaxed fully against him. She nestled her head against Slade's jaw and shoulder, content. "Yes, I want more of what we have, Slade. I want to be your partner and best friend."

"So do I," he murmured, nuzzling her soft, nearly dry black hair. "I have an idea…"

Pulling away to look up at him, she said, "Yes?"

"Tomorrow morning when we go back to the meadow to pick up the trophy and money, let's announce our engagement." He saw joy leap into her face, her cheeks redden even more.

"I like that idea," she murmured.

Slade caressed her jaw and placed a light kiss on her smiling mouth. "The town will rock with shock. Gwen Garner will be miffed because we didn't tell her first so she could tell the whole town."

Laughing softly against his mouth, Jordana said, "Gwen Garner will have a *lot* to gossip about anyway." They laughed together over that thought.

The moments filled with silence, and Slade appreciated the woman he held tenderly in his arms. He was amazed at Jordana's strength, her fierce love for him and the devotion he'd seen in her eyes for him alone. Moving his hand down across her shoulder to her hip, he rasped, "I don't know what I did to deserve someone like you, Jordana. I honestly don't."

Leaning up on her elbow, her breasts brushing against the wall of his chest, she said, "You wouldn't, Slade. But I do. You're a man with incredible morals and values. Your word is your bond. You work hard, long hours…" She slid her hand across his dark haired chest. "You're humble, Slade, about everything. Maybe it was the way you were raised. I don't know." Jordana leaned down and whispered against his lips, "That just makes me love you even more, darling. Pride doesn't run you like it does a lot of other men. You're a complex man, Slade." Jordana placed a nibble on his ear and then lifted her head. Meeting his smiling expression, she added, "And I like a complex man. I want my life to be entwined with yours. We share so much already."

"We do," he admitted, liking the way her drying hair curled softly about her flushed features. "You've given me so much already."

"Well," Jordana said in a wispy voice, "I wouldn't have it any other way, Slade. We share an equal partnership."

"That money you won will go to saving our ranch."

Nodding, Jordana said, "And now, once we get married, my money will be mixed in with yours." She looked around the large bedroom. "Not only is the ranch saved, but so are we."

Nodding, Slade drew her back into his arms. Her long leg crossed his. He savored the warmth and womanly strength of her body against his. "I never thought I'd ever fall in love again." And then Slade amended, "Now, I realize I never really loved Isabel. It was all about sex. Once we'd burned through that phase, there was nothing left to replace it. We were like strangers. What I loved, she hated and vice versa." His mouth thinned, and he

LINDSAY McKENNA 291

cupped Jordana's shoulder. "It taught me a good relationship is like a cake recipe. Everything has to be there to make it work for the long-term."

Laughing softly, Jordana said, "I like your idea about a relationship being like a recipe. You're right," she murmured, touching his hard, unyielding jaw. "Something that you want to last forever is a mix of many things. Among them, being friends. You really have been a dear friend to me whether you realized it or not."

Hearing the sudden choke in her voice, Slade turned his head and dissolved into the tears he saw in her eyes. "I didn't know what a friend was until I met you," he admitted in a roughened tone. "I've got a lot to learn about a healthy relationship, Jordana." His mouth lifted a little, "But I've got a sense you're going to help teach me about the rest of that recipe."

"Not that I'm an expert," Jordana protested with a breathy laugh. "The key is we both want this to work, Slade. *That* is the difference. There's going to be a lot of compromises, but I love you and I'm willing to make them."

Touched deeply, Slade shook his head. "I don't know what I've done to deserve you, but I'm a grateful man."

Nodding, Jordana rested her head on his chest. She felt the wiry hair against her cheek and heard the drumlike beat of his powerful heart in his massive chest. There was such strength to Slade. As she closed her eyes and simply absorbed the moment, Jordana promised herself that she would show him over time why he was a man worth loving. "You're no longer a loner, Slade. You have me..."

THE NEXT MORNING at the awards ceremony, Slade stood with Jordana. They were surrounded by everyone who'd been either a spectator or contestant after the final horse and rider had finished the endurance ride yesterday evening. And after he'd announced their engagement, the entire crowd gave a collective gasp. And then cheers and applauding broke out. He stood with his arm around Jordana's small shoulders, the rope of Thor's halter in her other hand. The stallion, who stood next to her, his bare back gleaming in the early morning sunlight, tossed and snorted as if to agree with the happy crowd.

"Well," Judge Amy Talbot said into the microphone with a smile, "I'd say this is a marriage made in heaven, Slade. Now, we'll have *both* of you on the pro circuit to watch out for!" Everyone burst into good-natured laughter.

Jordana grinned and looked up at him. Slade looked so ruggedly handsome in his tan Stetson drawn down across his serious features. He wore a black leather vest this morning, gussied up for the ceremony. The red bandanna that was always around his thickly corded neck was in place against the clean, pressed white cowboy shirt. He'd even put on his best pair of Levis and his fancy ostrich hide cowboy boots he wore only for special occasions.

Slade gave the crowd a sheepish grin. Taking the microphone from the judge, he said, "I hadn't thought of that, Amy."

The forty-year-old red-haired woman shook her head and took back the mike. "Well, *we did*, Slade! You two are going to be double-barreled trouble out there on the circuit. It used to be we only had you and Thor to worry about, but now, Jordana has shown she's got the moxie to win equal to you." She handed him the microphone.

"That's true," Slade said. He handed the mike to Jordana and said, "Tell them about Stormy."

Jordana told the crowd about her mustang mare who would show up on next year's circuit. She saw the merry crowd laugh and clap some more.

Amy said, "Well, let's give Jordana her due, Slade." She handed over the ten-thousand-dollar check. "Congratulations, Jordana. You earned every cent of this!"

Taking the check, Jordana saw Curt Downing standing nearby. His brows were puckered, and he was clearly still angry about the loss. She held it up in the air, and the group applauded more. Turning, she handed it to Slade. "With this money, Slade's ranch will be safe from foreclosure," she told the crowd, her voice growing raspy. "I rode Thor for him to try and save his home. I just want to thank Slade for having faith in me that I could do this," and her voice cracked. She turned and gave Thor a pat. "And this horse ran his heart out for me. They're *both* champions!" The crowd roared with approval as she turned and gave Slade a quick hug. He embraced her, his eyes suspiciously bright.

As Jordana drew away, she saw Griff McPherson hovering on the edge of the crowd. She hadn't seen him before. He was looking around, as if hunting for someone in particular. That was strange. Her heart went out to the younger twin. Looking up, she saw Slade had spied him, too. Some of the happiness faded from his eyes. He led her off the stage so second- and third-place riders would receive their accolades and checks. As they stood to the right of the stage, they both clapped for Downing, who was not happy. He took the check and stalked off the stage without a word. There were some catcalls and boos from the crowd. Slade shook his head. Downing was always a sore loser.

After the ceremonies, there was hot coffee, hot chocolate and Danish pastries for the crowd of one hundred and fifty people. Slade and Jordana were the focus of the crowd, and well wishes came from everyone. Andy Patterson, who had won third place on his half-Arabian gelding, called out, "Hey! When's the big day, Slade? When you going to get hitched?"

Jordana laughed and looked up at Slade. "Slade and I have to set a date, Andy," she said.

"How about you make the date the same as the Tevis Cup ride? That way, someone else gets a chance to win it!"

The crowd rocked with laughter and applause. Slade grinned. "Now, Andy," he chided, his voice booming over the crowd, "I was thinking that *after* the Tevis Cup Ride, we'd get hitched."

Groans collectively rose from the crowd. Andy smiled and called out, "Hey, that's a *great* idea, Slade! You're gonna have to send all of us invites because we're all gonna be there to try and beat you and your bride!"

Never had Jordana felt so happy or fulfilled as right now. The endurance riders were a small, tight-knit community. Everyone knew everyone else. She saw how happy they were for them. Slade nodded and promised to send the invitations. It was a joyful celebration.

As the party finally broke up around ten that morning, Slade finished shaking hands with the last of the well-wishers. He and Jordana walked toward the truck.

"Slade?"

Turning, he saw his twin coming up. Griff looked

nervous. Automatically, Slade put his arm around Jordana and drew her close.

"Griff?"

Griff halted in front of them. "I want to just say congratulations to both of you," he began, his voice sincere.

Jordana knew what it cost the twin to say that. After all, he still legally owned half the ranch. Reaching out, she touched his arm and whispered, "Thank you, Griff. We appreciate your care." And she did. Glancing at Slade, however, she saw no change in his frozen, dark features. There was still a war going on between the brothers. Her heart ached for both of them.

"Well, I just wanted to let you know I got a job."

"Really?" Slade growled. "Where? McDonald's?"

Griff stiffened a little but held on to his anger. "No, brother. I was just hired as a wrangler for the Horse Emporium. I'll be moving hay and feed for them. And I found a room for rent in town, so I'll be moving out today."

"Good," Slade bit out. He was relieved but wasn't going to say so. Griff looked like a cowboy to others. But he doubted he had the spine to stay the distance. "Being a wrangler is nothing but hard, constant work."

Nodding, Griff said, "I'm willing to do it."

Relieved, Jordana released his arm and said, "That's great, Griff. Stay in touch with us?"

He gave Jordana a slight smile. How like her to be the peacemaker between them. Tipping his hat, he murmured, "I will. Thank you. And congratulations on your engagement. I'm really happy for both of you."

Slade stood there tense and unyielding as his twin turned and walked away. He felt Jordana's warm hand moving slowly up and down his back as if to soothe him. "I'm okay," he growled, walking to the truck with her.

"I know you are," Jordana said lightly. "The good news is Griff has a job."

"The better news is he won't be at our ranch," Slade bit out, opening the truck door for her.

Sliding in, Jordana said nothing. As they slowly drove the horse trailer with Thor out of the meadow, she watched as Slade began to relax. There were such untended wounds between the brothers. And they wouldn't be healed quickly. As they moved out onto the highway that would take them back to the ranch, Jordana slid her hand across Slade's massive thigh.

"Give yourself time with Griff," she counseled gently. "He's hurting like you, Slade. There are a lot of bridges to be rebuilt between you two over time."

Shrugging, Slade's hands tightened on the steering wheel. "He doesn't belong out here, Jordana. He never will. And he wants the ranch. I know he does."

"Don't be so sure," she whispered, patting his thigh. "I think he's going to try to make it out here on his own, Slade. There's no job for him on Wall Street anymore. The country is in the deepest recession it's ever seen since the Great Depression. He looked happy to get that job. I feel he'll make a go of it."

Mouth tightening, Slade said, "You're kinder to him than I am."

"I don't have the family baggage you two do, that's why."

Giving her a quick look, he saw the peaceful look on Jordana's beautiful face. His anger was snuffed out. Reaching out, he gripped her hand and gave it a squeeze. "We'll cross those bridges as they come. Right now, all

I care about is loving you. If I have you, I have everything."

Nodding, Jordana understood. She returned the squeeze to his large, powerful hand. "Life is never easy, Slade, but it got easier for us because we love one another." And then she added, "Forever."

* * * * *

Joan Johnston is the *New York Times* and *USA TODAY* bestselling author of more than fifty novels with more than fifteen million copies of her books in print. She has been a director of theater, drama critic, newspaper editor, college professor and attorney on her way to becoming a full-time writer. You can find out more about Joan at joanjohnston.com or on Facebook at Joan Johnston Author.

Books by Joan Johnston

Hawk's Way: Jesse
Hawk's Way: Adam
Hawk's Way: Faron
Hawk's Way: Garth
Hawk's Way: Carter
Hawk's Way: Falcon
Hawk's Way: Zach
Hawk's Way: Billy
Hawk's Way: Mac
Hawk's Way: Colt

Visit the Author Profile page
at Harlequin.com for more titles.

HAWK'S WAY: GARTH

Joan Johnston

PROLOGUE

"So how did Mom and Dad meet, Charlie?"

"That's a long story, Zach, and it's time for you three kids to get to bed." Charlie One Horse, the ancient part-Comanche housekeeper at Hawk's Way, ruffled the hair of the seven-year-old boy sitting on the rawhide stool at the foot of his chair. Zach Whitelaw was the spitting image of his father, Garth. He had black hair that hung over his forehead and dark brown eyes that could be equally serious and mischievous.

"I wanta hear, too," Falcon said. Garth's six-year-old son was stretched out on his belly in front of the fire-place, his head resting on his palms. He had his father's black hair, but his eyes were the same blue as his mother's. Falcon possessed bronzed skin, high cheekbones and a sharp blade of nose passed down from his Comanche great-great-grandmother.

"Me, too!" four-year-old Callen chorused. Garth's youngest child, the only girl, had her mother's delicate features, but her father's black hair and dark eyes. She wriggled around in Charlie's lap so she could see the old man's face. She put a hand on the Indian's weathered cheek and said, "Please, Charlie?"

Charlie glanced from the three children to their parents, who were sitting on the sofa across from him. Garth had his arm around Candy, and her blond head lay nes-

302   HAWK'S WAY: GARTH

tled against his shoulder. His big hand clasped hers. They were the image of a loving, caring couple. It hadn't always been that way.

"So you wanta hear how your mom and dad met, do you?"

"You bet!"

"Sure do!"

"Uh-huh!"

"And after I finish you'll all go to bed without arguin'?"

Three heads nodded vigorously.

"Well, now, let me see," Charlie began as he tugged on the rawhide that held one of his gray braids. He chose his words well, knowing there was no way he could tell those three innocent faces the truth. "Long about eight years ago, your father was a hoss wrangler, just like he is now. And your mother, why, she was a rich girl. One of them gen-u-ine Texas deb-u-tantes. Now, one day..."

Garth's hand tightened on Candy's as the old man began to speak. Their eyes met and held. As Charlie told a story of how they had met and fallen in love, the two of them remembered how it had really happened.

CHAPTER ONE

GARTH WHITELAW HAD only one use for women, so he
didn't have much to do with the decent sort, like the lady
heading straight for him now. He avoided meeting the
widely spaced, speculative gray eyes that sought him
out along the show ring at the spring quarter horse sale
in Amarillo. But he felt a definite tightening across his
loins as he perused her long, jeans-clad legs and sylph-
like figure.

He couldn't help admiring the grace of her walk or
the way her long blond hair shifted across her shoulders as she moved. His appreciation was balanced by
the knowledge that where this particular woman was
concerned, the growing bulge behind his fly had damn
well better stay zipped in his jeans.

Candice Baylor was a genuine Texas debutante, the
daughter of one of the richest men in the state. Garth
had first met her three years ago, when she was seventeen. She and her father, Evan, had come to his northwest
Texas ranch, Hawk's Way, to look over some championship cutting horses Garth had for sale.

Initially Garth had been amused when Candy tagged
along behind him everywhere he went. He had a younger
sister who had taught him patience, so he answered all
Candy's eager questions with brotherly indulgence. Be-

cause she was clever and interested in everything he did, it was easy to be tolerant.

It soon became clear to Garth that his horses weren't the only thing that interested Candy Baylor. Unless he was very much mistaken, the girl had caught a bad case of puppy love. She began flirting with him, sending coy, come-hither looks from beneath lowered lashes.

Garth was annoyed by her antics because even though he knew what she was doing—and despite the fact that she was entirely too young for him—he had felt the first stirrings of arousal. He had scowled mightily at her, but even that hadn't discouraged her.

Garth frowned as he remembered how, the night before she was scheduled to leave the ranch, Candy had confronted him in the downstairs room that served as both office and parlor. She had been dressed for bed and wore a thigh-length belted aqua silk robe over matching long silk pajama bottoms. She might only have been seventeen, but Garth had seen a woman's shape beneath the sensually draped fabric.

Candy claimed she couldn't sleep and just needed someone to talk to. Garth had given her several crude, broad hints, but she hadn't left him alone. So he had settled back in his chair with a whiskey in hand to watch the show, certain he could handle anything this spoiled little rich girl could dish out.

Candy had wandered around the room touching his things—vicariously touching him. She sought out the collection of trophies he had won in cutting horse futurities and fingered the delicate designs. She picked up a photo of Garth with his two younger brothers, Faron and Jesse, and his sister, Tate, from the mantel and tenderly traced his image. Then she ran her hand the length of the pine mantel, which drew her slowly, inexorably toward where he sat in one of the two leather chairs that faced the stone fireplace.

Frustrated by the arousal he couldn't control, Garth fought fire with fire. As she stood before him, he let his gaze insolently run the length of her, stopping to admire the firm, high breasts and flat belly before following the length of her pajama-clad legs to her bare toes. When he looked back up at her face, she was blushing a fiery red.

But she didn't run. He felt a grudging respect for her because he knew the same look had warned off older, more savvy women. Candy had merely turned and strolled, hips sashaying, to the chair across from him. Instead of sitting down normally, she had curled herself into the leather chair with her feet underneath her. She had rested her elbows on the arm of the chair and cupped her chin in her hands.

"Why haven't you ever gotten married?" she asked.

Garth had fielded that question from a lot of women during his thirty-odd years. He gave her his usual cynical response. "Why buy the cow when the milk's free?"

She wrinkled her nose in disgust. "That's an awful thing to say! A man gets other things from marriage besides sex."

"There's nothing else I want or need from a woman."

"What about children?"

Garth's lips flattened. "If I could be sure they were mine, maybe I'd want some."

"What do you mean, if you could be sure they were yours? Whose else would they be?"

"Some other man's," Garth responded curtly.

"No wife of yours would—"

"You're right. No wife of mine would. I'd kill her

first," Garth said in a harsh voice. "But don't fool your-self. Lots of wives cheat on their husbands." His own mother had cheated on his father. His younger brother—half brother—Faron had been the result.

"What about companionship?" Candy demanded. "A wife can be a friend, someone to share your hopes and dreams and troubles with."

"I've got lots of friends." He smirked and added, "Of course, none of them are women. I figure there are bet-ter things to do when you're with a woman than talk."

She blushed again, an enchanting pink flush that raised the ridge in his jeans. He was ready to concede the battle to her and leave the room, but she asked one more question.

"What about love?" she said in a quiet voice.

"What about it?"

"Haven't you ever been in love with a woman and wanted her to love you back?"

His lips curled in a sardonic smile. "I'm not the kind of man women fall in love with."

She swallowed hard and said, "I love you."

Her gray eyes were huge in her face. He had never seen such a look in a woman's eyes. This was differ-ent from the admiration of his physical body, his broad shoulders and narrow waist, his straight nose and mouth, his black hair and deep brown eyes, which he had often seen from the women who wanted him—for sex or his money or to show off on their arms. This was some-thing more.

Garth felt a pain in his chest, like there was a great weight on it, making it hard to breathe. For one brief in-stant he wanted nothing more than to gather her up in his arms and hold her tight, to reach out and accept the love she offered.

But it was an instant only, and the fact he had even considered holding to his bosom what he knew was just one more female viper made him all the more harsh when he finally responded to her words of love.

"What you're feeling isn't love, little girl. It's good old-fashioned lust. Since you've been asking for it ever since you walked into this room, I figure it's about time you got it." He noticed his hand was shaking when he set down his whiskey glass, so he quickly balled it into a fist.

When he rose to his full height she looked up at him, frozen like a rabbit in a gunsight. Her face had bleached white and her hands had dropped into her lap. He reached out to grasp her wrists and slowly drew her to her feet.

Garth waited for Candy to stop him or show the least sign of fear or resistance. What he wanted her to do was run from him, back to her rich daddy, back to the safe haven of her room upstairs.

He was less surprised this time when she did not.

Candy laid her hands on his bare forearms. Then she turned her face up to his. Her innocent gray eyes were filled with love—and trust.

Garth had never felt so confused. His flesh burned where she touched him. Desire sent blood rushing through his body, engorging a shaft that was already rock hard. He wanted her like he had never wanted another woman. But he was equally determined that he wasn't going to take her. She was just a rich kid with a bad case of puppy love—which he was about to cure.

His mouth was hard, almost brutal, when it captured

hers, and his tongue raped and ravaged the inside of her mouth.

Sweet. Dear God, she's so sweet!

Garth was disturbed and disgusted when he felt himself responding to the young girl in his arms. He was a bastard, but not enough of one to take advantage of a teenage virgin. He pressed his mouth harder against hers—hard enough to scare the bejesus out of her—until he tasted blood.

He felt her begin to struggle in his arms and reached out for her breast, the most crude, most possessive male gesture he could make. He cupped the warmth of her through the slippery silk, and in spite of the strong urge he felt to caress her, forced himself to tighten his hold beyond what a girl of her little experience would find comfortable. This wasn't making love. This was sex. Down and dirty. The kind he might have with a woman who wanted it a little rough.

"No, Garth!"

When Candy jerked away, he let her go. She nearly fell when he released her. She stood panting, her parted lips still moist and swollen from his kisses. Her eyes... her gray eyes were wounded, full of pain and disillusionment. She wiped her mouth with the back of her hand, leaving a streak of blood across her cheek. He felt acid in the pit of his stomach.

"Why?" she asked in a ragged voice. "I love—"

He cut her off with an obscene oath. "Don't use that word to me! Foolish little girl! You're just a rich kid playing grown-up. Come back and see me when you're woman enough to handle what I have to offer."

He kept his eyes hard, his lips curled into a sneer. Even then she hadn't run. He had watched the tears brim in her eyes, watched her try to blink them back before one finally spilled down her cheek. It was plain she wanted to say something to him, but she couldn't talk because she had her teeth gritted to control her trembling chin.

For several tense moments he stood there feeling an urgent need to comfort her. He forced himself to remain where he was. What he had done was for her own good. But the tightness in his chest was back.

At last she swallowed and said, "You're the fool, Garth Whitelaw, to throw away an offer of love. You're going to end up a bitter, lonely old man.

"But I thank you for making me see that giving my love to a man like you, a man who can't—or won't—give love in return, would be like standing in front of a Brahma bull, waiting to get stomped. I know when it's time to make a break for the fence. Believe me when I say I'll be glad to put some distance between us!"

She turned and marched from the room, shoulders back, head held high with a dignity and courage he couldn't help but admire.

He hadn't seen Candice Baylor again before she left Hawk's Way or at any time since that night. Until now. Here she was headed straight toward him, a friendly smile on her face as though that night had never happened. At least they were on neutral territory at the fairgrounds in Amarillo. It was doubtful she planned to make a scene in a public place, although that had happened to him once or twice in the past with other women. His lips flattened in displeasure as he recalled such a moment.

"Hello, Garth."

He had forgotten how husky her voice was. The sound

rasped over his flesh, lifting the hairs. He didn't know what to say, so he said nothing. An awkward silence followed. Candy was close enough that he could smell the perfume she was wearing, the light scent of lilacs. He felt his body tightening in instant response to her allure and swore under his breath.

She froze and her face paled.

Garth clamped his back teeth and stood in silence.

"I need to talk to you," she said at last.

"If you want to buy a horse, see the auctioneer."

"Not about that."

Garth refused to help her by asking what she wanted. He watched the expressions chase across her face. Frustration, then anger, then determination.

"I'd like you to join me for a drink at the hotel across the street," she said.

"I didn't think you were old enough to drink in a public place."

She flushed painfully, but her chin came up a notch. "I'm not. I'll have a glass of tea. I have a proposal I'd like to make to you. I thought we might as well get away from the noise and bustle of the sale. Will you join me?"

Garth listened to the auctioneer's patter over the microphone and the sounds of horses neighing. People were going right on with their lives, unaware that he was being confronted by a specter from his past.

He knew it would be a mistake to go with her. Despite the three years that had passed since he had seen Candy Baylor, he was still attracted to her. She was definitely not a child anymore. Her voice, her face, her body had all matured. She was a woman now.

And probably not a virgin anymore.

He tried not to think about that, but couldn't get the

idea out of his head. He would never have taken her innocence, but now that she was an experienced woman, why not have her? He wondered if she would be willing. His lip curled cynically. Why else had she sought him out? Probably she was taking him up on his offer to come back when she was ready to have an adult relationship with him. He sure as hell wasn't going to turn her down.

"I don't have much time," he began. He watched her face closely and saw the disappointment she couldn't hide. "But I can spare you a few minutes."

The smile was back, and a brightness in her light gray eyes that made his gut twist. He wanted her. His mouth was so dry it was hard to swallow. His body felt taut, stretched on a rack of desire.

It was a damn good thing they were having a drink at the hotel, he thought. At least that way it wasn't far to the nearest bed.

CHAPTER TWO

CANDICE BAYLOR WANTED one thing from Garth Whitelaw—and it wasn't sex. That was a good thing, because from the look on his face as she had approached him, he wasn't the least bit happy to see her.

Her last encounter with Garth had cured her of her childish infatuation with the wrangler, but even so she couldn't help admiring the man. He stood well over six feet tall, and his lithe body was all muscle and sinew. He moved with the easy grace of someone who has spent his life depending on the strength and coordination of his body.

Over the years since that night in the parlor at Hawk's Way, Candy had tried to figure out what it was about Garth Whitelaw that had caused her to fall in love with him. She had watched him with the horses he bred and trained and seen that he was capable of gentleness, infinite patience and compassion. Her only mistake had been in thinking that Garth would be able to transfer those emotions to human beings. He had turned out to be a hard, harsh and unforgiving man where women were concerned.

As they headed toward Garth's pickup truck for the ride to the hotel, Candy stole glances at the man she had once thought she loved. His face wasn't conventionally attractive. It was full of hard planes and gaunt hollows.

His dark brown eyes were feral, almost dangerous. He wore his black hair too long, down over his collar, and even his tan Western suit didn't make him look the least bit civilized.

His expression was brooding, his eyes hooded, his body taut with what Candy recognized as the first signs of desire. She felt a shiver run down her spine, aware of a sexual attraction to the rugged horseman which she thought had been put to rest forever.

Candy was grateful that the hotel was so close, since neither of them said anything to break the uncomfortable silence that had fallen between them in the truck. Once in the hotel restaurant, Garth took charge of ordering an iced tea for her and a whiskey for himself.

Candy didn't want to be interrupted when she told Garth what she wanted from him, so while they waited for their drinks to arrive, she asked about his family, whom she had met during her ill-fated visit three years before.

"Jesse and Tate are both married and have children," Garth said. "Faron…" He frowned and finished in a voice that didn't invite further probing, "Faron's gone to Wyoming on business."

"So you're all alone at the ranch now?"

"Except for Charlie One Horse."

"How is he?"

"As cantankerous as ever."

Candy knew Garth wasn't married, but she wanted to ask if he had a steady girlfriend. She resisted the impulse. It would bring back too many memories she wanted to forget. But she couldn't think of anything else to ask, either.

Fortunately, Garth picked up the slack. "I heard your

father's big black stud won another cutting horse futurity."

Candy smiled. "You mean Comanche Moon? That horse can stop on a dime and give you nine cents change," she said proudly. "There's a good chance he'll be World Champion Cutting Horse this year. Not that it'll be easy to beat Hawk's Honor. I know your stallion has proved he's a champion the past two years, but this year the title belongs to Comanche Moon."

"Any chance your father would let me buy him?"

Candy shook her head. "Comanche Moon isn't for sale. Dad wouldn't part with him for all the oil in Texas."

The waiter arrived with their drinks, and Candy fiddled with her tea, squeezing in lemon and stirring in sweetener to postpone the moment when she would have to make her proposal to the wrangler.

"All right," Garth said after he had taken a drink of whiskey. "Spit it out. What do you want?"

"I want to hire you to teach me everything you know about breeding and training cutting horses." She rushed on before he could interrupt. "If I want to be the best— and I do—I figure I need to learn from the best. That's you. As a rider, you've won every cutting horse competition there is. As a breeder, your horses have what it takes to win championships."

Garth was stunned by Candy's suggestion. It was a far cry from the sexual invitation he had been expecting. He was surprised at the sharp disappointment he felt that she wasn't seeking him out for more personal reasons. On the other hand, he was flattered by her obvious admiration for what he had accomplished with cutting horses. He was tempted to say he would take her on and teach her what he knew.

Two things stopped him. First, having her around would be a constant distraction from his work. There was no denying the way his body reacted to her. He wanted her, wanted to be deep inside her. If she came to Hawk's Way he would have her.

However, having her wasn't the problem. It was getting her to leave when he was tired of her. It was bound to get awkward if she stuck around to learn about cutting horses long after he had lost interest in having her in his bed. It never occurred to him that his interest in her wouldn't wane. No woman had ever held his attention for long after he had bedded her.

His second reason for refusing her was equally compelling. In Garth's experience, rich people thought they could buy anything with money. His mother, for one, had been tempted into an affair by the gifts of jewels and money a wealthy man had offered her. Garth Whitelaw wasn't about to hire himself out to anybody—especially not to some spoiled little rich girl.

Garth had been staring into his drink while he thought. Now he looked up and saw that Candy had caught her lower lip in her teeth. His belly tightened as he remembered the sweet taste of her. His voice grated with need when he spoke.

"I'm not interested. You go on back to college in the fall and finish your education."

Her eyes flashed with irritation, but her voice remained calm. "In the first place, I've graduated college. I went straight through and finished early. In the second place, I'm prepared to pay—"

"Keep your money, sweetheart. Now, if you'd like to make me a different proposition..." He let his voice trail off suggestively.

"Like what?" she asked hesitantly.

"Seems to me we have some unfinished business together."

Candy realized suddenly what Garth wanted from her. She felt the heat skating up her throat. She had hoped and prayed he had forgotten her youthful indiscretion. Here it was, back to haunt her. "I'm only interested in a business relationship, Garth. If you're worried about me making any other overtures, you can relax. I wouldn't dream of imposing myself on you."

"Unfortunately, I can't make the same promise. I find you a damned attractive woman. Now that you're not a virgin anymore, I can't guarantee I could keep my hands off you."

Candy opened her mouth to tell him "I am too a virgin!" and snapped it shut again. It would be too embarrassing to discuss such a thing, and he was bound to say something that would make her so furious she wouldn't be able to talk.

"What if I made it clear I didn't want anything to do with you?" she asked.

"I've never forced myself on a woman," Garth said. "I've never needed to." His smile was slow in coming, but no less devastating to her senses.

Candy pressed her thighs together, but that did nothing to stop the growing warmth between her legs. She was still determined to get what she wanted, even if it meant she would have to deal with Garth's sexual overtures. She could handle him. Especially since he had promised no force would be involved.

"Look," she said, "I'm willing to work with you on a purely professional basis if you'll just work with me."

"That's the point, sweetheart. I don't want to work with you."

Candy gritted her teeth to keep from snapping something back at Garth that would forever close the door to Hawk's Way. "I'll give you some time to think about it and—"

"I don't need time to think," Garth interrupted. "The answer is no. Not now, not ever."

"You are the most stubborn, most arrogant sonofa—"

Garth's eyes narrowed. "I think you've said enough."

There was something in his tone of voice that warned Candy he was at the end of his rope. One look at his face told her that words weren't going to change his mind. She hid her disappointment, not wanting to give him something else to throw back in her face. "All right, Garth. If that's the way you feel, I suppose I'll have to look elsewhere for someone to teach me what I want to know."

Garth wondered who she would find. Sam Longstreet at the Double Bar Ranch was good. He was a bachelor, too. Garth felt a sudden unreasonable jealousy, but forced it down. He stood when Candy did and reached out a hand to help her from the booth.

Candy slid out on her own. Her eyes met Garth's one last time, searching for any sign that he might relent. When she found none, she said, "Goodbye, Garth." Then she turned and walked away.

Garth stared after her, wondering if he had done the right thing. He sat back down and finished off his whiskey. Then, because he was beginning to think maybe he had been too hasty, he ordered another drink and nursed it while he tried to get the image of Candice Baylor out of his mind.

Meanwhile, Candy headed upstairs to the hotel suite

she shared with her father. She was glad he wasn't there, because by the time she arrived, she was on the verge of tears. Candy hadn't admitted to herself how much she had been counting on Garth Whitelaw to agree to her plan. She had tied up her hopes and dreams for the future in that one request. And it had been denied.

Candy slipped into her bedroom and closed the door behind her. She felt weary beyond words. She lay down on the bed and hugged a pillow to her chest, pressing it to her mouth to hold back the sobs that threatened.

It was dark when Candy's father knocked on her door.

"Candy? I've been waiting downstairs for you. I thought we were supposed to have supper together. Are you all right, honey?"

"I'm fine, Daddy." Candy quickly turned on a lamp and swiped at her eyes, which were red from all the crying she had done.

"Can I come in?" he asked.

She jumped up and crossed to the bathroom for a damp cloth. She dabbed at her eyes, trying to undo the ravages her tears had left. "Come on in, Daddy."

When she came out of the bathroom, her father took one look at her and said, "What happened? What's wrong?"

"It shows, huh?"

He opened his arms and Candy crossed into them. With her father's arms around her she confessed what she had wanted to do and Garth's rejection of her proposal. Of course, she didn't mention anything about Garth's personal interest in her. Evan Baylor was very protective of his daughter and would likely make things worse by confronting the younger man.

"It doesn't matter, Daddy," she finished. "I suppose

it was pretty presumptuous to think he'd be willing to teach me. I'll find somebody else."

"But Garth Whitelaw is the best!" Evan protested.

Candy shrugged and managed a smile. "Then I guess I'll have to take second best."

Evan's mouth firmed. He hadn't started out as one of the richest men in Texas, and he had learned over the years how to get what he wanted. What he wanted now was to take that look of defeat and despair off his daughter's face. Which meant he had to find a way to get Garth Whitelaw to reverse his decision.

"Don't you worry, honey," Evan said. "Maybe when Garth thinks it over he'll change his mind."

"He sounded pretty definite about his decision," Candy said.

Evan didn't bother arguing with her. "You still hungry?"

"I'd rather have something sent up to the room, if you don't mind."

"Not at all," Evan said. That would give him a chance to hunt up Garth Whitelaw and see about changing the man's mind. "You order whatever you like. I think I'll go out and get myself a good steak. See you tomorrow morning."

"Good night, Daddy."

"Good night, honey." Evan gave his daughter a hug and received a kiss on the cheek. He adored his only child. She was the light of his life. He would do anything to see her happy. His eyes narrowed in calculation as he began to examine his options.

Evan headed back downstairs. Candy had left Garth Whitelaw in the hotel restaurant. There was just a chance the man was still there. Sure enough, as Evan entered the restaurant Garth was just on his way out. He had his arm around a luscious-looking redhead.

"Hello there, Garth," Evan said. "I see you've got yourself some entertainment for the evening."

"Yes, sir," Garth agreed with a grin.

"I wonder if I could take a few moments of your time before you retire. I have a proposition to make to you."

Garth glanced down at the redhead. She wasn't the woman he wanted, as Evan Baylor's appearance reminded him.

Evan took advantage of Garth's hesitation to hand the redhead a hundred dollar bill. "Why don't you go have yourself a drink?" he said.

The redhead looked from Garth to Evan and smiled broadly. "Why sure, mister. Whatever you say."

Garth's brow arched as what he saw reinforced both his distrust of women and his belief that the rich used their money to get what they wanted. He eyed Evan warily, but when the older man gestured, he joined him in a booth in the hotel bar.

"What are you drinking?" Evan asked.

"Whiskey."

Evan held up a twenty, and a waitress quickly appeared. "Two whiskeys," he said.

Garth remained silent. He knew Evan Baylor well enough to appreciate the man's shrewd business sense. He figured Evan wanted something from him, and it wasn't too hard to guess that it might have something to do with his recent conversation with Candy.

Evan didn't wait for the whiskeys. He got right down to business. "What would it take for you to accept my daughter's proposition?"

"I'm not for sale," Garth said flatly.

"Of course not," Evan placated. "But there must be something you want that you can't get on your own. Some new piece of land to expand Hawk's Way. Some new mare. Some stud you'd like to have."

"Did Candy put you up to this?" Garth demanded.

"She doesn't know I'm here. In fact, she's willing to settle for second best. I'm not. There must be something I have that you want," Evan insisted.

Garth started to tell Evan Baylor to go to hell. Then he thought of something Evan had that he wanted very much. "Comanche Moon," he said in a soft voice.

Evan hissed in a breath. "That stud's going to be World Champion Cutting Horse this year."

"That's my price." Garth was certain the old man would never pay it. That was the only reason he had even suggested it.

"Done."

"What?"

"You teach my daughter everything you know about cutting horses, and I'll give you Comanche Moon."

"What if she quits before I've taught her what I know?" Garth knew ways to make that happen.

Evan stared down at work-roughened hands. He might be rich, but he still worked from dawn to dusk each day. And he had taught his daughter everything he believed about hard work and persistence being the roads to success.

"Candy won't quit," Evan said certainly. He looked up at Garth. "I'm so sure she won't quit that if she does, I'll give you the stud anyway."

Garth shook his head. "If she quits, I buy the stud at a fair price." He didn't want to cheat Evan, and he was pretty certain Candy Baylor wasn't going to be hanging around Hawk's Way for very long. He didn't plan to make it easy on the girl if she came to live at his ranch. He had already told her there was only one thing he wanted from her. If he didn't end up fulfilling his part of the bargain with Evan because the girl couldn't handle everything he threw at her, Garth wanted to pay for the horse.

"Done." Evan held out his hand to be shaken by the other man. He knew his daughter well. Garth Whitelaw was in for a big surprise if he thought the girl would quit.

"There's one condition," Evan said. He knew how upset Candy got when he used his money to get his own way. His daughter was just stubborn enough to refuse to go along with the bargain if she found out the truth about the deal he had made with Garth. "You can't tell my daughter that I had anything to do with your change of mind."

"That's fine with me," Garth said. After all, he had just gotten through telling Candy he couldn't be bought. He wasn't willing to admit—even to himself—that he had spent the better part of the afternoon seeking some way to get Candy Baylor alone at Hawk's Way.

"One other thing," Evan said.

"Now what?"

"I know your reputation with women," Evan said.

Garth stiffened. "What does that have to do with anything?"

"I don't want my daughter hurt."

The warning was there, and the threat also. Garth wasn't offended. He had every intention of taking Candice Baylor to bed, and no intention at all of marrying her, so he could understand her father's concern. Nevertheless, Garth didn't believe Candy was going to suffer from their relationship.

"Rest assured, your daughter won't find herself in any situation she doesn't want to be in," he said at last.

That wasn't much comfort, but Evan realized it was the only reassurance he was going to get. He had a lot of confidence in his daughter. She had managed to handle herself in some pretty tight situations. "All right," he said. "I suppose that's the most I can ask. I'll make sure Candy is downstairs for breakfast tomorrow. Say about eight o'clock?"

"I'll be there," Garth said. "Don't worry. I'll take care of making the necessary excuses for my change of mind. Your daughter won't suspect a thing."

CHAPTER THREE

CANDY STARED SUSPICIOUSLY at Garth. Against all reason, he had joined her and her father for breakfast in the hotel dining room. Then her father had suddenly remembered an appointment and left her alone with the rancher.

"What's going on?" she demanded.

Garth shrugged. "I changed my mind."

Candy sat stunned for a moment. Then she smiled. "I'm so glad." Her face lit up with happiness, but it didn't take long for a shadow to cloud her joy. Her teeth caught her lower lip and her brow furrowed.

"What changed your mind, Garth? My father didn't—"

"I figured I'd have a better chance of getting what I want from you if I had you closer to home," Garth said.

"Oh." Candy thought about that for a moment. The roguish grin on Garth's face left little doubt what it was he really wanted from her in exchange for the knowledge she wanted from him. "I think it only fair to warn you that I'm the kind of girl who doesn't have to be burned twice to learn it's dangerous to stick your hand in the fire."

"Meaning?"

"Meaning I plan to keep my distance from you at Hawk's Way."

"That's going to be a little difficult, considering the

fact we'll be working side by side every day," Garth pointed out.

Candy gave an exasperated snort. "You know what I mean."

"I'm afraid I do. Lest there be any misunderstanding, I'm agreeing to this arrangement because I want you in my bed. I'm going to do my level best while you're at Hawk's Way to convince you to join me there. Now that all the cards are on the table, do you still want to come?"

"Oh, I'm coming," Candy reassured him. "That was never in doubt. Only, as long as we're both being so honest, I think you should know that I'm cured of the love or infatuation or whatever it was I felt for you three years ago. I won't set my heart on a platter and watch you refuse it again. You're welcome to do your best to seduce me. But I'd never have sex with a man I didn't love. If you're smart, you won't waste your time trying."

"It's my time." Garth was irritated, infuriated and not sure why. He didn't want her love. Why the hell would she think he cared whether she offered it to him? All he wanted was the pleasure two consenting adults could enjoy in bed together. Candy's opposition only increased his desire for her and made the chase that much more interesting. She would give in sooner or later. He had never met a woman yet who hadn't.

"I'll expect you at Hawk's Way by the end of next week," he said.

"So soon?"

Garth arched a questioning brow. "Is there something you need to do before you start?"

"Not really." Candy thought of the spring charity ball she had been planning to attend in Fort Worth. She would have to call Edward Vargas and break their date. "No, no problem at all," she said. "I'll be there next Friday."

ON THE FOLLOWING FRIDAY, Garth was on tenterhooks from the moment he woke up. He couldn't sit still for breakfast, and Charlie One Horse kicked him out of the kitchen when he complained about the coffee.

"Get out of here and go to work," Charlie ordered. "Either that filly'll show up or she won't. Worryin' about it ain't goin' to change anythin'."

Garth saddled up a three-year-old quarter horse and began working him in the corral. A cutting horse was bred and trained to separate a cow from the herd and keep it from rejoining the other animals.

In olden days, as now, cutting cattle from the herd was a necessary function in order to brand animals or to dose them with medicine. Garth had the satisfaction of knowing that the sport for which he trained his horses also had a utilitarian purpose. Some horses were suited for the sport and thrived on the competition. Others didn't. The ability to stop and turn on a dime was of ultimate importance if the horse was going to be able to keep ahead of the cow.

Garth put the three-year-old through his paces, making sure to stop and back the horse at each turn so the animal kept his weight on his heels, giving his front end mobility. He gripped the saddle horn and hung on, giving commands with his knees while the horse leaped, dodged and wheeled with breathtaking speed to keep the cow at bay.

Garth was concentrating hard on what he was doing. It wasn't until he gave his horse a pat on the neck at the end of the workout that he realized Candy had been standing with her arms folded over the top rail of the corral watching him.

"He's wonderful!" she said.

"He needs more work," Garth countered.

Candy bit back the compliment she had been about to make about Garth's riding, certain he would only contradict her about that, as well.

Garth kneed the stallion toward Candy as she slipped through the wooden bars and approached him. When Garth stepped down from the saddle, Candy ran her hands knowingly over the quarter horse checking his conformation. She looked to see whether he had low hocks that could handle the abrupt stops, slides and pivots required of a cutting horse.

"He's a beauty," she said. "What's his name?"

"Stop and Go."

Candy grinned. "That certainly fits." She followed Garth as he led the horse into the barn to unsaddle him. "What were you teaching him today?"

"The basics," Garth said, unconsciously beginning the lessons he had promised to teach. "Traveling with the cow. Stopping, collecting, and moving his front end to stay with the cow."

Garth led the horse into one of the stalls. Candy closed the door behind him, then stood on the bottom rail and leaned over to watch while Garth unsaddled the animal.

"I noticed Stop and Go works with his head up. Does that slow him down?" she asked.

Garth shook his head. "All horses are different. Some work with their heads up, some down. What's most important is the stop that sets up the turn." Garth temporarily set the saddle on the side of the stall, slipped off the bridle and replaced it with a halter.

Candy stepped down off the stall door and opened it as Garth came back through with the sweaty horse.

"You can take him out back and hose him off now," Garth said.

Candy opened her mouth to say that bathing horses wasn't what she had come to learn but shut it again. She had made up her mind to follow directions and do what she was told. That way there was less chance of a confrontation with Garth.

A look down at what she was wearing made Candy grimace. The designer jeans, red silk shirt and matching red boots she had worn to travel in were a little fancy for hosing down horses. "Can you give me a minute to change?"

"Never mind. I'll do it myself."

Garth was being totally unreasonable, but Candy wasn't about to give him the opportunity to say later that she cared more about her clothes than the job. "Give him to me," she said. "I'll take care of him."

Candy accidentally brushed the crisp hairs across the back of Garth's hand as she took the lead rope from him. It felt as though she had been zapped with an electrical shock. She stared at the wrangler with a stricken expression.

Before she even considered asking Garth to teach her about cutting horses, Candy had convinced herself she was over her infatuation with the wrangler. Her reaction to the mere touch of his hand was a shock—both literally and figuratively.

Candy had believed herself no longer susceptible to Garth's powerful animal magnetism. Since she had firmly quashed the strong emotional feelings of three years ago, she had figured there was not much the cowboy could do to entice her into his bed. Thus, she was confounded by the surge of sexual excitement she had just experienced.

Candy stood frozen for a second, staring at the spot where she had touched Garth. For the sake of the horse, she forced herself to move slowly rather than jerking her hand away. But once she and Garth were no longer touching, she quickly headed out the back door of the stable.

"Don't get too wet," he called after her.

Candy shot him a look over her shoulder. "Don't worry, Boss. I won't melt." In fact, a dousing with cold water might be just what she needed to cool off.

As Garth watched the sway of two rear ends moving away from him, it suddenly dawned on him how quickly and easily Candy had insinuated herself into his workday.

One thing Garth hadn't considered when he told Candy he would teach her was whether she would be an apt pupil. It appeared that she was serious about learning the art of breeding and training cutting horses. Which added an entirely different dimension to their relationship.

All Garth's plans had evolved around the physical connection he planned to have with Candy. Now he was going to have to deal with her on intellectual terms, as well. He smiled wryly. That was certainly going to be a first for him. He had always kept business and pleasure separate in the past.

Garth stepped to the next stall and began saddling another horse, a two-year-old he had raised from birth.

He soon found that he had certainly been right about the fact that Candy would prove a distraction. The third time he let the colt get away with turning before he made a stop, Garth ended the lesson. He didn't want the horse to end up with bad habits because his trainer's mind had strayed to some female.

Meanwhile, Candy had turned over the cooled-down quarter horse to one of the hands working in the stable and headed back to the house for a change of clothes. The silk blouse hadn't survived the encounter. The red boots would be fine to work in, but she wouldn't be dressing up in them again. She figured she better find out where Charlie One Horse had put her suitcases.

Candy stopped and stared at the place that would be her home for the next several months. She had fallen in love with Hawk's Way the first time she had seen it. The ranch house was an imposing two-story white frame structure that looked a lot like an antebellum mansion. It had four twenty-foot-high fluted columns along its face and railed first-and second-story porches that ran the length of the house. The road leading to the house was lined with magnolias, while the house itself was shaded by the branches of a moss-laden live oak.

For all its grandeur outside, the house was very much a home. The oak and pine furniture that had been passed down from generation to generation showed the hard wear of frontier life. However, though gouged and scraped, it was kept polished to a fine sheen.

Candy pulled the screen door open and entered the kitchen. "Charlie? Where are you, Charlie?" When she got no answer, she headed upstairs. She expected to find her things in the guest bedroom where she had stayed the last time she had come to Hawk's Way. A glance inside the room showed it was bare.

Candy pursed her lips and began a search from room to room upstairs. Each room showed the personality of its former occupant, and Candy got images of Garth's siblings—independent, uncontrolled, unpredictable—as she passed from one room to another. Each step took her closer to the end of the hall, where she knew Garth slept. Sure enough, she found her suitcases in the bedroom next to his. Candy frowned.

She walked in and closed the door behind her, muttering her displeasure as she began stripping off her wet clothes. There was nothing subtle about the message Garth was sending. It was only a step or two from her bedroom to his.

Despite her anger at Garth's blatant manipulation, she had to admire the room itself. The canopy over the bed was trimmed in eyelet lace, as was the spread. The dry sink and chest were antiques, and the back of the rocker beside the bed was hand-carved. Garth had put her in a room that held a wealth of Whitelaw heritage. Candy could almost feel the love and hate, the hope and despair of the generations of Whitelaws who had slept in this room.

The view from the window took Candy's breath away. The mountainous Palo Duro Canyon area was rugged terrain that had once provided a haven for raiding Comanches. It was a landscape as harsh and unforgiving as the man who owned it.

She was just buttoning up a blue chambray shirt when the door opened.

"Candy? It's Garth. Are you in there?"

"Garth, I—" Before Candy could say she didn't have

her jeans on yet, Garth opened the door. She glared at him and said, "You could have knocked."

"I'm glad I didn't." Garth found himself treated to the sight of Candy's bare legs beneath the tails of a Western shirt. "I just came up to ask whether you'd like to take a ride with me. I have to check on some stock in the north pasture."

"I'd like that." She hesitated, then said, "I want to know why I'm not staying in the same room I used the last time I was here."

"The answer to that ought to be obvious. I wanted you close to me."

Candy's fists landed on her hips. "It's not going to make any difference where you put me. I'm not going to go to bed with you."

"Then it won't matter if you stay here," Garth shot back. His eyes slid to her legs where another inch or two of flesh had been exposed when her fisted hands gathered the shirt at her waist. His heart, which was already thudding from his race upstairs in search of her, picked up a beat.

For a few hectic minutes when he couldn't find Candy anywhere around the barn, Garth had feared she had packed up and gone home. He refused to admit how relieved he was to discover her here. He let his eyes feast on the sight of her.

"If you're through ogling, I'd like to finish getting dressed," Candy said.

Garth tipped his hat in acknowledgment of her demand, turned and sauntered out the door. He stopped just beyond the threshold and said, "If you're not at the barn in five minutes, I'm leaving without you."

Candy slammed the door behind him. She considered making him wait on her, then admitted he probably wouldn't. At which point she grabbed a pair of Levi's and jerked them on, tucked in her shirt and added a tooled leather belt. Then she sat down on the canopy bed, pulled on socks and stuck her feet into a pair of sturdy Western boots.

Four and a half minutes later she was standing at the door to the barn. Garth walked down the center aisle leading two saddled horses. He handed the reins of a bay gelding with four white stockings to Candy and led a coal-black stallion out of the barn for himself.

Candy checked the length of the stirrups and the cinch to make sure it was tight. Then she mounted and followed Garth down a dirt road that led to the north pasture. She was pleased to note that Garth had put her on a spirited animal, but she felt self-conscious as the wrangler evaluated her seat on the horse. She forced herself to relax. She had learned to ride before she could walk and had been a champion herself in several eighteen-and-under junior cutting horse futurities.

Still, she breathed a sigh of relief when Garth said, "I'm glad to see you've got an easy hand on a horse's mouth. That's one less thing I'll have to teach you."

"I'm willing to take pointers on anything you think could stand improvement," she said.

"That's good to know. Because I have a suggestion."

"Oh?" Candy tensed.

"Relax. I'm not going to bite you. At least, not anytime soon."

Candy laughed. "Be careful. I might bite back." She made the mistake of looking at Garth and saw the sudden leap of desire in his eyes. "Forget I said that," she muttered.

Fortunately they had reached the pasture where several mares and their foals were grazing along with some stock that was still too young to be ridden. Candy dismounted and, following Garth's lead, tied her horse to the closest fence post. Garth's stallion whinnied at the mares, who looked up and then went back to grazing again. Candy wished she could be so nonchalant when Garth demanded her attention.

She assessed the quarter horse mares and realized she was seeing the best of the best. She whistled her appreciation. To her surprise, one of the yearling colts began trotting toward her. Then she realized Garth had slipped through the fence and was holding an apple in his palm, waiting for the colt to approach.

After sidestepping and tossing his head several times, the yearling walked over to Garth and took the apple from him. As the chestnut-colored colt stood there munching, Garth handled the animal, running his hands over its neck and chest, down over the withers and back to the hindquarters, then down the legs and up again.

"Come here," he said to Candy in a quiet voice.

Candy joined him, and he began another lesson. He stepped behind her, took her hand in his and made the same journey as before. Only this time, his hand moved hers across the colt's sleek coat, pointing out the yearling's good and bad points for her edification.

At last he moved to the colt's head. "He's short between the eye and muzzle, has a wide forehead, a nicely defined jowl and a straight profile. His eyes are wideset, and his ears are set forward and close to each other. Damn near perfect."

Garth let go of Candy's hand at last, but he didn't step back. Their bodies were aligned so that each could feel the other's heat. Candy forced herself to focus on the horse, not the man standing behind her. She scratched the blaze on the colt's face and said, "You didn't comment on the way his neck meets his shoulder."

Garth had his right hand on the colt's withers and reached past her with his left to run a hand down the colt's neck, effectively trapping her between his arms. "It might be a bit low, but not enough to make a difference," he said at last.

Candy felt Garth's moist breath against her cheek when he spoke. She turned slightly and realized that their mouths were only inches apart. She raised her eyes to his and saw they were hooded, the dark eyes lambent. She was appalled at the desire that pooled between her legs. Her breasts felt full and achy. Her nipples were erect.

Candy stood frozen as Garth lowered his mouth to hers. She was prepared for violence. It was what she expected, and it would have freed her from his thrall. His lips barely touched hers before they retreated, only to return for another taste. She kept her mouth closed, but he made love to her lips, kissing first one edge and then the other of her mouth before sliding his tongue along the seam.

Candy moaned when she felt Garth's tongue slip between her lips. The warmth, the wetness, made her feel weak. She needn't have worried about falling. Garth's hand slid around her waist and turned her to face him, sealing their bodies together from the waist down. There was no mistaking his arousal, which only intensified her own disjointed feelings.

Candy pressed the heels of her hands against Garth's chest with the thought of pushing him away, but instead her fingers curled into his cotton shirt, clutching him tight.

Candy was in way over her head. She knew how sexually experienced Garth was, and that she had to guard against his persuasiveness. But it was that experience which made him so successful in his seduction. Whenever she seemed reluctant for him to go a step further, he backed off. So a love bite on her throat that drew a guttural groan from her was followed by teasing kisses that had her melting in his arms.

His fingers tunneled into her hair and held her still for a ravishing kiss, then slid down to her nape and gently massaged the tender flesh there.

Candy was far more innocent than Garth knew. Her disastrous experience with him three years ago had kept her from letting things get very far with the men she had dated in college. No man besides Garth had ever touched her.

So when Garth's hand slid up to cup her breast, it recalled the memory of how he had hurt her in the past. She cried out in anticipation of the pain and jerked herself from his grasp. Her cry frightened the colt, which turned and kicked up its heels.

Garth grabbed her and threw them both out of the way of the colt's slashing hooves. He took the brunt of the fall, protecting her in his arms. When they finished rolling, he was lying on top of her in the grass.

Candy stared up at him, eyes wide with fright.

"You damn fool! Don't you know better than to shout like that around a horse?" Garth said between gritted teeth.

"I was—"

"What were you yelling for, anyway? I know damn well I didn't hurt you!" he ranted.

"Not *this* time," Candy retorted.

She watched a muscle work in Garth's jaw, but his tirade abruptly ended. She gave his shoulders a push. "You can get off me now."

Garth took most of his weight off her, but he didn't free her. The grass was surprisingly cool beneath her, and several blades tickled the back of her neck. She closed her eyes and turned her face away, unable to bear the taunting look on his face. But he didn't allow her to hide from him for long. He grasped her chin and turned her face toward him.

"Open your eyes, Candy."

"No, Garth."

He lowered his body so that he was cradled between her thighs. He was aroused again. Or still. Candy didn't know which, but it hardly mattered.

"Open your eyes," he demanded.

She blinked against the sun's glare and stared at him in defiance. "Let me up."

"In a minute. First, we have a few things to get settled."

"I don't want to hear anything you have to say."

"That's too damn bad," Garth said. "I think what just happened between us proves you're not indifferent to me."

Candy's lips pressed flat. She couldn't deny the rush of passion she had felt in Garth's arms. Or the fact that she had enjoyed every moment of his kisses. But she still wasn't sophisticated enough to accept the fact that she could feel sexual desire for a man she wasn't even sure she liked.

When she remained stubbornly silent, Garth commanded, "Talk to me, Candy."

"What do you want me to say? That I enjoyed what happened? I did. That I want to repeat the experience? I don't! You're pushing too far, too fast, Garth."

Garth eased his body away from hers. Her outburst was something he understood. A woman liked a little courting before she succumbed to a man. He was willing to play the game, now that Candy had told him the rules. "Sure, sweetheart. Whatever you say."

Garth rose and pulled Candy to her feet. He began dusting her off, but she slapped his hands away. "Leave me alone. I can take care of myself."

She swatted the last of the grass from her fanny, then turned back around to face Garth. "What are you grinning at?"

"Can't a man smile when he's happy?"

Candy scowled. She marched past Garth toward where she had left the gelding tied and heard Garth following close behind her. She felt the heat of him, smelled the musky scent of aroused male that even three years later had the power to make her remember the taste of him. Candy turned, forcing Garth to stop in his tracks.

She jabbed a finger at his chest and said, "Don't push me, Garth. You won't like what I'll do."

Garth's grin widened. "Try me."

Pushed to the limit, Candy took him at his word. Her hand arced and her open palm hit his cheek with a loud crack. She was appalled at the clear imprint of her hand on his face and the dark flush that quickly followed. Garth's eyes narrowed, and his lips flattened, but he made no move to retaliate.

Candy trembled, shaken by the attack, which had surprised her as much as it had Garth. She swallowed over the sudden thickness in her throat. "I... I didn't mean..."

"Forget it," Garth snapped. "We'd better be getting back to the house. Charlie will have supper waiting for us."

Candy mounted her horse and rode back to the ranch house in silence. She couldn't imagine what had caused her to react so violently to Garth's provocation. She had never hit anyone before in her life.

When the ranch house came into sight, Candy realized that if she didn't want to have to apologize in front of Charlie One Horse she had better do it now. "I'm sorry."

Garth eyed her askance. "It's not the first time I've been slapped."

Candy flushed. "It's the first time *I've* slapped someone," she retorted. "Are you going to accept my apology, or not?"

"Apology accepted."

As they dismounted at the stable, Candy had the awful feeling that Garth wasn't the sort of man who easily forgave and forgot. She was bound to him and Hawk's Way for the next several months, at least until she had learned enough to feel confident about opening her own stable. Now they were engaged in a war of nerves. He was determined to have her; she was determined to resist him.

Candy had been certain she could hold her own against any efforts Garth made to seduce her. As she had just discovered, things weren't turning out quite like she had planned. She made up her mind that she, for one, wasn't going to be the next tempting morsel on Garth Whitelaw's plate. Because as she knew from bitter experience, the wrangler ate up little rich girls, and spit them out when he was done.

CHAPTER FOUR

CHARLIE ONE HORSE was bent over, checking the pot roast in the oven, when Candy came through the kitchen on her way upstairs. She mumbled something about washing up and disappeared in the direction of the stairs. Charlie took one look at Garth's face as he stepped through the screen door and poured him a whiskey from the bottle he kept over the stove. "What you been doin' to that girl got her so mad she whacked you?"

Garth rubbed his cheek, wondering how Charlie knew he had been slapped. To his chagrin, he felt several scratches left by Candy's nails. "Stay out of it, Charlie." Garth sat down at the heavy oak table in the center of the kitchen. He downed the finger of whiskey and held out his glass for another.

"She ain't like them other women of yours," Charlie said as he poured the second whiskey.

"Candy knew what she was getting into when she agreed to come here," Garth said. "Let it go, Charlie. This is none of your business."

"Ain't nothin' ever my business, but I'm the one gotta put up with your bad temper when some female's givin' you fits."

"Charlie." Garth's voice held a warning tone that made the housekeeper look behind him. Candy was standing in the kitchen doorway.

"Are we eating in here?" she asked.

"You can forget the silver and crystal," Garth said. "You're not a guest at Hawk's Way anymore."

Candy stuck her hands in the pockets of her jeans to hide her agitation. "I wasn't expecting any special treatment. I was just asking where supper is being served."

"I'm afraid I have to disappoint you there, too," Garth said. "The food's on the stove. Every man helps himself."

Charlie shot Garth an incredulous look. That was the first he had heard of such a practice. When the family was home they ate supper in the dining room. Charlie usually served the meal, although Tate or Faron sometimes took a turn.

Charlie picked up a pair of pot holders, took the pot roast out of the oven and plopped it on top of the stove. He looked pointedly at Garth. "Here it is. Dig in."

Garth gave Charlie a baleful stare which the old man ignored.

Charlie took out two plates and filled them with roast beef, potatoes and carrots. He handed one plate to Candy and took the other for himself, then made sure they had silverware and glasses of tea. He settled on a chair on the opposite side of the table from Garth and pulled out a chair next to him for Candy.

"Delicious," Candy said as she dug in. "You really are a good cook, Charlie."

"Thanks, girl."

Garth was torn between his hunger and his pride. Finally he got up and served himself a plate of food. "We'll start work at dawn tomorrow," he said to Candy. "You might as well learn how and what we feed our stock."

"Don't you hire people to take care of that sort of thing?" Candy asked.

"Sure," Garth said. "But somebody has to tell them what to do. Parasite prevention, fresh water, proteins, vitamins and minerals and the right amount of forage are all as important as the right amount and kind of feed."

Candy felt a little overwhelmed. "Am I going to learn all that?"

"That's up to you. But it's as true of horses as it is of humans—you are what you eat. If you want healthy animals, you have to pay attention to nutrition."

Candy nodded her head in understanding. "I see what you mean. All right. Is there some sort of literature that explains all that?"

Charlie exchanged a look with Garth. Apparently there was more to the spoiled little rich girl than met the eye.

Garth had known Candy was clever. Now she had proved she was also inquisitive, which was not a bad trait for a pupil. "Sure," he said. "I've got lots of stuff you can read. If you come into the parlor with me after supper—"

Candy nearly choked on a bite of food. Charlie slapped her on the back, but it took a moment for her to stop coughing. She wasn't about to follow that beast back into his den anytime soon.

Garth swore under his breath when he realized that Candy's memory of their encounter three years ago was as vivid as his own. He stood, leaving his food half finished. "I'll put the books on my desk. You can get them on your way upstairs later. I'm going out."

"Where you goin'?" Charlie asked. "You gotta be up early in the mornin'."

"None of your business," Garth snapped. He grabbed his hat from the rack by the back door and slapped it on his head, letting the screen door slam behind him. Then he turned right back around and stomped back through the kitchen into the parlor. They could hear books dropping on his desk. A moment later he returned. "Don't stay up late reading," he snarled. Then he was gone.

"Wonder what got into him," Charlie muttered.

Candy wasn't about to explain. She was grateful for Garth's willingness to provide the books, which led her to believe that even if he intended to pursue her, he also intended to uphold his end of the bargain.

She stayed in the kitchen long enough to help Charlie with the dishes, even though the old man said he could manage. "Things are easier when there's another pair of helping hands," Candy said as she scraped the remains of Garth's supper into the disposal.

Charlie handed her his plate and said, "I didn't think rich folks did their own dishes."

Candy smiled wryly. "My father raised me to believe in the work ethic. If he spoiled me, it was by making me believe that I could have anything I wanted if I was willing to work hard enough for it."

"So why you want to go into the horse-raisin' business?" Charlie asked.

"There's a lot of history and tradition involved with cutting horses. I want to be a part of it."

"You got all the money a gal would ever need. Why not just buy up a ranch and let somebody else manage it for you?"

"I want the satisfaction of breeding my own horses and training them to be champions. That's why I came here." She refused to admit to any other reason than her stated one, even to herself.

"Then you better get on out of here and get to those books," Charlie said. "I'll finish up."

Candy didn't want to leave, but she found herself unable to fight both Charlie and the desire to dig into the materials Garth had left for her on his desk.

It felt strange stepping into the parlor. Looking back, she wondered where she had gotten the courage to confront Garth Whitelaw and tell him she loved him. She felt extreme embarrassment—and a great sense of loss—when she looked back on that evening.

The fireplace was as cold now as it had been that long-ago night, no more than a blackened hearth. She walked up to the mantel, above which hung a map that delineated the vast borders of Hawk's Way past and present. Someday she would have a place of her own, and in the years to come her children and grandchildren would be able to point back to the moment when she had taken that first step.

Candy crossed to the rolltop desk where Whitelaw business had been conducted over the past hundred years. There sat a stack of books and pamphlets nearly a foot high. She picked up the one on top and read: *Horse Feeding and Management.* And another: *Rules of Thumb for Equine Feeding.* And another: *Feed a Horse Like a Horse.* She thumbed through a thick book as she crossed to the leather chair by the fireplace. She turned on the standing lamp beside the chair, sat down and put her feet up on the rawhide stool at its foot and began to read.

Garth was calling himself seven kinds of a fool for leaving the comfort of his home to drive around in his pickup. He hadn't had any specific destination in mind when he had left, only the desperate need to escape. So naturally he found an excuse not to go anyplace when all he really wanted to do was return home. Near midnight Garth decided that Candy must surely be in bed, and he would have the parlor to himself for a drink, which he sorely needed.

Because Garth believed everyone to be asleep, he entered the house quietly. He headed straight for the parlor, but was brought up short when he realized there was still a light on in the room. He crossed the threshold with matching amounts of reluctance and eagerness, afraid of what he might find.

She was there.

Candy was sound asleep, stretched out in his chair. One bare foot rested on the rawhide stool. The other was draped over the arm of the chair. Her boots were strewn like fallen soldiers beside the stool. A book lay open across her stomach, and her cheek rested on her hand on the arm of the chair.

She looked young and vulnerable, and he felt a sudden anger that she should be there waiting for him. He approached her like a wolf drawn by the bait, but wary of the steel jaws of the trap waiting to snap shut on him.

He knelt beside the chair and softly called her name. "Candy."

She made a sound in her throat which he took to be a subconscious acknowledgment of his presence, but otherwise she didn't move.

He knew he should wake her up and send her to bed, but he couldn't resist the opportunity to look at her at his leisure. He had never before noticed the tiny wisps of hair at her temples or the mole just below her ear or the slight jut of her chin. Her lashes created a feathery crescent along cheeks that bore the tiniest of freckl

The fingernails that had scratched him were her own, cut short and covered with a clear polish.

He ran a finger over lips that looked as sweet as strawberries. She instinctively turned her face toward his caress, much as a baby might when nudged by a mother's breast. Garth's physical reaction was powerful and instantaneous. He bit back the oath that sought voice. The last thing he wanted was to wake her up so she could see him on his knees looking every bit like he was worshiping at her feet. Not that he was. He just found her fascinating to look at.

He picked up the book on her lap, closed it and set it on top of a stack of six or seven beside the chair. Apparently she had done a lot of reading while he was gone. The more he learned about Candy Baylor the less certain he became of who she really was. None of the growing list of adjectives he could apply to her left him feeling the least bit satisfied. He didn't want to admire her intelligence or her curiosity or her determination. He wanted to enjoy a romp in bed with her.

Garth knew he could probably arouse Candy enough while she slumbered that by the time she was completely awake she would gladly join him in bed. He found himself strangely reluctant to take advantage of her that way. Which made him wonder what it was about Candy Baylor that kept him from acting the way he normally would with any other woman.

She wasn't the most beautiful woman he had ever known, though she was pretty enough. Perhaps it was the way she looked at him with those light gray eyes of hers that caused that achy feeling in his chest. Not that she used them to flirt with—at least, not this time around. They were clear and honest and there was nothing of the deceit he had expected—and often found—in other women.

Perhaps it was the fact that she absorbed everything he taught her like a sponge. Or that she didn't mind getting her hands dirty. Or ruining an expensive silk shirt. Or eating supper at the kitchen table when he was idiot enough to suggest that that was how they did things at Hawk's Way.

He wondered what would have happened if he had taken her up on her offer three years ago. What if he had made love to her—really made love to her—both giving and accepting the love she offered in return?

Garth felt his stomach clench and recognized the feeling as cold, stark fear. He had seen how his mother's unfaithfulness eventually destroyed his father. The old man had gotten drunk every night to forget the pain. One day he hadn't quite sobered up before he went to work and had come off a bucking horse and broken his neck. Garth had been left with the responsibility of holding both Hawk's Way and the family together.

Garth had made a vow that he would never let himself care for any woman enough that she could destroy him the way his father had been destroyed. In the years since his mother's infidelity he hadn't allowed himself to even think of a woman in terms of love.

Until he had met Candy Baylor.

Garth hadn't realized the emptiness, the loneliness he had felt over the past three years until she came back into his life. It was getting harder every day to convince himself that all he felt for her was desire.

Which made him all the more convinced that what he ought to do was get her bedded and out of his life before his feelings for her made him as vulnerable to a broken heart as his father had been.

Garth considered leaving Candy where she was. One look at the awkward angle of her neck convinced him that if he did, she wouldn't be much use to him in the morning. He slid one arm under her shoulders and scooped up her legs with the other. As he stood, she rolled down his arms and settled against his chest. Her face burrowed against him, and she said something unintelligible in her sleep.

In vain, Garth fought the feelings of possessiveness and protectiveness that rose within him. He hugged her a little closer and dropped a kiss on her forehead. "Come on, sweetheart. It's time for bed."

"Good night," she mumbled.

He carried her up the stairs and down the hall. The hardest thing he had ever done in his life was to stop at her bedroom door rather than traveling two steps farther to his own. He reached out with two fingers and dragged the spread off the bed before he laid her on it. She immediately curled into a ball on her side and murmured a sigh of satisfaction.

He would have loved to undress her, but he didn't trust his willpower that far. He pulled the spread back up over her shoulder, set the alarm clock beside the bed for 5:00 a.m. and left the room, closing the door behind him.

The next morning, the look on Candy's face was sheepish when she arrived in the kitchen for breakfast.

"Did you put me to bed?" she asked Garth.

Garth grunted his assent.

"Thank you. I guess I fell asleep. I'm sorry to be a bother."

"Next time go to bed when you're tired," he said.

Candy winced at the irritation in his voice.

"Did you learn anything?" he asked.

Candy gave him an excited recitation on equine digestion that ended with, "I had no idea all of that went on inside a horse."

Garth couldn't help smiling at her enthusiasm. She talked the whole distance to the barn and asked surprisingly astute questions as he and one of the hands, a young man named Tom Handy, fed the horses in the stable.

"Who feeds the horses in the north pasture?" she asked.

"Tom will take care of that. We've got other business to do today."

"Oh?"

"How would you like to take a turn on Stop and Go?"

Candy stared at him. "You're going to let me ride him?"

"I'd rather you started with a horse who knows what he's doing while I teach you the basics. Then I'll give you a horse of your own to bring along from scratch," Garth explained.

Candy hadn't expected to be allowed to work one of Garth's horses so soon. Although when she thought about it, how else was Garth going to teach her to train cutting horses except to put her on an animal and give her instructions about what she was doing right and wrong?

Two hours later, Candy was having second thoughts about riding, cutting horses and Garth Whitelaw, in that order.

Garth touched her constantly. All under the guise of teaching her, of course. The position of her hands, the angle of her heels, the shape of her shoulders, nothing escaped his notice. When he wasn't touching her, he was barking orders.

"When the cow goes, you go. When the cow stops, you stop. Back the horse up to reinforce the stop!"

Candy had grabbed the saddle horn and hung on, using her knees to let the horse know what she wanted from him.

"Stay down in the saddle. Push your pelvis forward. Not like that! Hold up there."

Garth marched out to her and put a hand on her rear end and a hand on her belly. "Tuck in your rear end. Sit deep in the saddle and stay with the horse's movement. Understand?"

Candy was so flustered by the feel of Garth's hands on her where no other man had ever dared put them, that she couldn't find her voice to object.

"Understand?" he demanded.

Candy nodded. "You can take your hands off me now."

Garth seemed to realize suddenly where his hands were. To Candy's chagrin he drew them away slowly, making his touch a caress. She closed her eyes and bit her lip to keep from moaning.

When she opened her eyes again, Garth was on the other side of the fence. Apparently he had recognized the danger, as well.

"Concentrate on getting the horse to travel with the cow. Keep his head aimed at the cow's shoulder."

Candy nudged Stop and Go with her knees.

"Don't pressure the cow!" Garth warned.

Candy backed the horse off slightly.

"Now you're too late!" Garth remonstrated. "Travel with the cow. Travel with the cow!"

Candy was more exhausted than Stop and Go when the training session was over, but she believed both she and the horse were doing better. She waited for a word of praise from Garth. It didn't come.

"Unsaddle him and wash him down," Garth ordered. "When you get done, come back and you can watch me with the two-year-old I'm working."

"Yes, sir, your highness," Candy muttered as she rode past Garth out of the corral.

She hadn't thought she had spoken loud enough to be heard. An instant later Garth had yanked her out of the saddle, and she was standing on the ground in front of him.

"There's no royalty around here, sweetheart. Just hard-working cowboys. If you've got a problem with that, we can finish the business between ourselves, and you can skedaddle on home."

Garth emphasized his point by pulling Candy into his arms and kissing her hard. Candy kept her teeth clenched, but he used his hands on her cheeks to force her mouth open so he could thrust his tongue inside. He wasn't gentle, and she had the feeling he wanted her to fight him.

Candy was smarter than that. She kissed him back. She slipped her tongue into his mouth and tasted him the way he had tasted her. It was a toss-up which of them was more surprised by what she had done. Desire speared through her, powerful and demanding.

She forced herself to think, rather than feel. This was a war of nerves as much as a seduction. She was determined not to succumb to the desire that demanded satisfaction. If anybody cried uncle, it wasn't going to be her.

Every place Garth touched her, she touched him back. Shoulders. Arms. Chest. Buttocks.

Both of them were gasping when he broke the kiss at last.

"Damn you, girl! You've left that horse standing there with the sweat drying on him. Take care of him!"

Candy was furious at Garth's accusation. He was as much responsible for the horse being left unattended as she was. But she wasn't about to lose her temper and give Garth a reason either to send her packing or seduce her further. "Next time stay out of my way!" she snapped as she crossed past him.

Garth stared after Candy as she picked up the reins and led the cutting horse back around behind the barn. He was shaken by how close he had come to having her right here in the open. Never had he become aroused so quickly or so completely from a woman's touch. When he was with her he felt like he was riding the edge of a steep cliff. It wasn't going to take much more to shove him off.

Similar thoughts were running through Candy's mind. She had never understood the power of her passions. It wasn't the least bit comforting to know that all Garth had to do was touch her and she responded. From the way things had gone today, every lesson was going to be a trial.

Over the next several weeks Candy realized that she had been mistaken about her feelings for Garth. To her horror, she discovered that the infatuation she had felt for him at seventeen wasn't gone at all. It had always been there, buried somewhere beneath the embarrassment and humiliation she had suffered that evening in his arms.

Every time Garth touched her—and he touched her as often as he could find an excuse—she was forced to deal not only with her body's instant reaction to his physical presence, but the growing knowledge that her heart and mind were equally involved with the man.

Candy knew the day was coming when Garth would push her too far, and she would have to make a choice. Candy couldn't decide whether it would hurt more to make love to him when she knew he didn't love her, or to leave and know that she could never come back.

During breakfast on the Fourth of July, Charlie One Horse announced that he was spending the holiday in Amarillo where he could see the parade and the fireworks.

"You two wanta come along?" Charlie asked.

"We've got work to do," Garth answered him.

Candy laughed. "It's a holiday. Surely we can—" The fierce look in Garth's dark eyes cut her off.

Garth turned to Charlie and said, "We'll be staying here."

Charlie shrugged. "Suit yourselves."

When Candy heard Charlie's rattletrap truck heading down the magnolia-lined lane, a frisson of alarm ran down her spine. It dawned on her suddenly that the old man had provided a much-needed buffer between her and Garth. Now that buffer was gone.

The difference was immediately noticeable. There was a subtle tension between them that made the horses skittish. Stop and Go performed badly, and Candy had to bite her tongue to keep from apologizing for what wasn't her fault.

"That's enough."

Garth's order, coming as it did long before sunset, told Candy she wasn't the only one who had noticed the difference. He followed her inside and watched her with hooded eyes while she unsaddled the horse and put away the tack. Then, for the first time since she had come to Hawk's Way, Garth joined her when she took Stop and Go out back to rinse him off.

Naturally, with Garth watching her, Candy was all thumbs.

"I'll do that," he volunteered.

Candy gratefully handed him the hose and was surprised when he turned it on her.

She stared at him aghast. Water dripped from her eyelashes, nose and chin. Her blouse was plastered to her body. "What did you do that for?" she spluttered.

Garth grinned. "I figured you needed to cool off, too."

It only took Candy two seconds to reach Garth and another two seconds to wrestle the hose in his direction. The two of them drenched each other, laughing over who was getting the wettest.

"We'd better go get dried off," Garth said at last.

Candy followed the direction of his gaze. She looked down and realized he could see her bra through her shirt. From the avid look in Garth's eyes, she knew he was seeing more than a hint of lace. If she could see his nipples through his soaked shirt, she suspected her bra wasn't doing a much better job of keeping her concealed. A flush rose from her throat to stain her cheeks.

Candy decided that going into the house with Garth right now wasn't such a good idea. "What about Stop and Go? We can't leave him here like this."

"Tom can take care of him."

Candy froze. It was unheard of for Garth to leave an animal untended that either of them had ridden.

"Let's go," he said.

Garth held out his hand to Candy. There was no mistaking where he was taking her, or what he had in mind when he got there. This was it, Candy thought, the moment of truth. Should she go with him, or dig in her heels and stay where she was? It was a decision she had been dreading for weeks.

She knew there might be pain waiting for her at the end of the road. Garth had rejected her love once before. But there was no denying the strength of her feelings, then or now. When all was said and done, Candy followed her heart. She placed her hand in Garth's. When a woman was in love, there really wasn't any choice at all.

CHAPTER FIVE

GARTH HEADED STRAIGHT for the house. They were both drenched, so to avoid leaving two sets of wet tracks on the tile floor in the kitchen or on the hardwood throughout the rest of the house, he lifted Candy into his arms and headed upstairs. He didn't even hesitate when he passed her bedroom door, just continued on to his own.

Garth set her down with her back to him and put his hands on her shoulders. Whether he did it to comfort her or to keep her from fleeing she wasn't sure.

Candy had never been in Garth's room, but she looked at it now, searching for anything that would tell her about the man she loved.

The first thing she noticed was how neat it was. That didn't really surprise her. Garth was a man who liked to be in control. He would want things where he could find them.

She was glad to see the pictures of his family, his sister and brothers, in frames on the various wooden surfaces around the room. There was also a picture of an older man, whom she supposed was Garth's father. She wondered why there was no picture of his mother.

Candy found hope in the fact that family was important to Garth. It was proof that he could care for people as much as he cared about horses. Whether he could love one woman and commit himself to her for a lifetime was another matter altogether.

His room was full of antiques, pieces of Whitelaw history that had been handed down from father to son. She had never doubted that Garth valued the traditions of his family. Which made her wonder whether he had ever considered how he could pass on those traditions to another generation of Whitelaws when he had so little respect for women and no use at all for a wife.

He slept in a huge four-poster bed covered with a patterned quilt. She stared at the bed, unable to take her eyes off it.

"Candy?"

His voice was low, intense, as demanding as it was challenging.

She suddenly had second thoughts about what she had come here to do. "I suppose there have been a lot of women in this bed."

"Yes, there have."

Candy's heart dropped to her feet as she thought of all the women Garth must have brought here.

"My mother, my grandmother, my great-grand-mother—"

Her heart swelled with joy. So this bed was reserved for Whitelaw women. Surely the fact that he had brought her to this room, to this bed, meant he felt something special for her. And maybe, just maybe, she would be able to get him to admit those feelings.

Candy turned slowly to face Garth. In his dark eyes, whether he knew it or not, was a need so fierce it sent a shiver of anticipation running through her.

"Make love to me, Garth."

He had been in such a hurry to get them here, she expected him to be impatient. Candy wouldn't have been surprised if he had simply ripped off her clothes and taken her in a fury of desire. It was infinitely worse waiting the endless moments it took him to undo her shirt one button at a time.

The wet cotton clung to her skin as he pushed the shirt off her shoulders. Candy shrugged and tugged at the sleeves to help him rid her of the garment.

With practiced hands he unsnapped the catch of her bra and pushed it out of his way—reminding her how experienced he was and how little she knew about what was to come. She caught his wrist when he reached for the zipper of her jeans.

"Your turn," she said in a shaky voice. Candy reached up and began unbuttoning his shirt. Her fingers were trembling, so it took longer than it should have, but he didn't interfere with her efforts. At long last the buttons were free, and she reached up to shove the shirt off his shoulders. Her hands skimmed across flesh that was smooth and warm. She felt his muscles bunch beneath her fingertips in response to her touch.

Intrigued by Garth's reaction, she slid her hands across his chest, playing with the dark curls there. They formed a triangle that headed down into jeans that hung low on his hips. His belly contracted as she skimmed past it.

He grabbed her wrists with enough strength that she shot a surprised look at him. His dark eyes were hooded, his nostrils flared for the scent of her, his facial muscles taut.

"Did I do something wrong?" Candy asked.

"I want to take my time," he said. "The way you were heading, things would have been over too damn fast."

Candy shivered again, only this time from the chill caused by the air-conditioning on her damp skin.

"Come on." Garth took her hand and led her toward a large, modern bathroom attached to his bedroom. Before Candy could object he had both her and himself completely stripped. She caught one quick—and somewhat awe-inspiring—glimpse of aroused male before he propelled her into the shower and followed after her.

The warm water felt wonderful. Candy closed her eyes and luxuriated in the feel of it on her back and shoulders. Her eyes blinked open when she felt Garth's hands on her, as well. Every feeling was new and exquisite, and yet it felt so right to be here with him that she welcomed each sensation.

Garth's hands slid over her breasts to her belly and then around to her buttocks. He tightened his arms around her, fitting their bodies together. There was no mistaking the hard length of him, even for someone as inexperienced as she was.

"Candy," he murmured. His mouth nuzzled against her brow as his hands slid up her back to hold her tight. "You taste sweet, girl."

Candy's flesh burned everywhere it met his. Her hands roamed over his back as she caressed him the way she had yearned to all those years ago. "Garth, I—"

Candy hesitated, uncertain whether she ought to admit she was a virgin. It didn't really matter, she reasoned. In a few more minutes she wouldn't be one anymore.

"What is it, sweetheart?"

"Shouldn't we be doing this in bed?" she asked in a husky voice.

Garth laughed, a deep, resonant sound she could feel

because he was holding her so close. "I just wanted to make sure you didn't catch a chill."

This time Candy laughed. "Believe me, I'm warm now."

Garth wasted no time getting them out of the shower. He wrapped Candy in his white terry-cloth robe and dried himself with a large towel which he knotted around his waist. He picked her up again and carried her into the bedroom.

"I can walk," Candy protested.

"I know, but I like the feel of you in my arms." Garth stopped beside the bed and bent so she could reach the covers. "Get the quilt, sweetheart."

Candy reached out and pulled the patterned quilt away to reveal pristine white sheets. She froze, thinking how they would look stained with virgin's blood. She opened her mouth to tell him the truth, and he kissed her quick and hard. The ferocity of the kiss left her gasping.

A moment later she was in bed and Garth was lying beside her. She might have wished for darkness, because she felt naked even with Garth's robe surrounding her. But she wouldn't have missed for anything the look in Garth's dark eyes as he reached out and spread the two halves of the robe and feasted his eyes on her.

"You're so beautiful."

Candy was overwhelmed with sensations as Garth's callused fingertips explored her body, beginning at her collarbone and heading downward between her breasts. He circled them, teasing her nipples before trailing his hand down across her belly.

Candy's body arched upward under his caresses. She pulled the towel away from his hips so flesh met flesh. Then she grabbed hold of Garth's shoulders and held on.

His dark eyes never left hers as his hands, and then his warm, wet mouth, roamed her body. She made a small sound in her throat as Garth's hand slipped down between her legs.

Instinctively she tightened her thighs to prevent his invasion.

"Relax, sweetheart. You're acting just like a—"

Candy did the first thing she could think of to distract him, so he wouldn't realize the truth. Her hand slid down his belly and encircled him. She was surprised to discover he was hard and soft all at the same time.

"Whoa, Candy! Go slow, sweetheart."

Candy had no idea what the difference was between fast and slow. But she forced herself to relax, and his hand slid between her legs.

Candy gasped at the intimate contact as he slid a finger inside her.

"You're so tight. Just like a—"

Candy could see it was going to take constant distraction to keep him from getting suspicious. She did what came naturally. She pulled his head down and kissed him to shut him up. She moaned deep in her throat when his tongue mimicked the thrust and parry of lovers truly joined.

His voice was harsh when he broke the kiss. "Dammit, Candy! I want to be inside you."

"I want you, too, Garth," she murmured breathlessly.

He spread her legs with his knees and thrust hard.

Her body resisted for a second before the barrier tore, and he sank to the hilt inside her. Candy bit her lip until it bled, but a whimper of pain escaped.

Garth muttered an oath. "A virgin! I should have known. What a fool I am!"

Candy wrapped her legs around Garth and held tight to his shoulders. "It's done now, and there's no going back. Please, Garth. Make love to me."

"I'll hurt you."

"No, you won't."

Garth knew he was making a mistake. He ought to get out while the getting was good. He hadn't asked if she was protected, he had simply assumed she was. The kind of woman he normally took to bed wasn't about to take the chance of getting pregnant. Candy had been a virgin. It was a good bet she hadn't taken any precautions to prevent pregnancy, and he sure as hell hadn't, either.

But right now he wanted her with a need that was beyond anything he had ever felt before in his life. Stopping was out of the question. If there were consequences, he would deal with them. "All right, little rich girl," he said. "You've got what you wanted. Now let's see how you handle it."

Garth moved slightly and saw her wince. "Dammit! I *am* hurting you!"

He started to withdraw, but Candy stopped him again. "It's all right, really. It's just... I'm not used to... You're so big that I—"

She flushed a bright red.

Garth chuckled. "All right, sweetheart. Let's start over again."

She arched a questioning brow. "Is that possible?"

He nudged his hips against hers, and Candy felt a spiral of desire twist inside her belly. Her breasts tingled. It appeared it was more than possible.

"I'm not in any hurry," Garth said with a grin. "Let's go back a few steps."

Candy didn't understand at first what Garth meant.

Five...fifteen...thirty minutes later she was writhing with pleasure beneath him. He was still inside her, but there wasn't a spot on her body he hadn't caressed, licked, bitten, sucked or kissed.

Of course, she hadn't been idle. She had learned how to touch him in ways that pushed him close to the edge. His body was covered with a fine sheen of sweat, and she could see the strain in his face as he delayed the culmination of his own pleasure to make sure she reached the pinnacle of desire.

He seemed in no hurry. He drove her to the edge only to back off again. At last she thought she would go mad if he didn't finish what he had started.

"Now!" she insisted. "Now, Garth!"

Those were the words he had been waiting to hear. Garth thrust slow and easy at first, but Candy wouldn't allow him to be gentle. Her fingernails left crescents in his flesh as she arched under him. He slipped a hand between them and found the tiny nubbin that was so sensitive by now that it took only a bare touch to set her off.

He felt her squeezing him, the tight muscles contracting around him until he could barely stand the pleasure. It was Candy's guttural cry of delight that freed him to find his own satisfaction. His head arched back and his body tautened as he released his seed in powerful racking spasms.

As Garth relaxed his weight on top of her, Candy wrapped her arms around him. She felt good. She felt wonderful. She felt loved.

"I love you," she whispered.

She felt him stiffen immediately. He took his weight on his palms and stared down at her.

"I don't want to hear that any more now than I did

three years ago," he said in a harsh voice. "That was sex, sweetheart. You asked for it, and you got it."

Candy turned her head away to hide her distress. It was impossible to speak over the lump in her throat.

Fool! Fool! You should have known he had no heart. You should have protected yourself better!

Maybe he can change. Maybe all he needs is a woman to love him just for himself and not ask anything in return.

Right! And if you believe that, I've got a spavined horse I'd like to sell you.

"I'm not asking you for anything," she managed to say.

"That's good. Because I'm not offering anything," he said. "You should have told me you'd never been with a man!"

"Would it have made any difference?"

"Damn straight! I don't make a habit of deflowering virgins!"

She smiled slightly. "But you do it so well!"

"That isn't funny!" he snarled.

Her smile widened. "Oh, I don't know. I find the idea pretty amusing."

"I could have hurt you!"

"But you didn't." She put her hands on either side of his face and forced him to look into her eyes. "You brought me a great deal of pleasure. I'm not asking for any more than that, Garth. Truly I'm not. I know you don't love me." She swallowed to try and force down the thickness in her throat. "But you enjoy making love to me. If it's what we both want, where's the harm?"

Garth knew where the harm was. The harm was that he wanted her as much now—more now—than he had

before they made love. That had never happened to him.
Once the chase was over, he usually tired of the woman
quickly. With Candy, all she had to do was look at him,
and he was hard all over again. At his age that was nothing short of miraculous.

He told himself he might as well take advantage of her
while she was here. Once she learned what she needed to
know to run her own stable of cutting horses she would
be gone. He felt that same awful weight on his chest he
had felt three years ago. He rolled onto his back and
pulled her on top of him.

He tunneled his hands up into her hair and tugged
her mouth down to his. He kissed her fiercely, letting
her feel his anger and his frustration. Her hands soothed
him as they spread across his chest and set him on fire
at the same time. How was that possible?

His hands slid down her back to her buttocks. He
grabbed hold, leaving fingerprints where his hands had
been as he lifted her and impaled her on his shaft.

Garth sighed in satisfaction as he slid inside her. Wet.
Warm. Tight. How could she be ready for him so soon?
His lips twisted. Probably the same way he was ready for
her. They were made for each other. Man and his mate.

His mate.

Garth denied the strength of his feelings for Candy
Baylor. She was just like every other woman. She wasn't
to be trusted. Give your heart to a female, and she would
crush it beneath her high-heeled boots. Garth Whitelaw
was never going to fall for any woman. Least of all some
spoiled little rich girl.

Garth sat up and pulled Candy's legs around him. His
hands tangled in her hair, and he held her captive for his
kiss. His tongue searched her mouth for the sweetness

that he couldn't seem to get enough of. He groaned as her tongue slipped into his mouth, tasting lips and teeth and seeking equal pleasure.

Garth took Candy to sensual heights she had never imagined as they made love through the afternoon. She reveled in his touch, and touched him in return. The loving was fierce and wild and left them both overwhelmed by tumultuous feelings that threatened an already-fragile relationship.

At last Candy lay asleep in Garth's arms, exhausted by the day's pleasures. Garth lay staring at the ceiling, appalled by how vulnerable he felt. He had never before experienced what had happened in this bedroom with Candice Baylor. He had exhausted himself and her, and still he wanted her. The truth could no longer be denied. His need for her was more than sexual. It seemed to come from deep inside.

He couldn't bear the thought of any other man ever laughing with her, holding her, loving her. His feelings were totally irrational, of course. But he knew he would kill the man who touched her. Such powerful emotions left him feeling agitated. And angry.

He shook Candy. "Wake up!"

Candy woke from a dream in which Garth had just told her he loved her, so there was a soft smile on her face as she looked up at him with sleepy eyes. "What is it, Garth?" Her hand smoothed over his chest, luxuriating in the feel of him.

Garth cursed when his body—wrung out from a day of making love to her—immediately hardened with need. He grabbed a handful of Candy's blond hair and pulled her head back at a painful angle.

"What's wrong, Garth?"

She didn't struggle, didn't swear or strike out against his strength. She lay there in his arms, looking up at him with love and concern. Garth felt that now-familiar tightening in his chest. He forced himself to ignore it. He was fighting for his life.

"I'm not the marrying kind," he said through gritted teeth. "I want one thing from you. Just one thing!" He laid her down and thrust inside her.

He cried out in an agony of pleasure as Candy arched up to receive him, welcoming him, taking all of him and asking for whatever more he had to give.

She was a witch, and he was ensorceled by her. That was the only explanation for the excruciating need he felt for this particular woman. There was no time for thinking once he was inside her, or for talking, either. He thrust and she parried, taking and giving pleasure, fast and hard and deep, until he heard her cry out and joined her in reaching a plateau of pleasure beyond any they had sought or expected to find.

As he lay panting above her, his body sweat-slick and musky from their lovemaking, he said, "So long as you're at Hawk's Way, you belong to me."

"All right, Garth."

Her demure response did little to ease Garth's anxiousness. "Anytime you want to cut and leave, it'll be fine by me."

"We have a deal," Candy said. "You promised to teach me what you know about cutting horses."

"And I will."

"Then I don't see that we have anything to argue about."

Garth stared at her suspiciously. There was something wrong with her logic, although he hadn't yet figured it out. "Just so we understand each other," Garth said. "From now on you'll sleep in here with me."

Candy snuggled closer to him. "All right, Garth."

Garth pulled her tight and closed his eyes. A few moments later, sated at long last, he slept.

Candy was wide awake.

She stared beyond Garth's shoulder to the framed picture of the older man, a man without a woman by his side. She knew some people would tell her she was tilting at windmills to even hope that she could change Garth's attitude about women—about having a wife.

But he had brought her here to the bed of his forebears, and when he had discovered her virginity he hadn't tossed her out. In fact, he had made love to her again and again. Sex was a strong lure, one women had used for aeons. Candy was not above using every source of ammunition she had to lay claim to her man.

She would love him so much he wouldn't be able to live without her. She would succeed where every other woman had failed. She would wait him out. Sooner or later Garth would have to admit that what they had done wasn't *having sex,* it was *making love.* Then he would ask her to be his wife.

She just had to make sure all that happened before she learned everything she needed to know to start her own stable. Otherwise, he might kick her out before she was ready to go. Well, Garth's deft, capable pupil might suddenly have to become all thumbs.

CHAPTER SIX

"HE'S SO SAVAGE! How can you hope to tame him?" Candy's eyes anxiously sought Garth's, then skipped back to the black stallion that was rearing and kicking and screaming his fury in the corral. "Is there a way to make him trust humans again?"

"It will take time. And patience. Maybe even that won't be enough. Señor Santos sent Midnight to me because none of his men could do anything with the horse."

"What made him so mean?" Candy asked.

"Probably somebody beat him once upon a time. Santos bought him at auction, but the horse had gone through three or four owners by then, so there's no telling, really."

Candy was aghast. "Beat him! How could anyone be so cruel?"

Garth's lips pursed. "You're living in a dreamworld if you think there aren't people out there who mistreat animals. It's too bad. Santos said if I couldn't tame that black beast he'd have to put him down."

"Oh, no, Garth! You can't let him be killed!" Candy grasped the wrangler's arm as though to stop him from such an action. She felt a jolt of electricity the instant she touched him. Candy stared up into Garth's dark eyes and saw that he was as aroused as she was by the simple contact. "You can tame him. I know you can!"

"I don't have the time to waste," Garth said. "Santos didn't tell me what bad shape the horse is in, or I never would have let him ship the stud here."

"I've got the time!" Candy said. "I'll do it. If you'll just tell me what to do."

Garth frowned. "I don't know. You need to concentrate on learning what you came here to learn."

Candy flushed with embarrassment. Garth hadn't said it aloud, but over the past week her learning curve had dipped considerably. She had manipulated the slowdown purposely, of course. But Garth didn't know that.

"I—I can learn," she stuttered. "This is important to me, Garth. Please let me try."

Garth scrutinized the magnificent quarter horse stallion. "He's a good-looking animal. It would be a shame to put him down."

"It's settled, then," Candy said. "I'll work with him." She put her arms around Garth's waist and hugged him. "Thanks, Garth."

Garth folded Candy into his embrace. "Don't think it's going to be a picnic, because it isn't."

"Oh, I know that. But if Midnight can be tamed, you'll show me how to do it."

"I'm glad you have so much confidence in me." Garth was appalled by how good her compliment made him feel. It was one more sign of what he had begun to recognize as his growing dependence on her. He wasn't sure how it had happened, because nothing had changed in his life. At least not where outward appearances were concerned.

He still worked from dawn to dusk, only with Candy by his side. After supper in the dining room—he hadn't been stubborn fool enough to insist they keep on eat-

372 HAWK'S WAY: GARTH

ing in the kitchen—he and Candy would retire to the parlor where she would read and he would work on the business end of his business. Then they would retire to his bedroom, where he would make love to her once or twice or sometimes even three times in a night.

She was always willing, and she had learned enough over the past week to incite him to passions even he hadn't known he was capable of. He felt his loins tighten as vivid memories of their lovemaking replayed in his head. The tastes, the scents, the sounds all combined to bring him to full arousal.

"Damn!"

Candy looked up at him. "What's wrong?" Then she looked down and said, "Oh. Again?"

"Again. Always. Constantly."

She grinned. "I think it's kind of cute."

He shook his head and laughed. "You would." His body concealed hers from the cowboys who were working nearby. He slipped his hand between them and cupped her breast, running his thumb across the nipple, which peaked instantly.

Candy made a tiny, kittenish sound in her throat and repaid him by sliding her hand across the hard ridge in his jeans. "Two can play that game," she teased.

They touched each other, hands pressing, pinching, playing, always careful to keep what they were doing hidden from the men who worked around them.

Only they might as well not have wasted their time. There wasn't a cowhand at Hawk's Way who didn't know the boss had a soft spot for Candy Baylor, and any look crosswise at her was a sure way to find oneself booted off the ranch.

Candy was breathless by the time Garth called a halt

to their sensual play. He simply pulled her into his arms and hugged her tight.

"We've got work to do, woman," he growled in her ear. He turned her and gave her a little shove in the direction of the stable.

As they fed the horses their evening ration of grain and alfalfa hay, Candy asked, "Will you tell me what I should do first, where I should start, to tame the stud?"

"I'd leave him outside in the corral, give him some room to move around. Don't hedge him in too close."

Candy nodded her head. She could do that.

"You should be the one to feed and water him, no one else. Talk to him when you do. Keep it soft, something soothing."

"All right."

"Then you can start tempting him to come closer with something sweet. Sugar works. Leave it where he can find it at first. On the fence rail, maybe. Then make him come to you for it."

"Won't he try to bite me?"

"He might. When the time comes, watch yourself."

"Then what?"

"When he starts coming to you for the sugar, you'll have a chance to touch him. Take your time. Move slow. Don't crowd him. Let him get to know you."

"And when he gets to know me, I can put a rope on him," Candy concluded.

"Hell, no, woman! You'd undo everything you've done so far."

Candy stepped out of a stall and stuck her hands on her hips. "How long before I can put a rope on him?" she demanded.

Garth shrugged. "It'll take time. Maybe a few weeks. A month. Six months. Maybe never."

"When will I know for sure?"

"You'll know when you know," Garth said. "There's no predicting these things. It all depends on the horse, on his history. If he can't let go of what happened in the past, of whatever it was that made him the way he is, he'll be useless to himself and everybody else."

"I see," Candy said thoughtfully. "Oh, I see."

Candy looked at Garth with new eyes. She couldn't help seeing the similarity between the battle she was fighting in her attempts to gain Garth's love and trust and the challenge of taming the wild stallion.

She was determined to win the stallion's confidence. She would do whatever was necessary to save the animal from destruction. And if she could win one battle, surely she could win the other.

"All right, Garth. I'll do what you say."

"You just be careful," Garth said. "That beast is dangerous. He'll destroy you if he can."

Candy was struck by Garth's warning. So, too, could *he* destroy *her,* if he only knew it. But she was her father's daughter, and she wasn't used to giving up or giving in. She would tame the stallion *and* the man. Just wait and see if she didn't!

Garth put his arm around Candy as they walked back toward the house. "By the way," he said, "we'll be having company for the Labor Day holiday."

"Oh?"

"My sister Tate's son is being christened. The whole family will be coming here for the occasion."

Garth felt Candy hesitate, then slow to a stop. She

turned to face him and asked, "Where do I fit into that picture, Garth?"

"You'll be staying with me, of course. Just like you have been for the past week."

Candy shook her head. "I don't think so."

"Why not?" Garth wasn't happy about the irritation in his voice. It indicated just how great was his need to have her in his bed.

"I don't want your family thinking—"

"Don't worry. They won't say a word." He would give them fair warning that Candy was different. He couldn't—wouldn't—tolerate his brothers saying the things about Candy that they had said about other women he had from time to time brought to Hawk's Way.

"But they'll know," Candy protested.

"Know what?"

That I'm sleeping with you when you haven't once said you love me, Candy thought. She didn't dare say that aloud.

"How soon did you say they'll be here?" she asked.

"Labor Day."

Only three weeks in which to get Garth to admit his feelings for her.

Candy didn't waste any time following Garth's advice, either with the horse or with him. She kept one rule in mind at all times.

Give him some room to move around. Don't hedge him in too close. With that understood she moved on to the second point Garth had made.

You should be the one to feed and water him, no one else. She was the only one who fed and watered the stallion. Things were a little more difficult when it came to feeding Garth.

Charlie One Horse normally prepared meals. Candy decided to take the bull by the horns and tell Charlie what she was trying to do. She caught him in the kitchen preparing supper.

When she was done, the old Indian tugged on the beaded rawhide thong that held one of his braids and asked, "You really think this is goin' to work?"

"It has to," Candy said.

Charlie was skeptical that Garth would ever trust another woman after what his momma had done. Mona's infidelity had occurred at a very impressionable time in Garth's life. But he had seen with his own eyes that Garth treated Candy differently than he had other women. And Charlie had been the one to wash the blood-stained sheets that had told their own story.

"All right," Charlie said at last. "I ain't gone on vacation yet this year. I'll tell Garth I'm takin' three weeks off. But that's all. I ain't missin' the christenin'."

"I'd never ask you to do that," Candy said. She gave the old man a kiss on the cheek and watched his ruddy face turn even ruddier. "Thank you, Charlie."

"Aw. Didn't do nothin'."

"How soon can you leave?" Candy asked.

Charlie chuckled. "I'll be gone 'fore supper, if that's what you're askin'."

"Thanks again, Charlie."

"Good luck, girl," Charlie said. As she left Charlie to run upstairs and change her clothes he muttered, "You're gonna need it!"

While she cooked supper, Candy went over in her mind the rest of what Garth had said about taming the stallion. *Talk to him. Keep it soft, something soothing.*

Garth wasn't in the best of moods that evening. As

Candy set his plate in front of him he grumbled, "That old buzzard didn't even give me a day of warning. Who's going to do the cooking around here?"

"I am."

Garth eyed her skeptically. "You can cook?"

"Of course I can."

"You've already got enough to do. How are you going to handle any more?"

"I'll manage," Candy said. "Don't worry about me, darling." Candy let the endearment drop in a husky, breathless voice.

Garth looked at her sharply, but he didn't deny her the right to call him by such a term. Candy joined him at the table and waited for the conversation to start. She soon discovered how much Charlie had contributed to the dinnertime talk. Charlie usually asked one or the other of them how the day had gone, and then they would answer him. Candy had never noticed before that she and Garth had been talking to Charlie, not to each other.

Their time in the parlor after supper each evening had always been comfortable because they were together, even though very little dialogue passed between them. Candy recognized the importance of Garth's lesson. She needed to talk to him, to establish some sort of communication with him beyond the exchange of knowledge that consumed their days and the lovemaking that consumed their nights.

"Tell me what it was like growing up at Hawk's Way," she said.

Garth seemed startled by the request. She was afraid for a moment he wouldn't respond. Then he said, "There was a lot of work to do. I did it."

"There must have been some time for play," Candy chided.

"Not much," Garth muttered.

"But there were so many of you—your father and your brothers and sister—to do the work, and with the cowhands—"

"We couldn't afford hired help when I was growing up," Garth interrupted.

"Oh. Hawk's Way is so large and successful now, I thought it must always have been like this."

"It's always been a big spread," Garth conceded, "but we've been through a lot of hard times. There's oil on the property, but the bottom fell out of the market, if you'll recall. We raised beef for a while, but that's another market that isn't too dependable. Then we took a chance on raising rodeo stock. It wasn't until we started breeding and training championship cutting horses that we could afford any outside help."

"I had no idea," Candy said. It gave her a whole different image of what Garth's childhood must have been like.

"I saw a picture of your father upstairs. You must miss him a lot."

An agonized look crossed Garth's face and was gone so quickly Candy thought she must have imagined it.

"He was a good father. Until my mother killed him."

"What? Faron told me three years ago that your father came off a bronc and broke his neck. Are you saying he lied?"

Candy waited for Garth to answer her question, to explain his provocative statement, but his features turned stony and he remained mute. At least she knew now why there was no picture of his mother upstairs. Finally, she couldn't stand the suspense any longer.

"I don't want to intrude on what must be a painful episode in your life—"

"Then don't," he said in a harsh voice.

Candy reminded herself this was supposed to be *soothing* talk and decided to change the subject.

"Tell me more about your brothers and sister."

Almost immediately his expression softened. "My brother Jesse's a renegade," Garth said. "We were too close in age, so we knocked heads after Dad died. Jesse left to find his own way."

"How long was he gone?"

"It was years before we heard from him again. He was a Texas Ranger until he married a widow named Honey Farrell. Now he has two stepsons and a daughter of his own, and he and Honey run their ranch, the Flying Diamond, in southwest Texas.

"My sister Tate is as independent as they come. Did you know she ran away from home?"

"You must have been crazy with worry," Candy said.

"I was. But at twenty-three she decided she'd had enough of her overprotective older brothers."

"Twenty-three!" Candy gasped. "You're kidding, right?"

"I'm afraid not," Garth said with a rueful laugh. "She was gone for a couple of months before my long-lost brother Jesse called out of the blue and told us Tate had moved in with some rancher in south Texas. My brothers and I showed up the next day and made things legal."

Candy was aghast. "You forced her to get married?"

"She was pregnant," Garth said flatly. "But it wouldn't have mattered whether she was or not. She was an innocent when she met Adam Philips. He shouldn't have taken advantage of her. Anyway, everything turned out all right. Tate and Adam are bringing their son, Brett, here to be christened."

Candy bit her tongue to keep from making the retort that leapt to mind. But if Garth wasn't making the connection between Adam's treatment of Garth's sister and Garth's treatment of her, she would be wasting her breath to point it out to him.

"What about the brother I met three years ago, Faron?"

"You mean my brother the lover?" Garth said with a chuckle.

Candy laughed as she recalled the way Faron had flirted with her. "That's the one. You said he was away on business. What kind?"

A hard, closed look reappeared on Garth's face. "Faron's in Wyoming meeting his stepmother."

Candy's brow furrowed in confusion. "What? How can Faron have a stepmother if he's your brother?"

"You figure it out." Garth's tone of voice made it clear he was done with that line of discussion. He was also finished with supper. He picked up his plate and carried it out to the kitchen, leaving Candy sitting alone.

She wouldn't have called her efforts a total success, but she had learned more personal information about Garth over supper this evening than in all the time she had spent at Hawk's Way. That achievement gave her the confidence to go on to the next step in Garth's training program.

You can start tempting him to come closer with something sweet. Sugar works. Leave it where he can find it

*at first. On the fence rail, maybe. Then make him come
to you for it.*

Candy picked up her plate and headed for the kitchen
after Garth. He had already rinsed his plate and stacked
it in the dishwasher and was making himself a cup of
coffee.

"I'll have one of those," Candy said as she rinsed her
own plate.

Garth took out another mug and poured her a cup. He
handed it to her, and she took a sip before setting it down
on the counter. She walked up to Garth, put her hands
around his waist and leaned her cheek against his chest.

"Mmm. This feels good."

Garth said nothing. Candy's hands slid down over the
contours of his buttocks and back up the center of his
spine to his nape, where she played with the hair that
hung over his collar. She turned her face slightly and
nipped his flesh through his shirt.

"Sonofabitch," Garth muttered.

Candy released him and walked away as though she
hadn't felt the blunt ridge in his jeans. She used her
hands to lever herself into a sitting position on the heavy
oak table. Then she spread her knees and leaned back
on her palms.

Come and get your sugar, darling.

Garth approached her slowly until he stood between
her legs. He grasped her thighs and pulled her toward
him until the heart of her was pressed to the heat of him.
Then he pressed her shoulders down until she was lying
flat on the table.

*When he comes to you for the sugar, you'll have a
chance to touch him. Take your time. Move slow. Don't
crowd him. Let him get to know you.*

Candy didn't move a hair when Garth reached for the snap of her jeans. Nor did she take her eyes off him as the zipper rasped down. He placed his hand flat on her belly and slid his thumb down so it just grazed her mound. She gasped. But she let him have his way.

He stepped back and pulled off her boots and socks. Then he reached his hands into the back of her jeans and began pulling them down. She lifted her hips slightly to help him. She lay before him naked from the waist down.

His dark eyes were almost black, hooded with desire. A muscle jerked in his cheek. He was breathing hard, as though he had been running. She wasn't breathing so well herself.

He pulled her to the edge of the table again and spread her legs so that she was totally exposed to him. Candy resisted the urge to cover herself. Instead she reached out and covered his hands where they lay on her naked thighs. She trailed her hands up his arms.

She knew what was coming. He left her plenty of time to refuse as he lifted her up and lowered his mouth to kiss her nether lips. Her hands tightened on his arms as a thrill of pleasure raced through her. Her eyes never left his face as he made love to her in this new and very different way. The sensations were exquisite, unbearably exciting, unbelievably arousing. He possessed her totally, absolutely, bringing her to a climax so powerful she trembled afterward.

She wanted to tell Garth what she was feeling. How wonderful the gift was that he had given her. But she couldn't catch her breath, and wouldn't have known what words to use anyway. She lay before him, her heart in her eyes, telling him in the only way she could that she loved him. That she wanted to spend her life with him.

How long before I can put a rope on him?

It'll take time. Maybe a few weeks. A month. Six months. Maybe never.

She managed to sit up. He was still standing between her legs. She reached out for the snap of his jeans but his hand was there to stop her. She waited to see what he would do. What he would say.

He only muttered, "Sonofabitch." Then he picked her up in his arms and headed upstairs. "Come on, woman. Let's go to bed."

Garth loved Candy with his whole body, in every way he knew and some he made up on the spot. He had nearly gone crazy when she had loved him the same way he had loved her in the kitchen. It had been wonderful. Beyond anything he had ever imagined it could be. He could feel her waiting for the words of love. He could almost hear them ricocheting off the walls. But he didn't speak them.

Neither did she.

Candy lay in Garth's arms, replete. But not satisfied.

When will I know for sure?

You'll know when you know. There's no predicting these things.

Candy had to figure out what it was that had made Garth so reluctant to commit himself to a woman. He had given her several clues. First, there was the fact that he had no picture of his mother anywhere in the house. Second, he had said that his mother killed his father. Finally, there was that story of Faron having a stepmother, because he had a different father.

It came to her in a flash, so obvious that she wondered why she hadn't suspected it before.

Apparently, Garth's mother had been unfaithful to

his father. Faron had been the result. And Garth had never trusted another woman to be any more faithful than his mother.

At least now she knew what she was up against.

If he can't let go of the past, whatever it was that made him the way he is, he'll be useless to himself and everybody else.

Candy felt overwhelmed by her sudden knowledge. How was she going to change Garth's lifetime of distrust? What could she possibly do to convince him that she would never be unfaithful to him? It just wasn't possible.

She remembered the last of Garth's warnings when he had told her how to tame the big stud.

You be careful. That beast is dangerous. He'll destroy you if he can.

Candy turned into Garth's arms. She felt them close tight around her. At least for now he was hers, and she was his. She would hold him with the only ropes she had. Somehow, someday, she would find a way to reach him. She was sure of it. She would start tomorrow with that black beast in the corral and prove it could be done.

CHAPTER SEVEN

CANDY HAD WON several battles with the savage black stallion, but she was losing the war. No matter how hard she tried, the animal refused to trust her. Her failure left her feeling desolate because she had tied all her hopes for a life with Garth to her success with the incorrigible stallion. They were both turning out to be unbelievably stubborn males.

She had gotten only so far with Garth and no further. She couldn't explain it exactly, but it seemed like the more they made love, the more distant he became. Not that he desired her any less. In fact, their loving sometimes seemed almost desperately passionate, as though they had only these moments, these very few moments, to love each other.

And maybe this summer would be all they ever had together.

Candy held out the sugar to the black again. "Come here, you big beastie. Come here and take what I'm offering you. Everything is going to be all right. No one's ever going to hurt you again."

The black horse stomped a hoof and shook his head.

"You don't believe me, do you?" She slumped against the corral. "Neither does he. He doesn't trust me any more now than he did the day I came here. He wants me. But he doesn't trust me."

Garth's family was due to start arriving any day and Candy hadn't yet made up her mind what she was going to do. She couldn't bear to have Garth's family think she was just another one of the women moving through his life. Yet he had given her no encouragement to think that she would ever play a continuing role in his future.

She stepped onto the bottom rail of the corral and leaned over, holding out her hand with the cube of sugar in it. The stallion neighed and stood his ground.

"Come here, you bullheaded mule," she crooned to him.

The horse took two steps forward and stopped.

"That's it, you willful devil," she purred. "Come and get it."

Suddenly she felt Garth's dark, brooding gaze on her. She turned to face him and lost her balance. He caught her as she fell.

The stallion raced back to the other side of the corral.

"Dammit, Garth! I almost had him," she exploded. She tried to wrench herself from his grasp, but he refused to let her go.

"Whoa, there, girl! I came to tell you Jesse and Honey are here with their kids. I thought you might like to come and meet them."

Candy took one look down at the ragged jeans and dirty shirt she had been working in all day and groaned. "Look at me. I'm a mess."

"I wouldn't say that." Garth tightened his arms around her. "You look fine to me," he whispered.

She shivered at the feel of his warm breath against her face. "You'd think I looked fine no matter what I was wearing—or wasn't wearing. I wish you'd reminded me they were coming today, Garth. I wanted to make a good impression on your family."

"Why bother? They'll be leaving in a few days anyway." He brushed her long blond hair out of the way and kissed her nape.

Candy hid her face against Garth's chest. How dense could a man be? If she married him she would certainly be seeing his family more than just this once! But that was the problem. Garth apparently didn't see a future that included her.

"Hello there."

Candy jerked herself from Garth's embrace at the sound of a deep male voice. Her face flushed scarlet as she turned to face a man she realized must be Garth's brother. She crossed her arms protectively around herself. "H-hello."

"I'm Jesse. You must be Candy Baylor. Garth was telling us about you."

Candy shot a glance at Garth. Exactly what had he been saying? She took the hand Jesse offered and shook it. "It's nice to meet you, Jesse."

She compared Jesse to his brother and noted Jesse's skin was a darker bronze, his features broader, blunter. He had the same thick black hair as Garth, the same dark eyes—only Jesse's seemed more remote.

Garth reached out to put a hand back around her shoulder, but she stepped out of his way.

"I have to go change," she said. "It's getting on toward time for supper."

She hurried past them and headed for the kitchen door.

Candy took one step inside the house and froze. It looked like an army had invaded. There was a collec-

tion of baby furniture stuck in corners and baby para-
phernalia littered the counters and table. She should have
realized the kitchen was the very place where everyone
would congregate. To her dismay not only did she find
Honey there, but Tate and her husband, Adam, as well.

She recognized Jesse's wife, Honey, right away because Garth had said she had long, curly blond hair and
striking blue eyes. Tate was a delicate version of her
brothers, with short-cropped black hair and friendly
hazel eyes. Blond-haired, blue-eyed Adam was clearly
no Whitelaw.

Candy opened her mouth and shut it again, unsure
where to start.

Charlie stepped into the breach. "All you folks, this
here is Candy Baylor. She's workin' at Hawk's Way this
summer, learnin' all about cuttin' horses. Candy, these
folks are Jesse and his wife, Honey, and Tate and her
husband, Adam. Them babies in the cribs is Lauren and
Brett. Honey and Jesse's two boys, Jack and Jonathan,
are upstairs. You'll meet them later."

Candy shook hands with the men, and despite the
condition of her work clothes, got a hug from each of
the women. She resisted the urge to go look at the babies. "It's nice to meet you all," she said. "I hope you'll
excuse me. I need to clean up a little."

"Sure," Tate said. "Hurry back down. I want to hear
what my big brother has been doing all summer."

"Giving orders," Candy muttered.

"What was that?" Tate asked.

Honey rescued Candy from having to reply by putting a hand on her shoulder and heading her in the direction of the door. "Go on and change. We'll still be
here when you get back."

Candy took her time in the shower. By the time she got back downstairs, dressed in a clean pair of jeans and a Western shirt—the same thing the two women in the kitchen had been wearing—everyone had resettled in the parlor. Apparently the two boys were still playing upstairs.

Honey was sitting in Jesse's lap on a chair in front of the fireplace. Adam and Tate were sitting close beside each other on the couch. Garth was standing with an arm resting on the thick pine mantel above the stone fireplace. They were discussing—arguing—the merits of two brands of horse feed.

It wasn't the adults who interested her. Like a lodestone, Candy approached the antique cradles in the corner that held the two babies. She tucked Brett's blanket around him, then tentatively reached down to caress the black curls on Lauren's head.

"Go ahead and pick her up," Honey said. "She won't bite."

"Are you sure you don't mind?" Candy asked.

Honey didn't answer, just got up and crossed to the cradle. She picked up her daughter and laid her in Candy's arms. "Be sure to support her head."

"What if I drop her?"

"You won't," Honey said as she settled herself back in Jesse's lap.

Candy had always loved babies. Maybe it was because she had never had any brothers or sisters of her own. Unfortunately, she had come into very little contact with small children during her twenty years. She was fascinated by Lauren's tiny fingers and her equally tiny fingernails. She laughed when the baby grasped her hand.

"She's so strong!"

Candy looked up and found herself staring straight into Garth's dark eyes. She didn't know when he had crossed from the hearth. She hadn't heard him coming. But then, she had been totally involved with investigating the baby.

Garth felt his stomach fall all the way to his toes at the sight of Candy with a child in her arms. She looked so…maternal. He had never planned to have a wife, and he would never bring a child into the world without the benefit of marriage. He had long ago resigned himself to the fact that he would never have children. He had settled for the idea of standing on the sidelines, of being a fond uncle.

Now he could see how he had cheated himself all these years. Of the joy of having his own child. Of the opportunity of sharing that bliss with a woman he loved. It hurt. Lord, it hurt.

His jaw tightened. He might never feel the joy of having his own child, but he would likewise never be destroyed by the pain of a woman's betrayal. He could survive the former, but not the latter.

"Do you want to hold her?" Candy asked.

The hell of it was, he did. "Sure," he said.

Candy laid the baby in his arms. To her surprise Garth seemed perfectly comfortable. "You look like you've done this before."

He shot a glance over his shoulder at Tate. "I put a diaper or two on my sister over the years."

Tate blushed. "Good grief, Garth. Do you have to remind me of that?"

"I somehow can't imagine you diapering a baby," Candy said to Garth with a grin.

"Mom died when Tate was born," he said in a harsh

voice. "Dad fell apart and Charlie was busy with Jesse and Faron. That left me."

There was a long silence.

"I didn't know," Candy said. "That must have been hard on you."

Garth laid the baby back in the crib and returned to his place by the mantel. "She kept me up a few nights. But it was worth it."

Candy saw the look Garth exchanged with Tate. There was love there, and concern. Love for family wasn't the same as romantic love, but she couldn't help feeling optimistic. Surely there must be a way to convince Garth that loving a woman didn't have to end in disaster.

The sound of footsteps in the foyer alerted them to the fact that someone else had arrived.

"That'll be Faron," Garth said. "We're in the parlor, Faron," he called to his brother.

Candy took her time looking at the third Whitelaw brother. She had met Faron before but saw him differently now that she knew he had a different father than the other Whitelaw men. His eyes were an unusual gray-green color. He had black hair, like the rest of the Whitelaws, but his facial features were more refined. He was unbelievably handsome.

Faron wasn't alone. He had two women with him, an arm around each of them. "This is my grandmother, Madelyn Prescott," he said. "I call her Maddy."

The younger woman with Faron, an elegantly tall blonde with stunning violet eyes, was clearly uncomfortable. The woman seemed on the verge of fleeing the room. Faron introduced her as his stepmother, Belinda Prescott.

"That's the ugly stepmother?" Jesse whispered. His

wife elbowed him in the ribs to shut him up. That saved
Candy the trouble of kicking him.

Obviously the whole family knew of Faron's illegit-
imate birth. But it was clear there was something else
going on between him and his beautiful young stepmother.

Garth spoke first in what had become a very awkward
situation. "I'm pleased to meet you, Belinda."

Candy knew Garth well enough by now to hear the
sneer in his voice. It was plain what he thought of the
beautiful young woman who had married a rich man old
enough to be her father. *Not much.*

Candy couldn't stand it. She reached out and grasped
Belinda's hand.

"Hi. I'm Candice—Candy Baylor. I guess you and
I are the only two people here who aren't family." She
smiled, giving Belinda the welcome Garth hadn't.

"I'm working at Hawk's Way this summer, and I can
imagine how you must feel, meeting this rowdy bunch
for the first time."

"They are a little overwhelming," Belinda said.

Candy watched as Faron stepped up and put his arm
around Belinda to support her. He reached out his hand
to Candy and said, "I don't know if you remember me."

"Of course I remember you," Candy said. "Last time
I was here with my father you yanked my braids at the
breakfast table."

Faron grinned. "Guilty. Was that only three years
ago? You've grown a little since then."

The longer Garth watched his brother flirting with
Candy, the more irritated he got. Faron was a man who
loved women. And they loved him. Garth wasn't about
to let Faron work his wiles on Candy. "I think it's time

you showed Maddy and Belinda where they'll be staying," he said.

The moment the three latest arrivals headed upstairs, Garth turned to Candy and said, "You come with me. There's a mare due to foal in the next day or so that needs to be checked."

Candy was furious that Garth had ordered her to come with him like some hired hand rather than asking her if she wanted to go. Besides, this was the first she had heard about a foaling mare. She wasn't sure Garth hadn't made the whole thing up to get her out of the room. Candy would have argued if Garth's brother and sister and their spouses hadn't been sitting there with ears perked up listening.

"All right," she said. Once they were out of earshot she planned to give Garth a good piece of her mind. But Garth was striding so fast it was all she could do to keep up with him.

The instant they reached the barn, Garth turned on her. "What the hell did you think you were doing in there?"

Candy was completely taken aback by his attack. "What are you talking about?"

"I'm talking about the way you were flirting with Faron."

"Flirting with—"

"He's right, though, you have grown up a lot in three years. I've noticed the difference myself. You're not a kid anymore, are you?"

He grabbed her wrists and pinned them over her head, then backed her up against the rough wooden wall, grinding his hips against hers. To Candy's surprise, he was aroused. To her utter horror, his violent actions caused a rush of desire to flood her body.

He put both of her wrists in one hand, then reached down to free the snap on her jeans. He unzipped them and yanked them down past her buttocks, then freed himself.

"Garth, I don't—"

"You belong to me. No one else. You're *mine!*"

He punctuated the word by thrusting inside her. Candy's body undulated to accommodate his intrusion. His mouth found hers and his tongue forced its way inside. There was nothing gentle about his lovemaking. It was hard and fast and desperate as it had never been before.

It was rough, but it wasn't rape. Because Candy participated wholeheartedly in everything he did. She sucked his tongue into her mouth and parried with her own. She arched her body into his, forcing him to give and give until at last he cried out in exultation. Her own body shuddered in response.

He released her hands at last and pulled her tight against him. He hid his face at her throat. They were both panting with exhaustion, and if either had tried to move they both would have fallen. At last he let her go.

Candy felt bereft when he turned his back on her. She heard his zipper and realized that only the tails of her shirt kept her decent. She turned away to tuck in her shirt and rearrange her jeans. What must he think of her? She had been totally wanton!

Garth shoved all ten fingers through his hair. He had never lost control like that with a woman. Never! He dared a glance at Candy and saw that her lips were swollen, her face flushed. He felt his body responding at the sight and swore loud and long.

Candy's face suddenly bleached white. She knew Garth was wishing she had never come here. She knew he was going to send her away right now, today. And she knew she would go rather than face his family when he felt about her the way he obviously did. "I guess you want me out of here," she said.

"There's a mare that needs looking after," he said. "Unless you're ready to quit and go home."

Candy could hardly believe her ears. There actually *was* a foaling mare! And he wasn't sending her away. "I'm not a quitter," she said. There were things that needed to be said about his irrational fear of Faron's charm, about the way he had made violent love to her. But she knew now there would be time enough later to say them. "Let's go see about that mare."

The pregnant mare had been separated from the other animals at the far end of the barn. In the later stages of the birth she would lie down, but right now she was restlessly pacing the stall.

"Is this the first time she's foaled?" Candy asked.

Garth shook his head. "Second. She had some difficulty the first time, but got through it all right. I have the vet on call in case she has trouble again, but I'm not expecting it."

Garth stepped into the stall and talked soothingly to the mare. "Easy there, Starlight. You're going to be fine. Take it easy, girl." As he ran his hands over the mare's sides he called to Candy. "Come in here a minute."

Candy walked quietly—if not calmly—up beside him.

"Put your hand here."

She did as he asked.

"What do you feel?"

Candy's brows rose in surprise. "Contractions."

Garth nodded. "Right. I don't like the fact she's so restless. I think I'll stay with her tonight. The company might calm her down."

"What about your family?" Candy asked.

"They're all ranchers themselves. They'll understand my stock comes first."

"If you're staying, I'm staying," Candy said. She would much rather spend the time with Garth than endure the speculative looks of his brothers and sister and their spouses.

"Suit yourself," Garth said. "If you ask Charlie, he'll fix us some sandwiches and a thermos of coffee to tide us over tonight. I'll get some blankets from the tack room."

Candy took her time getting back to the kitchen. At the last minute she checked to make sure no sign remained of her lovemaking with Garth in the barn. To her chagrin, her shirt was hanging half in and half out of her jeans. She stopped and tucked it in neatly, then shoved her hands through her hair in hopes of straightening a few of the tangles.

Candy stood at the screen door and watched the antics inside with amazement. Everybody seemed to be in the kitchen helping with supper. Perhaps *helping* was the wrong word. They seemed to be *playing* catch with a raw potato. Tate threw it to—or was she throwing it at?—Faron, who caught it and tossed it to Jesse, who tossed it to Honey, who tossed it to Adam, who tossed it back to Tate. Tate then handed it to Charlie One Horse, who cut it into four pieces and dropped it into a pot of water on the stove.

Candy took advantage of the laughter that followed to quickly step inside.

"Where's Garth?" Faron asked.

"He's in the barn," she answered. "He sent me in to let you know we're going to be spending the night there."

Faron cocked a brow. "Oh, really?"

Candy flushed as she realized Faron had misinterpreted her words. "There's a mare foaling," she rushed to explain. "Garth thinks it would calm her down to have company. So we're going to stay with her."

Faron looked at Tate, who looked at Jesse, who looked back at Faron. Garth had brought a lot of women to Hawk's Way, but he had always kept ranch business and his personal pleasure separate in the past. To be honest, none of the women Garth had ever invited to the ranch would have been willing to spend the night sleeping on a blanket in the hay, let alone baby-sitting a nervous mare.

So the three of them took a second look at Candy Baylor.

Candy tried to ignore the measuring eyes she felt on her as she crossed to Charlie One Horse. "Garth said you'd fix us up a thermos of coffee. I'll make us some sandwiches, since we won't be here for supper."

She was on her way back out the door when Tate stopped her.

"You don't have to spend the night in the barn if you'd rather not," Tate said. "My eldest brother can be something of a bully."

Candy appreciated Tate's concern, but she hurried to reassure the young woman that she wasn't acting under duress. "I came here to learn everything I can about managing a place like Hawk's Way. I'm looking forward to watching this birth. I've never seen a foal born before."

"Never?" Tate asked. "It can be a pretty messy proposition. Are you sure you want to be there?"

Candy nodded her head. "Garth will be there."

Candy didn't realize until the words were out what she had revealed to Tate. Her absolute confidence in Garth. Her absolute certainty that if he was by her side, there was nothing she couldn't handle.

Tate smiled. "Well, well."

There was nothing more Candy could say without making the situation worse than it already was. "I'd better get going. Garth will be waiting for me."

She flushed when she realized how that sounded.

"I mean," she corrected, "he'll be getting hungry."

That was even worse.

"For *supper*," she stressed.

Tate burst out laughing. She nudged Candy out the kitchen door. "Don't worry about us, we'll all be fine. I just hope that mare delivers in time for you two to come to the christening tomorrow."

"Oh, Garth would never—"

Tate shook her head. "I'm afraid you don't know my brother as well as you think. The ranch comes first—always. You won't find anyone here who doesn't understand that. I think all of us love Hawk's Way, but to Garth... It's all Garth will ever have."

Candy heard the caution in Tate's voice. Garth's sister was telling her that while the rest of the Whitelaws might marry and have families, Garth would not. Candy was being warned not to offer Garth her heart, because he would most likely break it.

Candy understood. But she didn't agree. At least, she

didn't want to agree. She had seen signs that Garth might let her climb over, step across or otherwise breach the wall he had built over the years to keep himself safe from hurt. She refused to be discouraged by Tate's well-intentioned warning.

"I'll be careful," Candy said.

Before Tate could say anything more, Candy clutched the thermos and the bag of sandwiches close and hurried out the screen door.

The contrast between the sunlight outside and the dimness of the barn left Candy blind for the few seconds it took her eyes to adjust. She called out to Garth, but got no answer.

"Garth?" she repeated. Still no answer. She felt a sudden anxiety. Something was wrong.

She rushed a few steps farther into the barn, even though she was still having trouble seeing. Which was when she tripped over the wheelbarrow.

Garth saw the sandwiches and thermos go flying in one direction while Candy went the other. He got to her just before she hit the ground. She clutched at him, and it was all he could do to keep from falling with her.

With effort he regained his balance and stood her on her feet. She was still trembling, so he kept his arms around her. His own heart was beating fast from his terror at seeing her about to crack her head on the cement floor. He tightened his grasp, aware of what a narrow escape she'd had.

"Lord almighty, woman! How did you miss seeing that wheelbarrow?" he said angrily.

"Where were you, Garth? I called and you didn't answer," she retorted no less angrily.

"I was trying to make someplace comfortable for you to spend the night," he snapped back.

They glared at each other for another moment before Candy lowered her eyes and hid her face against Garth's chest.

"I thought something had happened to you," she murmured. "I guess I panicked."

"I guess you did," Garth said in a husky voice. He felt a heaviness in his groin, a growing tension that arose from holding her in his arms. He wanted her again.

His need for her frightened him more than he was willing to admit. Once again he pushed her away. To protect himself. And ultimately, to protect her.

Garth let Candy's feet drop and held on just long enough to make sure she was steady on them before he said, "I didn't hear the thermos hit, so maybe it landed in some hay. See if you can find it without falling down again."

Candy was stung by Garth's insinuation that she was clumsy. She marched over to the stall where the thermos had indeed landed safely on a pile of hay and picked it up.

"Here it is," she said. "Catch."

That was all the warning Garth got before she threw it to him. He had already picked up the bag of sandwiches and was forced to drop it again in order to catch the thermos.

Candy walked over, picked up the bag of sandwiches and held them out to Garth. "You dropped something," she said in a sweet voice.

Garth opened his mouth and shut it again.

Candy laughed at the look of chagrin on his face.

Garth turned his back on Candy and headed toward

the stall next to the one where the mare was treading. "Come on. Let's eat."

Candy thought twice about following him. She didn't understand how Garth could be so gentle one moment and so harsh the next. And lately he had no sense of humor. But she was hungry, and going back to the house for more sandwiches would require an explanation she would rather not make.

She found Garth sitting on a thick pile of hay he had covered with a wool blanket. He was leaning back against the side of the stall. He had a cup of coffee in one hand and a roast beef sandwich in the other. Candy joined him, but kept to the farthest edge of the blanket. She helped herself to a cup of coffee from the thermos and grabbed one of the sandwiches.

They ate without conversing. Candy focused her attention on the mare.

"Starlight seems a little quieter," she said.

"Her labor's stopped."

"Is that normal?"

"It happens sometimes."

"Shouldn't we call the vet?" Candy asked anxiously.

"Not yet. We'll wait a while and see if it starts again."

But "a while" turned into several hours. Garth maintained a stony silence that discouraged conversation. Candy wasn't about to let him sulk all evening.

"Mrs. Prescott is very beautiful, don't you think?"

"Faron's stepmother? She's pretty enough."

"And very young."

Garth grunted an assent. "Not what Faron was expecting, that's for sure."

"Then it's true?"

"What's true?"

"Faron had a different father than the rest of you?"

The skin stretched tight across Garth's face. His fists bunched at his sides. "I try not to air the family linen in public."

"It must have been awful for you," she said.

"I survived," he said in a harsh voice. "I told you I don't want to talk about this."

"Why not?"

"You're asking me why I don't want to discuss the fact my mother was a whore!"

Candy scrambled to her feet. "How can you say such a thing about your own mother?"

Garth rose to his feet and towered over her. "Because it's true!"

"People make mistakes—"

"That ruin lives," Garth said ruthlessly. "My mother killed my father as surely as if she'd put a knife in him."

"He was bucked off a horse. He broke his neck. Your mother had nothing to do with that!"

"He was drunk! He was drunk a lot after he found out what she'd done."

"But he forgave her!" Candy protested.

"How the hell do you know that?"

She fisted her hands on her hips. "Tate is proof of it!"

"Tate is no proof at all," Garth countered.

"Why not?" Candy demanded. "Your father had to make love to your mother to get her pregnant again."

"He didn't make love to her," Garth said in an anguished voice. "He raped her."

Candy's face bleached white. "Oh, no. Oh, my God, no!"

"Are you happy now?" Garth put the heels of his

hands to his eyes. "I've never told that to another living soul."

A moment later Candy's arms were around him. There was nothing she could say, so she said nothing.

Garth refused her comfort by physically removing her hands and stepping away from her. But now that the dam had been breached, he was unable to stop the flood of words that followed.

"Jesse and I were supposed to be spending the night with friends. I'd forgotten my jackknife, so I came back. Mom and Dad were arguing. She was begging him to forgive her, to let her make amends. He told her he would never forgive her. He could never forget, either, because Faron was there to remind him every day of what she'd done. But he still intended to exercise his marital rights.

"She told him to stay away from her. That she couldn't bear for him to touch her anymore if all he wanted was sex.

"But he wouldn't be denied. He was stronger than she was. I... I couldn't leave without being discovered. So I heard it all. Her screams. His shouts. And her tears.

"He was sorry afterward. He begged her to forgive him. You see, his betrayal of their love was every bit as wrong—as horrible—as hers had been.

"There were complications, and my mother died in childbirth when Tate was born. And my father...my father cried. He was sorry she was dead. He didn't want to live without her. I think he found a way to kill himself."

Garth's voice had become progressively more guttural, his tone of voice more bitter, more cynical, until finally it ended in a harsh rasp.

Candy had listened in shock and horror to the ghastly circumstances that had molded Garth into the man he was. She felt an awful sense of despair. After hearing such a story, how could she hope to convince Garth that he could trust her? More frightening, how could she trust him not to turn on her as his father had turned on his mother?

"Garth, I—"

"Get out of here."

"I only want to offer you—"

"Sex? Sure, I'll be glad of it. It'll help me forget. That's what you want, isn't it? To make me forget my mother betrayed my father, and that he loved her so much he got himself killed rather than live without her!"

Garth took one step and grasped a handful of her silky blond hair. He yanked her head back so she was forced to look up at him. His arm snaked around her and pulled her tight against his hips.

Candy struggled with all her might. There was no way to deceive herself that this was love. It was something violent, something painful. And it would kill forever any feelings she had for him if she let him go through with it. She was certain Garth knew exactly how she felt, certain that he was driving her away to save her because he feared, as he had all these years, that if he ever loved a woman he might turn out to be just like his father.

"Garth, stop!" she said. "You aren't like him. You aren't! And I'm not like her. Don't make it impossible—"

"It *is* impossible! Don't you see that?"

"No!" she said fiercely. She fought back the tears that brimmed in her eyes.

"Don't fool yourself!" he said with a sneer.

"You're the fool, Garth Whitelaw. And I'm not going to stay here and let you do something you'll be sorry for later." She stomped hard on his instep. He yelped and let her go.

Candy raced from the barn, not looking back to see whether he was chasing her. She didn't stop until she reached the kitchen door. She paused then, to make sure there was no one inside to see the tears that fell in hot tracks on her cheeks.

She snuck in past the parlor where she saw the two mothers nursing their babies. It struck fresh pain in her heart to see her secret dreams played out in front of her and know she would never be a mother sitting there in front of the fireplace at Hawk's Way with Garth's baby at her breast.

She tiptoed up the stairs and closed her bedroom door behind her. She stared at the bed, knowing she would never be able to sleep.

Candy had to think what to do next. Maybe the time had come to leave Hawk's Way. She wouldn't be able to stand seeing Garth in pain and knowing he refused to reach out for the comfort—not necessarily sexual—she was willing to offer.

But maybe she ought to stay. And give him comfort whether he wanted it or not.

It was a long night. She was grateful for the sunrise, but she still hadn't made up her mind what to do. She would at least stay at Hawk's Way long enough to attend the christening. After that...well, she would see.

CHAPTER EIGHT

CANDY WAS THE first one down to the kitchen in the morning and started the bacon for breakfast. She put an apron over the simple jersey dress she had chosen to wear to the christening. It felt strange to be wearing nylons again. She had almost forgotten her other life as the debutante daughter of millionaire Evan Baylor.

Candy was soon joined by Charlie One Horse.

"Where's Garth?" he asked. "I figured the two of you would come in together for breakfast."

"I spent the night upstairs. I have no idea where Garth spent it. You're welcome to go find him. I'm cooking breakfast."

"Women," Charlie muttered. "Can't live with 'em, can't live without 'em."

They weren't alone for long. Jesse and Honey and Adam and Tate soon showed up with the babies. This time Honey's two gangly boys, Jack and Jonathan, were with them. Candy thought dinner the previous night had been chaos—breakfast was even less civilized.

Tate and Jesse starting tossing eggs back and forth. One of them missed, and Candy turned to find raw egg dripping down the front of the refrigerator. Shells lay cracked and broken on the tile floor, which was layered with a fine dusting of the flour Honey was using to make biscuits on the counter beside the stove. Both the babies were gurgling, and Madelyn was rocking their cradles, trying to keep the noise level down.

They took turns eating as the fried eggs were done. Charlie had already cracked two eggs into the pan for Faron when he realized Faron and Belinda hadn't come down yet.

"Tate, go call your brother," Charlie said.

Tate stepped to the kitchen doorway and yelled, "Faaarrrooon! Your eggs are done!"

"I could've done that," Charlie muttered.

Moments later Faron appeared. "I'm hungry as a bear. Where's my breakfast?"

"Still in the pan," Charlie replied.

"Where's Garth?" Faron asked Candy.

"Why ask me?" she retorted.

"I thought you two—"

"You thought wrong!" Candy said.

At that moment, Garth stepped into the kitchen from the interior hallway. Obviously he hadn't spent the night in the barn, either. He was dressed for church in a dark Western suit with a crisply ironed white shirt that set off his tanned skin and dark features. Lord, he was a good-looking man!

Candy pointedly turned her back on him and focused her attention on the stove.

She missed seeing the flash of pain in Garth's eyes, but Charlie One Horse did not. He shook his head in disgust and muttered, "Women."

Garth felt like a wounded animal, defensive, ready to lash out. He stared at his brothers and sister, daring them to say something, anything that would give him the excuse he was looking for to explode. Fortunately for all of them, Belinda chose that moment to make her entrance.

Every male eye in the room turned to stare at her. She had put her long blond hair up in an elegant twist, and she was wearing a sheath that outlined her figure, even though it concealed her from neck to knee.

"You look absolutely gorgeous," Tate said.

Faron slipped a protective arm around Belinda's waist and said, "And she's as nice as she is beautiful." He had obviously laid something other than a maternal claim to his stepmother, and was challenging his family to say anything about it.

This time it was Charlie One Horse who stepped in to diffuse the tension. He put a hand around Maddy's shoulder and said, "I 'spect I gotta vote that this here is the purtiest woman in the room."

Candy looked over her shoulder in time to see Maddy's blush. There could be no arguing that Charlie's compliment had made the grandmotherly woman glow.

Not to be outdone, Jesse announced, "Honey is the sweetest!"

Adam countered with, "Tate is the cutest."

That left Candy as the only woman in the room who hadn't been complimented. She stood by the stove, spatula in hand, staring at Garth and waiting.

Say it. Lay some claim to me. Name me yours, and I will be. Do it, Garth!

She willed him to speak, but he said nothing.

At last he turned to Tate. "We'd better get moving if we're going to be at the church on time. Finish up your breakfasts. I'll go get the car." He turned on his heel and stalked out the screen door, letting it slam behind him.

Candy's face paled. A moment later she left the kitchen with the excuse that she had to put on some more lipstick.

"But she hasn't eaten yet," Jesse protested.

Honey jabbed him in the ribs. "Hush."

When it came time to leave for church, there could be no doubt in anyone's mind that a rift had developed between Candy and Garth. She made a point of riding to church in a separate car. However, Faron maneuvered things so she was forced to sit in the pew beside Garth during the christening ceremony.

Candy had never been so aware of him. He was like a package of dynamite set to explode. All that was needed was a spark to set him off. Candy didn't intend to light that particular fire. She planned to ignore Garth for as long as it took to get back to the house and get her bags packed.

The incident this morning had finally made up her mind for her. Garth wasn't going to change. He could no more let go of the past than the black stallion that had refused to surrender his fear and his fury. She had learned everything she had come to learn. It was time to leave.

Only Garth apparently had other ideas.

Garth's family was celebrating the christening of Brett Patrick Philips with a picnic under the moss-laden live oak that shaded the back lawn. Candy stayed just long enough not to be rude, but excused herself from a game of softball that was forming and headed upstairs.

She was in her room packing when she heard someone knocking—pounding, really—on her door. Her heart began thumping with an equally powerful force.

"Who is it?"

"You know damned well who it is!" Garth shouted. "Open the door, Candy."

"I'm busy, Garth."

The door swung open so hard it crashed against the wall. She stood staring at him with wide, wary eyes.

He took one look at the suitcase on the bed and said, "What the hell do you think you're doing?"

What she was doing was perfectly obvious to both of them. "I'm packing."

"Why?"

Another stupid question. "Because I'm leaving."

"Starlight is in heavy labor. I need your help."

There were at least three men in the backyard who could have helped him, and she would have guessed that several of the Whitelaw women would have been equally capable of delivering a foal. Garth had the vet on call, as well. But she didn't point out to him the absurdity of his statement.

Candy supposed she owed Garth an explanation for why she could no longer remain at Hawk's Way. It wasn't going to be easy or pleasant making it, but it would allow her the mental peace she needed to get on with her life. A life without Garth Whitelaw.

She finished folding the jeans in her hands and laid them on top of the rest of the clothes in the suitcase. "All right, Garth. I'll come with you. We need to talk."

When he reached out to her, she avoided his hand. She could feel the tension in him as she crossed past him and out her bedroom door. "Have you called the vet?" she asked as they reached the bottom of the stairs.

"He's taking care of another emergency. He'll get here as soon as he can."

Candy felt a small chill of alarm. Maybe Garth's tension wasn't all directed at her. Maybe he was anticipating trouble. As she stepped through the screen door she said, "Maybe Faron or Jesse should be the one to help."

"There's nothing they know that I don't," Garth replied. It might have sounded like bragging if Candy hadn't known it was very likely the truth.

Candy stopped at the door to the barn. "What is it you need me for?" she demanded.

There was a long silence before he said, "You started this. I thought you should finish it."

His response was vague enough that he could have been referring to any number of things. "*You started this.*" Started *what?* The foaling of the mare? The taming of the stallion? Learning the art of breeding and training cutting horses? She suspected that where Garth was concerned, *this* referred to her relationship with him. Well, if he wanted to see a formal ending to the latter, she could and would provide it for him.

"All right, Garth," she said at last. "I'll see it to the end."

Her *it* was as vague as his *this.* Nevertheless, she was certain Garth understood her.

When Candy got a good look at the mare, her alarm increased. She turned to Garth and said, "She seems to be in a lot of pain, Garth. Is that normal?"

"Some pain is normal." He shoved a hand through his hair. "But not this much. There's something wrong." He whooshed out a breath of air. "I just hope the vet gets here in time to make a difference."

Candy realized suddenly why Garth had wanted her here. He was concerned about the mare. With his brothers or sister he would have had to maintain the stoic facade of uncaring. It was a mask he wore to hide his feelings—his very real and vulnerable feelings—from them. Last night had been a breakthrough of sorts.

Today, for the first time—too late?—Garth was allowing her to see behind the mask.

A short half hour after Candy arrived at the barn, the mare went down. It was clear she was struggling to deliver the foal without much result.

"Shouldn't we call the vet again?" Candy asked, her fear apparent in her voice.

"He said he'd come when he can. Doc Stellan knows I wouldn't have called him if I didn't need him. He'll be here as soon as he can get here."

They were both sweating from the heat. Garth had his sleeves rolled up so he could check on the mare's progress occasionally. They left the mare momentarily alone in the stall so Garth could wash up at the sink in the barn.

"I should have called Doc Stellan the first time Starlight's labor stopped," Garth muttered to himself. "I shouldn't have waited."

"How could you have known?" Candy said, trying to ease his guilt.

"It's my job to know!" he snapped at her.

"You can't know everything!" she snapped right back.

"I sure as hell was mistaken about you," he retorted. "I thought you might be different. But you're just like every other woman—"

A screaming neigh cut him off.

"It's Starlight!" Candy cried.

The two of them set off running for the stall that contained the mare. For a moment they stood stunned.

Starlight lay on her side, clearly too exhausted to do what was necessary to complete the birth process. The tiny foal lay on the hay, still in its birth sac.

Candy had never seen Garth move so fast. He was

on his knees beside the foal an instant later. He tore the sac away from the foal's mouth and nose with his hands and reached inside its mouth to clear the passage so the animal could breathe freely. But that wasn't enough.

"Breathe, damn you!" he demanded of the motionless form in his arms.

Meanwhile, Candy tended to the mare. Starlight was weak, but she was still alive. "Keep fighting, girl," she crooned to the mare. "You can make it. Keep fighting and everything will be all right."

Candy watched as Garth tried several ways to resuscitate the foal, even using his own breath to try and revive the tiny being. She could see now that the filly had a white star on its forehead that was an exact replica of the one Starlight bore.

At last Garth laid the foal down in the straw. His back was to Candy, so she couldn't see his face. But there was no mistaking the way his body heaved with silent grief. She stroked the mare the way she wanted to comfort him.

Until she realized the mare was also dead.

"Garth? *Garth?*"

Garth swiped at his eyes before he turned to face Candy. He saw the horror on her face and looked at the mare. Starlight had hemorrhaged, and he had been so busy with the foal that he hadn't noticed what was happening.

"She's dead, Garth. Starlight is dead."

"Hell. Dammit to hell!"

Candy wanted to hold Garth. She wanted to be held by him. But neither of them moved for what seemed a very long time.

"Candy, I—"

His dark eyes were full of so much pain. She crossed

the distance between them on her knees. Then she was in his arms, and he was holding her tight, pressing kisses to her face and neck.

"Hold me," he said. "Hold me."

"I am. I will."

Candy didn't know how long they stayed like that. Her heart nearly broke when she felt his tears against her cheek. He *could* feel. He *did* care. Only he wasn't able to let his family see his vulnerability. He had needed to be strong, to hold his family together, to be a parent when his own parents were no longer there to do their jobs.

When at last he let her go, Candy searched out Garth's face, hoping the mask wouldn't be there. But the vulnerable man who had cried for the loss of a mare and a foal was gone. In his place was the Garth Whitelaw who wanted a woman for one purpose, and one purpose only.

In that moment she hated him. He had let her glimpse the man he could be, given her hope when she had been hopeless. And made it all the more difficult to say what she knew must be said.

"I'll be leaving in the morning."

"No one's stopping you."

That hurt. As he had known it would when he said it. Candy swallowed over the lump in her throat. "I want to thank you for everything you've taught me."

"There's more you have to learn," he said.

"It would take years to learn everything. I know enough to get started on my own. I thank you for that."

"Tell your father when you see him that he can send Comanche Moon here anytime it's convenient."

"Why would he send Comanche Moon here?"

"Your father and I had a little agreement."

Candy's lips flattened. "What sort of agreement?"

Garth shrugged negligently. "I agreed to teach you everything you wanted to know, and he agreed to sell me Comanche Moon at a fair price. The bargain is concluded the day you leave Hawk's Way."

"Were lessons in the bedroom part of the deal?" she asked in a scathing voice. "How could you? How could you blackmail my father that way?"

"He came to me," Garth countered. "And I'm paying a fair price for the horse."

"And that makes it all right?" she demanded. "I hate you! I don't think I could ever loathe anyone as much as I loathe you right now. I can't wait to get out of here!"

Candy surged to her feet and nearly fell again because her legs refused to hold her. Garth half rose to help her, and she shoved his hands away.

"Don't worry. You'll get what you bargained for. I'll make sure my father ships Comanche Moon here the instant I arrive home. Goodbye, Garth. And good riddance."

She left the barn at a walk, determined not to flee like the wounded animal she was. But her walk turned into a trot, and her trot into a run. She saw Garth's family as blurs of color as she sought out the safety of her room.

Garth stood unmoving for a long time. He didn't know why he had driven her away. He had come so close, so close to letting her see how much he cared for her. At the last instant he had turned away from the tenderness she had offered him. He was like that big black beast, unable to let go of the past. And it was destroying him, as it would one day destroy the beast.

Garth kept his distance from his family the rest of the day. He ordered Tom Handy to take care of removing the dead mare and foal. He was too afraid he might break down and cry if he saw them again. He called the vet and told him not to come.

Then Garth saddled up a horse and went riding across the vast acres of Hawk's Way, through canyons and gullies as he crisscrossed the rugged terrain. He rode without stopping until both he and the horse were exhausted.

It was nearly midnight when he arrived home. He breathed a sigh of relief when he saw the house was dark. There was a light on in the kitchen, but Charlie usually left a light burning in case someone got hungry during the night.

Garth was headed for the parlor and two long fingers of whiskey, but he ran head-on into Charlie One Horse when he stepped inside the kitchen door.

"Where you been?" the old man asked.

"Riding."

"Case you hadn't noticed, today was supposed to be a family celebration."

"I wasn't in much of a mood to celebrate," Garth said in a curt voice. "I lost Starlight and the foal both."

"Candy told me what happened."

Garth didn't want to ask, but he couldn't help himself. "Is she still here?"

"Where else would she be?"

Garth breathed a sigh of relief, although he knew he'd only had a reprieve, not a pardon.

"Women," Charlie muttered. "You gonna marry that girl?"

Garth's dark eyes were bleak. "She's decided to leave Hawk's Way."

"Mistake lettin' her get away."

"What am I supposed to do? Hog-tie her to keep her here?"

Charlie opened the refrigerator and began looking for something to snack on. "You admittin' you wanta keep her?"

"I want her," Garth said.

"You wanta marry her?" Charlie asked again.

"I want her," Garth repeated stubbornly.

Charlie shook his head again. "Gotta do better than that. Else you're gonna lose her sure. Can't get that filly without promisin' marriage. No sirree, Bob. With a girl like Candy, it's gotta be marriage or nothin'."

"You finished saying your piece, old man?"

"I'm finished."

"Then I'll be saying good night."

When Garth was gone, the old man shut the refrigerator door and stared at the ceiling. "Sure thought that filly had him lassoed good and tight. Ah, well, she ain't gone yet."

Meanwhile, Garth found the whiskey in the parlor and poured himself a glass without turning on a light. He crossed and sat in the leather chair before the fireplace and put his feet up on the rawhide stool that had held generations of Whitelaw boots. He stared into the glowing embers that were all that was left of what he was sure must have been a roaring fire earlier in the evening.

He sipped his whiskey trying to dull the pain. He thought about what Charlie had said. Would proposing marriage keep Candy Baylor from leaving tomorrow morning? He recalled the words she had shouted at him.

I hate you. I can't wait to get out of here!

Somehow he didn't think a marriage proposal would be very welcome right now.

Garth didn't know how long he had been sitting alone when Faron slumped into the leather chair beside him.

"What are you doing sitting here in the dark?" Faron asked.

"I could ask you the same thing," Garth responded.

"Women," Faron said in a tone reminiscent of the one Charlie One Horse had used.

Garth grunted an affirmation of the sentiment.

Neither of them said anything more, each caught up in his own thoughts. Occasionally, Garth drank from the glass of whiskey he held in his hand.

Without either of them knowing quite how it happened, Faron was spilling out his problems with Belinda Prescott. He had fallen in love with his stepmother but was unsure whether she loved him. They were both working hard to repair the ranch where Belinda lived so it could be sold, when all Faron really wanted to do was marry Belinda and settle down at King's Castle and raise children.

Garth urged Faron to keep the ranch. And to pursue Belinda, if that was what he wanted.

"What are you doing hiding down here? I never thought you were a coward," Garth challenged.

Faron took enough umbrage to say, "I'm not the only Whitelaw sitting in the dark. What's the story between you and Candy Baylor?"

"None of your business," Garth said brusquely.

A slow smile grew on Faron's face. "Well, well, big brother. How the mighty have fallen."

"What's that supposed to mean?"

"You figure it out. I'm going upstairs where I hope there's a lady waiting for me. You can sit here alone in the dark all night if you want. But I suspect there might be a lady somewhere waiting for you, too."

"She'll have a long wait," Garth retorted.

Faron laughed. "Good night, Garth. Sleep well."

"Get out of here and leave me in peace."

"I'll leave, but I doubt you'll have much peace until you seek out a certain blond-haired, gray-eyed woman."

Hell and damnation! Garth wanted desperately to follow his youngest brother's advice. He wanted to go to Candy, to seek forgiveness, to beg her to stay. But that would mean admitting to her, and to himself, just how much he needed her. And that was still far too dangerous a proposition.

So he would have to let her go. When he thought of the life stretching out in front of him, it seemed bleak indeed.

Garth threw his whiskey glass against the stone hearth with all the pent-up anger and frustration he was feeling. The shattering glass sounded like an explosion in the silent house. He waited for his family to rouse, to come down and demand an explanation for his violent act.

But they slept on. Unaware of the turbulence in his mind and soul as the one women he had ever loved, would ever love, walked out of his life.

Tomorrow. Tomorrow before she left he would confront her one last time. He would tell her what he was feeling. He would lay his future happiness in her hands. He would give her his heart and wait to see if she broke it.

CHAPTER NINE

HE WAS TOO LATE. When Garth knocked on Candy's door the next morning, she was already gone. Soon after that a long-distance call came for Faron and Belinda. A corporate buyer wanted to see King's Castle. They had to cut their visit short to return to Wyoming. Because the other two couples had driven to Hawk's Way from their southwest Texas ranches, they left right after lunch to try and miss the worst of the Labor Day traffic.

By late afternoon, Garth's family was gone from Hawk's Way, and he was alone. He avoided Charlie One Horse because he didn't want to hear the old man's "I told you so."

Since his brothers and sister had left the ranch and gone their own ways, Garth had managed to keep the loneliness at bay. He had stayed busy, and having Charlie One Horse around gave things a sense of continuity. But after Labor Day that changed. Garth was aware there was something—someone—missing in his life. The days felt hollow, empty of all joy.

Within a week, Evan Baylor's prize stud arrived in a horse trailer, along with a note from Evan saying that once he received Garth's check for the agreed upon amount, their agreement would be fulfilled. Garth now had what he'd bargained for. But not what he wanted.

He wandered around Hawk's Way, trying to find a

focus for his days, feeling the awful loneliness of the nights. For the next week, he couldn't seem to find the time to write that check to Evan Baylor. He had thought there was nothing that could make him change his mind about trusting a woman. He was discovering that in this, too, he had been mistaken.

Two weeks to the day after Candy had left him, Garth awoke with a purpose that drove him like a whip. "Hurry up with that breakfast, Charlie. I've got a lot of traveling to do today."

"You goin' someplace?"

"I'm taking Comanche Moon back to Evan Baylor."

Charlie gave Garth a speculative look. "You thinkin' 'bout makin' a trade?"

"I might be."

"Good idea," Charlie said. "You need that filly a lot more than you need that stud."

Garth grinned. "For once I have to agree with you."

The grin didn't stay on Garth's face for long. In fact, his look was downright grim by the time he arrived at Evan Baylor's doorstep. The drive to the B Bar Ranch outside of Dallas was long and grueling. The terrain was flat, the weather hot, and he had never seen a more welcome sight than Evan Baylor's Spanish hacienda.

The ranch house had thick, white-washed adobe walls that kept the heat out. He stepped through an arched doorway into a house that was dark and cool. The furniture consisted of heavy Mediterranean pieces accented by Navajo and Hopi Indian decorations. The living room was spacious and there were several arches inset along the walls adding to the Spanish flavor of the room.

Garth stood with his hat in his hand waiting to see Candy's father. He wasn't sure what his reception would be, but he was willing to insist that Evan Baylor talk to him.

Evan was cordial, if not friendly. "I'm surprised to see you, Garth. What's brought you over this way?"

"I've come to return Comanche Moon. I left him at the barn."

Evan arched a brow. "I always keep my bargains, Garth. You earned the horse. He's yours."

This time Garth heard the irritation in the older man's voice. "I didn't hold to my part of the bargain," Garth said.

"Oh?"

"I told your daughter about our agreement."

"Oh." Evan pinched the bridge of his nose. That explained Candy's cold behavior toward him for the past two weeks. She hadn't told him much about what had happened at Hawk's Way, except to say that she had learned a great deal. And that she never wanted to see Garth Whitelaw again for as long as she lived.

"I want to talk to her," Garth said.

"What makes you think she's here?"

There was a pause. Then, "Is she?"

Evan realized the futility of that sort of deceit. Garth would keep looking until he found her. "Candy doesn't want to see you."

"Too damn bad. I want to see her, and I won't take no for an answer."

"Now, look here, young man—"

"Either you ask her to come here, or I'm going to go hunting for her."

"Like hell!" Evan said. "You'll have to go through me first."

"If I have to, I will," Garth threatened.

"That won't be necessary."

Both men turned to face Candy, who was standing in one of the arched doorways. Garth had been hungry for the sight of her, and he ate her now with his eyes. He noticed changes in her appearance. There were smudges under her eyes that told him she hadn't been sleeping well, and her jeans hung on her, which told him she hadn't been eating right, either.

But her gray eyes flashed fire, and her chin jutted pugnaciously. She might have been bucked off, but she was raring to get right back on and apparently willing to use spurs, if that was what it took to stay there.

"I'll talk to him, Daddy."

"Do you want me to stay?" Evan asked.

Garth didn't bat an eyelash.

"No, Daddy. I'll be all right."

Evan looked from his daughter to the man who had come seeking her. "Call if you need me." Evan made it plain with a look he shot at Garth that although he was leaving them alone, he wasn't going far.

Candy followed her father's progress from the room, then turned to Garth. "Say what you came to say and get out."

Garth wasn't a man used to making explanations. Nor apologies. For Candy he was willing to do both. If only he could get the words out. But wanting to explain how he felt about her and being able to do so were two different things.

"I didn't figure you for a quitter." What he had intended as a compliment came out sounding more like a taunt.

"I'm not!" Candy retorted, stung into speaking.

Garth stared at her, trying to say with his eyes what he wasn't able to express in words.

I want you back at Hawk's Way. I need you in my life.

What he said was, "If you want to be the second-best wrangler in Texas, you've got a lot more to learn."

Candy bit down on an oath that sought voice. She had control of her temper. Barely. She wasn't going to allow Garth to provoke her into losing it. She was incensed by the mockery in Garth's voice and frustrated by the fact that he seemed determined to ignore the intimate relationship that had developed between them at Hawk's Way.

Candy had hoped and prayed every night since she left Hawk's Way that Garth would see the error of his ways. She had dreamed that he came after her and asked her to marry him. Well, he was here. But he wasn't following the script she had written for him. And she was just furious enough to take him up on his challenge.

"We'll just see who's a quitter!" She marched to the door through which her father had left and called, "Daddy! Come here, please!"

Evan came on the run. He looked worriedly from his daughter to the stony face of the man who had come to get her.

"I'm going back to Hawk's Way," she announced.

"Are you sure that's what you want to do? You aren't being forced or—"

"No one's forcing me into anything." She met Garth's glacial stare with fiery eyes. "I know exactly what I'm doing."

Candy hoped she was right. The risk of giving Garth a second chance was great, of course. But the rewards, if she could get past that cynical shell he used to protect himself, would be even greater. Just coming here, she realized, had been a huge step for Garth.

"I'll go pack a few things," she told Garth. "We can leave as soon as I'm done."

Once Candy was gone, Evan eyed Garth speculatively. "Would you like a drink?"

"I could use one," Garth admitted. "But I've got a lot of driving to do yet today."

"A cup of coffee?"

"That sounds good."

Evan led Garth into the decorated tile kitchen and poured him a cup of coffee from the pot on the stove. "Make yourself comfortable." He urged Garth to sit at the small wooden table set close to the wall and took the chair across from him.

"You broke my daughter's heart," he said.

"It wasn't my intention to hurt her."

"Yet you did," Evan said. "You'd better be damn sure of what you're doing, young man. Because you won't get another chance with my daughter."

Garth took that to mean Evan wouldn't allow it. He didn't argue with Candy's father. He took a sip of the coffee, which was hot enough to burn his tongue, and kept his thoughts to himself.

Evan was worried. Candy had been miserable in the two weeks since she had returned from Hawk's Way. His gentle probing had revealed little about what had happened to bring her home. She had mentioned Garth but had refused to discuss the man. Garth's arrival explained a lot of things Evan had been wondering about.

Obviously his daughter and Garth Whitelaw had been having a love affair. It was difficult as a father to allow Candy to leave again with the wrangler. But she was a grown woman, and she knew what she wanted. Evan had always known he was going to lose his daughter someday. He would never know what Candy saw in a man as hard as Garth Whitelaw. But then, Evan hadn't known why his wife, Roberta, had chosen him, either. Nonetheless, they had enjoyed a loving and happy relationship for as long as Roberta had lived.

Evan interpreted Garth's sudden appearance at the B Bar as a good sign. The fact that Garth had returned the stallion was an even better sign. The young man's insistence on seeing Candy and his refusal to be deterred from his purpose was the best sign of all. Evan needed those signs to justify letting his daughter go with this man who had hurt her so terribly. He hoped Candy knew what she was doing. Because Evan was sure Garth Whitelaw had the power to break his daughter's heart.

"I'm ready," Candy said, joining them in the kitchen.

Garth rose and took the suitcase from her. "I left the truck at the barn." At Candy's questioning look he added, "I brought Comanche Moon back."

"He didn't keep his part of the bargain," Evan explained. "He told you I arranged for him to teach you in exchange for the horse."

"Was that all you arranged?" Candy asked.

Evan looked hurt that she would even ask. "Absolutely."

"We'd better leave if we're going to get back to Hawk's Way tonight," Garth said.

There wasn't much to see once it got dark, and neither of them wanted to listen to the radio. Candy sat with her arm resting on the open window, staring out at the shadowy landscape.

"I've been doing a lot of thinking since you left Hawk's Way," Garth said at last.

"Oh?" Candy's heart began to beat a little faster.

"I... I've blamed every woman I ever met for what my mother did to my father."

Candy remained silent.

Garth swallowed over the knot in his throat and kept talking. "I always figured that if I never let myself love a woman, she could never hurt me."

"So you never loved anyone," Candy said in a soft voice. *Not even me?* she wanted to ask. That was entirely too dangerous a question. The fact that Garth had come after her was significant. It didn't mean he had let go of the past. Only that he wanted to try.

Neither of them said anything more until they could see the lights of Hawk's Way in the distance. Candy turned to Garth and said, "What is it you want from me, Garth?"

I want you to love me. But he couldn't yet say that to her aloud. "I don't know," he said gruffly. "I want you. I always have." *I always will.*

Candy sighed. Trust a man to focus on the physical. "That isn't enough, Garth."

"I know," he admitted with a sigh easily as large as her own.

Candy took a deep breath and asked, "Do you really think you can change?"

Garth met her eyes with a bleak look. "I don't know."

It might not have been a very satisfying answer, but it was an honest one. Candy realized that only the test of time would tell whether Garth could put the past behind him.

When they arrived at Hawk's Way, Charlie One Horse

was nowhere to be seen. Garth carried Candy's suitcase up to her room—the one next to his. She looked at him askance, but he did no more than set down the suitcase and back away to the door.

"You know where everything is," he said. Then he closed the door between them.

Candy frowned. She knew Garth had been aroused. She had seen the glitter in his dark eyes, the tautness of his body when he passed by her, not to mention the ridge in his jeans. Yet he hadn't tried to seduce her. She was confused by his restraint. But not discouraged.

In fact, Garth's unusual behavior continued over the next several days and weeks. His eyes never left her, and when she caught his glance the heat was enough to warm her deep inside. But they continued tiptoeing around each other, afraid to wreck the fragile balance in their relationship.

Candy went back to work with the black stallion. She got up before dawn each day to make time for an extra session with the animal. She was close to earning his trust. She just knew it!

At last the day came when she held out her hand, and the stallion walked up to take the cube of sugar from her. Of course he instantly danced away again. But if he had done it once, Candy knew that sooner or later he would do it again. It was only the first step, but it was a big one.

"I didn't think that would ever happen."

Candy whirled to find Garth directly behind her. She smiled up at him. "He's a lot like you."

"How's that?"

"Afraid to trust."

Garth stiffened. Candy had just stepped over the invisible line they had drawn regarding discussion of their relationship. "I suppose next you'll be holding out a cube of sugar to me," he said in an acid voice.

"I would if I thought it would sweeten you up any," she retorted. When she tried to leave, Garth caught her wrist and snapped her back around to face him.

"Where are you going?" he demanded, terrified that she might be leaving him again.

"I have work to do."

"Nothing that can't wait." Garth had stayed away from Candy as long as he could. Simply touching her had brought back memories of how she felt in his arms. "Come with me." He paused and added, "Please."

"When you put it that way," she said, "I find myself inclined to join you."

Garth picked her up in his arms and headed for the house.

"Garth!" she said with a breathless laugh. "Everyone will see us."

"Let them look. I don't care."

He took the stairs two at a time, and by the time he reached his room, Candy was as aroused as he was. When Garth let her feet go, she laced her hands around his neck and urged his head down for her kiss.

The first touch of Garth's lips sent a shiver through Candy.

"Garth."

It was all she said, but it was enough to send the blood pumping through Garth's body. He wasn't feeling patient, but he forced himself to slow down. His mouth trailed over her temple, down her cheek to her ear. Her head fell back and he kissed her throat. He sucked hard enough to put a love bruise on her, branding her as his.

It was a savage, primitive thing to do, but he wasn't feeling very civilized at the moment.

Candy wasn't aware of the pain, only the pleasure of Garth's mouth on her flesh. Sensation streaked through her, until she was quivering with desire.

They shed their clothes like winter coats in springtime, and then they were standing naked before each other.

"You are so beautiful," Garth said as he reached out reverently to cup her breasts. He lowered his head to suckle her, and Candy's whole body arched toward him.

Her hands landed low on his hips and slid around to his buttocks. Her fingernails left crescents as she held on for dear life.

Garth picked her up and laid her on the bed, mantling her body with his. Moments later he was inside her. She was wet and tight and welcoming.

"You have no idea how wonderful this feels," he said with a satisfied groan.

"Oh, I think I do," Candy said. She moaned deep in her throat.

Garth put his hands on either side of Candy's face and forced her to look at him. His voice was fierce, his dark eyes savage. "Don't ever leave me again, Candy. I need you."

It wasn't a declaration of love, but Candy suspected it was as close to one as Garth Whitelaw had ever come. She put her hands on either side of his face. "I love you, Garth."

She was afraid he would turn away from the words, as he had in the past. This time his face bore a look of exultation.

Garth didn't say anything more. Neither did she. But

there was something different about this loving. Something deeper. More powerful. More moving than anything that had passed between them before.

Afterward, they lay close in each other's arms, until their panting eased and they could speak again.

"Will you spend the night here with me?" Garth asked.

Candy remembered what Garth had said when she had first asked him why he had never married. *Why buy the cow when the milk's free?* But she couldn't bring herself to leave him. If he didn't love her enough to marry her, she would know soon enough. And if that turned out to be the case...

She might not have a lifetime with Garth; she might have only the next few days or weeks. She planned to make a lifetime of memories for the day when she might be forced to leave him.

Candy snuggled closer to Garth and laid her arm across his chest. She angled her nose under his chin until she was comfortable and said, "I'll stay."

Garth pulled her snug against him. This felt right. It felt good. Surely it was safe to love her. Surely he would find a way to convince her that she belonged with him without having to say the words. Because it simply wasn't possible for him to speak them. It ought to be enough to prove to her how he felt.

Garth fell asleep trying to convince himself that Candy didn't—wouldn't—need to hear the words to know he loved her.

CHAPTER TEN

CANDY SUCCEEDED BEYOND her wildest expectations with the black stallion. In a matter of weeks, he was not only coming to her for sugar, but she had put a halter on him and was leading him around.

"I think I'll call Señor Santos and tell him I've decided to collect on the fee he offered me, after all," Garth said when he caught Candy standing inside the corral stroking the stallion's neck.

"What fee?"

"He said if I could get Midnight to stand at stud I could breed him to the mare of my choice."

Candy stammered, "B-but we don't know how he'd act with a mare. He might savage her."

Garth grinned. "I don't think so. Midnight's problem was with humans. Nobody could handle him to get him close to a ready mare. I feel certain he'd know what to do if the situation arose."

"But—"

Garth's voice hardened. "I say he's ready. I'm going to have him cover Starlight's firstborn tomorrow afternoon."

Candy paled. Since the death of Starlight and her second foal, Candy had sought out Starlight's firstborn, a five-year-old mare out of Starlight by Hawk's Sanctuary. The mare's name was Hawk's Star and she was beautiful, a rich glossy black, with a star on her forehead. Candy had befriended the horse, and although she would have been more than happy for Midnight to prove himself, she didn't want it to be with Hawk's Star.

The thought of the savage stallion covering the mare left her feeling physically ill. "I'm afraid," she said.

"Of what?" Garth asked.

"That he'll hurt her."

"I admit the mating of two horses sounds wild and brutal, but it isn't usually. I'll keep an eye on Midnight to make sure he doesn't get vicious with Hawk's Star."

Candy swallowed hard and said, "If you're going to be there, then I want to be there, too."

Garth eyed her sharply. "Are you sure?"

"Midnight knows me best. He'll respond best to me if it's necessary to separate the two horses."

Garth snorted. "Once he's with her, his mind won't be on leaving."

"Nevertheless," Candy said, "I want to be there."

For someone who wanted to possess her own stable and breed her own stock, Candy had been strangely reluctant to observe the mating of stallion and mare. She had studied Garth's stud books to see which stallions he put with which mares, and looked to see the results in their offspring. She understood what assets Garth was looking for in an animal, and how he chose one horse to be bred to another.

But it seemed profane somehow to stand by and watch while a stallion covered a mare, even though she knew it was done for the protection of both animals. The mare might lash out with her hooves at the stallion, or he might savage her in return. In the wild, one animal could run away from the other. In a corral, there was no escape.

The humans who had put them there together had to rescue the one that needed help.

It didn't help her peace of mind when Candy discovered the next afternoon that Hawk's Star had never been bred before.

"She'll be scared. She'll fight him!"

"No, she won't," Garth reassured her. "She's ready. I've had them in side-by-side corrals all morning. She's been flirting with that stud like a two-dollar—" Garth cut off the vulgar reference he had been going to make and finished, "She's been flirting with him all morning."

"She's so small," Candy protested.

"She'll be fine."

"He looks so wild."

"He'll settle down."

"It's her first time."

"There has to be a first time for everyone."

The sexual tension in the animals had been transmitted to the humans. Candy's body felt stretched and full, and she was aware of every move Garth made. She wanted him, had unconsciously sent out sensual lures to him all day. Like the mare, she teased Garth and then moved away, making it necessary for him to follow her.

Garth's mouth was dry as a bone. His body was strung taut as barbed wire. He wasn't sure if Candy was aware of how she was teasing him, taunting him, but he damned sure wasn't going to wait much longer to do something about it.

If the truth were known, Garth was as anxious about putting the two animals together as Candy was. The difference was, he had previously observed the wildness, the naked ferocity of the act that was coming. She had not.

Garth opened the gate, and Candy led Midnight inside the small breeding corral. She left the halter on Midnight so he would be easier to catch, but disconnected the lead. She stepped out, and Garth closed the gate behind her. Tom Handy was there to help, if help was needed.

But Hawk's Star wasn't in the least shy. And Midnight knew exactly what he wanted. The stallion quickly covered the mare. Even with both horses willing, Candy was unprepared for the violence of the coupling. She couldn't bear to stay and watch. She headed for the house at a brisk walk. As soon as she was out of Garth's sight, she broke into a run.

Garth was torn between his duty to stay and his desire to go.

"I'll keep an eye on the horses," Tom offered.

Garth nodded abruptly and headed in the direction Candy had gone. Charlie's truck was missing, so he knew there was no one else in the house besides Candy. Garth ran up the stairs and stopped to catch his breath in front of Candy's bedroom door.

"Candy? I'm coming in." Garth didn't wait for an invitation because he wasn't sure he would get one. Candy was curled up on her bed, her face hidden in her pillow. He sat down beside her and touched her shoulder. "Candy?"

The instant he touched her she turned and launched herself into his arms. "Oh, Garth!"

Garth had never had much to do with crying women and now he knew why. A man felt downright helpless in the face of a woman's tears. All he could do was hold her tight and tell her everything would be all right. Garth felt her anguish, and if there had been a way to do it, he would have taken her pain on himself. He had to be content with murmuring words of comfort.

"Even though it looks wild and rough, the coupling isn't hurtful to the mare," he said.

Garth pushed the hair back from Candy's face and kissed her brow. Then he kissed away the tears at the corners of her eyes and on her cheeks, until his lips found their way to her mouth.

It was the gentlest, the softest kiss Candy had ever felt, and it touched her to her core. A steady warmth built inside her. She shivered when she heard the stallion's neighing scream and the mare's sharp whinny in reply.

Candy looked into Garth's dark eyes and saw a fierceness there every bit as savage as the stallion. And like the mare, she had no intention of denying him. Candy returned Garth's kisses with an urgency she didn't understand. She only knew it was necessary to couple with Garth now, to love him as she had never loved him before. Because time, her precious time with him, was finally running out.

"Love me, Garth. Please, love me." It was a plea from the heart, an urgent wish not just for the physical act, but for an emotional commitment.

Garth didn't answer her in words. She hadn't expected him to. He stripped her and himself and laid her out naked for his admiration.

"You are so perfect," Garth said in a husky voice. "Your breasts high and firm. Your belly flat. Your legs strong and slender."

He worshipped her with words. His hands adored her. His mouth cherished her. His loving was as tender as it had ever been.

But the passions running high between them put tremendous pressure on Garth's restraint. Until at last he gave rein to the demands of his nature. Man's possession of his mate was every bit as violent as that of any other animal.

Candy arched up to receive Garth as he covered her with his body. She gasped as his thrust impaled her. Her hands clutched at his shoulders as he began to move inside her. Candy was insensate with desire as she undulated beneath him.

Her fingers clawed at him.

His hands grasped at her.

Her legs circled him and held on.

His mouth claimed hers and clung.

At the moment of ultimate pleasure, Candy's wild cry of fulfillment urged Garth to his own release. His shout of exultation was no less feral than hers.

The tumultuous coupling expressed all the unspoken love each felt for the other. But in the aftermath, only she was able to say the words that expressed what they had shared.

"I love you, Garth."

There was a long silence, one that begged for words of response. Candy waited. But Garth remained silent.

Candy lay in his arms and felt only despair. Her dream that Garth would one day love her seemed doomed to remain unfulfilled. Oh, he could desire her. And he could demonstrate that desire. But because of his past, he was unable to trust—ultimately to love—any woman. She had to face the fact that he never would and go on with her life.

Candy slipped out of Garth's embrace and left the bed, looking for the clothes he had scattered when he had torn them from her.

Garth's eyes were closed, his body completely relaxed. He was enjoying the languor of a sexually satisfied male. He was aware Candy had left the bed, but he expected her to return at any moment. His arms felt empty without her. He knew she had wanted him to speak his love aloud. But it was still a very new emotion, and he felt too vulnerable to say the words.

But he knew now that he loved her. He felt almost giddy with the knowledge. Someday he might even be able to tell her so. Garth took a breath and let it out.

When Garth felt the weight on Candy's side of the bed, he thought she was returning. Then he heard two clicks. He shot bolt upright and stared at what he found.

Candy was completely dressed. She was packing her suitcase to leave.

He grabbed for his jeans and yanked them on, leaving them half-unbuttoned as he stalked around the bed to confront her. "What the hell do you think you're doing?"

"I think it's pretty obvious what I'm doing. I'm packing."

"Why?"

"I'm leaving."

"Why?"

Candy closed her eyes and took a deep breath. She let it out, opened her eyes and said, "I thought I could wait forever for you to love me. I can't. It hurts too much."

"I care for you," Garth managed to say.

"Oh, Garth." Candy knew it was more than he had ever said to any woman. But it wasn't enough upon which to build a lifetime together. "That's not enough," she said at last.

"What do you want from me?" he demanded. "I've

done everything I can to show you how I feel," he said in a savage voice.

"I want the words. I want you to say it out loud. I wouldn't even mind if you shouted it to the heavens," she said with a sad, wry smile.

But Garth said nothing.

Candy returned to packing.

Garth wanted to rip the clothes from her hands. Wanted to throw the suitcase across the room. Wanted to fold her in his arms and never let her go.

He watched her close the suitcase and snap it shut on the bed. When she walked out that door, he would lose her forever.

Garth faced a moment of truth. He had to let go of the past—or let go of Candy. When it came right down to it, the choice was amazingly easy.

"I love you, Candy."

The words had a harsh, grating sound, but they were the sweetest Candy had ever heard. She stared at Garth, her heart in her throat. She was afraid to believe what she had heard. "Say it again."

"I love you."

"I wasn't hearing things?"

"No, you weren't. I love you, Candy."

"Oh, Garth!" She launched herself into his arms from halfway across the room. He caught her and swung her around with abandon. His mouth found hers and his tongue thrust inside, laying claim to her.

"You're mine now," he rasped. "Now and forever."

"And you're mine," she said just as fiercely. "Now and forever."

"We'll have children, lots of them," he promised.

"Oh, I hope so," she said. "In fact, I think we already have one on the way."

Garth stared at her, stunned even though he had always known it was a possibility. "What?"

Candy laughed. "I said we already have one on the way."

Garth sobered, only now realizing just how much had been at stake. And how close he had come to losing it all. He would never take that chance again. He would say the words often, until Candy would never again doubt his love.

"I love you, Candy."

"And I love you, Garth. Everything will be all right. You'll see."

He took her to bed again. This time the loving was tender. At the moment of climax he said the words that sealed their fates together.

"I will always love you," the wrangler promised her.

"As I will love you, always and forever," the rich girl promised in return.

EPILOGUE

"Eight—uh—nine months later you was born, Zach. Three months after that, Hawk's Star foaled a fine colt with a star on his forehead."

"And Mom named him Midnight Star," Falcon piped up.

"Yessiree, that's the one." Charlie One Horse looked down at the little girl asleep in his arms. Zach lay sprawled on the floor in front of the fireplace. Falcon sat cross-legged at Charlie's feet. "And that's the story of how your mom and dad met and fell in love."

Zach rolled over to face his father and asked, "Is that how it really happened, Dad?"

Garth kissed Candy softly on the mouth and said, "Trust your uncle Charlie, boy. It happened just the way he said. I took one look at your mom, and I knew she was the woman for me. Now it's time for all of you to get to bed."

"Do we hafta?" Falcon asked.

"You can barely keep your eyes open," Candy chided. "Come on now."

She herded the two boys ahead of her while Garth retrieved his daughter from Charlie's lap.

"She's sleepin' like an angel," Charlie said as he gave up his burden. The old man marveled at how tenderly

Garth held the girl. He wanted to be a fly on the wall when the first beaus came calling on Callen Whitelaw.

Garth caught up with Candy and slipped his arm around her waist. Charlie heard them laughing together as they followed their sons up the stairs.

"Yep," Charlie muttered to himself as he watched them disappear, "that sure is the way it happened, all right. And the wrangler and the rich girl lived happily ever after."

* * * * *

WE HOPE YOU ENJOYED
THIS BOOK FROM

HARLEQUIN

ROMANTIC SUSPENSE

Danger. Passion. Drama.

These heart-racing page-turners will keep you guessing to the very end. Experience the thrill of unexpected plot twists and irresistible chemistry.

4 NEW BOOKS AVAILABLE EVERY MONTH!

SPECIAL EXCERPT FROM

(H) HARLEQUIN

ROMANTIC SUSPENSE

*After a suspicious death on her team, environmentalist
Emma Copley knows someone needs to investigate.
When the authorities won't, she decides to do it herself,
despite Beau Kingston's warnings. He may have a
financial incentive to stop her investigation, but he
certainly doesn't want her hurt. Can they trust each
other long enough to find the real culprit?*

Read on for a sneak preview of
Deadly Texas Summer,
the latest thrilling romance from Colleen Thompson.

She looked up at him, her expression stricken. "You don't
believe me either, do you? You don't think I can prove
that Russell was on to something real."

"I'm reserving judgment," he said, keeping his words
as steady as he could, "until I see more evidence. And
you might want to consider holding back on any more
accusations until you've recovered from this shock—and
you have that proof in hand."

"Oh, I'll find the proof. I have a good idea where, too.
All I have to do is get back to the turbines as soon as
possible and find the—"

"No way," he said sharply. "You're not going out
there. You saw the email, right? About Green Horizons'
safety review?"

She gave him a disgusted look. "Of course they want to
keep everyone away. If they're somehow involved in all

this, they'll drag out their review forever. And leave any evidence cleaned and sanitized for their own protection."

"Or they're trying to keep from being on the hook for any further accidents. Either way, I said no, Emma. I don't want you or your students taking any unnecessary chances."

"I'd never involve them. Never. After Russell, there's no way I would chance that." She shook her head, tears filling her eyes. "I was—I was the one to call Russell's parents. I insisted on it. It nearly killed me, breaking that news to them."

"Then you'll understand how I feel," Beau said, "when I tell you I'm not making that call to your folks, your boss or anyone else when you go getting yourself hurt again. Or worse."

She made a scoffing sound. "You've helped me out a couple times, sure. That doesn't make me your responsibility."

"That's where you're wrong, Dr. Copley. I take everyone who lives on, works on or sets foot on my spread as my responsibility," he said, sincerity ringing in his every word, "which is why, from this point forward, I'm barring you from Kingston property."

Don't miss
Deadly Texas Summer
by Colleen Thompson

Available March 2020 wherever
Harlequin Romantic Suspense
books and ebooks are sold.

Harlequin.com

HRSEXP0220

SPECIAL EXCERPT FROM

H HARLEQUIN

INTRIGUE

*Sheriff Jamison Wyatt has never forgotten Liza Dean,
the one who got away. But now she's back, and she needs
his help to find her sister. They'll have to infiltrate a crime
syndicate, but once they're on the inside, will they
be able to get back out?*

Read on for a sneak preview of
South Dakota Showdown *by Nicole Helm.*

Chapter One

Bonesteel, South Dakota, wasn't even a dot on most maps, which
was precisely why Jamison Wyatt enjoyed being its attached
officer. Though he was officially a deputy with the Valiant County
Sheriff's Department, as attached officer his patrol focused on
Bonesteel and its small number of residents.

One of six brothers, he wasn't the only Wyatt who acted as an
officer of the law—but he was the only man who'd signed up for
the job of protecting Bonesteel.

He'd grown up in the dangerous, unforgiving world of a biker
gang run by his father. The Sons of the Badlands were a cutthroat
group who'd been wreaking havoc on the small communities of
South Dakota—just like this one—for decades.

Luckily, Jamison had spent the first five years of his life on his
grandmother's ranch before his mother had fully given in to Ace
Wyatt and moved them into the fold of the nomadic biker gang.

Through tenacity and grit Jamison had held on to a belief in
right and wrong that his grandmother had instilled in him in those
early years. When his mother had given birth to son after son on the
inside of the Sons, Jamison had known he would get them out—
and he had, one by one—and escape to their grandmother's ranch
situated at the very edge of Valiant County.

It was Jamison's rough childhood in the gang and the immense responsibility he'd placed on himself to get his brothers away from it that had shaped him into a man who took everything perhaps a shade too seriously. Or so his brothers said.

Jamison had no regrets on that score. Seriousness kept people safe. He was old enough now to enjoy the relative quiet of patrolling a small town like Bonesteel. He had no desire to see lawbreaking. He'd seen enough. But he had a deep, abiding desire to make sure everything was right.

So it was odd to be faced with a clear B and E just a quarter past nine at night on the nearly deserted streets. Maybe if it had been the general store or gas station, he might have understood. But the figure was trying to break into his small office attached to city hall.

It was bold and ridiculous enough to be moderately amusing. Probably a drunk, he thought. Maybe the…woman—yes, it appeared to be a woman—was drunk and looking to sleep it off.

When he did get calls, they were often alcohol related and mostly harmless, as this appeared to be.

Since Jamison was finishing up his normal last patrol for the night, he was on foot. He walked slowly over, keeping his steps light and his body in the shadows. The streets were quiet, having long since been rolled up for the night.

Still, the woman worked on his doorknob. If she was drunk, she was awfully steady for one. Either way, she didn't look to pose much of a threat.

He stepped out of the shadow. "Typically people who break and enter are better at picking a lock."

The woman stopped what she was doing—but she hadn't jumped or shrieked or even stumbled. She just stilled.

Don't miss
South Dakota Showdown *by Nicole Helm,*
available March 2020 wherever
Harlequin Intrigue books and ebooks are sold.

Harlequin.com